She put the phone down and looked at the number as if it had been written by a stranger. Then, when she could move again, she wandered out into the kitchen and, in a dream, pulled a beer from the fridge, opened it and began to drink. She sank into a chair, watching blindly as Fleabag dug his claws into the wallpaper and skilfully removed a strip of it in the shape of the Isle of Man.

Rob's brother? The one who looked like a bouncer and had a nasty tendency to state unpleasant truths without knowing it? The one she'd thrown wine over at Maggie's party? *He* wanted to take *her* out to dinner? She looked over at the cat for an answer.

'What the hell was that all about?' she demanded.

Linda Taylor worked for the Civil Service in London, Angola and as a vice-consul in Sri Lanka before teaching in Japan. On her return, she read English at Oxford. *Reading Between the Lines* is her first novel and was the 1998 winner of the RNA New Writers' Award. She lives in Oxford.

Reading Between the Lines

LINDA TAYLOR

ARROW

Published in the United Kingdom in 1999 by
Arrow Books

1 3 5 7 9 10 8 6 4 2

First published in the United Kingdom in 1998
by William Heinemann

Arrow Books Limited
Random House UK Limited
20 Vauxhall Bridge Road, London SW1V 2SA

Random House Australia (Pty) Limited
20 Alfred Street, Milsons Point, Sydney
New South Wales 2061, Australia

Random House New Zealand Limited
18 Poland Road, Glenfield, Auckland 10, New Zealand

Random House South Africa (Pty) Limited
Endulini, 5a Jubilee Road, Parktown 2193, South Africa

Random House UK Limited Reg. No. 954009

A CIP catalogue record for this book
is available from the British Library

Papers used by Random House UK Limited
are natural, recyclable products made from wood grown in
sustainable forests. The manufacturing processes conform to
the environmental regulations of the country of origin

Printed and bound in the Great Britain by
Mackays of Chatham PLC, Chatham, Kent

ISBN 0 09 927232 6

This book is for my mum, Sue,
for all her help and kindness

I am indebted to the following
for their support and friendship

Ian Burnell, Christina Jones, Rob Marshall, Jane
Gordon-Cumming, Marina Oliver, Hilary and John
Johnson, and the RNA. Elizabeth Wright, Darley
Anderson, and all at the Darley Anderson Agency.
Lynne Drew at Heinemann. My sister, Julie Taylor,
my stepfather, Geof Ward and my mum, Sue Ward.
And my love and thanks to Tristram Compton.

Chapter One

Bugger it, she thought. That's all I need. All it took was a man like that to walk into the room, and everything changed.

One minute Julia had been oblivious of her baggy jeans, sagging at the bottom because she should have washed them a week ago, her rollneck sweater which had stretched over the years from its original size to something more like a knitted marquee, and the fact that she wasn't wearing make-up. She never did on a Thursday night.

But then Vivienne had led the heavenly vision into the small room where the volunteers were sitting quietly, side by side with their students, listening to them read under their breath, interjecting occasionally with noises of encouragement. Julia had looked up, looked down, looked up again, and wished she could slide off her chair and crawl under the table without anyone noticing.

'This is Rob. Hello, everyone? Can I have your attention just for a minute?'

Vivienne's eyes were bulging like Maltesers under her velvet cloche hat, which for some reason, she never took off for the class. Julia had begun to wonder if she was hiding a monstrous bald patch underneath it. It did mean that Vivienne always ran away on time at the end of the class, leaving Julia to grapple with six layers of jumpers, a ten-foot scarf and an anorak, and therefore to check the room and turn out all the lights.

Rob. Despite the polish that Vivienne applied liberally

1

to her Oxford accent, his name still sounded dangerously like 'Rub'. Julia felt a flush coming on, which she knew would turn her face into an overripe fruit. God, what was wrong with her? The last thing she'd rubbed with any semblance of vigour was a persistent stain on her kitchen unit. There was no need for the association racing through her mind now.

'Rob's coming to join us. Rob, I'm sure you won't remember everyone's names straight away, but I'll go round the group anyway.'

She did. There were eight of them tonight, four tutors and four students, although the numbers didn't always work out so perfectly. They were dotted around the room; four of them sat around the large table in the middle, two pairs off to either side.

'Brenda's working with Alec over there, then there's Fiona and Kieran, and here we have George, he's working with Shirani, and lastly Julia. She's been working with Mack since last week, haven't you, Julia?'

'Yes,' Julia obliged weakly.

The gorgeous Rob nodded at everyone, a lock of hair as thick and rich as molasses loosening itself to flop over eyes that were as clear as the Aegean and just as calm. He shook his hair out of his eyes charmingly.

'Hi.'

Julia looked down again quickly. What the hell was she thinking of? Well, she knew the answer to that one, and it involved a jacuzzi, a bottle of champagne, and some strawberry-flavoured massage oil. So the question should really be, why? It had been a long time. Too long, she realized now. Far too long.

She tried to pull herself together. Vivienne swept Rob away to show him the little kitchen which led off to the side of the corridor. Julia heard her explaining sweetly where things were, Rob's low interruptions sending

2

vibrations through the walls. His vocabulary seemed to be limited to 'Yep', and 'Righto', although Julia knew from experience that Vivienne tended to have that effect on most people. She added a bucket of cornflour to anybody's stream of consciousness. Her body glowing, she tried to turn her attention back to vowel clusters, resisting the urge to put her hands over her ears as she heard another rendition of 'Yep. Righto' arrowing down the corridor.

'You all right?'

She flashed a forced smile at Mack, conscious that she probably looked like a gargoyle.

'Fine. Where were we?'

Mack leaned back on his plastic chair, stretching his long denim legs under the table. She noticed the splashes of paint there again. Why couldn't she do something really useful with her life, like he did? A proper job, like decorating people's houses. If she got out more, she wouldn't be having this violent attack of lust as if she was an adolescent at her first disco.

'D'you want to break for a minute? You look a bit flustered.'

She shook her head.

'No, I'm just a bit warm. I think they've turned the heating up in here this evening.'

'Feels okay to me.'

'Well, it must be a hot flush then. I'm an old lady, you know.'

She tried to be flippant. Mack stared at her.

'If you say so. You wanted me to read that list of words, then?'

'Yes, you go ahead. Remember, they've all got "ou" sounds in them.'

He pulled his chair up to the table again, and crouched over the printed list of words she had found for him. His white-blond hair, shoulder length and twisted into rope-like strands, fell over his face. She could tell by his profile that he was struggling. She resisted the urge to prompt him, and let her mind wander instead.

Of course, she knew that Rob had turned up as a tutor, not a student, because Vivienne had shown him the kitchen, and the volunteers took turns to make the tea for everyone at the half-time break. But other than that, it was impossible to tell from glancing round the room just who was teaching who. It had been the first thing to strike her when she herself had turned up, wet behind the ears, last term. One of the shocks in store for her as she had ardently launched herself into the world of literacy teaching was that those with difficulties were so good at getting round them. Take Mack, for example. He strode in last week, a crash helmet under his arm, shaking off a thick leather jacket, and glanced around with an air of self-possession that reminded her of Peter Stringfellow walking into one of his clubs and assessing the totty. Vivienne had put the two of them together and Julia was now going through the process of putting him at his ease, and sounding out his abilities. Last week, it had all gone very well and she was just getting into her vowel clusters this week when gorgeous Rob had walked through the door.

She distantly heard Mack stumbling through the list as her ears strained down the corridor and into the kitchen, wondering why Vivienne was taking so long with Rob. Vivienne was married, for God's sake, with two toddlers. It wasn't fair. And what was more disconcerting was that for six months now Julia had relished her Thursday evenings up at the adult centre. For one thing, through-out the winter months she left home in the dark and got home in the dark. That meant that she could throw on a pile of crumpled clothes and an anorak, wind her thick scarf right around her face, and leg it up to the old school without making any effort to look beautiful. And when she did unwind herself in the warmth of the classroom, there was nobody there who worried about her saggy jeans, or her shapeless jumper, or her albino eyes and blotchy face produced by the wind that hurtled round the car park they all trekked across to get to the class. Up until now, of course.

Rob had ruined all that for her. Deep resentment stirred in her veins as she heard a distant 'Righto' floating through the air. She supposed they had another student lined up for him, and he'd been asked to come along for the first night just to observe, as she had done. She heard a clatter of mugs coming from the kitchen. She stiffened. Usually in the tea break they all sat back and had a chat. It was a communal moment that gave everyone a chance to get to know each other a little better. But she didn't want to hear about Rob. Looking at him was bad enough.

'Julia?' Mack was looking at her without expression. 'Dangerous, isn't it?'

She jumped. Was he psychic?

'What's dangerous?'

'The word. The last one on the list. Dangerous, isn't it?'

She expelled a breath.

'Yes. Well done.'

She mentally kicked herself in the shins. She was here to do a service, to do some meagre good and to try to 'put something back into society', for what it was worth, and she'd spent the last ten minutes wondering what Rob looked like without his clothes on. It didn't help matters when he appeared back in the room, cleared his throat, and addressed the group.

'Er, hi everyone. Vivienne says, who's for tea and who's for coffee?'

Julia sneaked a good look at him while he was

concentrating on the others' requests. He was simply the most wondrous man she had ever seen. His eyelashes entered the room half an hour before he did, his lips were full and sensual, his jaw wide and solid. His body was perfect, strapped into an open-necked white shirt (white enough to show off an olive skin) with a navy blazer thrown over the top, and thighs bound by black denims. Quite tight. Tight enough for her to answer the question she had been pondering over. She ran her fingers round the collar of her sweater, and let some cold air in. He turned melting green eyes to her.

'Julia, isn't it?'

Foolishly flattered to the soles of her feet that he had remembered her name, she breathed her reply.

'Tea, please. One sugar.'

He nodded, not holding her eye, not lingering over the becoming glow spreading over her cheeks, but merely turning back to the kitchen to make the tea. As he disappeared, the room gradually came back into focus again.

'Shall we stop for a bit, then?'

'Oh, yes, Mack. You must be tired. It can be quite exhausting to concentrate like this, can't it?'

'I'm fine, but you look knackered.'

'Thanks,' she muttered ungraciously.

'No, I mean it. I'm used to concentrating anyway. When I paint.'

'Ah, yes. It must be quite absorbing.'

'Yeah. It is. What do *you* do, anyway? When you're not doing this.'

She peered at him out of the corner of her eye. She was aware that Vivienne and Rob had reappeared with a tray and were handing the mugs round. She didn't want Rob to know what she did. At that moment, she wanted to be a marine biologist, or an astrophysicist. Anything at all

6

that might make her sound enigmatic in a brilliant kind of way.

'Nothing very interesting.'

'I don't believe you,' Mack said easily, picking up his mug and blowing over the top.

'Then try,' she gritted, taking her mug from Vivienne and giving her a tight smile.

'Okay, I'll try and guess.' Mack sipped his tea.

'No, don't.'

'Er, a model?'

'A model?' She swung round in her chair and glared at him. 'Are you taking the p—?'

She gulped and caught Vivienne's disapproving eye as she settled down with Rob on the other side of the table. She would have to watch herself. Vivienne used to teach in a primary school and she applied the same principles to teaching adults as she did seven-year-olds. And that meant that words like 'piss' were definitely taboo.

'I'm sorry, Mack,' she murmured. 'I'm not feeling very well.'

'Thought not. Anyway, I'm not taking the piss. It seemed a reasonable suggestion. You've got the face and the figure for it. You could have been a model. Have you ever done anything like that?'

'No. I used to be a little girl, and then I grew up. That's the story of my life.'

Mack fell silent. Julia stared down into the blurred reflection of her eyes in her tea, not stopping to wonder how Mack had any idea what her figure was like under three hundred yards of knitting. At this rate, she'd be surprised if Mack even bothered to turn up next week. If she continued to heap her bad temper on his head like this, it would be amazing if he lasted the evening. She'd have to make a bit more effort. However laid-back he was trying to be about attending the class, she knew that he must be finding it hard.

Vivienne's conversation with Rob opened up. Julia heard Brenda, a heavy, apple-cheeked woman who looked as if she'd been catapulted out of Hardy's Wessex, shoot a question at him.

'What do you do, Rob?'

'Er, postgrad. At the Uni. Bit esoteric, I'm afraid.'

Julia caught Vivienne's discomfort. It was an unwritten rule that vocabulary was generally kept simple, out of respect for some of the students who had trouble keeping up. As it was, Shirani, whose first language was Urdu, had acquired a glazed look in her eyes.

'What're you studying?' Mack asked, lounging in his chair.

'An unknown eighteenth-century author.' Rob cleared his throat again, as if he sensed that the group had become subdued. 'I'm researching someone no one's ever heard of, and editing a book that no one's ever going to read.'

'Sodding students,' Alec rumbled under his breath, dipping his nose into his tea.

'What's wrong with being a student?' To Julia's surprise, it was Mack who piped up again. 'Shouldn't people try to improve themselves? Isn't that what we're doing?'

'But what's the point if nobody's going to read the book?' Alec said with unrelenting logic, looking up from his tea. He was a gaunt man, prone to making startling statements, especially when he'd been on the whisky. They were all used to him. But Rob wasn't. He looked very uncomfortable. 'Get a proper job. Do something useful. I would, if I had your education. Which I haven't. Obviously.'

Rob blinked at an alarming rate, his eyelashes

flapping. Julia wondered if an earthquake had started in China.

'Wh-what do you do, Alec, isn't it?' Rob said.

Brave man, Julia thought. They all waited.

'I *was* a plumber, but I couldn't get the work.' Alec pursed his lips, not venturing any further information. He played with the corner of a piece of paper on the table with great concentration.

'You still got the tools?' Mack asked. Alec shrugged, his head disappearing into his thin shoulders. ''Cos if you have, you can come and fix my immersion. I'll pay you the going rate.'

'All right,' Alec squinted back over the table. 'Give me your address at the end.'

'Great. I'm sick of cold showers.'

Vivienne beamed at everybody from under the velvet rim of her hat. Her expression said, that's nice, isn't it, boys and girls? Rob shifted in his chair, seeming quite relieved that he hadn't been thumped.

'I thought Rob could sit with you and Mack for the rest of the session, Julia?' Vivienne was all encouragement as she widened her eyes at Julia. 'We'll have a new student joining us next week, but for now it might be useful for him to see what you're doing.'

Julia shot a painful look at Rob. He cocked his head on one side, the sleek lock of hair wavering for a moment, then deciding to flop again. The thought of cold showers suddenly seemed very appealing.

'We're doing vowel clusters,' she stated, as if in dissent.

'Fine,' Rob said, looking none the wiser.

'But we'll all enjoy our cups of tea first, won't we?' Vivienne said, slowly and clearly.

They grunted individually, although Julia thought that Vivienne would have preferred it if they'd chorused, 'Yes, Mrs Hunt'.

9

Julia sat uncomfortably listening to sporadic burblings of conversation as she counted down the seconds to the end of the tea break. It was cramped on her side of the table as it was. Behind them was a long unit which she constantly backed her chair into. He'd have to sit on her left, she decided, but then he wouldn't be able to see what Mack was doing. No, he'd have to stay where he was, and watch them from a distance. That way, the tight black denims would be safely out of reach. She startled herself with the thought. Had things really got so bad that she didn't trust herself to sit next to him without groping his thighs? The answer to that was obviously yes.

The next thing to ask herself was, how had things got so bad? Over the last year or so she'd settled for a few fantasy romances to help her sleep at night. An Australian rugby player, Grant from *EastEnders* and Dr Greene from *ER*. It hadn't seemed to be a problem. She could summon them at will, and dispose of them as she drifted off to sleep without all the hassle of having to rustle up breakfast for two from stale bread and margarine in the morning, or worry about whether she'd broken wind in her sleep. She had told Mack she was an old lady, and she felt like one. The stark truth was that she was thirty. Old enough to have her job applications ignored, young enough to want to crawl over the table right at this minute and rip Rob's crisp white shirt from his body.

But, she reminded herself, it was all her own fault. She was the one who'd decided to give up her safe, steady job in a huge insurance company in central London and rush up the M40 to become a 'mature' student. And now that dizzy experience was over. Just because life wasn't knocking on her door and asking her to play a prominent role in it at the moment was no reason to be churlish. But she felt extremely churlish, and it got worse when Rob took the mugs that Vivienne was collecting and offered to go and wash them up. He would have to be domesticated and thoughtful as well, wouldn't he? Great.

She returned to the planet as Mack let out an airy sigh beside her. She glanced at him, stretching in his chair. Just for a moment, she envied him. She should have done a City and Guilds in something. Plastering, perhaps. Or floristry, that might have been fun. Something which an employer actually wanted to see on her CV, rather than her degree in Medieval English. It had been a breathtaking experience, but who the hell wanted to know what the moral of *The Summoner's Tale* really was? She had often pictured herself at imaginary interviews giving a fine speech in a flawless accent:

'Lordynges, ther is in Yorkshire, as I gesse, a mersshy contree called Holdernesse, In which ther wente a lymytour aboute . . .'

'That's very interesting, Miss Cole, but can you do spreadsheets?'

Rob returned to the room, and looked for somewhere to sit.

'Stay where you are,' Julia issued, rather more menacingly than she'd intended. He hovered, looking majestic. 'What I mean is, if you sit opposite us, you'll have a better view.'

'Righto.' He plopped back down into the chair, and pulled it up to the table, all attention. She turned to Mack again, conscious of completely forgetting about his existence every thirty seconds or so.

'Is this all right with you, Mack? You don't mind if Rob watches us?'

'Kinky.' Mack shrugged. She frowned at him. She didn't need him getting frisky on her.

'Right then. We'll try something a bit different.' She fished into her folder for a photocopy she'd taken earlier in the week. 'Here are some words. They've all got different sounds, some are quite straightforward, and some of them are quite complicated. Let's just see what you can do.'

'Complicated words?' Mack raised an eyebrow. 'Like "esoteric", you mean?'

'Sort of.' She nodded, holding her breath. She really was behaving like a bulldozer tonight. Normally she'd have been much more reserved, much less quick to make assumptions. Many of the students she'd seen in the classes were very bright, and very articulate, and from her session with Mack last week, she knew he was quick off the mark. She pushed the sheet towards Mack, and he sat up and began to crouch over the table again. She waited quietly, her skin buzzing as she felt Rob glance at her from time to time.

'Er, I think that's, no, it can't be.' Mack sniffed.

'Go on, have a go,' she urged.

'Orgasm,' Mack said.

She lurched over the table and grabbed the sheet, her eyes scanning the first word frantically. She set it down again in relief.

'Not quite. Try again.'

'Er, it's still orgasm, I'm afraid,' Mack said, looking up at her without expression.

'How many letters does the word have?' she asked tensely. Turning into Vivienne at this moment and acting shocked wouldn't help matters. In any case, she wasn't shocked, she just didn't want to hear words like 'orgasm' while Rob was sitting within grabbing distance. It was turning her face into a loganberry again.

'Er. It's got eight letters.'

'Okay. And how many letters has "orgasm" got?'

'I'm not sure. I'll try and write it down, shall I?'

'Good idea.'

She nodded at Rob to demonstrate that this was a good tactic, and found him staring at her like a rabbit stuck in a headlight. Was the word 'orgasm' disturbing him as well? Well, what did he expect from these classes? She could imagine, because she'd been through the process as well, but the students were adults, after all. She could hardly see a man as worldly as Mack settling down happily to read Janet and John. She suspected he wouldn't give a stuff whether the dog got the ball or not.

'I've written it down,' Mack said, and pushed his lined pad under her nose.

'That's only one letter,' she said, reading it. 'R?'

'That's right. Aaaaaahhhh!'

He'd produced such an ardent simulation of an orgasmic groan, that the entire group looked up and stared at them. Julia blinked at him. Now, without doubt, he really was taking the piss. Vivienne appeared, and smiled over Rob's shoulder uncertainly.

'Everything all right?'

'How do you spell orgasm?' Mack enquired.

'The word is *organism*!' Julia yelled, worried that Vivienne was about to faint. 'O-R-G-A-N-I-S-M. Okay?'

Vivienne departed with a white face and shot silently down the corridor as if she was on greased castors.

'Look, perhaps we'd better do something else.'

'Why?' Mack looked at her, his dark blue eyes all innocence. 'I nearly got it right, didn't I?'

'All right,' she said carefully. 'Choose another one from the list.'

She sat back in her chair and waited, refusing to look at Rob. She was aware of him shifting, crossing his legs, and settling again. He cleared his throat nervously. She was doing a great job, Julia thought. By the end of the session

13

she would have ensured that neither Mack nor Rob ever set foot in the centre again.

'Bonking,' Mack said.

'I think that's unlikely.' Julia desperately tried to stay cool, looking over his shoulder at the letters. 'No, look there's an "a" there.'

'Ah, I've got it. Banking.'

'Yes.' She remained tense, her throat tight. 'Another one?'

'Erection,' Mack said.

'Right, that's enough. Give me that sheet.'

She grabbed it from him, stared at the list and confirmed to herself that the word was, in fact, erection.

'Who wrote this bloody thing?' She screwed it up and dumped it in her carrier bag. 'We'll forget the longer words for now.'

'Shame. I was getting quite good.'

She peered at Mack suspiciously. Throughout, his face had been dead straight, but there was an odd look in his eyes. For some reason he'd taken control of that last exercise, and used it to amuse himself.

'What we try to do, Rob,' she persevered without looking over at him, 'is to allow the student some time to read and to write in each session, if possible. So, do you want to write something now, Mack?'

'What sort of thing?' His body language was still relaxed, but she saw his pupils widen anxiously. She softened her expression. He was a tall, broad-shouldered man, probably only in his mid-thirties, and she was in danger of forgetting that they weren't bandying remarks about in a pub, where they both might feel equally at home. He was probably feeling extremely vulnerable, and it occurred to her that Rob's erudite presence might not be helping him.

'Well, why don't we leave you alone for a bit, and see

what you come up with? You could write about yourself, or your work, or try to write to a friend. It's up to you. Don't try to make it too long, and I'll come and have a look at it before you go.'

He inclined his head, just enough to show that he assented, but it was obvious that he wasn't happy. She got up, and gestured to Rob to follow her. She walked steadily down the corridor, and seeing that Vivienne had gone from the kitchen, went inside. Summoning all of her self-control, she turned back to Rob, and tried to address him as if he was a normal human being. Standing in front of him, it wasn't easy. He must have been six foot two or three, and even though she pulled herself up tall, he loomed over her head.

'This is only Mack's second week, and I'm still sounding him out,' she instructed officially. 'He's very nervous, but he's trying not to show it. Sometimes you have to remember as a tutor that listening is as important as talking.'

'Righto.' Rob lolled against the kitchen units, looking Julia up and down. She tried to imagine that she wouldn't lose a beauty contest to a bag of potatoes at that moment, and kept her head high. Rob's marble brow was furrowed as he analysed what was before him. 'Haven't I seen you somewhere before?'

She faltered. It was a disturbing question. How could she have been seen by him without seeing him back?

'I – surely not?'

'I think I have. In the Union bar. Or the King's Arms? Did you used to drink in there?'

'I might have done,' she defended.

'Ah.' His face cleared. 'So you're a student as well, are you?'

'I was. Not any more. The end of my course put paid to that little escapade. I graduated last year. And yes, before

15

you ask, I am a *bit old* to have just done my degree.'

'I wasn't going to say that.' He stood up straight.

'Really? You're an exception then.'

His tongue probed his cheek for a moment, as if he wasn't sure what it was safe to say next. She wished she could slap herself without him seeing. Why was she being so rude? It was because she fancied him, and he was obviously too young and too spectacular to look twice at her. And although she'd washed her hair that morning, the wind and rain on the walk up to the centre had ensured that it had now settled into a perfect parallelogram.

'So, what are you doing now?' he ventured.

'Nothing,' she bit.

'Righto.' He folded his arms. 'Shall we talk about the weather then?'

'Why do you want to teach basic skills?' she demanded. 'Surely your research keeps you busy?'

'Yes, but I feel out of touch with the real world. It's easy to get sucked into it all. You know what it's like. Libraries, college dinners, student bars. And some of the younger students get on my nerves. They haven't got a clue what's really going on, have they?'

'And you have, I suppose,' she whistled at him.

'And you're assuming I haven't?' he asked her back, raising his eyebrows at her.

'At least I'd been out there and worked for a living. At least I didn't walk into university as if it was my God-given right.'

'Hmmn.'

'And I may not be doing anything interesting right now, but at least I didn't just drift into postgrad because I was too scared to face the alternatives.'

'I see.'

It went very quiet. Julia could hear the murmurs still

coming from the classroom. What annoyed her most was that she did know what he was talking about, but she wouldn't admit it to him. Her first term at the University had been a total culture shock. From a life where she had spent every waking moment worrying about late trains, unpaid electricity bills and her next month's rent, she had thrown herself into a second adolescence, where her function was suddenly to write essays and read the books she had only had time to snatch glimpses of in her lunch hour. And there was a social life that had swept her off her feet. Not that it had been easy. The pressure had been enormous – mostly coming from inside herself – to try to perform brilliantly, to justify giving up her job, to try to convince her old friends that she had done the right thing.

But that was then. And this was now. Nobody had warned her about the crashing identity crisis that came afterwards. And what really irked her was that a year down the line, everybody around her seemed to think that she'd had her fun, and now she should go back to London and back to the job where she really belonged. Except that she didn't. Not any more. And the problem was, she didn't belong anywhere else either. She snapped herself back into the present, and found that Rob was looking at her with something akin to interest.

'Sorry, I was thinking,' she said, not sounding sorry.

'So was I. I was thinking that you make an awful lot of assumptions when you first meet someone. Are you always like this?'

'Always like what?' she said, dodging his analysis.

'It's just that it's not what I expected from someone doing this kind of work. Don't you have to keep an open mind? That's what they told me when I was interviewed.'

'I'm not narrow-minded,' she insisted, squirming under his very open stare.

'How old are you?' he asked.

'Thirty,' she replied as if it really proved something. 'Why, how old are you?'

'I'm twenty-nine. I know, I don't look it. But I started out late as well.' He smiled at her surprise, and her stomach turned into a spin dryer. 'So now that we've established that we're both fossils, can we start again?'

'Oh.' Twenty-nine? He didn't look twenty-nine. She'd assumed he was one of the beautiful young people who swanned around Oxford as if a street-map had been handed to them along with their birth certificates. 'I – I'm not saying all postgrads are like that,' she said lamely.

'How about a drink after the class? I'd like to talk to you.'

'You would?'

'Yep. So what do you say?'

What did she say? She froze. Words, her fair-weather friends, dumped her without ceremony and ran away.

'I think the word you're looking for is "yes",' he prompted, his lips still curling.

The cheek of it! No, she wasn't going to have a drink with him. Not now, and not ever. Or at least, not until she'd lost a stone, firmed up her thighs and bought a matching set of silk underwear.

'No. Sorry, I've got to go straight home.'

'Righto.' He seemed dangerously unconcerned.

'Maybe next week?' she said, hating herself for wanting a second chance. He didn't answer, but glanced distractedly over his shoulder. He looked back as if he hadn't heard her.

'I was just wondering if we should see what Mack's written?' he suggested politely.

She glanced at her watch, her quivering heart plummeting into her boots and landing with a thud. It was nearly time to clear up.

They found Mack staring round the classroom, tapping his biro on the surface of the table. She made her way round to him and sat down again. He had already packed away his pad of paper.

'So – did you manage to write anything, Mack?'

He looked at her, his deep-set eyes meeting hers squarely. For the first time in his presence, she felt very uncomfortable. What had she said? Had she patronized him? Her guilty conscience convinced her that she had earned that look. Something she'd said, or done, had upset him.

'I, er, if you want to show it to me, I can help you with it.'

'I didn't write anything,' he said.

She sat helplessly as he stood up, heaved his leather jacket on to his shoulders, and fished his crash helmet out from under the desk. He shrugged his haversack over his back, and made his way round the table to the door. Oh hell. She'd scared him away, and not surprisingly. She put a hand to her warm forehead, and stood up, ready to follow him out to the corridor and apologize.

He stopped at the door, and turned back to look at her. Then to her total surprise, he winked at her.

'See you next week,' he said.

After Julia had succeeded in strapping herself back into her extra jumpers and winding her scarf protectively around her head, the others had left ahead of her, chatting as they pushed back out into the open air. She picked up her carrier bag and switched off the lights, stopping to stare back into the empty room before she left. She could still feel Rob's presence all around her. He had left a cloud of charged particles which made her hairs bristle, like the thickening atmosphere before an electric storm. Chances like that came and went, she decided. Like buses. And she wondered, just for a second, why she had always assumed that another one would be along soon.

Chapter Two

When Julia got home she found that Fleabag had answered the phone again.

She picked him up and held his compact black body over her head, rubbing his ears with her forehead.

'You're a sod. I'm going to pull your whiskers out with a rusty pair of tweezers.'

He purred back, and reached out his paws to pat her nose. She slumped on to the sofa with him, and ruffled his fur. He should be growing bigger by now, she thought. He was ten months old, and although he was getting wider, he didn't seem to be getting any longer. He was like a Koi carp, adjusting to the size of his environment. She supposed if she ever got rich and moved out of the bedsit he'd expand, but they'd both have to put up with it for the time being. Maggie, as usual, was more succinct. She called him Dudley Moore. Fleabag got bored, and bounced off to climb into her plastic bag. She collapsed on to the floor to dial 1471.

It was a small bedsit to have a cat in, but it had been unfurnished, and the landlady probably wouldn't mind even if she knew, Julia told herself. Dr Gimble was a seventy-three-year-old retired academic who lived in a village outside Oxford. She rarely visited the bedsits personally. She'd had the old house converted about ten years ago, and there were six bedsits in total, Julia's on the ground floor, which meant that Fleabag could escape through the door at the back of the kitchen that led out to the ramshackle shared garden. Julia assured herself that the rent the old lady got from the six bedsits was more than enough to pay for the occasional strip of wallpaper that Fleabag decided to remove with his claws. She had had moments of doubt, though, when she first got him home. The woman who was fostering him for the Animal Sanctuary had said, 'He's a bit crazy. You don't mind that, do you?'

'Of course not,' Julia had gurgled, snuggling the tiny sooty package in the crook of her arm, and gazing indulgently into the milky eyes.

For the first few months, he ricocheted round the walls endlessly like a little black bullet, seemingly untroubled by earthly matters such as friction and gravity. Even after she had marched him up to the vet to put an end to his romantic aspirations, the rebounding continued, although at a slightly subdued speed. But now, at least, he had stopped thumping her head with his paw and yowling in her ear to demand breakfast when he heard the milk float at five in the morning, and was sleeping through to seven o'clock, like a good toddler.

She stuck the receiver under her chin and waited for the computerized voice to give her the number, praying that it wasn't her mother's. She had to be calm when she talked to her, and she certainly wasn't calm at the moment. And when her mother rang, it was to get a progress report. Seeing as there wasn't any progress, there was nothing to report. Thankfully, it was Maggie's number. She replaced the receiver, and crossed her legs, opening the can of cheap lager she'd picked out of the fridge. She took a gulp, and felt a bit better.

Maggie had been in her year, doing English as well. They stuck together because they both felt too old to be students, and because they liked each other.

Julia had first met Maggie when she had walked into the student common room, her legs shaking with fear, to get a cup of coffee and to meet the others. She hadn't been so overwhelmed since her first day at school. She had just filled a cup and was trying to hold it with jittering hands when a woman of indeterminate age with long, blazing red hair had come and stood next to her, rolling a cigarette, and asked her if she fancied a game of pool.

They had taken over the table, Julia revealing that she had misspent her youth, Maggie letting on that she'd been a barmaid for thirty years and honed up her potting skills during quiet spells in the pub. She'd left her grammar school in Leeds with seven O levels and gone out to work, she told Julia. It was the thing to do then. Nothing else had entered her mind. It was only much, much later that she'd gone along to an evening class, for fun, initially. She'd thought it would fill the aching gap left by the kids. Her teacher took her essays seriously, and told her she was good. He pushed her to take exams. She'd battled through the barrage of complaints at home, that the ironing was strewn in heaps around the kitchen, that the hall needed hoovering, that dinner always seemed to be a last-minute effort on her part. She sat up in the kitchen, reading and taking notes until her eyes smarted with exhaustion, while her husband fell asleep in front of the television. She passed her A levels, not just adequately, but with flying colours. Her teacher pushed her to go further. Finally, she confided, she'd pulled together the courage to apply to university. She had grown-up children who thought she was being selfish, and a husband in Leeds who thought she was suffering from a diagnosable mental disorder. From the moment they met, Julia and Maggie became allies.

Originally, Maggie tried to make it back to Leeds at the weekends, but as Pete got more and more fed up and the kids went off to do their own thing, she spent more time in Oxford. By the time she'd finished her course, Pete had confessed to an affair with the woman next door, and their marriage appeared to be over in all areas other than the legalities. Now Maggie was sharing a house in Summertown, north of Oxford, with a brace of undergraduates coming up to finals who alternately feared her and worshipped her. She was working in a bar again, and trying to get her erotic stories published.

Julia dialled her number. One of the undergraduates, a softly spoken boy called Fabian, answered the phone.

'Hi, she's just coming. By the way, I'm supposed to tell you we're having a bash here tomorrow night, if you want to come.'

'A bash?' Julia wasn't in the mood to be vomited on.

'Well, just a handful of friends. And some food. It'll be civilized, I promise. No fag ends in the beer cans. Maggie's going to do us a curry.'

'Really?' Now that was worth going for. 'Yes, I'll come. How's the revision coming on?'

'Oh.' The boy's voice faltered. Julia felt a flash of sympathy. 'I'm not on to revision yet. I'm still on vision. I've got an essay crisis tonight. I'll never get it done.'

'Yes, you will.'

'No, this time I've really fucked it up. I've got to read the complete works of Shakespeare by ten o'clock tomorrow morning.'

'You'll do it,' Julia said confidently. She'd realized herself early on that survival at Oxford depended on your ability to bluff. She knew that he'd appear to have read the complete works of Shakespeare by the time he staggered in to his tutorial, and that was where the skill really lay.

'See you tomorrow, then.'

'Hello, love.' Maggie's voice broke on to the line. 'I was trying to leave a message about the party for you, but Dudley Moore got there first again. He had the nerve to purr at me.'

'You love him really,' Julia said. 'He's only a toddler, remember.'

'You wait till you've had kids and then tell me that!' Maggie guffawed loudly. 'Anyway, are you going to come? I thought I'd have one of my curry evenings. Fabian needs cheering up, and I thought if I did some food it'd stop the kids getting too drunk.'

'Of course I'll come. You've got to stop calling them kids, Maggie.'

'They don't mind. Do you, *Fay*-bian?' Julia smiled. Poor Fabian. Maggie never stopped teasing him about his public-school accent. She heard him say something about whippets in return. Maggie chuckled. 'He's going to bring some people from St Anne's. And I think Naomi's going to bring a friend. Fay-bian seems to think she might have one now.'

'Maggie!' Julia breathed. 'She's going to hear you one day.'

'Oh, she's all right really. She just needs a bit of gingering up, that's all. A party might bring her out of herself a bit. It's not natural, hiding herself away in her room all the time.'

'She's probably scared of you.'

'Of me? No, I feel sorry for the poor lass.' Maggie became pensive. 'You know her mum and dad are in Malaysia? She never sees them, even in the holidays. Sometimes I think I should adopt her. Anyway, how was the class?'

Julia picked up her beer again and took a deep slurp before answering.

'There was a bloke. I mean, a new tutor. He's called Rob.' She stopped. What more was there to say?

'A-ha.' Maggie leapt to her own conclusions. 'And he's a bit of all right, is he?'

'Well, yes. But nothing happened.'

25

'Nothing happened?' Maggie blasted a laugh down the line which terminated in a rattling cough. 'What *might* have happened? You make it sound as if you might have enacted the *Kama Sutra* on the desks.'

'I was rude to him. I mean, really offhand. And he asked me if I wanted to go for a drink after the class, and I said no.'

'And?'

'Well, that's it. I just opened my mouth, and instead of the word "yes" coming out, I said "no".'

'So why – hang on a minute, love. *Fay*-bian! Are you going to start reading those bloody plays or not? Well, get up to your room then, lad, before I take a hand to you.' Julia heard the door swing shut in the background. 'What was I saying? Oh, yes. Why did you say no, then, if he was nice?'

'I don't *know*. Oh, Maggie, it's hopeless. I don't know what came over me. Thursday nights are never going to be the same again.'

'Good thing too. You need a bit of spice in your life.'

'If I want spice, I'll come to your curry evenings. I don't want to feel like this. It's just not convenient.'

'Sex isn't convenient.'

'Will you stop talking about sex? I've got to work with this man.'

'Look, love, it's not really my place to say it, but it might just do you good. You've been a bit uptight recently.'

'I haven't!' Julia denied, stopping to frown at her uptight voice.

'Well, you have actually. I don't mind, you can be whatever you want with me, but I don't get the feeling that you're very happy with the way things are going. I mean, it's as if you've lost your way, lass. I haven't seen you fired up about anything since we graduated. You

26

need—' Julia heard her stop to light a cigarette. 'You need something to get you going again. Give you a bit of momentum.'

'Momentum?'

'You know what I'm saying. You're young, Julia. You've got everything ahead of you.'

Julia drained the can of beer. It was difficult to feel old when she was talking to Maggie, whose richness of experience sometimes made her feel that she hadn't even fought her way out of her Babygro yet. But she didn't feel young either. At least, she didn't have the energy and optimism that were supposed to come with being young. And she had a pile of job rejections to prove that the world wasn't exactly her oyster. It made Maggie's encouraging remark irksome, and she found herself snapping in response.

'What about you, Maggie? You're happy doing what you're doing. And you got a much better degree than me. If anyone should have any momentum, it's you, but you're not exactly setting the world on fire, are you?'

Maggie paused imperceptibly. Julie instantly regretted her words. Maggie was always the one who raised everybody else's spirits. She was Good Old Maggie. Julia knew it didn't mean that she was deliriously happy about her own predicament, she was just better at getting on with things than anyone else she knew. She heard Maggie laugh, and relaxed again.

'Listen, when the world reads all about Tracey's adventures with Timothy and his Torrid Twin, it *will* catch fire. Or at least it'll smoulder a bit. That's if anyone sees fit to give my genius the attention it deserves.'

'I'm sorry, Maggie, it's just me. I'm just not ready to shoot off in any particular direction. And the last thing, the very last thing I need at the moment is any sort of – of well, romance, I suppose.'

'It won't do any harm, will it?'

'Yes, it will,' Julia asserted, clutching her beer can. 'I'm not ready.'

'Julia? Is this all about Bill, really?'

'Of course not.' Julia felt a familiar graze over an old, deep wound. She felt sorrow, followed by anger. The pain passed. 'That's all history. God, it's a million years ago, Maggie, why did you have to bring that up?'

'Sorry, Julia.' There was a pause. Julia stared at the blank wall and listened to Maggie exhaling smoke. 'Listen, I really am sorry. I just hope you've put it all behind you. You can't let it hold you back.'

'It's not holding me back. It's been years. It didn't stop me getting my degree, did it? I really don't want to talk about it.'

She never wanted to talk about it. She had told Maggie all about her old life and why she had wanted to leave it behind and change direction, one night in the very first term, when they had got drunk and sat in Maggie's room until four in the morning. Now she wished she'd never mentioned it. It was in the past, dead and buried.

'So what's he doing, this Rob?'

'He's a postgrad student,' Julia swept quickly on. 'Researching some obscure eighteenth-century author. He didn't say which college he was at.' Because she hadn't asked. She hadn't asked him anything about himself. 'And he's twenty-nine.'

'Bit old,' Maggie mused aloud. 'You've got to get them young, you know. Much more stamina.'

'Maggie, I suppose Timothy and his Torrid Twin *are* over the age of consent, are they?'

'Just about.'

'You're a dirty old lady, you know that, don't you?'

'Don't call me old! I'm not even fifty. Not yet.' Maggie's voice tailed off. Julia knew that in another two months she would be fifty, and suspected that she'd never let any of them know just how much it scared her. 'Why don't you bring Rob to the party?'

Julia gasped, and then laughed, grabbing Fleabag as he trotted up to her and stroking him roughly as a form of therapy.

'Don't be daft. I don't even know his number, or where he lives.'

'Shame. You should have asked him which college he was at, at least. Haven't you learned anything from me?'

'Quite enough, thank you.'

'Still, he shouldn't be so hard to track down. Can't be that many twenty-nine-year-old hunks about researching unknown eighteenth-century authors.'

'This is Oxford, Maggie. Get real. There are thousands of them.'

'I could ask Fabian,' Maggie steamed on. 'He's got some friends in the MCR. They'd probably know him.'

'Don't you dare!'

'Well, I'll see you tomorrow then. I'm bushed, and I'm going to turn in.'

Julia drank another beer before she went to bed. In the bedsit upstairs, the Dutch couple began to make love, and she braced herself for impact. She felt deflated and empty now. Damn Maggie and her ideas. Why should Bill still be in her life at all, even by name?

In bed later, her hands wandered over her warm stomach, feeling the flatness. It had been so many years ago. It seemed like a different life, with somebody else living it, as if the memories weren't even hers to own.

A loud thump from the ceiling, followed by a series of ecstatic shouts, distracted her. Fleabag crawled on to her head, and settled down to sleep with his paws reaching down her cheeks like sideburns. Thump, thump, thump. She waited for Annelies to reach orgasm, so that she could go to sleep. It was taking longer than usual tonight. She turned impatiently on the pillow, finding Fleabag's stomach covering her face. She realized that she couldn't breathe. She swivelled back again to stare straight up at the ceiling. Thump, thump, thump.

'Oh, get on with it!' she cried into the air.

Seconds later, Annelies screamed with delight, her cries subsiding into the night.

'Netherlands, *douze points*,' Julia muttered acidly, closing her eyes tight.

The following evening, as she was about to get ready for the party, Annelies knocked on the door of Julia's bedsit, and asked her if she'd feed the fish at the weekend.

'Going pot-holing again?' Julia smiled in a friendly fashion, trying not to look as tired as she felt.

'We're going to climb up an escarpment in the Peak District,' Annelies enthused, her thick accent booming with a zest that made Julia feel faint. 'You know what to do, don't you?'

She handed over her keys. Julia always fed the fish for them at the weekends while they went away. They were always trying to climb up something, or squeeze themselves down into something else. She didn't know how they ever had any calories left after their strenuous week-night activities, but before she could ask Annelies if she and her boyfriend were on steroids, she'd bounced away up the hall stairs, her blonde pony tail pogoing rhythmically on her back.

Julia closed the door. Of course she'd feed the fish. Because she never went anywhere. She took herself back into the main room which led off from the small kitchen, and sorted through the pile of jumble again.

It was a student party, so she shouldn't have to worry too much about what she wore. But after being discovered wearing her baggy green jumper yesterday, she wasn't going to take any chances. And this time she'd wear her clean jeans – the ones that didn't hang around her figure like a denim nappy. She had a slow bath in the bathroom she shared with the bedsit across the corridor. Mercifully, the other bedsit was still unoccupied at the moment, and she was relishing having the bathroom to herself. She wallowed, washing her hair twice for good measure, while Fleabag sat next to her shampoo bottles and gazed down at her naked body with a disdainful look that was crushing. Together, they plodded back to get changed.

She squeezed her body into her jeans and an equally tight black T-shirt, pulling a thick leather belt around her waist. She had a vague memory of someone paying her figure a compliment. Who was it? Mack. His words swilled around her brain again. She should have been flattered that he suggested she could be a model instead of snapping at him like a Jack Russell. It wasn't as if she was so used to flattery that she found it tedious. Fleabag started to complain loudly as she thrust her head under the hairdryer. She mouthed endearments at him while she tried to brush the long brown strands into some sort of order. It was definitely time for a trim, but she couldn't afford one. She'd have to get Maggie to do it again, but Maggie had no concept of a straight line.

She stared at herself in the wardrobe mirror, and felt stirrings of regret. What if she'd never given up her job? By now she'd have a car, a mortgage and a decent set of clothes, and she'd be able to afford to have her hair cut by someone who knew how to do it. As it was, she got sporadic work teaching English in the private colleges dotted around Oxford that paid well by the hour but never by the week, and periods in between of thinking time. At the moment, she was deeply enmeshed in a period of thinking time.

But the clothes made her look younger than she felt, and she pulled on her old brown leather jacket, cruelly rejecting her anorak and tossing it into a corner. She flicked her hair over the collar, and decided that it was better to be going to Maggie's curry evening with a bunch of teenagers on a Friday evening than to be rattling home on the Underground surrounded by grey suits. There was no going back.

Maggie answered the door, and threw herself out on to the doorstep before Julia could make a move to go in. She looked terrific, all five foot two of her. It looked as if she'd put a new rinse in her hair, giving it a subtle hint of copper. She'd left it loose to drape over her slim shoulders. And she was wearing the billowing purple shirt and long, slim skirt she saved for special occasions. A touch of make-up, never too much, mostly carried by a vibrant lipstick. Julia instantly felt as bland as a cup of weak tea. Maggie clutched her arm, and waved her auburn eyebrows wildly.

'He's here!' she hissed. 'I thought I'd better warn you.'

'What are you talking about? Who's here?'

'What d'you mean "who"? *Him!* He's divine, isn't he?'

'Divine? That's not a word out of your dictionary!' Julia laughed at Maggie's face, contorted into some sort of message. 'Who the hell is here?'

'Your bloke from the class. Rob.'

'You're not serious.'

It was clear that Maggie was serious.

'Look, I'm sorry. I should have asked you, but I didn't really think for one minute that Fabian would really know him. I just asked if he or any of his friends knew about a postgrad called Rob, and he said he'd talked to him at the English faculty. So when he saw him again this afternoon, he just asked him to come.'

Julia's head was spinning. She gripped her bottle of

wine by the neck, and pretending it was Maggie, silently attempted to strangle it.

'You've set me up!'

'No! He doesn't know about you coming. Fabian just asked him anyway, and didn't expect him to turn up, but he got here about ten minutes ago.'

'Have you got enough curry?' Julia realized as soon as the ridiculous question was out that she was in shock.

'Just as well I have,' Maggie said. 'Because he's brought his brother as well.'

She followed Maggie through the dark hall of the spacious terraced house, and into a living-room which seemed full of people. She passed them in a blur, vaguely aware of a delicious smell tickling her nostrils, with only one thought in her mind. She had to get into the kitchen, open this bottle of wine, and drink it.

Fabian was making a punch in an industrial-sized saucepan teetering over the edge of the cooker. Maggie ran up to him.

'Not the whole bottle of whisky, dickhead.'

'Eee by gum,' he retorted in a cultured voice.

'Give me that bottle. I know you all used to drink like fish at Westminster, but my liver's not up to whisky punch without the punch.'

'Only because you've spent your whole life in a pub,' he parried. 'Your liver's probably the size of a Space Hopper by now. My liver's only just starting out in life. I've got to educate it.'

'Open Julia's bottle of wine, and pour her a drink, there's a love.'

Fabian flashed Julia a welcoming smile. He really was cute, she admitted. His curly brown hair looked more like a beret than anything organic, and he possessed a marvellous pair of brown eyes that were the same deep colour. He had a hooked nose that he'd broken in a rugby

33

match six months ago, and it still headed down his face in an uncertain trajectory. He was lanky, but in another ten years he'd be really something, she decided.

'I gather you know Rob?' he said, looking back at the punch as he stirred it.

'Yes,' she said breathlessly. 'And you do too. Fancy that!'

'Nice bloke. He helped me with Shakespeare.'

'You did get the essay done, didn't you?'

'Yep. Got to the tutorial, and found it was put off until three this afternoon. I was having a fag outside the library, and Rob tipped up, so he read my essay for me, and told me which bits were crap.'

'You mean it wasn't all crap?' Maggie winked at Julia and, giving up on Fabian, opened the bottle of wine herself.

'Considering I read *The Tempest* in forty-five minutes flat at six o'clock this morning, I thought it was bloody miraculous.'

'And what did your tutor say?' Julia asked.

'I think he fell asleep half-way through it. He just said, "Fine, fine." And that was about it.' Fabian looked up as a handful of students burst into the kitchen waving beer cans. 'In the fridge. Hi Liz, Katie. Grab yourselves a drink.'

'Where's the curry, Maggie?' a hungry voice asked.

'All on burners in the dining-room. Just go through and help yourselves.'

'You've been busy.' Julia took the glass of wine Maggie passed her, noticing she'd chosen a very big one and filled it to the top. She took a grateful sip. 'You're so much more organized than me.'

'I learned years ago to do it all in the afternoon,' Maggie said, fishing out a cigarette paper and forking tobacco into the crease. 'When the kids grew up I nearly went bonkers. So I started cooking exotic meals. That was before A levels, of course. Not that Pete ever appreciated it. He used to say, "What's this foreign muck?" And I used to say, "Pete, if you don't like it, just throw it on the floor." Do you know, there's nothing you could educate about that man, not even his sodding taste-buds? When A levels came along, I tried to cook what I could in the afternoons and hope the Red Lion wouldn't sack me for falling asleep standing up behind the bar at night. Here, Fay-bian, why don't you go and put that Pulp album on, get things going a bit? There's nothing I like better than to see a load of public schoolboys' bums jiggling about.'

'Okay.'

He sauntered off.

'Pulp? God, Maggie, you make me feel like an old fogey.'

'Well, you are, aren't you? Have some more wine.' Maggie squeezed a centimetre into the top of the glass.

'Are you trying to get me drunk?'

'Yes. So that you can talk to Rob. Mind you, his big brother's a bit scary. Watch out for him.'

Julia leaned back against the sink.

'His big brother? What the hell did he bring his brother for? And where are they, anyway?'

'Must be eating in the dining-room. Rob said his brother'd come up for the weekend, so he thought he might as well bring him along. I don't mind.'

'Is he like Rob?' The idea of Rob in double vision was a little too much to take.

'Not a bit. He looks like a bouncer. Fairly scared the stuffing out of me when I opened the door. Perhaps he's brought him along for protection.'

'But Rob doesn't know I'm here. Why should he need protecting from me?' Julia complained, her skin prickling again.

35

'Not from you, from me. If you don't want him, I'll have him.'

Maggie was called away as Fabian yelled for her to come and explain to his friends what she'd cooked. Julia hung on in the kitchen as the music throbbed through from the living-room, the sound of conversation swelling into a loud buzz. She downed her wine, Maggie's words echoing in her head. She wondered for a moment if she might be serious. Maggie's general rule was that she looked, but she didn't touch. But Maggie was a woman too. And she was on her own now. She drained her glass, and found the bottle again in the bottom of the fridge, splashing in a refill, and watching the pale liquid rise precariously to the rim. She giggled. Perhaps she could hide in the kitchen all night? If Rob stayed in the dining-room on the other side of the house, he'd never know that she was at the same party. And perhaps after Fabian had finished his saucepan of whisky punch, he might be on for a bit of baby-snatching . . .?

'Is there anything left in that bottle? Or shall I open another?'

She jumped, spilling her wine over her hand, and looked up guiltily. The strident voice had cut through her thoughts. She was suddenly aware of the picture she created, squatting on her haunches, carefully edging as much wine as the laws of physics would allow into her own glass. The man in front of her was probably in his thirties, and looked like a bouncer. It could only be one man. Rob's elder brother. She stood up, swaying a little, and without thinking, stuck her glass in her mouth and took another deep slurp.

'I'll help myself,' he said, prising the bottle out of her hands, and glancing at the label. His face stiffened. 'On second thoughts, I'll open the bottle I brought. If it's still here.'

'I haven't drunk it, if that's what you're thinking,' she said.

He looked at her again. She blinked back. He was a daunting figure, with shoulders like breezeblocks, and a very imposing stare. If it was Rob's brother she was looking at, he certainly had none of his elegance. And none of his charm. He had an aura about him that was vaguely threatening. But he did have a hint of green in his eyes, just a smear across a tawny background. He turned back to the kitchen units, and fished a bottle of red wine from the collection.

'Here it is. I won't have to fingerprint you after all.'

'That's a relief.' It sounded very authentic, coming from him. Perhaps he was a policeman? She pitied the criminals. 'Don't you like white, then?'

'I'll stick to this.' He eased the cork from the bottle, sniffed it, and poured himself a glass. He concentrated on it for a moment, and took a small mouthful, savouring it. She had the urge to laugh at him.

'There isn't a spitoon, I'm afraid. You'll have to make do with the punch saucepan. Who knows, you might improve it?'

To her relief, he swallowed.

'Not bad,' he said. 'So, are you a student as well?'

The way he said 'as well' sounded disparaging. She put herself on her guard.

'I was, until last year.'

'Postgrad?'

'Er, no. I was a mature student.'

'Come up here to find yourself, did you?'

Definitely sarcastic. She frowned at him.

'What exactly do you mean?'

'I just find it interesting that most mature students are people in their thirties from the Home Counties who suddenly find the need to study Psychology or English, usually so that they can wallow in self-analysis.' His gaze didn't waver. 'So which are you? Psychology or English?'

'English,' she said in mock-obedience. He sipped his wine, nodding approvingly to himself. 'Admiring your own taste in wine?' she added politely.

'Yes. I have got good taste, in most things.'

'And modest with it,' she continued sweetly. 'Nothing like your brother, are you?'

'Do you know Robert?' His sharp glance confirmed her suspicions.

'I've had the pleasure of meeting him, yes. As I say, you're nothing like him.'

'No, I'm not. How do you know Robert?'

'We—' She was about to tell him about the class, but she suddenly felt defensive about it. Let him think she was nothing but self-indulgent if he wanted. 'From the library. We shared an interest in the human condition.'

'Very useful to the world at large.'

She took a breath. She had heard it all before, but it was still infuriating to have to justify herself to a complete stranger.

'If you take a broader view of society, yes. It depends what you mean by useful, doesn't it?'

'Typical answer from an English student.'

'Thank you,' Julia replied in the most acidic voice she could muster.

'So what are you doing now? Teaching?'

God, she hated that. It was one thing that was almost as bad as her mother trying to force her back into her old job. As soon as she admitted to studying English, the next assumption was that she would teach.

'Actually, no.' It was only half a lie. At the moment, she was unemployed. Apart from her voluntary work. But she wasn't about to explain her life away to him. She had no desire to prolong the conversation with him for longer than was absolutely necessary. A few civilities, and she could go and find Maggie. 'What do you do?'

'Evading the question. That means you're still unemployed.'

She pulled herself up, and gave him an indignant look.

'Actually, what that meant was that it's none of your bloody business.'

'Definitely unemployed. And feeling guilty about it.'

She was momentarily speechless. She recovered herself with a very large gulp of her wine.

'So what do you do, then? Or are you going to evade the question as well?'

He gave her an odd smile, a light of humour in his eyes. She watched incredulously.

'I don't evade questions, I usually put them. I'm a lawyer.'

'For the prosecution, no doubt,' she said. 'So how does a nice guy like Rob come to have a git like you for a brother?'

'A git?' He smiled again. 'You think I'm a git just because I'm not full of admiration for you because you've pulled yourself through a degree as a *mature* student? I beg your pardon, an *Oxford* degree, which makes it more spectacular, doesn't it?'

'I don't think so, but I'm flattered if you do.'

'So what were you doing before you discovered yourself?'

'I worked for a big insurance company. In the City.' She ignored his additional dig, but it rankled at her.

'And the rat race wasn't good enough for you?'

'You're the lawyer. You should know all about rats. Why don't you tell me why it *is* good enough for you?'

'Or were you tending a broken heart? Is that it? Did a man disappoint you? Was it a failed romance that drove you to wallow in poetry at the taxpayer's expense?'

She gasped. A blurred vision of Bill's face fled across her memory, the pain, the nausea, her own tears, spilling down, week after week, with no hope of receding. Her throat tightened, and then she came back to the kitchen, to a man leaning casually against the cupboards, firing her life back at her, pigeon-holing her, belittling her achievements, insulting her in any way that occurred to him.

She stepped forward, and threw her glass of wine in his face.

'Julia? Guess what? Rob says he knows you . . .' Maggie's artless introduction ceased. Julia looked round, clutching her empty glass with an iron grip, to see Maggie standing in the doorway. Beside her, Rob's eyes went from her white face, to his brother's, dripping with wine, and then back again.

'Hi, Julia. I see you and Leo have already met.'

Chapter Three

'Here's a tea towel. It's the only clean one left, but you'd better have it. Wipe yourself down, duck.'

Julia watched in a daze as Leo rubbed his face with the tea towel that Maggie had given him. He emerged, blinking the wine from his eyes. Maggie bustled around, producing another bottle of white wine, taking Julia's glass from her hand, filling it up, and giving it back to her.

'Drink that. You look as if you need it.'

'Yes, do *drink* it, please,' Leo said, still looking bleary.

'I wouldn't waste two glasses on you, don't worry,' Julia said stiffly, her senses returning.

'At least it was cheap wine,' he said. 'It'd be a shame to throw the decent stuff in my face.'

'You'd have got whatever I had in my hand at the time,' Julia continued, her burst of anger subsiding. At least he didn't seem to be reacting with anger himself. But he was a lawyer, after all. He probably had a skin as thick as tarmac.

'What have you been saying, Leo?' Rob looked at him with caution.

'The wrong thing, obviously,' he answered drily, dismissing his brother and looking straight at Julia. 'I don't even know your name.'

'No, you don't,' she answered. 'Well! I've worked up quite an appetite. Time to hit the food I think, Maggie. Is there any left?'

'You'd better be quick,' Maggie said, picking up her

cigarette papers. 'The last time I looked, Fabian was jumping into the Chicken Ceylon with his snorkel and flippers on.'

'Fine. I'll take my wine with me just in case I need it. You should enjoy chatting to Maggie about thirty-year-old mature students from the Home Counties, Leo.' She gave Leo a frosty glance and stalked out, leaving the kitchen behind her, and pushing through the ever thickening mass of bodies towards the dining-room.

Maggie had done more than been busy, she'd been a marvel. The table, prudently covered in a paper cloth, was crowded with dishes filled with thick sauces, now half-devoured, of every shade of autumn red. Julia grabbed a plate, heaved a mass of rice on to it, and decorated it with three different curries, a selection of vegetable side dishes, and picked up a poppadam for good measure at the end. Then she sank into one of the chairs lined up against the wall, and stared at her pyramid-sized meal without appetite. She stabbed her fork into the mass of flavours, and stuck it into her mouth, emitting a muted moan in appreciation. She tried to relax.

It wasn't in her nature to lob wine in people's faces, but some sort of reflex action had set in, and she'd done it. Now Rob would have confirmed his suspicions that she was a virago. What of it? Did she care now? That brother of his was a prize bull. He was just lucky that she hadn't been able to reach the saucepan of punch, or she would have drowned him with it. She was as likely to win the affections of the gorgeous Rob as she was to gain the approval of his less than gorgeous brother. She might as well just accept the fact that she was destined for spinsterhood and have done with it. She continued to plough through the delicious meal, enjoying the time on her own while conversation from the vultures picking on the remains of the food drifted over her head. It was the sort of conversation she was used to overhearing at Oxford.

'So how was the tute?'

'Oh my God, complete nightmare! I thought I'd read up on Kant, but I felt like a fucking idiot.'

'Did you see Carrie in the bar last night? She practically raped Steve. But she was s-o-o pissed.'

'Do you think Grant's sexy?'

'Grant who?'

'*EastEnders*. Oh my God, don't tell me you don't watch it? It's brilliant.'

Her interest perked up a little, and she finished playing around with the last piece of chicken on her plate. She stood up slowly, added her plate to the pile on the table, reminding herself not to drink so much that she couldn't turn up tomorrow to help with the washing-up, and made her way back through the room.

In the doorway, she came face to face with Rob. She felt an instant surge of embarrassment.

'Rob! Look, I'm sorry I threw my wine in your brother's face—'

'Don't worry. It's the standard reaction to him. He probably deserved it.'

She assessed his expression. He seemed very calm, almost resigned. Such a beautiful face, so gentle compared to Leo's Rottweiler snarl. The music was reverberating now down the hall, and she sensed from the increase in temperature that people had started dancing. Curry, punch and dancing. It was a bit of a lethal combination. She hoped Maggie would be philosophical if anybody threw up. Or if everybody threw up. Rob was looking at her sympathetically.

'I shouldn't have brought him. He's been too busy to come up to Oxford before, and I was amazed he bothered

43

to come up this weekend, but he's got very strong opinions. I might have known he'd have a go at someone. I'm sorry it was you, though.'

'Your brother doesn't frighten me, Rob. He's probably having a go at someone else now. I didn't feel particularly special. I got the feeling that whatever he's suffering from is probably episodic.'

Rob expelled a breath.

'Yep, you're right. He's always been like this. I just have to put up with it.'

'Does he do this to you too?' Now she felt sorry for picking on him for doing research. It was obvious that he didn't get any support from Leo, and she knew nothing about his family. For all she knew he was struggling to research his unknown book that nobody was ever going to read without any support from anyone.

'He doesn't approve.' The tone of Rob's voice surprised her. 'He's never approved of anything I've done, and I don't think he's going to start now. It's a long story. I don't want to bore you with it. This is supposed to be a party, after all.'

'Oh, I'm not bored,' she said quickly. 'In fact, I wanted to apologize to you for being so rude last night. I don't know what came over me.'

Rob looked confused.

'I don't remember you being particularly rude?'

'I had a go at you for doing postgrad. And you asked me for a drink.' She raised her voice as the volume went up on the music in the next room. 'And I said no.'

'Righto.' He nodded. 'Don't worry about it. Another time?'

She laughed, the wine kicking in to her system.

'Well, we're here now. Shall we go and try Fabian's punch, or aren't you ready to die yet?'

'Frankly, the more pissed I get, the better I can cope

44

with Leo,' Rob said, looking down the hall. 'Let's go and get some.'

They found that the punch was providing a great source of entertainment in the kitchen. They picked up plastic cups and joined the short queue that had formed. Fabian was ladling out his conconction with great pride.

'Perhaps if you got Leo on the punch, he might feel less like spoiling for a fight,' Julia said in Rob's ear.

'Makes no difference. He's a sod. When he gets drunk, he's a drunk sod.'

'You poor lamb.' Julia pouted back at him. 'Just as well you don't see much of each other, then.'

'We used to. I lived with him in London while I did my degree.'

'I thought you did your degree here?'

'No, I was at King's. He's got a house in Notting Hill. I stayed there. My mother's abroad, you see. It was pretty tense most of the time. But he has helped me out. Financially, I mean, so I suppose I should be grateful to him. Still, he earns enough. You need all the help you can get when you're studying, don't you?'

'Of course you do,' she soothed him. He seemed in need of reassurance tonight, and since he was still six foot two, still gorgeous, and she was feeling half-drunk already, she was happy to provide it. They reached the cooker, and Fabian proffered a ladle of punch.

'Maggie told me to warn everyone that it's really strong,' he said without any sign of regret.

'Good news,' said Julia. 'Fill us up.'

They took their cups and filed back through to the living-room. The party had evolved into a living, breathing thing with a genetic code all of its own. The main light had been turned off, the music was loud enough to make muted conversation impossible, and a small crowd was bouncing up and down. Julia sipped her punch, pausing in between mouthfuls to acknowledge that it had the kick of a mule, and subsided into the wall. She thought she spotted Naomi, Maggie's other house-mate, in the middle of the bouncing crowd, and gave Maggie a Brownie point for perception. It gave her a shot of courage. If mousey Naomi could climb out of her shell and bounce with the best of them, why should she be coy? And Maggie herself was dancing, as Julia expected, drawing people in who stood on the sidelines, shaking her bright red hair, and looking as if jumping around with a room full of teenagers was the most natural thing in the world.

'D'you want to dance?' she asked Rob suddenly.

'Ah, no. I'm no good at it. No, I'll just be a wallflower, if you don't mind.'

She didn't catch everything he said above the noise. But she caught 'no', and saw his head shaking his reluctance.

'Oh, come on!'

'No, no.' Another polite shake of the head.

Her hand was grabbed, and she swung round to smile at Fabian, his shirt undone to his waist, his head tossed back as he rotated his hips erotically. She allowed him to drag her into the throng, and began to dance with him. As the room went up and down, she thought she spotted Leo standing in a corner nursing a glass of wine. She bounced again, and refocused. Yes, he was staring bleakly at the happy crowd with an expression that suggested he'd rather be undergoing a rigorous bout of colonic irrigation than being a guest at Maggie's party. And he and Rob seemed to feel no urgency to talk to each other. Rob had moved away to talk to one of Fabian's friends in the doorway, and Leo was, at that moment, looking straight at Julia.

A burst of high spirits overtook her. As Fabian leapt

towards Maggie and started to jive with her, Julia slipped away and went back into the kitchen. She filled a cup with punch, poured another one for herself, forgetting where she had put hers down, and took the two drinks back into the living-room. She skirted around the edge of the dancers, and found Leo, decorating the corner of the room with all the animation of a garden statue.

'Here!' she said, thrusting the flimsy cup at him. 'Drink this!'

He looked at her offering as if it might jump up and bite him. He indicated his glass of wine. She saw that it was nearly empty.

'Oh, come on, for God's sake! Why don't you just enjoy yourself?' Or go home, she added mentally. 'Everyone here's having a good time, apart from you. You look like a spare dick at an orgy, d'you know that?'

He took the cup, then shifted himself from his position, and put a hand on her elbow, guiding her away from the living-room, through into the conservatory which led away to the back of the house. The music was still loud, but the conservatory was empty apart from a slumped body in the corner that was either asleep or dead. He closed the glass door behind them, and the noise from the party became more muffled.

'I'm going to apologize to you,' he said. 'I'm not sure what I said, but I obviously upset you.'

'Go on, then,' she said, sticking her nose into her cup of punch.

'Go on, what?'

'Apologize.' She smiled. 'I'm waiting.'

He squinted at her.

'I just did.'

'No, you didn't. You said you were going to.'

He gave her a long, assessing look. She decided his eyes looked like grass stains while she stared un-

47

flinchingly back at him. His jaw tightened, then relaxed again.

'I'm sorry I upset you. I'm not at home in this sort of environment. I'm too old for frolics like this, and they get on my nerves.'

'Why did you come then?'

'Because—' He eyed the punch, then surprisingly took a sip from it. Unsurprisingly, he grimaced. 'Because Robert and I don't seem to be able to hold a conversation without it degenerating into an argument. He told me when I got here this evening that he'd been invited to a party, and it was very clear that he wanted to go. So I went along with it. I don't want a confrontation this weekend.'

She tried to keep her balance in front of him. The punch was zipping past her stomach via a ring-road and going straight to her head.

'So why bother to come up to Oxford at all? You could have stayed in London, and spent your weekend drinking expensive red wine and doing sophisticated things. I expect that's what you usually do, isn't it?'

'He's my brother,' he said flatly.

'But if all you've done is come up here to demoralize him, it's a pretty pointless exercise, isn't it? Or do you get your kicks out of demoralizing people?'

'You don't know anything about our relationship,' he said sharply.

'It's pretty obvious that you don't approve of students. Although you must have been one yourself once, mustn't you?'

'A long time ago. I grew out of it. Now, I accept my responsibilities.'

His tone of moral hauteur furrowed its way under her skin, and dug in deeply.

'Unlike me, I suppose,' she added for him. 'Well, for

48

your information, when you were a lad, lounging around university and going to student parties, I was working for my living. I went straight into a job when I was eighteen, and I stayed in it until I came up here to study. And Maggie's been working all her life. What's more, she held down a job in a pub all the way through her course as well, so that she could make ends meet. So before you start lecturing me again about the bloody taxpayer, just bear in mind that I've been one, and I probably paid for my course in advance before I even got here!'

He braved another mouthful of his punch, watching her as she spoke.

'I suppose you've got a point,' he said obliquely.

'And don't give me this "You're not doing English, are you?" crap either. I don't see what's so wrong with trying to gain some sort of insight into the human condition. It's better than screwing money out of people for a living, and preying on other people's misery, like you do.'

'Thassright. You tell'im.' The drunken slur coming from the dead body in the corner was followed by a loud belch. The body slumped back into sleep. Julia stifled a wild laugh. Leo glanced coldly at the crumpled form, strewn inelegantly across the cane chair. He looked back to Julia with an eloquent expression.

'And this is what you want to spend your time doing now? Hanging around teenagers who can't handle their drink? Sitting around kitchens littered with cigarette ends and half-drunk beer cans? Trying to pretend that the world outside doesn't exist?'

'Oh, don't tell me about the world outside.' She shook her hair back and glared at him. 'I know exactly what's out there.'

'So you're hiding from it, is that it?'

She stuck her plastic cup into her mouth, and bit the rim as she sucked up another pungent mouthful. She really was feeling very drunk, but his comments were hunting her through the haze like truth-seeking missiles. She gazed at him steadily over her cup, wondering why he wouldn't just go away and leave her alone, forgetting the fact that she had sought him out again. She pulled the cup away, forgetting to stop biting on it, and was left with a mouthful of plastic. She looked stupidly at the cup, a chunk taken out of the side, neatly serrated with her teeth marks.

'Ooops,' she said, fishing the offending piece of plastic out of her mouth and wondering where to put it. Leo shook his head, and made an impatient noise.

'This is exactly what I mean. You people are in a world of your own!'

'You're just jealous,' she asserted, wondering why her taking a bite out of a plastic cup by mistake had somehow proved his point.

'I can assure you that I'm not. I wouldn't live like this if I was paid to do it.'

'You are. You're bitter and twisted because your brother's actually enjoying himself, and you're stuck in a rut. Why don't you admit it? And you're jealous because he's got a place at Oxford.'

'I hardly think that's a factor. Where he studies is immaterial. The fact is that he's running away from his responsibilities, and he damned well knows it. That's why he dragged me to this bloody student party, instead of listening to what I had to say to him.'

She clutched her cup, now sure that she was visibly swaying backwards and forwards. A pair of turf-coloured eyes, half brown, half green, wobbled in front of her.

'Well I can't say I blame him,' she said. 'I think if you were coming up for the weekend to see me, I'd probably arrange to be out when you arrived.'

'It's hardly likely that I'd come all this way to see you, is it?' he shot back.

'No,' Julia agreed. 'So why don't you just let me get back to the dancing, and leave you here to wallow in your misery? I only wanted to give you a cup of punch. I have this instinct that makes me take pity on the afflicted. I didn't particularly want to offer myself up for another dose of your disapproval.'

'Do what you like,' he said, standing up straight and looking down his nose at her. 'Take a leaf out of my brother's book. Indulge yourself, and hang the consequences.'

'Thank you. I will.'

She swung away from him, teetering slightly before keeping her balance, and letting herself out of the conservatory and back into the throb of the party. She very pointedly shut the door behind her, leaving Leo alone with the dead body. They deserved each other, she decided.

She spent the next couple of hours immersing herself in the fun, exchanging nonsensical comments with people she vaguely knew, dancing a little, downing another two glasses of punch – or was it three? – and letting herself go with the flow. Why shouldn't she have a blast now and then? At least she was unwinding, burning off some of her pent-up energy, and feeling happy again. It may not have been the most cultured way to spend an evening, but she was enjoying it and, she realized now, she had needed it badly. Too much time to think, to worry about where she was in her life, what she should be doing, was making her uptight. Maggie was right. As usual.

Some time in the early hours, she found Rob standing next to her. She leaned against him and slurred up into his face.

'Where's your delightful brother? Has he got off with someone in the loo?'

Rob snorted. She could tell by the way that he was clinging on to the wall that he was as drunk as she was.

'He's gone home. Miserable bugger. I gave him a key, and sent him away.'

'Oh, good.' She grinned inanely. 'Perhaps he'll get run over on the way.'

'Hope so.'

'So now your chaperone's gone, you can enjoy yourself properly.'

'Yep.'

'So, who're you going to get off with, then?' she teased him.

'Can't do that. Leo won't approve.'

'Oh, sod him.' She leaned more heavily against his shoulder, half-meaning to move away, but her body failing to respond to instructions. 'You can do what you like, can't you?'

'Bit tricky. He's in the spare room, next to mine. He'd hear everything.'

'So—' Her hormones took control of the proceedings. 'Why can't you go home with someone else? I mean, he's got a key, hasn't he?'

'What, someone like you, you mean?'

Somewhere deep inside her alcoholic haze, her pulse began to hammer loudly. Rob was looking down at her face, his eyes bright. He was so, so gorgeous.

'Yes,' said a voice that sounded like hers. 'With me.'

Julia woke up and wondered why she was wedged against the wall. There was a taste in her mouth like well-used cat litter, and her head hurt. She tried to wriggle, and realized with a jolt of shock that she was almost naked. Her arms and legs were bare, but she was still bound up in her underwear. She tried to turn over, and felt a warm human back against hers.

A flash of panic assailed her. Who had got into her bed in the night? She struggled round violently to face the intruding lump of flesh, and focused on a mass of gleaming brown hair, and a broad pair of tanned shoulders. She could hear a faint snoring sound.

For a moment, she froze in utter horror. Then, piece by small piece, a jigsaw began to put itself together in her head. It started with the corner pieces, then went along the straight edges, then a couple of vaguely recognizable features came together in the middle. But there were still big unsightly gaps in it. She reached out a hand, and shook the shoulder that was embedded in her under-sheet.

'Rob? Rob! You've got to wake up.'

The body stirred, groaned, and turned slowly on to its back. Rob put a hand up to his eyes and left it there. There was a long silence, interrupted only by his moans.

'Rob?'

'It's Julia, isn't it?'

'Yes,' she said, faintly perturbed by the question.

'Oh God. I feel like shit.'

His moans increased as Fleabag decided to leap from the wardrobe on to the bed, landing with a thump on Rob's stomach. He prowled up to the pillows to sniff the intruder.

'I hate cats,' Rob muttered, trying to turn over again.

This was more disturbing news. Julia squeezed her eyes together tight and opened them again. Rob was still in her bed – a single bed, with no room to escape from him. She would have to edge her way down the bed and climb off the end. Not very elegant, but from what she could remember from the previous night, none of her behaviour had been very elegant. Fleabag opened his mouth and blasted a miaow at her, bluntly reminding her that his breakfast was well overdue.

'All right, sweetheart.' She sat up, her head pounding in response. The pain momentarily subsided. She pulled herself out from under the duvet, and slid down the bed to drop off the end. Very quickly, she grabbed her towelling dressing gown, and flung it on. Whatever had happened last night, she wasn't about to be scrutinized in the cold light of day in a pair of dishcloth-grey knickers and a matching bra, with a screaming hangover. She pulled her fingers through her hair, disturbed to find that most of it had conspired to form a knotted beehive on top of her head, and quietly followed Fleabag through to the kitchen. She closed the adjoining door behind her, desperately in need of a moment of privacy.

The kitchen danced around in front of her eyes. A slant of bright sunlight was firing its way through the window in the back door and glancing across the white units. She winced. She stumbled to the cupboard, and pulled out a tin of cat food. Then she filled up the kettle, pausing at the sink to wonder whether she had thrown up in it last night. From a bleary inspection, she assured herself that the contents of her stomach must have remained *in situ*. That was some comfort.

She found the teapot. Forgetting to plug the kettle in, she spooned cat food into the teapot, and began to pour loose leaf tea into Fleabag's plastic bowl. Giving up on herself, she took two aspirins, and tried again. This time Fleabag got his breakfast. He launched into it noisily, causing her a serious burst of nausea. She sat down at the kitchen table and stared aimlessly into space for two minutes while the nausea subsided.

She could remember the party, most of it at least. And having an argument with someone – Rob's brother, that was right. She could distantly remember defending Rob to him. Vigorously. She cringed. Had she been really rude? Yes, but he had been ruder to her. That was all right then. Then she could remember Rob's face looming at hers, and— The next thing she remembered was being in a taxi, pointing out landmarks to Rob, and him telling her every few seconds that he lived in Oxford too and knew what everything was, thank you. God, the cab driver must have been gritting his teeth. Who had paid? Did it matter? Probably not. Then they'd come in, and she had a vague picture of a struggle. A struggle? Or was it passion? Plenty of bodily contact, anyway. She'd put some music on, very loud. Oh God, the clogs would have heard them! No, it was Saturday, and the clogs were up a mountain. That was lucky. Oh yes, she was supposed to feed the fish.

The kettle clicked and she slowly got up. Her body ached all over, but even in her confusion, she knew that whatever clumsy intimacy there might have been in her bedsitting room, the underwear which was now firmly in place had remained that way throughout. Even when she was anaesthetized to the point of oblivion, and with a man she might have picked out of a catalogue, it appeared that she still couldn't break the spell.

Oh hell, she thought, as she strained to lift up the kettle and fill the teapot. What on earth would Rob think of her now? Wasn't she the one who had propositioned him? She felt horribly sure that she was. And they hardly knew each other. Her mother would have fainted. She wasn't sure that she wasn't going to faint herself. How *had* she managed to bring him home with her?

She carried the teapot, milk and sugar over to the table on three careful, separate journeys. Then she took two mugs from the cupboard, and set them down. She set about pouring the tea, hearing sounds of movement from the next room.

Well, at least he was getting up. That saved the embarrassment of her serving him tea in bed, and him lying there, trapped, staring longingly across the room at his boxer shorts. The boxer shorts that he, at least, had apparently been brave enough to discard. In another few moments, the door opened, and he appeared. He looked distinctly dishevelled, his clothes at least back on in the right order. He still managed to look utterly desirable, but there was something else. He looked very unhappy. She gave him an uncertain smile, hoping that she didn't look as terrifying as she thought.

'I've made tea,' she said, nudging a mug towards him.

'Right.' He yawned elaborately, and closed his mouth again. He seemed unsure about what to do next.

'Look, have a cup of tea. And I've got aspirins if you want some.'

'Er, actually, I think I'd better get back.'

'What, right now? At least have some tea first?'

Her heart began to beat slowly with a sense of impending doom. She had thought, in an illogical way, as she made the tea, that he just might stay for a bit and talk to her. But he looked as if that was the last thing on his mind.

'Your cat slept on my shirt,' he stated. She could see there were a few black hairs dotted on the cotton.

'Oh, I'm sorry. He usually sleeps on my head. I expect there wasn't room for him last night . . .' She tailed off. It was too cosy to talk like this. She could tell that it wasn't welcome.

'Look, Julia—'

'It's all right,' she said brightly, picking up her mug and clutching it tightly. 'I know what you're going to say. We shouldn't have done it. Whatever it was that we actually did.'

'It's just . . .' He sighed, blinking slowly at her. 'I don't think I want a relationship right now.'

'Neither do I,' she said, easing the situation for him.

'It's the last thing I want. So you don't have to be embarrassed, okay? I don't expect we need to see too much of each other. I hardly go near the University buildings these days.'

'What about the class?'

'I won't tell them if you won't.' She tried to be flippant. It seemed to work.

'I just don't want you to—' He pushed a hand through his hair. Such lovely hair. Her stomach turned again. 'You know, I don't want you to expect anything. To hope for anything.'

'What sort of woman do you think I am?' She sat up straight, giving him an ironic look. 'I'm not planning to camp out in your garden. I'm a straightforward sort of person, okay? So relax. I was drunk last night, and so were you. And things obviously didn't go as far as they might have done. That's all there is to it.'

'Yep, I was. Appallingly drunk.'

Thanks, she thought. 'So you'd better get back to your brother, hadn't you, before he arrives with a shotgun.'

'Shit! Leo!' His face coloured, and he looked away from her quickly. 'Christ.'

'It's got nothing to do with him, has it?'

'You think so? Oh, he's going to love this.' He shook his head, and pulled his jacket together in front of his shirt.

'Why should he care? I expect he got a good night's sleep.'

'Yeah. Right. Well, I'll be off then. See you around.'

'Yes, see you at the class.'

He went. The door to the bedsit closed. She heard him pace down the corridor. The front door swung shut with a clatter.

She stared at the empty mug on the table. The hand that was holding her tea began to shake violently. She put her mug down carefully. The bedsit was suddenly quiet, eerily quiet. Fleabag appeared on the table, and tried to climb up on to her shoulder. She pushed him away.

'Not now.'

She got up, and walked slowly back into the main room. The sheets on the bed were rumpled, the pillows indented. The duvet was thrown back where he had got up and left it. The clothes that she had worn last night were scattered about the carpet. She began to pick them up and put them in a pile. Then she stopped and sank on to the bed, staring into space bleakly with her head in her hands.

Chapter Four

It wasn't until later in the day that Julia actually realized the phone was off the hook.

After she had cried herself into exhaustion, she had taken a long bath, and spent the rest of the morning cleaning the bedsit. She hoovered away all trace of Rob's presence, as if he might have left molecules of himself ingrained in the carpet, and piled the bedclothes into the washing machine. And she had scrubbed everything scrubbable with a solution of mild bleach. Then she threw open the door into the garden to let the cold March air sweep through the kitchen.

As she wrestled with her hangover, she replayed the events of the last three days through her head. She castigated herself furiously for having been so miraculously stupid. She had met the man on Thursday, spent the night with him on Friday, and by Saturday, they were no longer on speaking terms. It was, without question, the briefest, most unsatisfying relationship she had ever had.

She'd had one or two pointless flings before. They had happened at moments when she'd been busy doing other things, and she hadn't dwelt on them for any longer than they were worth. They were in the distant past, snapshot memories with no depth or focus. They had been before Bill. But then she had met Bill.

After Bill, there was nobody. Not in London, and not in Oxford. She'd had opportunities, some that she thought she even might take, but it never happened. And now she was thirty.

She realized, as she washed Fleabag's food bowl for the third time, that she wasn't able to have flings now. Not because any book of rules was telling her so, but because the disappointment she felt, mingled with distaste, and sprinkled with a topping of acute embarrassment, was something that she simply did not want to feel. She just wasn't the same person that she used to be. Trying to do the things she used to do was futile.

And if she was brutally honest with herself, she probably had lost her direction. She was waiting for a vocational flash of inspiration to assail her, and getting very frustrated that it refused to oblige. She could never decide from one minute to the next whether staying on in Oxford was a benefit or a drawback. There was nowhere obvious for her to move to, especially now that she had lost contact with most of her old friends. But sometimes she felt just like an old colonial, refusing to let go. And now she had added to her own dilemma by spending the night with a man she was destined to see at least once a week at the basic skills class. The one activity in her life that she could focus on.

And she remembered that she had spent most of her time with Leo standing up for Rob, although she hardly knew him. Although she didn't exactly expect him to thank her for it, it might have been nice if he'd acknowledged it. But regardless, he'd shot in and out of her flat on a horizontal bungee jump. She became more angry with herself as the day lumbered on. And as she squirted the wardrobe door with polish and rubbed at it with superhuman strength, she noticed that the phone was off the hook.

'Fleabag!'

He was out in the garden, quivering with excitement and squeaking like a rubber toy as he watched a flock of starlings gather in the cherry tree. Given the competition, he chose to ignore her. She slumped to the floor and put the receiver back, staring at it for a while. As long as it wasn't her mother. She couldn't talk to her today.

She went through the routine of finding out who had called. She listened to the information, and frowned. Someone had called at two fifty-seven a.m.? The number was Maggie's.

She hung on to the receiver. What the hell was Maggie doing ringing her at three o'clock in the morning? And more to the point, what had been going on in the room when Fleabag had answered the phone, and left it lying face up on the carpet only a few yards from her bed?

She dialled Maggie's number, and waited with growing tension.

'Maggie! You didn't call me last night, did you?'

'Hello, there. Have a good night, did you?' Her cheerful question suggested that she'd already provided the answer for herself. Julia groaned. She had a vague memory of dancing out of Maggie's house, her arm linked through Rob's. It was too much to hope that anyone who'd seen her might be suffering from amnesia today.

'I don't remember much about it, to be honest.'

'Well, at least Rob saw you home. That was nice of him. Perhaps you'll see each other again now?'

'You saw us leave together, then.'

'I rang the taxi for you. I expect you were too preoccupied to notice, though. It's a real bummer that that scary brother of his turned up again. You must have been spitting venom.'

'His brother? You mean Leo? When did he turn up? I mean, where?'

Maggie paused.

'He came here, love. Just after you'd left. Rob gave him

61

the wrong key, and he got fed up with waiting outside the house in his car, he said. So he came back to find him, only you'd gone by then.'

'I'm getting the picture,' Julia said slowly. 'So just who telephoned here at three in the morning?'

'Well, I had to give him your number. I guessed Rob'd probably stay a bit with you. Why, what happened? How come you didn't know he phoned?'

'Oh deary, deary me,' Julia understated.

'Something's wrong, I can tell.'

'Only that at three this morning I didn't hear the phone ring. Which means that Fleabag answered it without me knowing.'

'Was Rob with you?'

'You're catching on, Maggie.'

There was a silence. Then Maggie let out a gust of laughter.

'Oh, I'm sorry. I can't help it. When I think of the look on his face!' Julia listened to her doubling up, wishing she could find it all so funny. 'No wonder he looked so tight-lipped when he put the phone down. I just asked him if he'd got through, and he said yes, he bloody well had. Then he stormed out. I wonder where he went?'

'Well, he didn't turn up here.'

'I wouldn't have given him your address, would I? He must have slept in his car.'

'I can't imagine Leo settling for curling up in a car seat all night, can you? More likely he went back to London. I can just see him doing that. Sweeping down the M40 with a face like an iceberg. I hope he was breathalysed.'

'Oh dear, Julia. D'you really think he got an earful, then?'

'I don't think I want to talk about it, Maggie.' Julia took a deep breath. 'Rob left this morning as soon as he was conscious. He didn't even stay for a cup of tea. Just shot out the door with a face like death. I don't think I'm going to be seeing him again – socially, at least.'

'Oh, dear.' Maggie's voice softened with sympathy. 'Oh, I'm sorry. I thought he was such a nice boy, too.'

'I think he's still nice. He just doesn't want to go out with me,' Julia said starkly. 'I feel like a complete prat.'

'You're not a prat,' Maggie said sternly. 'And I don't care whether you were both drunk or not. He's not a kid, is he? At least he could have talked it through with you.'

'We're talking about a man, Maggie. They don't talk things through. When they sense a meaningful conversation coming on, they hit warp drive.'

'They're not all like that, Julia.' Maggie didn't sound particularly convincing.

'Well, it doesn't matter now. There's no point in giving it a *post mortem*, is there? But anyway, I wondered if I could come round and help with the clearing up? I would have called earlier, but I knew I wasn't fit to travel.'

Maggie accommodated Julia's verbal handbrake turn. 'Don't worry, the kids did it this morning. Hey, and guess what? I was on my way to the bathroom, and I saw this lad coming out of Naomi's room. He looked pretty shaken up, I can tell you. Who'd have thought it?'

Julia took herself to Tesco's to cheer herself up. Usually she felt better after a conversation with Maggie, but now she felt distinctly worse. The fact that her behaviour was no better than mousey Naomi's had not helped to boost her self-esteem. And to add to her own mortification over her unfulfilling one-night-stand, she now had the good news that they'd had an audience.

In the entrance to the store she passed the photo booth. For the first time she noticed a curious message plastered across the outside. It read 'Take your picture until you are happy'. Above it was a poster-sized sample photograph of a young man with bouffant hair who looked as if he'd spent a week under a drier. She was considering lunging through the nylon curtains and thrusting herself on to the rotating plastic stool when she realized that it wasn't in fact a miraculous cure for depression, but a more mundane reference to the fact that people can never believe that they are as hideous as their passport photographs prove. She picked up a basket, shaking off the four others that were attached to it, and aimed for Fresh Fruit and Vegetables.

As she lingered aimlessly over the Value carrots, her head filled with a stern voice ridiculing her for spending her time with kids half her age. Well, not quite half, but near enough. Perhaps she was hiding from the world. Perhaps the formidable Leo had been entirely right about everything, and perhaps that was why she had tried to drown him in white wine?

She coasted up to the Bakery, and filled her basket with plastic boxes of sticky cakes. Then she put them all back again. Turning herself into a human basketball wouldn't solve the problem. And now, suddenly, it did feel as if there was a problem. She headed for the Toiletries instead. It didn't strike her that she was pre-menstrual until she looked down and found her basket full of smelly things – everything from a bag of pot-pourri to a can of body spray and a pack of lavender soap. She couldn't face putting them all back again. Someone would be upstairs, watching the monitors linked to the security cameras, deciding that she was mad. She lugged the load on to Pet Foods, and spent the next fifteen minutes assessing the flavours in an attempt to decide which were the most appetizing.

'Stupid, aren't we?' came a cheerful voice at her right elbow.

She looked round. A woman with an unnaturally

healthy face was beaming at her.

'I'm sorry?'

'Trying to work out which are the nicest.' She nodded at the mountainous range of tins.

'Ah, yes. I suppose we are.'

The woman grinned in obvious conspiracy, and Julia smiled curtly. She didn't want to get into a nonsensical discussion in the middle of Tesco's. She'd come shopping to be alone. They both turned their attention back to the labels, and continued in their earnest endeavour. Some minutes later, Julia noticed peevishly that the woman had gone, whilst she herself was still comparing the merits of salmon and tuna with those of sardine and mackerel. It made her careful analysis seem like an inability to make a decision. She quickly threw both tins on top of her shopping and headed off to Wines and Spirits, now quite decided upon a four-pack of lager of any merit. She was loading the cans into her basket, when there was a tap on her shoulder.

She hesitated for a moment. If this was the grinning woman, about to say, 'Stupid, aren't we?' again, she would have to punch her in the face. She turned round cautiously.

'Hi.'

For a moment, she stood inertly, trying to place the face smiling at hers. Her brain clicked just before it became embarrassing.

'Mack! Oh, hi!'

She forced a bright, pleased-to-see-you look. He shifted a little. She tried to think of suitable mundane conversation that wouldn't reveal that she was in the middle of a major crisis. A question dribbled from her lips.

'What are you doing here?'

'Shopping.'

'Of course. Stupid question.'

'Just picking up a bottle, actually. I've got someone coming round and I want to impress them.'

'Ah.' She nodded slowly. Her stomach lurched again. Romantic evenings were the last thing on her mind. 'Well, have fun, won't you?'

She started to turn back, but his body language stopped her. He was leaning from one leg to the other as if he was shy of asking a question.

'What is it, Mack?'

'Er.' He sniffed, standing up straight. 'I – er. Look, d'you think this is a good choice?'

He held out a bottle of red wine for her to see. Slowly, stupidly, the penny dropped. So slowly and stupidly that her reaction was plastered across her face for him to see. She saw him stiffen.

'Forget it. I'm sure it'll be fine.'

'No, no. Let me have a look. I don't know much about wine, but . . .'

'But you probably know more than I do. Is that it?'

'I'm sorry, Mack. That's not what I meant—'

'The thing is, when I was in France, there was this wine I really liked. But I can't find it. Can you see if you can see it? It's usually got flowers on the label. It's a Beaujolais. Fleurie it's called. They probably haven't got it.'

She gave him a swift look, burying her surprise under fifteen feet of earth, before following him across the aisle to the shelves where the wine was stacked. She found the French wines, and scanned the collection.

'No, I don't think . . . Oh! It's here! There you are.'

She levered a bottle from the shelf and handed it to him with a glow of triumph. It wasn't cheap. He must seriously be setting out to impress someone. She saw a small smile tug at his lips.

'That's great. Great.'

She stood a moment longer, noticing his perforated jeans, his scuffed leather jacket, his mop of blond hair. And the fact that he was very tall. His head was bent as he looked intently at the label, as if trying to burn its image into his brain.

'Well, enjoy your wine, then.'

'Yeah. Good job I saw you, wasn't it?'

He winked at her, reminding her with a jolt that he'd done the same only two days ago, and headed off. He disappeared around the corner. She stood and stared after him.

Preconceptions! She abused herself violently. What had she been taught when she had gone to the training sessions in an attempt to get her initial teaching certificate? Don't assume *anything*.

She stirred, heaving her basket on to her other arm, and carted her bizarre assortment of goods, crowned majestically by a four-pack of Tesco's own lager, towards the check-out.

After she had assured Julia that there was no clearing up left to be done, Maggie rang off and stopped to roll a cigarette. The house was quiet now. Naomi had announced that she was going into town, and had gone. Maggie had a sneaking suspicion that she'd arranged to meet someone. Possibly the lad she'd frightened the life out of on the landing that morning. She wasn't sure who'd been the more startled, him or her. Well, good luck to the lass. She deserved a bit of happiness. And Fabian had gone back to bed after his heroic stint with the Zoflora. It was miraculous that only one person had thrown up last night given the power of Fabian's punch. But at least they'd had the decency to do it in the conservatory where they could open the double doors and give it a good airing.

Picking a shred of tobacco from her lip, she stared around the living-room, at the mustard velour sofa, the thin carpet, the cream woodchip wallpaper plastered with Fabian's posters. At least they gave the room a bit of life. Kandinsky, Fabian had said. Four years ago, she would have dismissed the meld of colours as pretentious crap. Pete would have snorted derisively down his nose at them. 'Just give me a paintbrush, stick it up my arse, and I'll give you a masterpiece,' is what he would say if he saw them.

She flicked her gold lighter, the one Pete had given her for their twenty-fifth, lit her cigarette and began to laugh. She knew what he meant. And she wasn't a complete convert herself. There were too many lines that the past had etched on her face for her to move on and leave it behind her. And there were still things to resolve with Pete – things that she was putting off, and after twenty-nine years of marriage she knew he was putting off too. At some point, they'd both have to face the situation they were in, but for now, she guessed he was limping through the present with one foot stuck in the past as well.

Her own living-room superimposed itself. She still thought of it as hers, even though she hadn't been back now for nearly a year. In some ways, it wasn't so different. She remembered choosing the velveteen curtains with Pete, fifteen years ago. They were almost the same shade of mustard as the sofa. They were very practical, the assistant had said. Kept out the draughts. And there were plenty of draughts in those years, when they used to turn off the gas fire downstairs so that the kids would be warm upstairs while they were doing their homework.

That house had seen them through their marriage. From beginning to end. When they got back from their honeymoon in Scarborough, Uncle Eric and Auntie Betty had given them a mattress until they could afford to buy a double bed. And when they did buy one, it was a divan, with drawers in the side that slid in and out like a dream. Could there be a happier woman than me, Maggie had thought, squeezing Pete's arm as Uncle Eric gave them a lift to pick the divan up in his van. They'd all squashed into the front seat, and he'd given them both a suggestive look.

'There's something about new beds,' he'd said. 'You'll see, Mags. You'll be pregnant within a month.'

She longed for the moment. The house had three bedrooms, and they were aching to be filled. She'd already made plans in her head for the decoration of the baby's bedroom. In time, of course, when they could afford it. When her pregnancy was confirmed, she came home from the doctor and took herself into the small bedroom at the front which she'd always reserved for their first. She wanted the baby to have the best that they could afford. Then she realized that what they could afford was far from the best. Instead of announcing the news to Pete that night, she kept it to herself, and took on an extra shift at the factory. When the smell of the raw meat going into the pies became too much for her, she took on an evening job as a barmaid instead. Pete hadn't been pleased. He didn't want a load of drunks looking down her cleavage, he'd said. So she'd explained that they were going to have a baby and they needed all the cash they could get. The next day, he'd gone to speak to the landlord of the Red Lion in person to explain why she couldn't work there any more. And he took on extra shifts himself to make up the difference.

She should have known then, Maggie thought, re-lighting her dead cigarette, that she wasn't going to be able to go the distance with Pete. The nights that Pete worked late shifts, she had worked in the Red Lion without telling him. It got a bit dodgy. On a couple of occasions, he'd got home before her, and roared like a bull to find the house empty. She'd told him she'd been round at her mum's, and her old mum, bless her, had covered for her. At least until she'd started to show. Then the landlord of the Red Lion had asked her to take time out until she was the sort of shape that the customers could stomach over eight pints of Tetley's. She'd accepted it all philosophically. After all, she'd only been twenty at the time. And she'd opened an account of her own, and put her own money into it, so that she could buy things for the baby. Yet another thing that she had kept from Pete, until he found her statements stuffed in her knicker drawer.

'What the sodding hell are these?' he'd yelled, hurling them at her.

'I just wanted to do something, by myself, to help us,' she'd said, sinking on to the bedspread, and crying with shame.

'And I'm not man enough to provide for my family, is that it? What I do isn't good enough for you? Well, I'll tell you what you can do. You can go to the bank tomorrow, and you can close this bloody account. And you tell them from me that Pete Ridley can support his wife and his new baby without his wife skivvying for him. D'you understand?'

'Yes,' she'd sobbed.

'Did you hear me? I said, Do You Understand?'

'Yes! I understand!'

And so Maggie had begun, at the age of twenty, to become adept at hiding her feelings from her husband. But in time, it became less important. She had Jason, then two years later Terry came along, and finally a little girl, Kay. She seemed to be losing Pete, but she had her three children. Beautiful children who she lavished with all the love that Pete didn't seem to need from her any more. He got a promotion, became a production line supervisor, and she supported him every step of the way. And her life was timeless. The children were always there. There was always something to be seen to, something to be mended. And before long, she wore Pete down with her requests to work again.

'Do what you sodding want, just stop nagging me, woman!' he ultimately announced, snapping her bonds with a single proclamation.

The Red Lion took her back.

Maggie wandered through to the kitchen and put the kettle on. She looked out of the kitchen window at the barren garden, at the conservatory doors opened wide to embrace the cold spring day, and smiled to herself. The Red Lion had stood by her through it all. Even when she had to change her shifts to make it to the evening classes, and did Saturday and Sunday lunch-times to make up, they accepted it. She'd dropped a tray of glasses one night, just coming up to her first exam, and Ian, the landlord, had told her she looked dog-tired. Instead of firing her, he sent her home to get some rest. She'd got home, stared at the heap of ironing that Pete had dumped on the kitchen table for her to find, and set up the ironing board on automatic pilot while she listened to *King Lear* on cassette. By the time it came to the paper, she knew the play off by heart. Once, she'd thought that Pete had turned the telly down in the other room so that he could hear it too, but when she'd asked him about it, he'd bitten her head off and switched over to the snooker.

She saw some life in the Red Lion. Things that she told Pete about, and that in the evolving years they laughed about together. And some things that she never told him about. But she was never unfaithful. It never entered her mind.

The kitchen door swung open, and she became aware that someone was standing in the doorway. She jerked herself back to reality. To what was happening now. It was Fabian, his chest bare, a pair of tracksuit bottoms slung around his lower body, clinging loosely to his hips. He yawned expansively, stretching his arms up to the flaking paint on the ceiling, revealing the downy dark hair under his arms. Then his arms retracted and spread over his chest. He rubbed himself lazily, then caught up his elasticated waistband in his hands, and flipped it back up to his waist.

Maggie watched him. Pulling herself up straight, she put on her habitual expression of patient indulgence.

'D'you fancy a cuppa? The kettle's on.'

She waited, her breath caught in her throat, for him to answer. He seemed to hesitate for a moment, and then he gave her a sleepy, warm smile.

'That would be lovely.'

She opened the cupboard and picked out two mugs. Thank God, she whispered to herself. It's going to be all right.

Julia stomped home with her shopping, riddled with guilt for spending money she didn't have on miscellaneous perfumed goods that neither she nor Fleabag could eat. As she stood at the pedestrian crossing, staring across the Cowley Road at her favourite newsagent, she remembered that she hadn't bought a lottery ticket. It was a hassle to squeeze her way into Mr Hussain's narrow aisles to get one from his stand at the back of the shop, but it would have to be done. After all, she thought, you never knew if your luck was going to change.

She stumbled into the shop, and was instantly greeted with recognition.

'Ah, Miss Cole. You have come for your ticket, yes?'

'Yes, Mr Hussain. I forgot to get it in the supermarket. Again.'

'Well, I'm happy then,' Mr Hussain continued to call over the heads of the customers he was serving at the counter. 'And while you're here, why not buy your other things?'

She gave him a weak smile and ploughed her way down the shop to the end. She did feel rotten for barging in with her bags full of cheaper and fresher purchases from across the road. Poor Mr Hussain. He was making a valiant effort to keep going in the face of the competition. But he did have one great advantage over the superstore, and she stopped for a moment to appreciate the wall of shelves laden with bags of spices and jars of exotic sauces. All twice the size and half the price of the brand names across the road. And he stocked things that she had never heard of. She had told Maggie about Hussain's as soon as she had discovered it, and she knew that Maggie now made the trek down to East Oxford for all of her more unusual ingredients. The fact that she had put some business his way alleviated the guilt a little.

She picked up a bag of cinnamon sticks and clung on to them, wondering what she would do with them when she got home. Then she filled in her numbers. Taking the slip back to the till, she saw that the customers had cleared. Mr Hussain gave her a big smile.

'And how is your life treating you, Miss Cole?'

She considered being honest, and decided against it.

'Fine, as usual. And you?'

'I can't complain. My wife says we must not complain. When you see people who are much worse off, don't you think? Why don't you have a newspaper, while you are here?'

'Oh, yes. I'd forgotten that as well.'

73

Hoping that he couldn't see the Saturday *Guardian* wedged into one of her shopping bags, she stooped over the newspapers and picked out a *Telegraph*, convincing herself that what she really wanted to do that evening was pore over the prize crossword. She added it to the bag of cinnamon sticks on the counter while he processed her lottery ticket.

'Mr Hussain, did you speak to your wife about the class?'

He looked up, his face rueful. He shrugged expressively.

'My wife, she has a mind of her own, you know?' He chuckled. 'Yes, I spoke to her, but the thing is—' He leaned forward and lowered his voice. 'She thinks that people will think she's stupid, going back to school. I say to her, when she watches the television, "Why don't you go and learn this language properly, like I have?" But what can I do? If she won't learn, she won't learn. But now, I tell you something. My son, he's sitting his GCSEs, and she cannot help him! And now, we have to go to the school, to talk to the teachers. You know, an evening for the parents? And she won't come! Because she thinks people will think she is stupid!'

'Oh, that's not true.' Julia paused with her purse closed, listening to him. 'There's a lady at the class I teach called Shirani, and she must be older than your wife. And she's been going for three years. She's made so much progress, you wouldn't believe it. If only your wife would give it a try.'

He shook his head, and poked the buttons on the till. The drawer popped open. Julia paid him, and while she was pushing her purse back into her handbag, she saw that she had an old leaflet advertising the classes lurking in the depths of the bag. She plucked it out, dusted the fluff off it, and handed it to Mr Hussain.

'Here. These are the details of the classes, and who to talk to if you want to come to one. Please read it to her, Mr Hussain. If you tell her about Shirani too, she might change her mind.'

He took the leaflet, and squinted at it. Then he tucked it away in his trouser pocket.

'I'll try. I can only try, can't I?'

Julia carted her shopping home, and as she pushed open the front door to the dark main hall remembered that she was supposed to feed the fish. She thumped into her bedsit, dropped the bags, picked up the keys, and made her way upstairs. She looked down as she twisted the key in Annelies's lock, and saw Fleabag sitting expectantly by her boots.

'You want to come in too? I suppose you can, as long as you don't shred anything.'

Inside, Annelies's bedsit was the same shape as hers, but it was darker, the light from the kitchen cast through a small sash window. In the main room, Julia stopped as she always did to look at the posters crowding the walls. Mountains, escarpments, craggy cliff faces. Punctuating the larger posters were smaller photographs dotted about. Annelies in climbing gear, Annelies in pot-holing gear. Annelies and her boyfriend in the Pyrenees. She felt a twinge of jealousy. It took courage to climb up a mountain. A real one or an imagined one.

She cursed herself for getting philosophical, and stared at the bed instead. So neatly put back together, a small, indefinable stuffed animal placed affectionately on the pillow, with a little satin heart stuck to its chest reading 'Amsterdam'. There was no evidence of the seismic activity that habitually took place there. But of course, there wouldn't be, would there?

Horrified with herself for being voyeuristic, she turned her attention to the fish. Fleabag had found his way up to the top of the tank, and was seated comfortably on the wire mesh, trying to push an oversized black paw through a hole the size of a two-pence piece. She grabbed him quickly, and dumped him on the floor.

'Don't you dare!' she scolded. He blinked innocent green eyes back at her. She pointed a warning finger at him and, heartened that he seemed to lose interest in the fish, bent her head to peer into the oblong tank.

Judging by the bulging eyes that looked back at her and the expressions of permanent astonishment, she wasn't the only one to have voyeuristic tendencies. Poor fish. What they must be exposed to in this room. She picked up the pot of food, and sprinkled the amount that Annelies had dictated over the wire. Instantly, the little gold shapes wafted up to the surface, and sucked in the multicoloured dots floating there. They were quite cute, she supposed. But she couldn't imagine swapping Fleabag for half a dozen fish. They didn't exactly respond to affection, did they? But then with a life like Annelies's, and a boyfriend with all the persistence of a pneumatic drill, she suspected there was no time to get soppy about animals. Even the kitsch little toy on the bed would be jettisoned across the room in the heat of the moment, abandoned and forgotten.

She gave the fish another half-pinch of food, to compensate for the irrational pity she felt for them, and steered Fleabag towards the door that led from the kitchen to the landing, all but booting him out ahead of her. She trudged back down the stairs.

Everybody seemed busy. Everybody but herself, of course. The clogs, as she'd privately named them for the sake of mental convenience, never seemed to stand still. Even when they were lying down. Vivienne had her family and her responsibility running the class, Rob had his research to bury himself in, Leo had his criminals to intimidate, Mack had his decorating, Mr Hussain had his shop, Fabian and mousey Naomi had their degrees to work for, and even Maggie had her part-time job at the pub and her salacious stories.

So what had happened to Julia? At what point had it all ground to a halt? Why was it that, having dreamt for all her adult life of breaking free from her restraints, of studying for the degree that had always eluded her, of opening doors of opportunity for herself, she now felt that she was shut in a room with the doors locked, as if the only thing left for her to do in life was to register for her old-age pension? Why hadn't the degree changed everything, as she'd thought it would?

She let herself back into her bedsit, and began to unpack her shopping without enthusiasm. If only, she thought as she piled the pack of soap, the can of body spray and the bag of pot-pourri into a heap on top of the cinnamon sticks, if only she hadn't compounded the problem with a disastrous attempt at a one-night stand. It had been a miserable start to the day, and it didn't seem to be in any danger of getting better.

She put the kettle on, picked up the *Telegraph*, and sat down at the kitchen table with the crossword. She pondered over it for a while. After fifteen minutes she was still holding her pen over the white squares, unable to solve a single clue. Her pondering turned to irritation. After half an hour, it erupted into anger. She tossed the newspaper to one side, and stared down at the clinically clean table top.

It was no use. She couldn't concentrate on anything else. She had to finally face up to the fact that she had a problem. While she'd been busy, studying, meeting new people, scrambling towards the next deadline, she'd been able to live for the moment, to enjoy every day as it arrived.

But the University experience hadn't changed her as much as she'd thought it would. She was still the same person, with the same past which had moulded and directed her. The problems she'd arrived with were still there, although she'd succeeded in filing them away for three years. It was like waking up after a vivid dream and realizing that the washing-up was waiting in the sink and the bin still needed emptying.

Maggie had told her that her life was still ahead of her. A life ahead of her that Bill had no part in. Bill, who was living his life without her. Wasn't it time that she dealt with him?

She sat quietly, and allowed herself to remember, her body rigid. She waited for a long time, without moving, until the fear had passed. After it, a quiet determination began to grow in her.

She had to try, at least, to do something about it.

Chapter Five

'You're a little depressed.'

Julia looked politely at the petite young doctor sitting on the other side of the vast teak desk. Even she seemed younger than Julia was. And look what she'd done with her life. Julia also noticed that she had an engagement ring on her finger. A healthy salary, a fulfilling career, and a fiancé to boot. What would she know about depression?

'I thought it might be something like that, but I wasn't sure. Can you give me something for it?'

Dr Baker flicked her heavy plait over her shoulder, and looked at the woman perching on the chair. She was trying to look comfortable, but the doctor could tell from her body language that she was very tense. She was clutching her handbag on her lap as if she was worried that someone was about to snatch it and although she was sitting up straight, her neck was straining. Every so often she darted a glance at the door, as if she couldn't wait to get out of the room. Or as if she was afraid of somebody walking in and finding her here. And she looked very tired, as if she hadn't slept for a couple of days. Otherwise, she had everything going for her. She was nice-looking, attractive in an unproclaimed, harmonious way, with tawny hair and eyes, a slim figure and an open face, and when she had checked the computer, Dr Baker had seen that her old registered address was an Oxford college.

'You've told me about your symptoms,' she began carefully, conscious that Julia Cole was a little older than herself. 'You've said you're not concentrating, spending a lot of time on your own, finding it hard to be enthusiastic about anything. And you're tired, sleeping erratically, and not eating well. Those are all symptoms of a form of depression.' She gave a comforting smile. 'I think not too severe in your case. Is there anything else you want to tell me?'

Julia surreptitiously glanced at her watch. She'd already been in with the doctor for ten minutes. Wasn't she supposed to be throwing her out and moving on to the next patient by now?

'Don't worry about the time,' Dr Baker interjected. 'We allow fifteen-minute slots for the patients here, and we run over if necessary. We believe in giving people as much attention as they need.'

'Oh.'

'So, do you want to say anything else?'

Julia watched the gold ring flash on the young woman's finger as she pushed a strand of hair neatly behind her ear.

'Congratulations.' She nodded at the ring.

Dr Baker smiled at her, her gaze steady.

'Is it a relationship you'd like to talk about?'

'To you?' Julia couldn't conceal her surprise. 'I'm sorry, that sounded rude. I just meant, can't you give me some pills or something?'

'It may be that you need something to buck you up, and that you'll be able to get on with things that way. From what you're telling me, this is a mild depression, and it might lift in time of its own accord. But if the cause of your depression is more deep-rooted, it'll be just papering over the cracks.' She hesitated a little. 'We can put you in touch with a counsellor, if you'd like that?'

'Oh, no. I don't think that's necessary.'

'Sometimes . . .' Dr Baker shifted in her seat, and sat

up straight again. This was a tricky one. But her gut instinct was telling her to persist. 'Sometimes we bury things, don't we? Things we don't want to think about?'

'Like the state of the economy, you mean?'

'No.' She smiled. 'I mean personal things. Things that have happened to us. Things that we might not have wanted to happen.'

Julia swallowed.

'Do we?'

'Yes,' Dr Baker said more firmly. 'We do.'

'Oh. Can I have some pills then?'

Dr Baker held the unwavering gaze of the tawny eyes for a moment. She was hiding something. And she was good at it. But not quite good enough.

'Can I call you Julia?' she asked.

'Yes, of course. Can I call you Dr Baker?'

'You can call me Caroline, if you want. You should understand that medical training isn't what it used to be, Julia. You should feel free to talk to me. Anything you say will be treated as strictly confidential. We're not just here to prescribe pills, you know. We're here to listen, too.'

Julia nodded.

'So . . . would you like to talk about anything?'

'I – what do you mean?'

'Julia. I don't want to push you if it will make you unhappy, but I wondered if you might like to consider counselling as a way to think things through. Depressions don't occur for no reason at all. The counsellors we refer people to are trained professionals, and very good at listening. That's if you want to talk.'

'It's nothing. It's just that I'm unemployed, that's all.'

Julia's eyes flashed. Caroline Baker felt a pang of doubt deep inside her. She was being too heavy-handed, crashing in where she wasn't wanted. Should she stop pushing? But Julia's face had turned from pale to white.

Her eyes were smarting, her body stiff. If she could just get her over this barrier, get her to give way to what she was feeling, that would be a start. It would give them something to work on, other than this brick wall of denial. And Caroline may have been a year or two younger than this woman, but she knew what denial was. She wasn't going to let it go. She leaned on the desk, and looked at Julia kindly.

'Is it something that happened in your past? To do with a relationship? Do you want to tell me about it?'

For a moment it didn't seem as if Julia had heard her. She sat perfectly still.

'What for?' she said breathlessly. 'If . . . I mean. You've already said that the counsellors do the listening. You just prescribe the pills, don't you?'

Caroline paused. She watched Julia twist the strap of her handbag around her fingers, pulling it tightly.

'Julia?' Her voice dropped to almost a whisper. 'Is this the first time you've felt like this? Have you been depressed before?'

'Yes,' she answered in a small voice.

'Did you see a doctor?'

'Yes. He told me to take up jogging, and read *Writing Home* by Alan Bennett. He said it worked for him.'

Caroline nodded, hiding her annoyance.

'Did anyone suggest to you then that you saw a counsellor? Did anyone ask you about it? Was there any follow-up?'

'No.' Almost inaudible.

'So,' Caroline swallowed the lump in her throat. 'Isn't it about time that you told somebody what really happened to you?'

'We're just popping out to the pub,' Naomi announced, sticking her head around the living-room door.

Maggie looked up from the magazine she was reading. Naomi looked different tonight. The light dawned. She was wearing make-up. It gave her thin face a new lease of life.

'Who's *we*?' Maggie raised her eyebrows.

'Er, just me. And Graham.'

'Graham?'

And she'd done something different with her hair. Usually it draped around her head like a tired old pair of curtains, but there was an indefinable quality – bounce, that was it – about the light brown strands tonight.

'Yeah. He was at the party, remember?'

Maggie squinted at her. Yes, she was blushing. Right on target.

'Graham, eh?'

'Yes, Maggie,' she said with elaborate patience. 'Graham who stayed over in my room, okay? And before you ask, yes, we were careful, and no, he's not an axe murderer and no, it won't put me off my finals. Anything else?'

'Just one more thing?'

'What?' She leaned against the doorframe, looking bored.

'Pick us up a bottle of brown ale while you're there, there's a good lass.'

'Eee by gum,' came the standard response. Fabian pushed into the room behind Naomi and gave Maggie a crooked grin. 'Haven't managed to wean you off the brown ale, have we? I suppose you'll be having your whippets sent down by Parcel Post, next?'

'You can shut up about my whippets.' She waved a finger at him. 'Or I'll start on at you again about public schoolboys and their homoerotic rituals.'

'Oh, those.' He collapsed on the sofa and flopped his legs over the end. 'Don't seem to have done me any harm.'

Maggie glanced up at Naomi and froze. The young woman was giving her a searching look.

'Thought you'd gone?'

'I'm waiting. For the money for the brown ale. I *am* on a student grant, you know.'

'I know, I know. Hang on a sec.' Maggie grabbed her bag and found a five-pound note in her purse. 'Get me a pack of baccy as well, will you?'

'Anything else?' Naomi said, holding out her hand for the money and refusing to budge from the door. 'A set of suitcases, perhaps? Some deluxe garden furniture? A family pack of condoms?'

'You'd probably better. But hang on to them,' Fabian muttered, closing his eyes.

'Hey, that's enough out of you.' Maggie got up and took Naomi the five-pound note. Naomi gave her a forced smile in return, and disappeared. The front door slammed after her.

'What's got into that girl?' Maggie shook her head. 'She never goes out in the week.'

'Or at the weekend,' Fabian added. 'We won't be able to call her mousey Naomi any more, will we?'

'It might be temporary. We don't want to rush into anything as significant as renaming her.'

'I don't think Graham's going to be temporary. I've got a feeling that two kindred spirits have found each other. I think we're just going to have to get used to it.'

'D'you know this Graham, then?'

'Yeah. Historian. Boring as shit.'

'Oh heck.' Maggie sat down again. 'I see what you mean.'

'As long as he doesn't move in, I don't care. I don't particularly want to bang into him in his shreddies every morning. It'll put me right off my bacon sandwiches.'

Maggie picked up *She* magazine again, and flicked it

84

back open at the page she was reading. She tried to get herself back into the article, about a woman who'd been crippled in a car accident, and had overcome untold difficulties to finally have her own baby. 'I had a right to be happy' cried the heading. She ran her eyes over it again, failing to find her place. Fabian didn't budge from the sofa, staring up at the ceiling. She looked up at him.

'Not going out?'

'Nope.'

'I thought you were going to the debate at the Union?'

'I can't. I've got an essay crisis. Professor Bastard Wilks has brought the tute forward to tomorrow. He says he's going to a conference on Friday. More like he's having a dirty weekend away and wants to take off early. Bastard.'

'Not everybody's life revolves around sex, you know Fabian,' she tutted at him.

He turned his head on the arm of the sofa so that he could see her. Luminous brown eyes, looking straight into hers.

'Really?' he said.

Her lashes flickered. 'You'd better start on your essay, hadn't you?'

'I can't work, Maggie,' he continued. 'I can't concentrate on anything. It's nearly the end of term anyway. He's not going to mind.'

'You've got to do it. Believe me, you'll regret it when you come to revise. You'll open your file, and there'll just be a big empty space there where the essay should be. Then you'll be sorry.'

'I don't think I'm going to be sorry,' he said, still looking at her. 'Anyway, I'm staying up for Easter, so I'll catch up then.'

'No you bloody well won't!' Maggie slapped *She* magazine down on the carpet. 'You're in your final year, Fabian, and I won't have you flopping about like a limp daisy at this stage. You've got to keep up with the work. You just won't have time to do it again.'

'And you know, because you went through this last year. I know.' He put his hands over his eyes again. 'I know, I know.'

'Then listen to me, because I can tell you, lad, when you get into examination schools and find that all you can remember are a couple of lines out of the *York Notes*, you'll look back on moments like this and you'll kick yourself. Bloody hard.'

He gave a ragged sigh, and she felt sorry for yelling at him. He was under so much pressure. She knew that. And she knew that his family expected him to walk out with a first, just as his sister had done three years ago. It was enough to put anybody into a state of paralysis. She softened towards him.

'*Fay*-bian?'

'What.'

'Look, I'm only trying to help. You need to take time off, we both know that. But not on your essay night. Not when you've got a tute tomorrow. Get it done, then you can relax tomorrow night, can't you? And you'll feel good about yourself, won't you?'

'Yes, Maggie. I'll feel really good about myself,' he repeated obediently.

She watched him with concern. He had pulled a cushion over his face, and was lying with it balanced over him. He lay perfectly still for several seconds, then he twitched. The cushion fell off, and he gave her a wide grin.

'You little bugger!' she admonished, picking up the magazine, and throwing it across the room at him.

'What's this? *Whippet's Realm*? *Me and My Whippet*?' He grabbed the magazine and waved it in the air, dodging her hands trying to catch it. 'Don't tell me, you've had a true story published? "I fell in love with a racing pigeon. Maggie Ridley tells all"?'

'Give it here, you little sod.' She began to laugh, falling over the sofa as her magazine shot out of reach.

'It were 'ard, in them days.' He mimicked her accent perfectly. 'Me and me dad were working at mill, wi' nought to eat but that old loaf of bread. But what a loaf it were— Ow! That hurts!'

'Stop taking the mick out of me. Give it here.'

She knelt on the edge of the sofa and stretched up to get the magazine. He wriggled so that he could hold it out behind his head. She lunged for it, leaning on his chest, trying to stop laughing so that she could aim straight. She took a swipe, and he jerked it away from her. She fell on top of him, instantly scrambling to get herself upright again.

'No, stay there,' he said. His arms had shot around her back, and he was holding her down.

'Let me go, Fabian.'

'No.' He shook his head. 'I don't want to let you go.'

'You've got to.' She was breathless. She struggled, but he held her firmly.

'Who says I've got to?'

She stopped struggling, and looked into his earnest face. Just for a second, she could almost imagine letting him hold her, forgetting the others, forgetting everything.

The telephone began to ring.

'Ignore it,' he said straight away.

'No, we can't. It's probably your mum. She'll want to talk to you.'

'Exactly. Ignore it.'

'No, Fabian!'

She pulled herself up with a sudden effort, and his arms relinquished her. She stood up and smoothed her hair down, rattled to the core. Fabian sat up, and looked at her.

'Maggie, what is it?'

'The bloody phone's ringing, that's what.'

'But—'

'I'll answer it.'

She walked shakily over to the telephone and bent down to the coffee table, once probably covered with a wood finish, but now bleached into a tortoiseshell effect by endless mugs of hot coffee being rested on it. She picked up the receiver. She must brace herself, be ready to deal with Fabian's mother. A woman who was so different from herself that they might as well belong to different species. What did she normally do? How did she normally deal with her? She must sound the same, that was so important. It came to her quickly. She joked, of course she did. She always joked, and his mother left long pauses after each of her comments. Pauses that she had no doubt were intended to make her squirm. She must be herself now. She must protect herself – no, protect *him*.

'Hello? War Office, who wants a fight?'

There was a pause on the line. 'It's Pete.'

She glanced at Fabian, and shook her head. He watched her for a moment more, saw her turn away from him and try to talk naturally, and then he got up, and went out of the room, closing the door quietly behind him.

'No, no it's all right, Pete. I'm on my own now. Fabian's gone to write an essay upstairs. What is it you want?'

She heard him draw a deep breath. Over the miles, she could see him standing in the hall next to the ledge he'd attached to the wall which they'd grandly called the telephone table, staring at the curtain which would be drawn over the front door to keep out the draught.

'I want a divorce,' he said.

Maggie gripped the phone until her knuckles went white. She gaped at *Couple Riding*, feeling the poster sucking her in, away from reality. For the first time, she saw every detail. The figures, entwined around each other, their cheeks pressed together, their arms holding each other tight, so tight, as the prancing horse carried them along. Through the ceiling a dull throb started up as Fabian put on his music. Her eyes shot upwards, to the flaking paint, the colour of stale cauliflower.

'Are you still there, Maggie love?'

A torrent of anger swept through her body.

'Don't you *dare* call me "love"! D'you hear me? Never, ever call me that again!'

She slammed the receiver down, her chest heaving, her breath coming in short, painful bursts. From above, the throbbing got louder, Fabian thumping backwards and forwards on the floorboards.

'Oh God,' Maggie whispered to herself, putting her hands over her face. 'What have I done?'

After her visit to the doctor, Julia found that she couldn't stop crying. The next day was as bad. She took the pills she'd been given on prescription. Some sort of anti-depressant, the doctor had said. She'd been warned that they'd take time to work, and she'd have to be patient. For the moment, at least, they seemed to be making her feel worse. But that could also be because she had spent over half an hour with the doctor, stumbling through her confused memories. In the end, she'd agreed to have an appointment made for her with a counsellor. Suddenly, it seemed like the right thing to do.

But knowing she was taking the right steps didn't stop the feeling of dread, and the feeling of fragility that had been growing inside her. She put off a trip to Tesco's to get some essential things, choosing instead to sneak to the shop around the corner where she'd be faced with fewer people.

She left the house, recoiling at the sound of a road-thumper kicking into its relentless routine at the end of the road. A small crowd of men were gathered around, one painting garish yellow lines along the path with mysterious intent. She would have to pass them to get to the shop, so she clamped her teeth together and braced herself.

'Hello, sweetheart!'

A voice hailed her above the chaos as she veered into the next road. She stomped on, muttering a forthright put-down under her breath.

In the shop, she found Mr Henderson, one of the more established occupants of the street, an elderly man with a rug of brilliant white hair, bending over the tinned meat pies. He creaked back up into a standing position, and stared over at her as she collected a tin of cat food. She sensed his attention, and turned to smile at him. She simply couldn't pretend that he didn't exist. The first time she'd met him, just after she'd moved in to the bedsit, she'd got stuck behind him on a narrow stretch of pavement, narrowed even further by the line of cars parked over the path. She was usually a fast walker, but behind his solid back, she'd ground to a halt. After several minutes of questioning the fact that he was moving at all, in any direction, she'd noticed that his shoes were in fact shuffling forwards, but with such hesitancy, that he was taking several steps to each side before he made any progress. It gave the impression that although he was wobbling a lot, he was fixed to the spot.

Feeling guilty that she'd been trying to pick a gap in the cars so that she could nip round him via the road, she'd tapped him on the back and offered to help him. He'd looked so deeply shocked, that she'd wondered if she'd offended him. But now, after several such encounters, she knew it was his habitual expression.

As he was now staring at her with the same startled look, she held up her tin of cat food and nodded at it.

'For the cat,' she said, realizing that it was a truly stupid thing to say.

'Eh?'

And, she remembered instantly, he was almost deaf. It meant that he shouted everything, and she had to shout back. She had seen the curtains twitching in the street before in response to their brief, but often disconcerting, exchanges.

'For – the – cat!' she said very loudly and clearly. If only she had thought of a less banal remark to make in the first place, it wouldn't be so embarrassing to have to shout it across the shop.

'It's cat food, isn't it?' he yelled back, looking at her as if she was a ridiculous person.

'Yes!' She nodded energetically, choosing to act like a ridiculous person. It was more simple that way. She sighed, and picked a carton of milk out of the fridge, making her way to the till. Mr Henderson began to wobble, showing the intention at least of heading in the same direction. He turned himself towards his goal clutching his tinned meat pie.

She paid for her goods, and waited for him. She could see him home at least, seeing as she walked past his house on the way back to hers. A pneumatic drill sporadically burst into life in the distance. It struck her that the men were working very close to Mr Henderson's. She was starting to pity him when she remembered that he was almost deaf.

'I'll – walk – you – home!' she explained at the top of

91

her voice as, having paid for his meat pie, he turned round slowly to face the door, and visibly jumped to find her standing next to him.

'Eh?'

'Come on.'

They made their way out of the shop, and began the momentous journey back round the corner. She fell into step beside him, stopping every so often to sway from side to side so that he wouldn't notice that what he was doing was unusual. After what seemed like several decades, they reached the workmen, now huddled together in some sort of secret conspiracy, leaning over one of their machines, and fiddling with it. Momentarily, the jarring of the drill had come to a halt, leaving the street strangely peaceful. She touched Mr Henderson's jacketed arm, partly to get his attention before she spoke, and partly just to remind him that she was there so that he wouldn't jump.

'I – wonder – what – they're – doing?' she called, questioning whether it was an over-ambitious effort given that his face had just straightened into surprise again. Unsurprisingly, given the volume of her comment, one of the workmen heard her and stood up, rubbing his back as if it was aching.

'Laying cables,' he supplied helpfully, taking the opportunity to give Julia the visual once-over.

'What for?' she demanded back.

'Cable television.' He stuck his hand on his hip. 'We're doing the whole street.'

She grimaced, realizing that they would have to drill outside her house as well.

'Eh?' shouted Mr Henderson.

'They're – putting – cables – in!' she repeated forcefully.

'Tell him the whole street's getting laid,' said a

younger workman, lolling casually on his drill with an inscrutable expression.

'Eh?'

'The – whole – street's – getting – laid!' she repeated at the top of her voice.

'Who's getting what?' he shouted back.

'THE – WHOLE – STREET'S – GETTING – LAID!' she bellowed.

A snort of laughter made her look back at the workmen, now sniggering as one. With a shock, she realized what she had just proclaimed. She hurriedly took Mr Henderson by the elbow and began to shove him towards his front gate.

'Who's getting laid?' he questioned loudly, looking extremely concerned.

'Just go home,' she muttered, opening his gate for him, and propelling him down the front path. She gave him a cheerful wave, mouthed a goodbye, and shot away, the guffaws of the workmen following her down the road as she accelerated home.

Inside, she put the kettle on, and sat down in the kitchen to stare out at the branches of the forsythia, now attempting to bloom, as they swayed unsteadily in the breeze. She considered her expedition to the shop, and its consequences.

Was she losing her sense of humour? Or was it just an off-day? How many off-days might she have to live through before it got better?

Tomorrow night, she was due back at the basic skills class. There she would have to face Rob again, and everyone else, and find the strength to see it through. But she could always ring Vivienne and tell her she had a cold? It would be easy to get out of it.

No, damn it, she would go, and she'd carry on. Rob couldn't know that their fumbled and pointless night had been a catalyst for her. She wouldn't hide from him, not now that she had begun to face her demons. There could be no hiding any more.

She made herself a mug of tea and contemplated the prospect of the rest of the day on her own. She thought suddenly of Mr Henderson, equally on his own in his house at the end of the road, heating up his meat pie. She supposed he had got used to being alone. But it was an odd thing to get used to. It was no wonder that he looked as if he had been assaulted whenever somebody spoke to him. She was close to understanding how he felt.

She wondered, as she pulled Fleabag on to her knee and kissed the top of his head, if Mr Henderson could possibly realize that he was the only person she was likely to have a conversation with that day.

Chapter Six

It was as bad as she'd expected. Rob ignored her, turning his attention to Vivienne's gushing introduction of his new student, a woman in her twenties with long, dyed, blue-black hair, black leggings and black Doctor Marten's. Whenever Vivienne paused for breath for long enough for the student, whose name was Sandra, to get a word in edgeways, she did so in a whisper, her thickly kohled eyes as huge as dinner plates. They disappeared off together into a small ante-room which was reserved for busy nights, when the class had to spill over from the main room. Vivienne eventually left them, closing the door firmly behind her.

It was odd, Julia thought as she sifted through her file and waited for Mack to arrive, that only a week ago she would have killed to have been shut in an airless room the size of a shoebox with Rob. Seeing him had disturbed her again. When she'd got to the class she'd found him flicking through one of the books on the shelves. It had struck her again how good looking he was, still so tall, his shoulders slightly stooped as he bent his head to read, his brown hair flopped over his eyes as he concentrated. She'd watched him as she unwound her scarf, waiting for him to look up and acknowledge her. She'd even been ready with a bright smile, just to prove that she wasn't going to be churlish, but his black lashes had remained downcast, covering the expression in those clear green eyes, and she'd been left fingering her scarf until the others had begun to crash in. She had thought he might at least have looked up and said something. 'Hello' would have been a start. But he'd waited, apparently totally absorbed in his book, until the others had started to arrive, and greeted them all brightly without acknowledging Julia at all.

It had had an unforeseen effect on her. She'd walked up to the class, her knees buckling at the thought of the next two hours, and had even thought of changing her mind and racing back home again as she turned the handle of the outside door. But his attitude made her angry, and her anger gave her strength. She would make it clear that she was able to deal with the situation maturely. Under the surface she was paddling like hell.

She was annoyed with herself too, given the reception she'd received, for bothering to think about what she wore tonight. She'd put a little make-up on, a pair of nicely cut wool trousers, and a cream sweater which was still the right size. And she'd stuck to her thick brown leather jacket in preference to the billowing anorak which made her feel like a grounded parachutist. But, she reasoned, she'd made herself feel better by bothering to look good, regardless of Rob's indifference. And Mack surprised her again by paying her a compliment when he lurched in, tossed his crash helmet under the table, and sank into his chair.

'You look nice tonight,' he said. He discarded his leather jacket on the back of the chair, flicked open the canvas flap of his haversack, and began to unload his pad of paper and a handful of tissues covered in engine oil on to the table top. 'Sorry I'm late. Had a problem with the gasket.'

'Thank you,' she said, stuck on his heartening remark. She watched him for a moment as he arranged himself. 'How was the wine?'

He looked at her and nodded without smiling.

'It was okay. Okay.'

'I thought you knew your Beaujolais. Wasn't it a good choice?'

'Oh, the wine was fine. Yeah. The wine itself was really nice.'

Her interest was caught.

'But the evening was only – okay?'

'Yeah. That just about sums it up.'

'Oh dear.' She tried to sound reasonably sympathetic. 'Wasn't your date impressed, then?'

'My date?' He stopped arranging things, and gave her a curious look. He chose not to answer, and she cleared her throat, somehow feeling that she'd put her foot in it again. He continued to assess her. 'So how was your evening?'

'On Saturday, you mean?'

'Yeah. Was your date impressed by the pink spray?'

She couldn't help smiling. In fact, the body spray had ended up stacked in the bathroom cabinet, and she wondered if she'd ever use it.

'My date?' she answered equally cryptically, quirking an eyebrow at him.

'Still,' he sniffed. 'It was a corking episode of *Family Fortunes*, wasn't it? I was on the edge of my seat all the way through. I couldn't believe it when they didn't get the car. And they were *so* close. Just one more top answer, and they'd have cracked it.'

'It was pretty nail-biting,' she conceded. 'And that woman with the frizzy hair was so annoying. As if cooking oil was something you might find in the greenhouse.'

'She was just panicking.' Mack pulled a sympathetic face. 'It must be pretty scary, waiting for that thing to go beep-boop at you. Still, that Les Dennis seems like a nice bloke, doesn't he?'

She stopped herself as she was about to launch into a full analysis of Les Dennis's skills as a game-show host.

'Hang on,' she said slowly. 'The Cribben family from Ipswich *did* get the car. You didn't watch it, did you?'

The corner of Mack's mouth was twitching, and she suddenly realized that he'd made all of his comments in a dead-pan voice. She'd fallen for it, head first. She mentally awarded him a point.

'It's all right,' he continued. 'Don't be embarrassed about staying in on a Saturday night. All I usually do is slump in front of the telly. I recorded all my favourite programmes this week. I just haven't had a chance to watch them yet.'

'Oh, and I've ruined the ending for you.'

'Just don't tell me how Tiggy from Surrey and Kevin from London got on in Lanzarote, otherwise you'll blow it for me. I was hoping to catch up with the video tonight, after the class.'

'You'd better get on with it. It's Thursday already.'

'I've been busy this week. I've had a job to finish.'

'Oh. Is there a lot of decorating work around at the moment?'

He looked at her again, that same half-ironic gaze, only his eyes giving the hint that he was amused by something.

'Well, you know what people are like. They always want something painting.'

'I suppose so,' she said, thinking of her faded wallpaper. It could do with brightening up. Perhaps if she got the cash together, she might even ask Mack to come and give it a face-lift.

'At least I changed my jeans tonight.' He nodded at his legs. 'I suppose you saw that they were covered in paint last week? I never actually told you I was a decorator, I don't think.'

'Perhaps you didn't?' She thought hard. Apart from the brief discussion they'd had on his first week, she hadn't really asked him about himself. 'No, you're right. You didn't tell me.'

'Observant, aren't you?' he said quietly, and opened his pad at the first page. 'I thought I would try and write something this week. I thought about it, you know, after the last time. I'm not going to get anywhere if I don't try, am I?'

'No.' She was relieved. She had been wondering, in the midst of her other preoccupations, how she might deal with him tonight. 'Well, it's up to you. You can either have a crack at something now, or we can do some reading now, and try to write after the tea break.'

'I think I'll write now.'

He sounded very positive. He shook back his mane of white-gold hair, and picked up his pen. He shot her another glance. 'It doesn't matter what it is, does it? Last week you said to do a letter, or something about myself. But I don't want to do that. Can I just write anything I want?'

'Of course,' she assured him. 'Whatever you want. Just don't be scared to make mistakes. I can try and help you with them.'

'Fine.'

He bent his head, and grasped the pen, concentrating on the blank sheet in front of him. She opened her file again, and leafed through the exercises, consciously ignoring his efforts to give him space. Instead, as the minutes ticked by, she wrapped herself up in making plans for future sessions. She tried not to think about Rob and Sandra, locked in their little room a few yards away. While she'd been talking to Mack, she'd managed to forget him, but hearing muted murmurs coming through the closed door, she couldn't help wondering if Sandra was suffering from the same hot and cold flushes that had afflicted her the week before. Jealousy darted through her, bringing with it another threatening surge of depression. She gripped the plastic edge of her file firmly. She had to stay on top of things.

She stared at the same page until she heard Brenda bursting in with the tea tray and announcing that it was break-time. She glanced at her watch, astonished to see that it was gone eight o'clock already. But then, Mack had been late, and they'd taken a while to settle. Thank God, it wasn't a total black-out. She wasn't going mad just yet.

To her relief, Rob and Sandra didn't emerge from their intimate cubicle to take tea with the rest of them. Brenda obligingly delivered the tea to them, and pulled the door to as she left.

'They're having a nice chat,' she said in a hushed voice to Vivienne who was hovering in her velvet cloche hat, itching to impart guidance and goodwill.

Julia piled sugar into her mug from the bag that Brenda had brought to the table explaining in her part-hearty and part-husky voice that she couldn't for the life of her remember who had what with what, and Julia wondered as she sipped her coffee whether the others were also being too nice to Brenda to admit that they hadn't got what they'd asked for.

'We'll all have to think about a nice little end of term party soon, won't we?' Vivienne said, slipping into a chair and, Julia thought, looking very happy now that she had thought of a suitable class announcement to make.

'When *is* the end of term, anyway?' Brenda rummaged in a handbag the size of a shed, and pulled out a battered diary. Several small pieces of paper slipped out of it and floated through the air. 'Oh, my lists!' she complained, grabbing at them.

Obediently, they began to make guesses as to when the term would end, searching for diaries or bits of paper they might have made a note on. Julia watched patiently. She had seen this ritual before. It caused endless confusion. The genuine problem was that the class terms didn't match those of the schools, which meant that everybody with children was misled completely, and those without children were left making wild guesses as to what seemed a reasonable date for the term to finish. And just as everybody was in a state of total bewilderment, Vivienne usually added her *pièce de résistance*. She'd done it before, and Julia waited for her to do it now.

'Well, it's up to you really. When would you *like* the term to end?' Vivienne said, adopting a helpful look, and being met with a row of blank faces.

'I don't mind,' the usually silent Kieran ventured in a soft Dublin accent. Fiona, who worked with him, and was usually equally silent, nodded to indicate that she also didn't mind.

'Oh, dear,' said Brenda, her cheeks glowing. 'I just don't know. Next week's too early, but in three weeks' time I've got to be at my sister's.'

'I've got a governors' meeting in a fortnight,' George said, popping the end of his biro and scribbling something in a NatWest diary.

'Can we go on, still working?' Shirani said, looking as persistent as ever. 'I don't like these holidays with nothing happening. Boring, isn't it?'

'Well, only if you haven't got young children, I suppose,' Vivienne said, looking faintly self-satisfied.

'My children've grown up now. It's boring, I can tell you, these holidays. Just my husband and me and the television. I like these classes. I like to be going some-where else. You know what I mean?' Shirani shrugged and, seeing Alec's sharp look, giggled to herself, waving her delicate hands. 'I know, I know, I'm talking too much. I shut up.'

'Talk all you like, gal. I'm used to it. You should hear my missus. Now *that's* talking.'

'We have to have a holiday,' Vivienne continued with a bland face. 'How about if we finish in a fortnight's time. Will that suit everybody?'

'I'll have to cancel my meeting,' George said.

'I'm sorry, George, but we can't organize everything around your governors' meeting, can we?' came Vivienne's sweet voice. George blushed, and popped the end of his biro energetically. 'Will that be convenient for everybody else?'

'Bit autocratic, isn't she?' Mack murmured to Julia.

She stopped listening to the continuing debate, and as the voices struggled on, she turned and looked at Mack.

'Autocratic?' she responded in a whisper.

'Yeah. The autocrat pretending to be a democrat. Bit scary.'

'Yes. She's scary,' Julia agreed, starting to giggle. Vivienne fixed her with a wide, brown stare.

'Did you want to say something, Julia?'

Julia pondered the question. Vivienne sounded so much like Dr Baker, trying to hook a wriggling fish with an invisible line, that she had an insane urge to burst out laughing. She restrained herself.

'No, no. Mack was just saying that a fortnight would suit him fine. Weren't you, Mack?'

'That's right,' he said with an earnest face. 'In fact, I think a fortnight's time for the end of term is a fantastic suggestion. It just sums everything up that I was thinking. It's just . . . a great idea.'

Julia chewed her cheek and held it firmly in place with her molars. Vivienne gave them both a lingering look of suspicion, and then pulled the class together again.

'That's good then, isn't it? Shall we all mark that in our diaries now, before we forget?'

'What if we don't have a diary?' Mack asked, apparently worried.

'Well then, Mack, you can make a note on a piece of paper, and remember to put it on your calendar when you get home.'

'I never thought of that,' he said, shaking his head, and picking up his pen. 'Awesome.'

'I won't be able to come,' Kieran said softly, displaying neither deep regret or deep joy. 'Sorry.'

'Never mind,' Vivienne said. 'In which case, it's up to you whether you make it or not, Fiona?'

'I probably won't be able to,' Fiona said, head bowed. Julia had never thought of her as a party animal anyway. She seemed to love her teaching, and she and Kieran had established a firm, if subdued, bond. She was probably secretly thrilled that Kieran had let her off the hook, Julia thought, glancing over at her petite body wedged next to Kieran's bulky form. They'd make a good pair, she decided, then slapped herself on the wrists.

'I hope we've all written the date down, now,' Vivienne continued in a firm-but-fair tone.

Julia turned her attention to Mack, etching something on to a clean sheet of paper, keeping her eyes away from Vivienne. It really was peculiar, this sudden burst of hysteria she was feeling. Mack inched his pad in her direction, and she read what he had written.

Hitlur.

She snorted, and quickly reached behind her to pull a tissue out of her jacket pocket so that she could bury her face in it and blow her nose.

'Aren't you going to make a note of the end of term, Julia? It's quite important really, because everybody will be expected to bring something to the party. You don't want to forget, do you?'

'It's okay,' she said through her tissue. 'I'll remember.'

'As long as we all do remember,' Vivienne said, with a sugar-coated note of warning in her voice. 'For some reason, this always gets us all confused, doesn't it? It's very simple, really. So, when is the end of term?'

There was a silence. Several people blinked, realizing that a response was expected.

'In two bloody weeks,' Alec almost yelled. 'Not next week, the week after.'

'Oh, I see. The week after.' Shirani nodded, looking very confused.

'That's the seventeenth. My governors' meeting's on the seventeenth,' George said, peering closely at his own handwriting and looking unsure of himself.

'That's a Wednesday,' Vivienne said curtly. 'And don't argue, because it's my anniversary.'

'Oh, that's nice,' said Brenda distractedly. 'So when's the end of term, then?'

'The eighteenth of March. Perhaps we could all talk about this next week, when we're more likely to remember?' Mack added his voice to the discussion, leaning back in his chair, and looking inappropriately calm. His last comment was directed at Vivienne. Her hands fluttered up to the rim of her cloche hat, and readjusted it.

'I find it's always best to give everyone plenty of warning,' she said with a little edge. 'That way, everybody knows what they're doing.'

After Brenda had cleared up the mugs, and they'd refocused on the session, Julia asked Mack to show her what he had written. He pushed his pad over to her, leaving her to open the front and find the page, a few sheets in, where there were several rows of conspicuously neat handwriting. She settled in her chair, and concentrated. His letters were looped, making it difficult to decipher, but it struck her instantly that his words were formed with a strong sense of pattern. She'd worked with students before whose handwriting showed a basic grip of rounded shapes and lines, but Mack's writing was artistic, and although she'd seen him pore over it, the impression was of flowing, linked letters, running into each other effortlessly. She began to read.

Ah but a mans reech shood xseed his grarsp
or wats a heven for. All is silvur grae plassid and purfekt
with my art. The wurs

She stared at the words. A warm rush of recognition filled her body. Inexplicably, her eyes filled with tears, and her throat became trapped in a clamp.

'I didn't finish it,' Mack said, leaning over her shoulder to look at his work again. 'I know it's all wrong. Isn't it? I've never tried to write it down before.'

'I—'

She pulled her tissue from her sleeve where she had inelegantly stuffed it, and blew her nose again. She coughed, and took a moment to compose herself. She took a deep breath, and mercifully, the urge to weep all over the table subsided. She turned to Mack over-brightly. He was waiting eagerly for her reaction, his body still slumped in apparent tranquillity, but a stirring in the depths of his eyes betraying his need for her response.

'It – er. Don't worry about the mistakes. It's often true that people read much better than they write, at least when they first come here.'

He nodded.

'We, er. You need to think about getting yourself a

dictionary. A learner's dictionary is a good idea, then you can look up the words yourself. I was going to suggest that you brought one along next week, so that we can start showing you how to use it. I can recommend one to you, and tell you where to get it.'

He nodded again.

'And, erm. I think we can see from this that we need to work hard on your spelling. There's a lot of promise here, but we can improve on what you've done.'

Again, just a silent nod.

Julia looked at him again, at his subdued expectation. She knew that he wanted a different response from her. She dropped her teaching face, and her eyes became soulful. She shook her head at him with intrigue.

'How do you know Browning?'

At last, he smiled broadly. Yes, she thought, that was the recognition he'd been waiting for.

'D'you like it?'

' "Andrea del Sarto"? Of course. It's a wonderful poem. The artist trapped by his own genius. I've always loved it. How did you – I mean, how is it that you know it?'

'My gran used to read to me. She loved poetry, my gran. She used to know these great long poems off by heart. And I used to ask her for my favourites. She did requests, you know, like Gloria Hunniford. She was brilliant at it.' He shook back his hair, and looked intently at the biro he was turning over in his hand. 'This was my favourite. I used to get her to repeat that bit, over and over, until I could remember it. I didn't understand all of it, but she told me what it was about. And I fell in love with it. Do you know what I mean? Have you ever fallen in love with a poem?'

She gaped at him, stunned into silence. He glanced at her under his hair, and laughed at himself dismissively.

'Course not. I'm talking crap. Sorry.'

'No. No, no, you're not talking crap. I know exactly what you mean. I'm sorry, Mack. You just surprised me.'

'You didn't expect a dunce like me to know anything about poetry, did you?'

'Who said you were a dunce? I didn't say that.'

'But I bet you thought it.'

'No.' She bent towards him on the desk, searching his face. 'I don't think that. There are so many reasons why students come here, Mack, and it's never because they're stupid. You've got to get that thought right out of your head.'

'Bit difficult,' he said quietly. 'When you've been called a dunce ever since you can remember. Or thicko. Or spastic. That one hurts, I can tell you.'

'Then you've got to start undoing the damage. Right now.' She stopped and thought for a moment. 'Do you want to tell me about it? Where things started going wrong for you?'

My God, she thought, I sound just like the bloody doctor. He flicked his eyes around the classroom. The others were intent on their exercises, concentrating in their pairs, oblivious of any other conversations taking place. But it was a small room, and not in the least private.

'Not here,' he said shortly.

He fell silent, and she watched him as he fiddled with his pen, stopping every so often to reposition his pad in front of him, his eyes cast down.

'Well, look. Let's carry on for now, shall we?' she urged him in a low voice. 'We can do another exercise, and you just tell me in your own time when you want to talk about your experiences? Perhaps you'd like to have a chat after the class?'

His face was a little flushed, she thought. She might be going too far, putting him off. Sometimes students did want to talk about their past experiences, and found it a great release to be able to be honest about what they'd been feeling, been hiding over the years. But sometimes they found it too painful. Sometimes, just getting on with the business of the class was therapy enough.

'Shall we do another exercise?'

'Yeah, let's do that.' His face re-emerged from his hair, once again coolly composed. He flashed her a grin, and relaxed backwards into his plastic chair, stretching his long legs under the table. 'We'll save poetry for another time, shall we?'

He retrieved the sheet he had written on, and stuffed it out of sight inside his pad. It appeared a casual action, but it was done a little too quickly and purposefully. Julia noticed, and was troubled by it.

They spent the remainder of the time going over an exercise on basic words, Julia explaining carefully what was required, and helping Mack through the principles. She felt uncomfortable as they worked on. She wasn't sure what was causing it, but it was as if she'd missed an opportunity, as if she'd been offered a chance to let Mack say or do something, and failed to see it.

The others began to wrap up the lesson, and she made a concerted effort to organize herself quickly so that she wouldn't be the last one left. She was still clipping sheets back into her A4 file when she felt Mack heave himself up beside her. He picked up his belongings, tossed his leather jacket over his shoulder, and began to move off.

'Mack? Are you going now?'

'Yeah. See you next week.'

She watched his back as he sauntered away down the corridor, and out of the building, the swing door slamming shut after him. This time, he didn't turn round and wink at her.

She slowly put her papers together, and tucked them

into her plastic bag. She pulled her jacket off the back of the chair thoughtfully. The classroom seemed almost empty. She could hear Vivienne ushering the loiterers towards the door. Oh well, she supposed Vivienne had appointed her lights monitor by default, so that was that. There wasn't any great hurry. Just Fleabag to feed, perhaps a phone call to Maggie, *Newsnight* to send her to bed with images of Jeremy Paxman dancing round her head. And hopefully she would sleep better tonight. Especially since she'd made it through the session without cracking up.

'How are you, Julia?'

She jumped round at the sound of the familiar voice, and her face instantly reddened.

'Rob! I thought you'd gone.'

'Just thought I'd hang on a bit. Thought I'd better ask you how you are.'

She continued to wrap her scarf round her neck, checked her bag again pointlessly to make sure she had everything, and made her way towards the light controls. Rob followed her.

'How did you get on with Sandra?' she asked casually, waiting for him to head into the corridor so that she could kill the classroom lights.

'Fine, fine. She's very nervous, though.'

I'm not bloody surprised, Julia thought peevishly. Poor cow probably had enough on her plate without having to undergo trial by temptation as well.

'She will be to start with. Just go very slowly, and you'll give her confidence. Can you flick that switch in the corridor that does the kitchen light? Thanks.'

She headed purposefully towards the outside door.

'So you're okay, are you?' he asked again, reaching the door with her.

She looked at him. He almost looked concerned. Or

was it guilt? Something was bothering him.

'Why shouldn't I be?'

'You know, after Friday, well Saturday. Whatever.'

'I hadn't forgotten, Rob.' She turned off the last light, and pulled open the heavy door. A burst of cold air met them, a sharp wind whipping around the car park. She waited for him to step out with her, and let the door go. She began to walk briskly in the direction of the iron gate that the caretaker had left propped open for the cars to leave. Rob walked with her.

'Sandra's quite interesting,' he commented.

'Only "quite" interesting?' she quipped archly.

'No, I mean, she's ... She was telling me, she's only twenty-three. You know, she's got a daughter? Four years old. Called Kylie.'

'So?' Julia increased her pace.

'So ...' He kept pace with her. 'So, it just made me think a bit.'

'What about?'

'I don't know. Everything, I suppose.'

'Right.' They reached the gate, and she turned to him, tucking her scarf inside her collar. 'This is where I head off towards Saint Clements. I'll see you next week.'

'Julia?'

'What?' She smiled politely.

'Are you sure you're all right?'

'Of course I am.' She paused, irked. 'Are *you* all right, Rob? It sounds to me as if you're the one with the problem.'

'Well,' he pushed his fingers through his hair. The breeze picked up a flurry of strands and blew them across his forehead. 'Actually, it's about Leo.'

'What about Leo?'

'It's about why he was so angry. At the party. I thought perhaps I should explain it to you.'

'I don't think I'm that interested,' she said curtly. 'I got the impression that you and Leo have some things to sort out. Surely that's between the two of you? I don't see where I come into it.'

'Well, look. D'you fancy a quick drink on the way home?'

She hesitated for a moment. In the yellow light cast by the overhead street lamps his hair looked soft and ruffled. The hair that she had so badly wanted to run barefoot through. And even in the dimness she felt a pulse of reaction to the searching look he was giving her, his eyes holding hers in appeal. He looked cold, vulnerable, in need of company. But a vision of herself on Saturday morning came back to her in a flash, sitting alone in her kitchen, staring at the empty mug that she had set out for him, listening to the front door slam. She had felt cold, vulnerable and in need of company.

'No, I don't fancy a drink. I'm tired, and I'm going home. I've got my own problems to deal with at the moment, so if you want to dump on someone about your relationship with your brother, you'd better pick someone else.'

'I wasn't – I didn't mean . . .'

She turned and walked briskly away from him, calling over her shoulder.

'See you next week, Rob.'

'Oh. Righto.'

She kept walking, her face set, and didn't stem her pace until she reached her front door and let herself in, leaning back against it. She had to keep her focus. She had to stay in control. Getting more involved with Rob on any level was only going to confuse matters now. He hadn't particularly wanted to go for a drink with her, she was sure of it. More likely, he'd had a bad weekend with Leo and was looking for a shoulder to cry on. If she hadn't seen the doctor, and started to unravel the web she was bound in, she might have offered hers. But not now.

Inside her bedsit, she flicked on the bar heater, and flopped down with Fleabag on the bed to watch the television. She grew calmer, sipping her mug of tea therapeutically, trying to stroke his head while he rolled on to his back and sank his needle teeth into her thumb.

She found her mind wandering as she gazed at the blur of colour on the screen. After a while, she got up, and went over to her lopsided bookcase. She dropped to her knees and scanned the spines of the books. After a painful search, she found what she was looking for. She prised the stocky book from the shelf, and flicked it open in her hand.

Browning's *Men and Women*, 1855.

She took it back to the bed, picked up her mug again, and leafed through the pages until she found 'Andrea del Sarto'. Fleabag climbed on to her back as she rolled on to her front on the bed, finally giving up his attempt to eat her hair, and settling around her shoulders like a fur stole. He began to purr loudly, the vibrations drumming through her neck. She fingered his paws as she read.

She'd studied Browning in her first year at University. She'd been lucky to have a wonderful supervisor, a woman who appreciated literature with her heart, unlike so many of the academics who processed the words through their brains like complex mathematical equations that demanded obscure answers which had no obvious connection to the question. She wondered if Mack's grandmother had been such a woman. What on earth must she have been like?

She read the poem through and stared at the television, her hands resting on the open book. It was odd, reading the poem again. Almost as if she was reading it for the

first time, the punctuated thoughts reaching into her life
– not the same life which she'd been living at University,
when she had been busy underlining phrases, analysing
their possible meaning. She now had a little piece of
Browning lodged into her consciousness to carry around,
words that would come to her over the next few weeks
and would make her stop what she was doing,
remember, and carry on. And Mack? Would he be doing
the same? Would he hesitate with a roller thick with
Brilliant White emulsion, stare at the wall, remember,
then slap the paint on?

She lay back on the bed and gazed at the ceiling, hardly
noticing that a rhythmic thumping was starting to drift
down from the bedsit above. She thought of Rob,
enthroned in the splendour of the Bodleian Library,
researching his unknown eighteenth-century author,
surrounded by pages and pages of printed words. And
she thought of Mack, rolling paint on to the walls,
remembering his grandmother's voice as she recited
poems to him. Perhaps she had been very wrong to
assume that she knew anything about either of them?

Chapter Seven

Julia was pulling up weeds in the back garden when she thought she heard the doorbell. It was Saturday, and the sky was a weak jigsaw-blue overhead, the sun floating about aimlessly in an attempt to warm the chill air. She'd sat in the kitchen that morning, chewing a piece of toast without appetite and assessing the scramble of weeds and brambles through her window. She made an impulsive decision to do something about it. With nobody yet installed in the other bedsit on the ground floor, either she was going to attack the undergrowth, or nobody would. She'd yanked open the door to the mouldy shed, and found a handful of rusty tools to play with. For the last two hours, throwing herself bodily into the task, she had been having fun.

She knew very little about gardening, but that didn't seem to matter. She knew a tuft of grass from a soggy crisp packet, and that had been the first test. She'd been tentative at first, wondering what the others upstairs might think when they peered out of their sash windows and realized that their nature reserve had been decimated, but her courage grew, and as she cleared the garrotting embrace of the brambles out of the way, she began to detect vibrant green shoots pushing up through the uneven mix of grass and earth.

From then on, she spared the life of what she liked the look of, and massacred everything that looked boring. She'd cleared an uneven brick path down to the wall at the end of the garden and hacked her way to the washing line so that it might one day actually be used. More disconcertingly, a mass of discarded green stuff which had started as a neat little heap had shot quickly through the undulating hills stage, and was now rising like the Himalayas at the end of the garden. She had had a vague idea that it would rot down, like a good compost heap, but she was starting to feel that it was too much to ask. A bonfire was out of the question – not, at least, without her bedsit gaining as much notoriety as the Pudding Lane bakery, and she was sure that the dustmen wouldn't take it away. But she could think about that later.

She stood up, stretched her back, and wiped her forehead, wondering if it had been her bell that had rung. She waited, and when the trill came again she plodded back through her open kitchen door, through the bedsit, and through the murky hall to the front door. She smiled to see Maggie.

'Come on in. I'm just doing a David Bellamy impression in the garden to amuse Fleabag.'

'Dudley sodding Moore.' Maggie stepped in, taking her cigarette out of her mouth. 'I phoned you about an hour and a half ago, and he miaowed at me. I guessed you probably didn't hear it, so I thought I'd pop round in case. You sure you don't mind, love?'

'Don't be silly. I'm suffering tannin withdrawal anyway. I'll put the kettle on.'

'What are they doing to your street? It looks like the Blitz out here.' Maggie gesticulated at the piles of rubble and dormant machines littered along the pavement.

'Don't ask,' Julia replied.

They went into the kitchen, and Julia kicked the back door shut. She filled the kettle.

'You look dapper today,' Maggie said, pulling out a chair for herself and sitting at the table. 'Lot better than you sounded last week. Must be the fresh air.'

'Well, the air is definitely fresh today, but I'm boiling now. I can't remember the last time I did anything really physical.' She stopped, was about to make a suggestive aside, and thought better of it. 'And seeing as I can't afford Vivienne Westwood's Lycra collection and the subscription to the trendy gym in town, I thought I might as well throw myself round the garden for a couple of hours. I might even decide that exercise is a "good thing", but the jury's still out on that one. I'll see first how many buckets of Radox Muscle Soak I get through tomorrow.'

'Does that mean I can't finish my fag?'

Julia gave her a saucer, and an old-fashioned look.

'Maggie, you can do what you like here. You know that.'

Julia pulled out two mugs and doled tea-bags into them, feeling something irritating her head and picking out a strand of bramble. She dumped it in the pedal bin.

'You didn't tell me I was in camouflage.'

'I didn't notice,' Maggie said. She tapped her thin cigarette against the saucer, and looked at it.

'You look nice in jeans,' Julia said, leaning back against the units. 'I don't think I've seen you in those for a couple of years.'

'Well, they still fit me. That's something.'

Julia looked at Maggie while she waited for the kettle to boil. She was looking good today. In a sweatshirt and jeans, her vibrant hair caught back in a ponytail, she looked ten years younger – that was if you could pin an age on Maggie, which you never could. And the jeans fitted her very well. Her figure was good anyway, curvy but not heavy. Julia often marvelled at how well she'd kept herself in shape. But today she seemed preoccupied. Usually, when they chatted, Maggie filled in the silences with comments, observations, one-liners, but she seemed content at the moment to sit quietly. The switch on the kettle clicked and Julia poured the boiling water into the mugs. Her mind wandered back to her own problems.

'I saw a counsellor on Friday, Maggie.'

'Did you, love?' Maggie looked round, all pre-occupation banished. 'I'm so pleased. I'm sure that's the right thing to do.'

'Yes, so am I now. It was pretty gruelling. The thing is, I went to the doctor, and she put me on some pills, for depression. Only mild,' she said quickly, flashing Maggie a glance. 'It's not deadly serious. But she said I should see the counsellor, just to assess things. You know.'

'I know. And what happened?'

Julia sighed. It turned into a shudder. She shook her-self up, bringing the tea and milk over to Maggie, and sitting down in the chair opposite her.

'Well, we talked. No, I talked. And she listened. And at the moment, I don't really know what it all meant. It's very confusing, but I'm going to see her again next week. I'm just going to see how it goes.'

'And you're going to be honest with her?' Maggie said, drawing her mug to her. 'About everything?'

Julia paused to put a spoon of sugar in her tea and stir it. She took a sip and set the mug back down. She couldn't take back what she had told Maggie. The words had bounced out, and left her behind.

'Yes,' she said carefully. 'I'm going to try. It was strange, though. All the things I thought she was going to ask me about? Well, she didn't. She asked me about my family, where I'd been to school, what my childhood was like. About Dad.' She shook her head, and fingered her teaspoon. 'That was weird. I hadn't thought about Dad at all, not for years and years, except fleetingly. Only at Christmas, and on his birthday. And the odd thing was, I ended up crying all over the place, not like an adult crying, trying to cover it up, but just like a child. Just crying and crying.'

'You didn't tell me about your Dad. I mean, apart from the fact that he left when you were a lass?'

'That's just it. I don't think there is anything more than that. But for some reason, it was like it happened yesterday. I just couldn't control myself. Poor woman. Being unemployed's pretty shitty, but I wouldn't have her job.'

Maggie sat back and fingered her lighter.

'It's what she's paid to do. Just remember that.'

'Oh, I know. It just felt strange. Then, at the end, she just made another appointment for me. I expected her to say something, or give me the benefit of her wisdom, but she didn't. So I just left, and came back here, and . . .' Julia expelled a long breath. 'I just don't know what to think. I don't know if it's really worth it.'

'Yes, it is. You've got to talk to someone, and I think you're very brave for doing it. I do, really. And sometimes you can't tell your friends everything, can you? There are always things you lock inside, because you think they're irrelevant, or because you don't want to bother anyone else. You're doing the right thing.' Maggie fixed her with a firm stare. 'You must go next week.'

'I will. I've got nothing better to do at the moment, have I? I'm hoping to get some work at Easter with the crammers. They'll be running revision classes for A level.'

Julia stopped and peered into her tea. At the moment, even the thought of the revision classes filled her with fear. She didn't want Maggie to know that. Maggie would only say, 'You can do it, love', and Julia knew that she *could* do it, in theory at least. That wasn't really the point.

'So, how are you?' Julia pushed her hair out of her eyes, and turned her attention to Maggie. 'How are *Fay*bian and mousey Naomi? Got over their hangovers from last week?'

Maggie pulled her tobacco pouch out of her handbag and set about rolling another cigarette. She didn't answer until she had manipulated the paper into a neat, thin stick, and placed it in front of her.

'When you came up here . . .' she began slowly, looking unusually hesitant. 'I mean, when you came to University, to be a *mature* student. What did you think would happen afterwards?'

'It's the million-dollar question,' Julia said. 'I didn't know, I just thought something would.'

'That's what I thought you'd say. You see, Julia, there are some differences between us, for all we've shared, for all we've found we've got in common.' She stopped to chuckle. 'For all the laughs we've had, and by God, we've had a few. Oh, it's been something else, hasn't it?'

Julia nodded, smiling. 'You might say that.'

Maggie put her cigarette between her lips, looked down at the lighter in her hands, and pulled the cigarette away, laying it back down on the table top.

'You see, the thing is, I *did* know what I was going to do afterwards. And I knew why I was doing it. It seems so daft now, but I had it all worked out at the time. I had a grand theory, Maggie Ridley's theory of how to save her marriage.'

Julia sat forward. 'To save it?'

'That's right. You see, there had always been something missing between me and Pete, and after a while, I wondered if it was me. Don't get me wrong. I wasn't a victim. I fought him all the way along the line, or I ignored him. It came to that. But then I thought, if I were happy, really happy, perhaps we'd both be happy?

119

And after the kids had gone, and Jason had got a kid of his own, I realized that it was down to me and Pete.'

She stopped, picked up the cigarette, and lit it.

'Go on, Maggie.'

'Well.' She breathed a practised plume of smoke away from the table. 'I looked around my living-room, at all the bits and pieces we'd gathered over the years, at the photos of the kids, and at the photo of my little granddaughter, and I realized that the next moment in my life that I was looking forward to – the only moment I was looking forward to – was three weeks away, when I knew that Jason was going to come round again with his family. And I had three weeks to live through until then. Three sodding weeks, up at the Red Lion and at home with Pete, wondering why his dinner was burnt up when he got home from darts. And I thought – can this be it? From now till I die? Till we both die? And I knew that if I was unhappy, we didn't stand a bloody chance. So I made up my mind, on the spot, that I was going to do something. Not just for me, but for both of us.'

'I – you never put it quite like that before.'

'No. Perhaps I saw that my plan was falling apart. It didn't take long, did it?'

'But you used to try to get home, didn't you?' Julia sat forward again. 'I remember you coming back on a Monday morning, absolutely knackered because you'd spent all that time on the train. And you used to sit there in your room on Friday afternoons, doing your essays before you went off for the weekend so that you could take time out. You did try, didn't you?'

'I tried. But it always took us a day to get to know each other again, and a day waiting for me to push off back to college. It was hopeless. I couldn't say anything right when I got home. Every time I opened my gob I was accused of being posh, or of trying to be clever, oh, anything at all. Pete hated me for it, I know he did.'

'But you're such a bright woman, Maggie. You couldn't have turned your back on this.'

'But in Pete's mind, it's not about being bright. He's bright. If you talked to him for more than five minutes, you'd know that. It's because I did something about it, but he didn't. It meant I'd betrayed him. He resented me so much.'

'That wasn't your fault,' Julia said, trying to understand. 'You tried to fulfil yourself. Pete shouldn't have resented you for that.'

'But I left him behind, love. That's the thing. I left him behind. If he'd left me like that, I might have felt the same. I deserted him and I deserted our marriage. If I were him, I'd have felt as abandoned as he did.'

'But you weren't him.'

No,' Maggie said. 'But knowing that isn't enough.'

Maggie walked away from Julia's towards the lofty heights of Magdalen College tower, the early spring sun shining overhead. She stopped on Magdalen Bridge, and leaned on the low stone wall, gazing down at the daffodils pushing their way through the thin coat of dead leaves in the grounds of St Hilda's College. Behind her, the traffic crawled with impatience towards the town; ahead of her was a garden of peace and tranquillity, of paradise.

She had stopped to lean on this bridge when she and Pete had come down to look at the colleges, when she had first tried to pluck up the courage to listen to her evening-class teacher, and to go for gold. She had tried to explain to Pete then how she felt. That ahead of her was the secret garden, the garden she'd never even realized was there, because nobody had ever told her. University was something that other people did, people on the television or in the news. Or other people's children, the children of people she didn't know. It had nothing to do with her. But somehow, the weeds had been cleared away, and she had been given a glimpse of the door in the wall. Then she had been offered the key, and taken her first tentative steps inside. And she had tried to leave the door ajar, to remember her way back.

But now the door had slammed shut, and she was trapped inside.

She turned back to the traffic and leaned back against the cold stone. She gazed up the creamy expanse of Magdalen Tower and rested her eyes on the perfect, intricately carved turrets, reaching up towards the sky as if they were growing towards the sun. Like her, she thought. Reaching into the air, and finding nothing to grab hold of.

She shivered, and began to walk briskly up the High Street towards the town. She might stop in Dillons on the way home, and pick up a new novel. Anything to take her mind off what was happening to her now.

She should have known that she wouldn't be able to tell Julia about it. Julia was a sweet girl, with a list of problems as long as her arm, and she knew that she would listen sympathetically and try to offer advice if she thought it was wanted. But Julia had too much on her own plate at the moment to be able to absorb Maggie's problems as well. It wasn't fair to expect it of her. She had the past to think about, and the present too. If only that bloke, Rob, had turned out to be the right one for her, he might have helped her to dispel all of that grief. But Maggie guessed that spending the night with him had only compounded Julia's problems, at least for the moment. What was it about getting drunk that made people forget who they were and what they were doing, and make stupid decisions about who to spend the night with – decisions that you'd never dream of making on the spur of the moment if you exchanged as many words with someone at the bus stop?

She walked through the shade cast by the thick wall of buildings, and glanced at the Examination Schools as she passed by. Her moment of triumph! They'd been met as they came out of their last exam by a horde of students from their college who'd dutifully doused them in champagne and covered them with flour while a pack of burly men in bowler hats frantically tried to stop them. She may have been Maggie Ridley, the barmaid from Leeds, but she'd been treated to the same bizarre rituals as the rest of them. And it had felt bloody good. For the first time in her life, she'd truly been one of *them*, one of the top notch, the privileged, the élite. Then she'd looked around for Pete, just hoping in her heart of hearts that he'd decided to come after all, to meet her and congratulate her, to share that fleeting, precious moment with her. But he hadn't been there.

She stiffened as she walked on, suddenly feeling the cold. Pete had been too busy entertaining himself with Chintzy Daphne, of course. Maggie's final exam had been the last thing on his mind. Bloody Daphne. If it had been somebody else, she might have understood. But Daphne had got right up her nose ever since she and Brian had moved next door. Daphne, whose son was a nuclear physicist one day, and Secretary General to the United Nations the next. Daphne, with her big bosoms and small bum. Daphne and her fake tan. Daphne and her garden furniture, and her Friday night barbecues. Bloody Daphne.

And in all that time, when she'd been at University, and suddenly found, to her unbridled shock, that men found her attractive, she'd stayed faithful to Pete. Even when younger, handsome men had paid her attention, she'd laughed them off, teased them away. But Pete had told her about Daphne when she'd gone home to visit him after her exams, and he also told her, after much prompting, that it had been going on for over a year. She'd felt like a fool to have thought that he might at least have waited for her.

So the next time she was tempted with forbidden fruit, she had it with whipped cream. It was so absurd, she almost laughed aloud. At least Daphne was the same age as Pete. They shared things – the estate, the neighbours, the chip shop in the arcade, the smell of the meat factory. At least his affair was in some way appropriate. What the hell would Pete say if he knew what she'd been doing? His face would turn purple and he'd probably be speechless, to begin with. All of his macho insecurities, his mid-life crisis, or whatever it was that was bugging him, would erupt into volcanic rage. He'd never expect it. He couldn't see how anybody else could find Maggie sexually desirable – not when he himself had gone off the idea a good few years ago. And if he knew that her lover was little more than a boy – a public schoolboy at that, with a slight lisp and an accent as clear and polished as a chandelier, with a father who was something important in the City and a mother who talked as if she'd got her nose caught in a mangle?

She drew a heavy breath, and pushed her way through Cornmarket, now jammed with Saturday shoppers. It was a manic day of the week, the pedestrians vying for space with the buses that trawled through, tempers fraying in all directions. She struggled up to Dillons, and hesitated outside. Did she really need to buy a novel, when her life was becoming stranger than fiction? At some point, she was going to have to ring Pete back and talk to him properly about a divorce. She glimpsed her reflection in the vast shop window as she hovered on the pavement, buffeted by shoppers pushing past. She did look good in her jeans. Julia was right. She shook back her ponytail.

She wouldn't talk to Pete today. She pushed open the glass door to the shop, and went inside.

Julia raced towards the phone as it began to ring, holding Fleabag off with one hand as she threw herself to the floor in a magnificent tackle and grabbed the receiver ahead of him.

'I won, you little sod!' she panted at him, ramming the telephone under her chin. 'Hello?'

She smiled at Fleabag and stroked his head as he sniffed the telephone with an air of disappointment.

'Julia?'

She frowned at the wall. She didn't recognize the voice. 'Who's this?'

'Julia, it's Leo. I don't suppose you remember – we had a conversation at a party a week ago.'

She stopped stroking Fleabag's head, and stared into his eyes instead. For a moment, she couldn't say anything at all, she was in such a state of shock to hear his voice again, and on the end of her telephone.

'I suppose you're wondering why I'm calling,' he said.

'Well, yes. Yes, I'm wondering that. Er – how did you get my number?'

'Your friend Maggie gave it to me after the party. I did try to ring you, rather late, I'm afraid, but I think there was something wrong with the phone. I found that I still had the number on me. I hope that you don't mind?'

Was he being disingenuous? It was so difficult to tell without seeing his expression. But then, there was a microscopic chance that he hadn't received an earful of drunken passion when he'd phoned that night. She decided to play the innocent.

'I'm not sure whether I mind or not. It depends on why you've rung, I suppose.'

'Right. I guess so.'

He sounded strangely reluctant to state his case, a quality she couldn't imagine him displaying in a court of law. She began to feel very wary. For some reason, both brothers seemed to think she was interested in the intricate details of their relationship with each other, which she found peculiar seeing as she'd known them for such a short time. Perhaps she should put him straight at once? She hadn't noticed 'mother substitute' written on her forehead the last time she'd looked. Then again, he might be playing the interfering older sibling. Did he think that she and Rob had something meaningful between them?

'Leo, I'm not sure what you want, but if it's about Rob, I should tell you that there's really nothing between us.'

'I know that.'

He sounded so sure that she was annoyed. She considered launching into a string of lies to disabuse him. But it wouldn't do anybody any favours.

'So, what can I do for you? I do find it a bit odd that you've rung me out of the blue like this.'

'Yes, well, I'm sorry. I wasn't sure if it was the right thing to do or not. It's just that I thought a lot this week about what you said, and I felt I should apologize to you again for being rude.'

Was that it? She hadn't thought to mark him down as someone who suffered from serial attacks of remorse.

'It's forgotten. I've heard it all before, anyway. You didn't say anything particularly original, I'm afraid.'

'No, well.' He stopped, and she thought she heard a muted sigh. Or he could be suppressing a burp. Difficult to tell.

'Thanks for the apology, but I haven't lost any sleep

126

about whatever it was you said, which to be honest, I can't really remember clearly anyway. So you'd better get on with whatever it was you were doing before you phoned.'

'There is one other thing.'

'What other thing?'

He paused then spoke again in an oddly polite voice.

'I wondered if you might have dinner with me.'

She sat back against the sofa and watched Fleabag hoist a leg into the air and begin a serious laundering of his bottom. It was a suitably poetic moment, somehow voicing her thoughts. Unfortunately, her shock was also audible.

'You've got to be kidding!'

His silence confirmed that her response was a little too direct. She tried to put her thoughts into a straight line, and deal with them one at a time.

'I'm sorry, Leo, that sounded awful. It's just, I don't quite know why you've asked me, but there's really no need to prostrate yourself to this extent. I seriously can't remember exactly what you said at the party, or even why I was offended at the time, but you really shouldn't worry about it. I'm sure you've got far more important things to do. Aren't there any criminals out there in need of a good prosecuting?'

'Oh yes, plenty of those.' He sounded vaguely amused, at least. 'But that isn't why I asked you. I actually rang because I would like to have dinner with you. Does that offend you?'

'Offend me?' She reached for Fleabag mid-wash and plonked him on her lap, rubbing his back with intense vigour. 'No, I'm not offended. I don't think.' She sought her brain for words, for an answer.

'Will you think about it, at least?'

'Er, I suppose so. It's just—'

'It's just so sudden, don't tell me?'

'It's not so much that. I just don't think you and I would make it in and out of a restaurant without killing each other. I mean, you'd only said a dozen words to me at the party, and I felt that I simply had to throw my glass of wine over you. It doesn't augur very well, does it?'

'I could wear a rain hat,' he said in a dry tone.

'Yes, but pizza would have more of an impact. This time, you might suffocate to death, and Maggie wouldn't be there with her tea towel to wipe the bits off.'

He laughed aloud, and she listened to the sonorous tone, intrigued. She hadn't realized that he was capable of laughing.

'Why don't I give you my number, and you can call me if you change your mind?'

She stared at the notepad and pen she left by the telephone. Her fingers refused to move towards it.

'You could do that, couldn't you?'

'Why don't I do that, then?'

'Okay.'

Her fingers drifted towards the pen, picked it up, and wrote down a London number.

'Well, I hope I might hear from you one day, Julia. I'm not a gorgon, whatever Robert might say. I think we might actually have an interesting evening, but I'll leave it up to you.'

She put the phone down and looked at the number as if it had been written by a stranger. Then, when she could move again, she wandered out into the kitchen and, in a dream, pulled a beer from the fridge, opened it and began to drink. She sank into a chair, watching blindly as Fleabag dug his claws into the woodchip wallpaper and skilfully removed a strip of it in the shape of the Isle of Man.

Rob's brother? The one who looked like a bouncer and

had a nasty tendency to state unpleasant truths without knowing it? The one she'd thrown wine all over at Maggie's party? *He* wanted to take *her* out to dinner? She looked over at Fleabag for an answer.

'What the hell was that all about?' she demanded.

Chapter Eight

'Do you like cats?'

Julia looked at Mack in surprise. She had briefly been letting her mind wander whilst he settled himself, her thoughts meandering aimlessly from anti-depressants to the workmen drilling outside her house, to Leo's telephone call. She blinked at him.

'Cats? Yes, I like cats. Why?'

He took off his jacket, slung it over his chair, and rolled up the sleeves of his denim shirt.

'I've got a bit of a problem.'

'With a cat?'

'Yeah.' He leaned on to his elbow, his hair falling smoothly around his face, and sighed. 'It's Elizabeth. She's pregnant.'

Julia's eyes widened.

'Elizabeth?'

'Yeah.'

'So . . . she wants to get rid of her cat before the baby's born, is that it?'

Was Elizabeth his girlfriend, she wondered? Perhaps the recipient of the carefully chosen bottle of French wine? She adopted a sympathetic look, just in case. She noticed that he was smiling, in a gentle, teasing way.

'Elizabeth is the cat,' he said.

'Oh! Oh, I see.' She nodded. Then she smiled back at him. 'Is she your cat?'

'Yeah. She's gorgeous. You should see her. I love tortoiseshells. I know they're really tetchy most of the time and they're real bitches, you know, to other people, but I love her. She's great. It's just the way she looks at me, just out of reach, and she really knows what I'm thinking. I'm sure of it. It's really freaky sometimes. And she plays blinkies with me.'

Julia leaned back in her chair to look at Mack properly.

'Blinkies?'

'It's this brilliant game. You blink at her, and she blinks back at you. It's some sort of language, I just don't know what it is we're saying to each other. And then – this is the amazing thing – just when you think she's doing it automatically, you change from a blink, to a wink.' He demonstrated, his dark blue eyes opening and closing. 'And then, she winks instead. She knows it's a wink, not a blink.'

'And she's pregnant.'

He exhaled slowly, looking weary.

'The thing is, she's so fluffy, I didn't notice at first. She's got this fantastically long hair, like a really elaborate picture frame all around her. She's like—' He stopped and thought for a moment. 'She's like the Mona Lisa. A tiny thing inside a huge case. Can you imagine what I mean? So I guess she's just been growing and growing and I haven't realized. I feel like a total bastard.'

'Why?' Julia laughed.

'Because I haven't been through the experience with her. I feel like I should have done. You know, given her special food to eat, or made sure she didn't exert herself, or something. I feel so protective of her. I can't explain it. It probably sounds stupid.'

For a moment, Julia felt absurdly emotional. Then she carried on, pushing away the dark memories, remembering where she was.

'So just how pregnant is Elizabeth?'

'Well, I took her to the vet as soon as I realized

something was wrong and he said that she's very pregnant. I was a bit worried that the journey would upset her. I didn't want her to lose the kittens.'

'You took her to the vet on your motorbike?'

He gave her a reproving look.

'No, Julia, I wouldn't do that to a pregnant cat. I took her on the bus. It's not too far.'

'Oh, I see.'

'And now I'm in a bit of a muddle. You see, I never meant to have a cat in the first place, but I rescued Elizabeth. She was just sitting in the road, only a couple of months old, and she was as skinny as a rat, with tiny eyes, all gooey. So I thought I'd just take her to the vet, have her sorted out, then find a good home for her. But it doesn't work out like that, does it?'

'No, it doesn't.' Julia sat forward, and listened.

'And she was a tough little thing. She had flu and the vet said she wouldn't live, but I tucked her into my jacket and took her home, and fed her on prawns and special kitten milk with extra vitamins, and she pulled through like a real trouper. And then, all this fur sprouted out. In tufts. I never guessed she'd have so much fur. But I should have taken her back to the vet, to have her done. You know.'

'Done,' Julia confirmed, nodding.

'Yeah. But I hadn't got round to it. I don't know.' He looked bewildered for a moment, shaking his head. 'They grow up so fast, don't they?'

'So, now you don't know what you're going to do with the kittens?' Julia suggested.

'That's it. I'm in a flat, not a very big one, and I've got a garden, so it's okay for Elizabeth, but I don't really think I can keep the kittens. Although the vet said she'd probably have a small litter.'

Julia looked at him thoughtfully. He continued to unpack his belongings, arranging them on the table as was the weekly ritual. So much compassion, she found herself thinking. Such a big heart. And yet, if you banged into Mack in all his black leather, waving his crash helmet in a dark alley, your first reaction would probably be to run for your life.

'So, er . . .' Mack finished his activity and looked at her again. 'I don't suppose you could give a kitten a good home, could you?'

'Oh, Mack. I'm sorry, but . . .'

'I can't vouch for the father, I'm afraid. There are two likely candidates. One's this really handsome geezer with black and white fur and a red collar. He's very well-to-do, and he's been sniffing around for a bit. Then there's this moggy, a real rough diamond with ginger hair and half his ear bitten off. I call him Wayne. Now he's really been interested, for a long time. So I think one of the kittens might be ginger. Have you got a problem with ginger hair?'

She laughed aloud, and shook her head at him.

'I haven't got anything against ginger hair. It's just that I've already got a cat.'

'Oh. That's a shame.'

He looked so disappointed that she wished she'd said something different.

'You'll find good homes for them, don't worry.'

'Yeah. I suppose. I'd just rather give them to people I know, people I could trust to look after them well. I thought you might be the sort of person to do that.'

'I would take one, Mack, if I hadn't got Fleabag. He's only ten months old, and my place just isn't big enough for another one. I'm sorry. Have you thought of anyone else who might like one?'

He shrugged, and flicked his pad of paper open.

'You were the only one I could think of at the moment. Never mind.'

She turned her attention to her file, pondering over his statement. She must have said or done something to make him think she was trustworthy. She wondered what it was.

They worked steadily through the session, pausing every so often to listen to giggles coming from the anteroom where Rob was ensconced with Sandra. Julia was relieved that Rob had greeted her in a normal way when she'd arrived. He seemed fairly friendly, at least not as ostensibly indifferent to her presence as he'd been the week before. Sandra had been pleased to see him, and Julia found herself wondering ungraciously whether Sandra would be more likely to deliver the sexual goods than she was. Then she castigated herself for being sordid. She suspected that even if the earth had moved for Rob in her bedsit, the outcome would be the same.

But just what had Rob said to his brother, and what did Leo make of their night together, if he knew anything about it? And what would Rob say to the fact that Leo had now asked her out? His incongruous invitation was intriguing her more and more.

'Listen, everybody!' Vivienne took centre stage, her eyes roaming the group expressively, her palms pressed together in the air. Julia's mind shot back to *Playschool*. She could picture Vivienne as a presenter, miming with her body. *You too can be a tree* . . .

'We all need to decide what we're going to bring to the party. We have all remembered that it's the last day of term next Thursday, haven't we?'

Julia sighed, and caught Mack's eye as he looked up from his reading. He winked at her, and turned his full attention to Vivienne, concentrating hard.

'We always have a little drink. Not too much, of course, seeing as some of us have to drive home, and some food. Shall we decide who's going to bring what?'

Oh God, Julia groaned inwardly. Another collective decision. It invited fifteen minutes of directionless debate, followed by long, silent spells of utter confusion.

'Why don't you just tell us what to bring, and we'll see what we can do?' Mack suggested, with an almighty surge of common sense, Julia thought.

'That's not the way we normally do things, Mack,' Vivienne explained, nudging her cloche hat with her fingertips. 'We all like to make a contribution. So, does anybody have any ideas?'

'I'll bring a bottle,' Alec said quickly, awarding himself the simplest job at once. He grinned at the others in acknowledgement.

'All right Alec, and perhaps the women can do some cooking. Shirani, would you like to do some samosas for us, like you did last term?'

'I can do that.' Shirani wobbled her head.

'I'll bring a bottle as well,' Julia said quickly and decisively, biting back her irritation at the assumption that the women should do all of the cooking. She didn't want to be landed with a disastrous week in the kitchen attempting to produce something that would meet with Vivienne's approval.

'Oh, but I think we might need you to bring some food,' Vivienne insisted, fingers fluttering. 'And we won't need two bottles, surely?'

'We'll need two bottles,' Alec said bluntly, rubbing his nose and looking away.

'Anyway, I can't cook,' Julia announced, challenging Vivienne with a bolshie stare. 'Unless you want me to buy something in Tesco's?'

'Home-made is so much nicer for these special occasions.' Vivienne returned the bolshie stare, her voice like honey. 'Can't you make a little effort, Julia?'

'I'll cook something,' Mack interrupted firmly,

swinging back on his chair. 'I love cooking, as it happens. So I'll bring some pâté, home-made of course, and some dips if you like. If someone else wants to bring some French bread, or something.'

Vivienne batted her eyelashes, looking nonplussed.

'How will you manage to carry it on your motorcycle?'

'I'll stick it down my jacket,' he returned. 'Anyway, Julia walks here, so she shouldn't have to carry loads of stuff, unless you're going to give her a lift up?'

Vivienne began to bounce up and down on the balls of her feet, looking decidedly uncomfortable.

'I don't go Julia's way, Mack. I simply haven't time to collect everybody on my way here. Why don't you offer to give Julia a lift on your motorcycle?'

Mack sniffed, and tapped his biro on the table top. He and Vivienne stared at each other for a moment. Although Mack's expression was placid, Julia sensed that he was annoyed.

'That's up to Julia, isn't it?' he said pleasantly. 'Anyway, I've said I'll bring food, Shirani's doing some samosas, and we've got two bottles of wine, so is there anything else?'

Vivienne was temporarily silenced. Julia watched with amazement. It was a rare thing, to see Vivienne's authority challenged. Julia herself had been close to uttering a few rude remarks in her time, but Mack was treating her to a dose of her own politesse. Julia simply hadn't thought of doing that.

'I'll bring some bread,' Brenda said, producing a handful of miscellaneous objects from her handbag, and looking deeply into it for her diary. 'I'll just make a note so that I don't forget.'

'And I can bring a nice ripe Brie, if we're having crusty bread,' George said, looking hungry. 'So I think that just about takes care of everything.'

Kieran and Fiona kept silent, seeing as they could not be expected to donate offerings to a party that they wouldn't be attending. Julia envied them for a moment.

'Oh heavens!' Vivienne exclaimed suddenly, swivelling round and staring at the closed door of the ante-room where Rob and Sandra had continued with their session in blissful ignorance of the democracy-in-action demonstration taking place in the main room. 'We haven't included everybody!'

'I'm sure they won't mind,' Julia ventured. 'We'll have enough now, won't we?'

'Julia!' Vivienne swung back again with an expression that only just managed to remain pleasant. 'I get the impression you're not trying to be helpful at all. I shall go and ask them now what they would like to bring. We wouldn't want them to feel left out, would we?'

Julia restrained a childish pout while Vivienne wrenched her hat securely on to her head, and marched off into the small room, closing the door behind her to make sure that nothing was overheard. When she had gone, Julia expelled a long sigh, finding that it was echoed by several of the others. There was a low murmur of restrained laughter. Then Alec scratched his head.

'What's Vivienne going to bring, then?'

When Julia got home, she sat down with a mug of tea, and stared at Fleabag. What had Mack called the game? Winkies? Blinkies?

She called his name in a silly, high-pitched voice to get his attention, then fixed him with a manic glare. After a few seconds, she produced an overt blink, and waited for results. He shifted on his back paws, sat down again, his eyes on hers. Nothing happened. She repeated the process, blinking slowly and deliberately at him whilst he watched her in apparent curiosity. Then, after a moment in which she became very conscious of staring at him rudely, he blinked back at her.

'Oh my God!' she exclaimed in astonishment. 'It works!'

Holding back a giggle, she repeated the activity several times, finding that he responded by imitating her blinks. Then, just when they had got into a routine, she winked instead.

She held her breath. For a long minute, he just looked back at her. Then, he winked.

'Fleabag, you're brilliant!'

She threw herself on him and hoisted him up into the air, draping him around her shoulders. He began to purr like a machine-gun. She fondled his paws in her fingers, and took him for a victory march around the bedsit. She had communicated with him in some unknown language, and it felt absolutely wonderful! She was so illogically filled with euphoria that she wished she had Mack's phone number so that she could ring him and tell him. It was a shame that she wouldn't see him until next week. By next week, Elizabeth probably would have had her kittens as well.

It was funny, she thought, how you could build up a portrait of somebody after only a few hours of contact. She still had a sketchy picture of Mack, but now she could imagine him going home, blinking at his tortoise-shell cat, stroking her long, soft fur. And he'd find time somehow this week to make a pâté and some dips to bring to the class. And he was holding down his job as a decorator as well, and perhaps going back to the supermarket at some point to try to find his favourite wine again. And, like her, he found *Family Fortunes* strangely compelling.

She smiled to herself and sank on to the sofa. Fleabag restlessly shot off to play with a lone woodlouse setting out on a perilous voyage from under the wardrobe to the kitchen door which, as Fleabag's accurate paw descended with a thump, proved to be fatal. She watched with distaste, deciding to leave nature to run its course, and noticed again that the notepad with Leo's number written on it was still face-upwards by the phone.

It would be easy to ring him and agree to have dinner with him. Having dinner with him itself would be a feat of monumental proportions. It was something she didn't feel up to doing. No, that was an understatement. She was terrified by the thought. It wasn't that Leo himself intimidated her, although she wouldn't want to be up on a shoplifting charge to find that he was the prosecuting barrister, but the way that he had telephoned her and asked her out was too reminiscent of an overture to courtship for her not to feel a flutter of panic. Picking somebody up at a party and pleading mitigating circumstances after the event – or non-event in Rob's case – was something, but actually planning a date, preparing for it, turning up to it, that was something else. And besides, this was the brother of the man she'd picked up at the party.

She thought about Rob again as she leaned back and stared up at the ceiling. Seeing him tonight, engrossed with Sandra, too preoccupied to chat to anyone else, made him seem very distant. There was no doubt that he was one of the best-looking men she'd ever seen. That, at least, was something. How long was it since she'd found a man attractive? Was Bill really the last one? He'd been handsome, dark haired, with a penetrating stare that alternately made her shiver with delight and discomfort. Perhaps Rob had been part of the process? Was she to expect that first came the stirrings of physical attraction again and that more interesting feelings might follow?

She snorted at herself, and Fleabag shot her a worried

look. She pulled an apologetic face. There was no point in getting analytical. She'd fancied Rob. So what? It didn't mean that anything else had to stem from it, which was just as well as it didn't look as if anything ever would.

Her eyes wandered back to Leo's phone number. Perhaps dinner wouldn't do any harm? She would think about it. After she'd seen the counsellor again.

Maggie peered at the slim liquid crystal display on the front of her typewriter. She pulled a face, and deleted the whole line.

She stopped to roll another cigarette, and stuck it between her lips without lighting it. It was hardly worth lighting her roll-ups when she was writing. She only rested them in the ashtray when she got a spurt on, they went out, then she had to go through the whole rigmarole of lighting them again. She decided just to chew the end of this one instead.

This story was so nearly finished. She called it a 'story', but there really wasn't any plot. There was a great deal of anatomical detail, much groaning and grunting, and not many euphemisms. She supposed she should be cringing, but she wasn't. It was just a way of expressing herself that might bring in a few quid, and it satisfied her sense of humour. After three years of immersing herself in polysyllables, it was something of a relief to be trying to work out how to spell 'oooh'. And she'd always made up stories in her head, just to keep herself sane half the time. Now she was having fun writing them down. And didn't most of the authors she'd written essays about start out by trying to make a few quid on the side? She ran the justification through her head again. She thought hard, chewed on the end of her cigarette, and rewrote the line.

She sat back and stared at the display. Then she

reached for her gold lighter, and lit the cigarette, blowing the smoke at her words. What a load of crap, she thought. As if Timothy would choose this moment to answer the door, only to find that the lady from Save the Children was coincidentally feeling as randy as he was. Perhaps it was just that some things were more likely to happen in California than in Bradford? But she'd never been to California, and hadn't felt it was honest to set the story there. She pulled the sheet from the roller, stared at it for a few, indecisive moments, then screwed it up and tossed it over her shoulder in the direction of the bin.

It wouldn't be so bad if any of the magazines had paid some interest in what she'd written. But she'd had a pile of rejection slips, and it was making her wonder if she was any good at this sort of fiction at all. She could tell the truth, she supposed. She drew on the acrid smoke, and pondered the story that might emerge. She laughed to herself, but the constriction in her chest didn't move. She stopped laughing, and felt a wave of sorrow sweep down and drench her.

So, she was escaping. Finding that she couldn't lose herself in a novel, that the sessions she was working at the pub weren't distracting her, and that her mind was in chaos, she had sat down at the desk in her room, and tried to finish the tacky story of Timothy and his twin. And it wasn't doing any good at all. Fabian was out, at the library, but she knew he'd be back at about five, and Pete was in Leeds, waiting for her to calm down and ring him up to talk about the divorce.

She smoked her way through the cigarette, took a swig of cold coffee, and edged a clean sheet of paper into the typewriter. With a flash of satire, she began to write.

My Life with Pete, by Maggie Ridley

She sat back and looked at it, trying to smile at herself,

but speared through with doubt. She swallowed. It was so long since she'd actually cried over anything, she thought she'd forgotten how to do it. But that was how she felt now, as if what was creeping up and down her throat was in fact the threat of tears.

She stubbed out her cigarette, and began to type, her fingers tapping the keys with a surge of newly released energy. She didn't stop to change or delete anything, she just wrote and wrote, changing the paper when it was full, until the urge to cry started to crawl back down her throat and settle in her stomach.

It was some time before she became aware that somebody was knocking at her door. She glanced round, feeling furtive. She turned over the sheets that she had typed so that the plain sides faced upwards, and tapped the sheet in the roller forwards so that it lolled over the keys.

'Come in?'

Fabian poked his head round the door, and looked at her uncertainly, waiting for her reaction. She hesitated, caught between the images of her wedding that she had been reliving, and the pair of dark brown eyes that were watching her. She breathed out slowly.

'Hello, love. Did you get much done?'

Relieved, he stepped in, and let the door swing shut behind him, his hands behind his back. His face creased into a smile as he suddenly produced a small package wrapped in gold paper, bound with a red ribbon. He held it out to her with a flourish.

'For you, madam.'

'Me?'

Maggie took the package, a flush rising in her cheeks, and gently pulled the ribbon. The paper fell away, and beneath was an ornate box, edged with gold. She recognized it as a very exclusive perfume. She caught her breath, looking up at Fabian's expectant face.

'On your income? You're barmy, Fabian!'

'I had some money transferred from my father recently. Don't worry about it, he's got stacks of cash. He never remembers what he's given me. So I decided that I'd spend it on you.'

'I – I don't know what to say.'

She placed the box carefully on the desk, and looked at it. It was so perfect, such an object of beauty in itself, that she didn't want to open it. He walked up to her, and stood behind her, resting his hands on her shoulders, and massaging the delicate bones with his fingers.

'You look knackered. Let me massage you back into life.'

She tried not to stiffen under his touch. She stared ahead at the drooping paper falling out of the typewriter. She'd just got to the bit where Betty's niece had thrown up on the wedding presents, and Pete's dad had been discovered unconscious on Rum and Blacks in the loo. Then the band had started up, and Pete had taken her hand, and led her on to the floor . . .

'Maggie? Is there anybody in there? You've been writing filthy stories again, haven't you? I can always tell. You get this glassy look in your eyes, as if you're stoned out of your box.'

She tried to lean back and relax. His fingers moved over her skin, teasing the tension away. She tried not to think about Pete's dad, or his mum, and how she'd always been so rude to her, only to regret it when she died of lung cancer ten years later. And the feel of the wedding dress, and the smell of alcohol and pipe smoke, mingled with lingering wafts of Betty's niece's vomit. She pushed it all away, back on to the page where she had left it, and fell back into Fabian's hands.

'You've got work to do,' she murmured, closing her eyes.

'I've been a very good boy today and written my essay,' he said, breathing near to her ear. 'Which means that I can take some time off tonight, doesn't it? You said I'd feel really good about myself if I did all my homework, and you were right. I feel really good about myself.'

'That's good.'

'What about you, Maggie?' His voice drifted over her. 'Do you feel really good about yourself?'

She didn't answer. His hand moved to caress her lapel, to touch the soft skin under her blouse. She flinched away. He delicately resumed his pressure on her shoulders, but feathered a kiss on her ear.

The door crashed open. Maggie and Fabian jumped, as one, away from each other. Maggie glared up with a red face. Naomi leaned against the door-frame, looked at Maggie and looked at Fabian. She was silent for a moment, then she shifted awkwardly.

'Your mum's on the phone, Fabian.'

'Can't you knock?' he retorted defensively.

'Sorry. I heard voices,' she said in a deadpan voice. 'I'll tell her you'll be down in a sec, shall I?'

She gave him a raise of her eyebrows and disappeared, her footsteps thumping away down the stairs. Fabian gave a low whistle.

'Shit. That was close.'

'For God's sake, go and talk to your mum,' Maggie said, leaning forward and putting her head in her hands.

'Maggie? You're not going to let that bother you, are you? Who cares if Naomi knows?' He paced across the room, and then back again, waving his arms in the air. 'In fact, who cares if everybody knows?'

'I care, Fabian.' Maggie turned to him, caught in anguish. 'At the moment, I care. All right?'

He leaned towards her, and grabbed her shoulders, searching her eyes.

'But I don't care! I've just realized that! I thought I did, but I don't! I really feel something for you, Maggie. It's not just infatuation, or any of the things you've been saying. I really care about you.'

He waited urgently for her to respond. She looked deeply into his brown eyes, at his soft, glowing skin, his beautiful full mouth.

'Oh Fabian,' she whispered. 'Go and talk to your mum.'

He waited a moment longer, then stood up, his eyes bright.

'I will, but I'll be right back. Don't go out, or get in the bath or anything.'

She laughed, despite herself. 'Just go!'

He stomped away, and her bedroom door swung closed again. She stared at it, listening to him lolloping down the stairs, imagining the polite strain with which he'd try to hold a conversation with his mother. A woman who was three years younger than herself, and a great deal more sophisticated. A woman to whom *petits fours* and soirées were second nature, who practically lived her life in delicatessens but who wouldn't be able to find her way round a launderette without a set of instructions. A woman who would pin Maggie down with an oyster knife and bludgeon her to death with a caviar chiller if she knew she was sleeping with her son.

She rolled another cigarette, and licked the gummed edge of the paper. She caught sight of her typed pages again, and pulled open a drawer, pushing them inside. She would deal with Pete soon, but not yet. He had bloody Daphne to entertain him while he waited for her to give her consent to the divorce. And if she didn't give it?

She lit her cigarette, noticed the paper left in the typewriter, and wrenched it out, stuffing it into the drawer with the others. It had been a bad idea to write about Pete. It only made him more real. Her eyes rested on Fabian's gift. A perfume that Pete would never have thought to buy her – would never have been able to afford. Her bedroom door flew open again, and Fabian thrust himself inside, slamming it behind him. He flung himself down on the bed, and covered his face with his hands. She twisted round to look at him with concern. His body was completely rigid.

'Fabian? What's up?'

'Oh fucking, fucking hell,' he moaned through his fingers.

'Fabian?' She stood up and looked down at him. He didn't move.

'Oh fucking hell.'

'I've got that bit. What's the matter?'

He removed his hands, and stared up at her, his huge eyes bleak.

'My parents are coming up to see me.'

Chapter Nine

Julia arrived at The Turf early, and ordered herself a gin and tonic. She paid, and chose a seat to one side, near the door, so that she could drink it quietly and watch people. She felt it gave her a momentary advantage.

She slipped her coat from her shoulders, and re-arranged the necklace that was sitting over the collar of her sweater. She'd dressed as simply as possible, without looking as though she'd popped in on her way to somewhere else. She'd put her wool trousers on, a pair of boots with a heel, to give her a bit more confidence, and a plain sweater that was casual but, with the necklace, quite smart. She'd left her hair loose. Hair could be a dangerous enemy at times like this. Too fussy and it would look as if she'd taken hours to arrange it. Too windswept and it might look too sexy. Hers was just newly washed and straight. It should be safe enough.

She pecked at the drink, gazing up at the low beams of the pub, her nerves pulsing steadily in her ears. She should have thought to get some beer in, she thought now, so that she could have a drink or six before she came out. She took a deeper sip of the gin. It was such a bad idea, being here, on a Saturday night. She should have suggested a week night to make it seem less significant. Even better, Leo probably wouldn't have been able to make it, and that would have been that. But he'd suggested the venue, insisted on paying, and she'd gone along with it.

She drained her glass, and was considering slipping another gin down her throat before he arrived, when a dark figure pushed through the wooden latched door, stooping to get in without crashing his head on the low doorway. He stopped to brush a sprinkling of rain from his hair, and looked around. She shrank back into the benched seat, hoping he wouldn't see her. She'd forgotten how scary he was, and in a navy cashmere coat, clutching a black umbrella, he looked twice as tall and twice as broad. She thought about crawling under the table and hiding there until he gave up on her and left, but it was too late. He saw her, nodded, and began to walk towards her.

She gulped, stuck her glass into her mouth, and sucked up a lemon pip, hoping that it was deeply infused with gin. After she'd seen the counsellor, she'd felt more like having this dinner after all, but now it seemed insane. She should get up, run past him, and out the door. Right now. She was still chewing on her lemon pip when Leo reached the table, looked down at her empty glass, and then, to her astonishment, smiled.

'Shall we have a drink here first?'

'Yes,' she said, a little too quickly. 'Mine's a G and T.'

He took off his coat, draped it over the stool opposite her and gave her a curious look. Then he went to the bar and ordered. She watched his back. It was very wide. He'd probably played rugby at university, she thought. And the opposition probably ran away. He was wearing a suit, a nice one, but it made him even more daunting. He returned with her drink and a whisky for himself, and sat opposite her.

'It hasn't changed in here,' he said, glancing around the dark room. 'This used to be a regular haunt of mine.'

She took her drink, swigged it, winced in realization that he'd got her a double, and at the same time, thanked him for it. Then she found her voice again.

'I didn't know you were here?'

'I did Jurisprudence here. Centuries ago, of course. At Queen's.'

'Oh.' She had a vague memory of accusing him of being peevish because his brother had a place at Oxford. He hadn't said anything then about where he'd studied. He could have done, but he didn't.

'It seems like a very long time ago. I went straight on to bar school afterwards, and I've hardly been back since.'

'Don't you like Oxford, then?'

He paused as he raised his glass to his mouth, and looked over the rim.

'It has its uses. And it's fine, in small doses. But London's where I live and work. After London, coming back to Oxford's like visiting a museum.'

'So that makes me an exhibit, does it?' She raised her eyebrows.

'You don't fit in here,' he said. 'Otherwise you would be an exhibit. You're just passing through, aren't you?'

She sat back and looked at him.

'I might be, or I might stay. I haven't decided. There's more to Oxford than the University, but it takes a little imagination to realize that.'

'Ah. So you live in East Oxford, then, with the "real" people. Somewhere down the Cowley Road.'

She frowned at him, already disconcerted to be the subject of his analytical brain, sifting the evidence and coming to confident conclusions.

'Saint Clements, actually. Not quite East Oxford. I'm surprised Rob didn't tell you that.'

He took a sip of his whisky, appeared to appreciate it, and set his glass down.

'I haven't spoken to Robert. Not since the weekend I was here.'

She was silenced for a moment. His comment took her

back to the problem she was pondering over. Had Leo overheard something very embarrassing when he'd rung her bedsit that night? She had played music very loudly when they'd got back. It was possible that he'd just got an earful of Tom Jones and had rung off in disgust. She was going to have to try and tease it out of him.

'I gather you were locked out that night, and had to phone me to try to find Rob?'

'Yes.' He stared at her, mud-green eyes oblique.

'I see. I, er. My cat has a habit of answering the phone. I'm afraid I didn't hear it ring.'

'No, I'm not surprised.'

Damn you, she thought.

'So, er. You must have heard the music playing quite loudly, then?'

'No,' he said slowly, picking up his glass and swilling the ice around. 'As it happens, I appeared to have broken into a conversation that was going on. That's why I hung up.'

She blanched, stunned into silence.

'Drink your gin,' he said. 'It'll put the colour back in your cheeks.'

'Now look here.' She sat up straight, recovering herself. 'I think you'd better tell me exactly what you overheard, don't you?'

'Do you really want me to, Julia? Or would you rather guess?'

'I can't bloody remember what was being said, okay?' she seethed, trying to keep her voice down. 'So will you stop playing games and come out with it?'

He sat back in his chair, resting his glass in his hands, and treated her to an assessing look.

'I expect you're wondering why I wanted to have dinner with you after you spent the night with my brother.'

It was a statement, not a question. Julia decided to challenge it.

'Who says he spent the night?'

'I do. I know Robert, and I know how drunk you were. You're not going to tell me I'm wrong, are you?'

'It's none of your damned business,' she bit, clutching her glass, and wondering just how much longer she could hang on to it without emptying it over his head again.

'Let me tell you something about Robert,' Leo said, sitting forward and holding her gaze. 'Something you may have worked out for yourself. He's very confused.'

She blinked at him in amazement, then she burst out laughing.

'Aren't we all?'

'Let me put it another way, then. I expect that Robert will have told you that he doesn't want a relationship right now. That the time isn't right, or something to that effect. That's what he usually does.'

'So what?' Her hair stood on end. 'I don't want a relationship either. There's nothing particularly wrong with that.'

'Oh dear,' Leo shook his head and took another sip of his whisky. 'I'm going to have to be blunt. Julia, Rob's gay.'

'You mean, he's happy?' Julia felt a bubble of hysteria rising in her throat. The gin was definitely hitting her smack between the eyes now.

'I mean, he's gay. He's still confused about his sexuality and every so often he takes off with a woman to try to convince himself that he can do anything he wants. The last time he did it, a little over three years ago, he ended up becoming a father.'

'What?'

Leo silently finished his drink, leaving Julia to sit

stupidly holding her glass and staring at him. For a moment, she wondered if he had slipped an illegal substance into her gin. Things had taken a decidedly surreal turn. No, she was just a little tipsy, and Leo was waiting for her to say something else.

'What do you mean, he's a father?'

'Do you want another drink?'

She looked down at her glass. She'd finished her gin already. She handed him the empty glass, and he took it, obediently drifting back to the bar to get refills for them both.

She stared down at the table while her body raged like a forest fire, and her brain froze over. He was gay, and he was a father? How? Where? When? What on earth had he been doing then, coming back to her bedsit as if it was a really good idea? How come she hadn't guessed that it wasn't really what he wanted? And above all, why did the one man in God knew how long that she'd decided not only to fancy, but to reveal her underwear to, have to turn out to prefer men to women? Leo, it seemed, had an interesting line in pre-dinner small talk. Ker-pow. She sat in shock, as if he'd stridden into the pub and clouted her over the head with a frying pan.

In minutes, which seemed like only seconds, Leo had returned, set a drink in front of her and settled himself back into his seat.

'I got you a single this time. You don't want to be too hammered to appreciate The Bath Place Restaurant's wine list, do you?'

She vaguely heard him, but looked up at him, her eyes filled with questions.

'What happened to the baby?'

'She's at home, with her mother. I look after them.'

'You do? *You*?'

'I help them, financially.' He sipped his whisky and

gave her a dry look. 'Well, you don't expect Robert to be able to support them on a student grant, do you?'

'Oh my God!' she breathed, more pieces of the jigsaw falling into place. 'No wonder . . .'

'No wonder I'm angry?' He shrugged. 'I'm not always angry. Robert's a good scholar. In many ways, he should be pursuing his research. But it's a difficult balance. For some men, becoming a father would have changed everything. But Robert had already come out to me, and to most people, before he knew that Emily was pregnant. It was unfortunate timing, but Emily wanted the baby and she had every right to go ahead.'

'But knowing that, Rob should be supporting his own daughter, surely?' she said, picking up her glass again. 'How old is she?'

'Two years and four months,' he said, with an accuracy that surprised her.

'You must see a lot of her, then?'

'She's my niece,' he said, with a protective edge to his voice. 'If I had a daughter as wonderful as she is, I'd do anything for her. But Robert doesn't share that view.'

'Does he—' She stopped and took a deep breath. The bustle of activity continued around them, leaving them in a private cocoon. 'Doesn't Rob see her?'

'Practically never. That's where we come to blows. He's running away from it all, not just financially, but emotionally too. You said when we first met that I was nothing like my brother. You were right.'

Julia sipped her drink and let the ice cubes rest against her warm lips.

'I, er . . .' Leo leaned forward, appearing to choose his words carefully. 'I don't want you to get the wrong impression. I haven't come here to tell tales about my own brother. I just thought you should know where you stood, if you don't already. Rob likes women, he gets on with women, and every so often he lets his feelings run away with him, he tries to make something more of it, but . . .'

'But he can't follow it through. It's not the way he is,' she finished for him. 'It's all right, Leo. I'm not about to start over-reacting. I've met all sorts of people, and . . .' She stopped, not wanting to erupt into a string of clichés.

'Okay, okay.' He smiled at her reassuringly. 'You're not a bigot and some of your best friends are gay. Relax, sometimes there's no other way to put it. I knew what sort of woman you were, Julia, and I knew how you'd react. I simply wanted to set the record straight.'

'Actually—,' she mused, thinking back to Rob's hesitant invitation to go for a drink – it must have been a couple of weeks ago, after the class. 'Yes, I think Rob was going to tell me himself, but I didn't give him the chance.'

Leo inclined his head with interest.

'That would be a positive development.'

She resisted the urge to laugh at him, suddenly formal again, as if he were considering a plea for mitigating circumstances.

'I think it's something to do with Sandra.'

'Sandra?'

'She's a student, at the literacy class we both teach at. He said she'd got a daughter who was about four years old. She's on her own with her, from what I can make out. That's right, he said something about it making him think, about life.'

'Literacy class?'

'Er, yes. That's where we met, actually. We're both volunteers there. And Sandra's his student.'

'Really?' Leo nodded slowly, holding her eye. 'Good. That's good. I think.'

She sat back on the hard seat and gave him a long

look. For the first time in her experience of him, he looked unsure of himself, as if he couldn't confidently predict the outcome of a situation, or as if something that he hadn't anticipated had happened. She suspected that it didn't happen very often. It made him more human. Perhaps even human enough for her to enjoy having dinner with him. She relaxed and smiled over at him.

'You might even say we were both doing something vaguely useful,' she teased him, the gin warming her spirits. 'But I wouldn't want to push you on that.'

'I'll withhold my judgement until I've had more time to examine the evidence,' he parried, his lips twitching.

'So I'm to be a witness this evening, am I?' She raised an eyebrow.

'More of an exhibit, I would say.'

'Oh God. Well, if I'm going to be examined by a forensic expert, I'd better be on my best behaviour, hadn't I?'

'Definitely.' He nodded. 'Especially as I forgot to bring my rain hat.'

'Don't worry,' she laughed. 'I've heard this restaurant's got a very good wine list. I'll be drinking what's in my glass.'

'The news gets better by the minute.' He inclined his head and raised his whisky to his lips. She watched him, deciding that he was really quite attractive. He wasn't spellbinding, as Rob was, but there was something about him. In fact, now she was genuinely looking forward to their meal together.

'So, Leo, brother of Robert, now that you've delivered all of your news, shall we go and eat something? Or is there anything else I should know first?'

He finished his whisky, and put the glass down, catching her eye.

'There is one more thing.'

'Oh God. What is it?'

'I don't want you to worry about the cost of the meal. This one's on me.'

'Don't worry, Leo,' she said, rising from her seat. 'I wouldn't have it any other way.'

Julia fell into her bedsit, a collage of her furniture and possessions swimming pleasantly about in front of her eyes. She fumblingly put the kettle on, and put her finger to her lips as Fleabag wailed at her.

'Sssh! You'll wake the clogs up!'

She hiccupped, pulling the mugs around until she remembered that she was actually trying to get one out of the cupboard, and dumped a tea-bag into it.

'Little Fleabag!' she cooed at him in a hoarse whisper. 'I'm a bit squiffy. You don't mind, do you? I've had quite a nice evening, actually. I'd never have thought it, would you?'

He wailed again, and she lurched around the kitchen until she found the cat food, and piled half a tin on to his plate. She teetered on her legs and fell heavily against the units, pushing the cupboard door closed with a crash.

'Sssh!' she said into the air. Then something pricked at her memory. 'Hang on, the clogs are down a well this weekend. It's okay, Fleabag, we can make as much noise as we like.'

He ignored her, tail up as he buried his nose in his food. She watched him, troubled by something she couldn't put her finger on. The clogs were away. Annelies had been in the bedsit on Friday night, saying something. Oh, balls! She hadn't fed the fish!

'Oh dear,' she mumbled, walking unsteadily across the kitchen and finding Annelies's bunch of keys on top of a pile of things to do. She waved them in the air. 'This is my St Peter impression, what d'you think, Fleabag?'

She hiccupped again, and frowned at herself. She hadn't been this drunk when she'd been with Leo, she was sure of it. The meal had been delicious, expensive and very pretty to look at, although far too small to mop up much of the alcohol they'd knocked back. She was relieved Leo wasn't driving after two whiskies, a very nice bottle of red and a glass of port. They'd managed to have quite a lucid conversation. He'd told her all about the chambers where he worked, about his gruelling schedule, and about the fact that he was a defence lawyer. That had surprised her hugely. He'd asked her about the literacy class and she'd talked about it. In a very witty fashion, from what she could remember. She frowned. At least, she'd thought she was being witty. Then they'd had coffee, and she'd agreed to a glass of port. That was silly, very silly. But she'd seemed reasonably steady when she'd said goodbye to him, and there hadn't been any funny business, no hanging around, or wondering whether to peck each other on the cheek. He'd just said goodbye and headed off down George Street towards the station, disappearing into a crowd of drunken students. And she'd quite happily marched off to the bus stop and come home. It must have been the fresh air. That and mixing her drinks, which was always a bad idea. That was probably why she'd nearly disappeared into a hole left by the workmen at the end of the pavement. It would have been a miserable place to spend the night.

'There are fish to be fed,' she stated severely, as Fleabag emerged from his food and looked at her to see what was going to happen next. 'C'mon then, fatso. Let's go and save them from starvation.'

She plodded up the stairs, stopping every so often to lean against the wall, and made it to the landing above.

She turned the key in the lock very quietly, not wanting any of the other residents of the house to hear her and find her in this state. She pushed the door, and let Fleabag in ahead of her, pausing to hiccup again, before following him in.

She flicked the lights, and leaned back against the door. She shook her head disapprovingly at the mess in the kitchen. She thought she was untidy, but Annelies was something else. There was a pile of washing-up in the sink, and magazines about mountains strewn all over the table. They must have shot off in a hurry this time. There was still a half-eaten plate of some sort of bean mix sitting around, something that only Dutch people would actually put in their mouths, she thought hazily.

She tromped through to the bedsitting room, put on the light, and turned her attention to the fish tank.

'Little, little fishy things.' She peeped at them, pushing her nose up to the glass. 'I'm so, so sorry I forgot to give you your dinner. Do you forgive me?'

They gaped back at her, grape-eyed and unforgiving. Suffused with guilt, she lifted the wire mesh from the top of the tank, and peered down at them from above.

'Little fishies. Are you hungry, sweeties?' She groped for the fish food, pulled open the top, and a shower of dots flew into the air. Exclaiming, she stuck her finger tips into the mixture, and began to sprinkle it over the water, watching with fascination as the psychedelic flashes shot towards the floating confetti and broke the surface with their lips to admit the food.

'Little cutie poos,' she burbled. 'Is your mummy away? Is she off bonking in Yorkshire again? Never mind, Auntie Julia's here to take care of you.'

'Julia? What are you doing?'

She screamed, threw the fish food into the air, and

jumped around all at the same moment, falling over and landing on her knees on the thin carpet. She stared at the bed in complete horror. Was she imagining it, or was Annelies sitting up in bed in a T-shirt, looking at her with an expression of total bewilderment? She blinked hard, her heart thumping in her chest, but Annelies was still there, looking surprisingly calm under the circumstances.

'Good God!' Julia managed to say. 'What the bloody hell are you doing in bed? I thought you were down a well?'

Annelies watched Julia scramble to her feet without moving from her bed. She seemed quite comfortable.

'I'm not pot-holing until tomorrow,' she said. 'I told you that, when I gave you the keys. I said I would give them to you early in case you went somewhere on Saturday. Don't you remember?'

'No,' Julia defended. 'I'm pissed.'

'Oh dear,' Annelies continued matter-of-factly. 'Well, you're not a burglar, so that's good. You can go now.'

'Right.'

Julia tried to get her bearings and point herself in the direction of the exit. Thank God Annelies's boyfriend wasn't with her tonight. Just what she might have walked in on, she couldn't bear to think. She began to stumble back towards the door.

'Look,' she turned round, feeling deeply ashamed. 'I'm so sorry, Annelies. I got a bit confused. I didn't mean to frighten you.'

'Oh, I'm not frightened.' Annelies shook her ponytail, settling herself back on the pillows. 'But don't forget to put the wire—' She stopped suddenly, looking over at the fish tank, her face a sheet of horror. Julia looked round quickly in the direction of her open-mouthed stare.

'Oh my God!'

She raced towards Fleabag and tried to grab him, but he leapt out of reach, something small, orange and unlucky clasped between his jaws. He fled into the kitchen. Julia looked back to Annelies, to say something, anything at all, but her white-faced shock was evidence that there was nothing she could say to make it better.

'I'll get it back. Don't worry.'

Julia shot through to the kitchen, throwing herself to the ground and trying to grab him. It was obviously too late. Even Julia's blurry vision identified that most of the fish was already down his throat, and the rest was destined to follow shortly. At least it was quick, she thought, feeling a brief rush of comfort.

'Don't come in, Annelies!' she called warningly. Annelies, it appeared, was still too stunned to move from her bed. 'Just stay there. I'll, erm . . .' She sought for words. 'I'll . . .' Honest ones.

'I'll buy you another one,' she admitted finally, laying her head on the lino in despair.

'Go away!' came an anguished shout from the bed. 'Go away, now!'

'Yes,' Julia muttered, lunging for Fleabag, who had now devoured the fish completely, and was looking pleased with himself. She hoisted him up, stuck him roughly under her arm, and fled out of the bedsit and down the stairs, throwing him ahead of her into her kitchen, and slamming the door.

'You absolute bastard!' she hissed at him. 'How could you do that? And don't you dare lick your lips! Don't you realize what you've done?'

He miaowed, and she gave him an evil look, going through to her main room to stare up at the ceiling. It was very quiet up there. She wondered if Annelies was capable of moving at all. She sank exhaustedly on her bed and fixed her eyes above, waiting for an explosion of some sort. Of anger, perhaps. Fleabag trotted in, sat down, and started to wash himself. She abused him again in a whisper, and waited. After a while, she heard footsteps across the ceiling. Annelies going to the fish tank. Probably putting the wire back on.

Why, why had she taken it off when Fleabag was there with her? Her head was spinning so much it was starting to hurt. An idea occurred to her, and she picked up the bottle of anti-depressants sitting by the bed. *Avoid alcoholic drink*. Well, that would explain it, then. It was a lethal combination. Lethal if you were one of Annelies's fish, anyway.

She began to giggle, putting her hand over her mouth to stop the noise. Fleabag blinked at her, and she glared at him, trying to look frightening. Her shoulders began to shake.

Finally, from the bedsit above, she heard the soft sound of Annelies weeping. She stopped laughing, and lay back on the bed, staring upwards. She would, without doubt, buy her another fish tomorrow. It was the least she could do.

Late on Sunday morning, while Julia was nursing a thick head with a quiet cup of tea and the omnibus edition of *The Archers*, there was a tap at her door. She crept over to it, and opened it. It was Annelies in a tracksuit, looking pale and red-eyed.

'Oh, Annelies. Please come in. I don't know what to say to you, but I'm just so, so sorry.'

Annelies came into the bedsit and hovered near the door. She'd lost her usual lustre, Julia thought, and it was all her fault.

'Can I get you a cup of tea or coffee, or something?'

She tried to look as remorseful as humanly possible.

She didn't share Annelies's taste in pets, but she knew what it was like to get attached to them. She'd probably given them all names, she mentally added, piling on the guilt. Annelies wandered over to the kitchen chair and sat down, heaving a deep sigh, and gazing out at the newly shorn vegetation in the garden. Julia quickly nipped over to the kettle, and flicked it on. It gave her a chance to do something constructive.

'Look, Annelies, if you tell me what type of fish it was, I'll get you another one. Isn't there a fish shop around here somewhere – I mean, a fish centre, or something?' She swallowed painfully. 'Fish shop' sounded too much like 'fish and chip shop'.

To her total disconcertion, Annelies put her head in her hands and began to cry. Julia stood for a moment, watching her, then she decided that comfort might be permitted. She tiptoed up to the stooped form, and patted her shoulders.

'There, there,' she said. 'I'll get another fish for you, don't worry.'

Annelies sniffed, and sat up, pulling a hanky from her tracksuit bottoms and stuffing it into her eyes. Then she began to howl again. Julia hopped back to the kettle, wishing that the anti-depressants had an instant effect so that she could pop one into Annelies's tea. She tried to remember how she had her tea. With lemon? It was something European, but she didn't have any lemons. She decided to leave it black, and padded back to the table, nudging the mug under her nose.

'Here, drink this.'

Annelies looked at the tea, and put out a shaky hand to pick up the mug. Julia tried to understand the depth of her grief. She must have been very profoundly attached to that particular fish. Perhaps the stomping across the ceiling last night had been Annelies working out which one had met its death in Fleabag's jaws. Still, she had five others to console herself with, Julia thought, and immediately felt heartless. Annelies took a sip of tea, and grimaced.

'Do you have any honey?' she asked weakly.

'Honey?' Julia's eyebrows shot up, but she immediately began a futile search in her jar cupboard. 'Er, I've got marmalade? I suppose it's not the same, is it?'

'It doesn't matter,' Annelies said, her voice breaking with emotion. 'Nothing matters any more.'

Blimey, Julia thought. This must have been some fish. Judging by the bleak despair plastered across Annelies's face, it was a fish in a million. Annelies looked as if life had simply lost its meaning.

'How about if I go to the fish shop – the fish *centre* right now? You could wait here, and I'd be back before you knew it. I think it's only a couple of streets away, and I know they're open on Sundays because when I first found it it was a Sunday and I had a look round.' She tried to sound coaxing. 'Why don't you tell me what type of fish you'd like? They've got all types.'

'It's, it's . . .' Annelies tried to speak, but had problems. Julia watched patiently. 'It's . . .'

She gave up, and started crying again. Julia watched with growing horror as Fleabag decided to come into the kitchen and sniff Annelies's legs. She shooed him away and he looked at her appealingly.

'Piss off,' she mouthed at him.

'Oh Julia!' Annelies's blotchy face appeared again from under her hanky. 'It's so awful. I'm so unhappy.'

'I'll get the fish now. You can wait here, and I'll be back in no time,' Julia decided, feeling that some action had to be taken before Annelies threw herself out of the window and realized that she was on the ground floor. 'I'll just get a pretty one, shall I?'

'It's not the fish,' Annelies blubbered. 'That just made it w-worse. It's – it's Stig.'

'Stig?' Julia paused as she was about to make a dash for the door. 'Your boyfriend?'

'He's not my boyfriend any more!' Annelies wailed. 'He's left me for s-somebody else!'

'Oh no.' Julia returned quietly to her seat. It all became clearer. She had started to think that Annelies was over-reacting, but she hated to say so. As Annelies blew her nose robustly, Julia wondered if there was anything she could possibly do. She could have gone out and bought Annelies another fish, very similar to the last one, so similar that you might not notice the difference. But a boyfriend? That was a bit more tricky.

'H-he's gone to the Alps. Without m-me. And taken h-her,' she stumbled on. 'That's why I was g-going to go pot-holing. To take my mind off things.'

'That sounds very sensible,' Julia said, trying to look motherly. 'I can see how pot-holing might take your mind off things. I think you should go.'

'He only told me last week,' Annelies continued. 'I think I was in shock. That's why I said I'd go p-pot-holing with my friends.'

'Right, well, I still think you should go away with your friends.'

'B-but they all know him. We used to do that all the time together. I can't go pot-holing. Stig used to go pot-holing with me! I can never pot-hole any more!'

She collapsed into tears again. Julia sighed, and gave up on her attempts to be sensible. Didn't she know herself what it was like to feel this way? Hadn't she once decided that breathing itself had to stop because the man she thought she loved was engaged in the same activity somewhere else? Annelies cried herself into exhaustion, and ultimately produced a series of soft coos, like a very tired woodpigeon. She blinked bulging eyes in Julia's direction. Julia smiled at her.

'So, Annelies,' Julia said. 'Let's start by emptying your bedsit of his belongings and having a bonfire in the garden, shall we?'

Chapter Ten

'And did it make you feel better?'

'It made Annelies feel a whole lot better, that's for sure. It was amazing, the things he kept in her flat, even though he hadn't committed himself to actually living with her. It just never occurred to him, while he was legging it up the Matterhorn with his new bit of fluff in tow, that she had to deal with those things. I mean, she'd have to look at them all the time. His toothbrush, underwear, shoes, cards he'd sent her and photographs all over the wall of the two of them together. Really personal things.' Julia shook her head. 'Poor Annelies. She had no warning at all. One minute it was service with a smile, the next, he was on the phone declaring that he was taking somebody else up the Alps instead of her. Pretty brutal, don't you think?'

'Do you think that warning her would have made any difference?'

Julia pondered, gazing at the thick net curtain flapping against the sash window. It was yellowing and badly in need of a wash. She shifted herself in the cushioned chair, and looked back at the woman asking her the question. She was a curious specimen, with hair the same colour as the net curtain, wide blue eyes, and lines around her mouth that suggested that over a period of time she had over-exercised the muscles that kept it shut. She knew what Mary Hanson was driving at.

'Yes. Because when you lose somebody that suddenly, it's as if they've died. You're left with a string of things you wanted to say, and never had the chance to. But by that time, their ears are closed, and they don't want to hear them. They might as well not be there. They might as well be dead.'

'How did you feel about the bonfire?'

'How did I feel about it?'

'When you stood next to it and watched Stig's possessions burning away, how did you feel?'

'Hot,' Julia said quickly. 'And very nervous. At one point the fence started sparking as if it was going to go up like a rocket, but we managed to control it. And I got rid of half the compost heap at the same time. It was all very satisfactory.'

Mary was evidently not amused. She just waited, her wide eyes patient, for Julia to give her a proper answer.

'Oh, I don't know. What can I say? I felt elated. I knew it was what she had to do. She couldn't go around dwelling on his things, hoping he might be doing the same. He was up the Alps, for God's sake. He didn't take a photograph album with him, just some boots, an ice-axe, a couple of woolly jumpers and a new girlfriend.'

'Do you think,' Mary began carefully, her eyes swivelling over to the flapping curtain. 'Is it possible that you were putting your own feelings on to Annelies? That you wanted her to do the things you hadn't done yourself?'

'I don't think it, I know it,' Julia stated, sitting forwards. 'I brooded and I didn't touch a thing, as if Bill was going to come back and take over from where we left off. My flat became a shrine to him. I even left everything exactly where it was, so that he could find the place as he left it.'

'And did he come back?'

'Of course not,' Julia asserted. She stopped, and heaved a deep breath. Again, the swell of discomfort rose in her stomach.

'And did it matter, do you think, that *you* didn't have a bonfire straight away?'

Julia started to speak, and stopped. Her throat was doing peculiar things again. If she tried to talk, she would cry. She mustn't do that again.

'I, um.' She chewed on her cheek, and looked straight at Mary. Eye contact would keep her in control. 'Yes, it mattered.'

'Do you want to talk about that?'

Julia shook her head, mute.

Mary Hanson watched her, and waited. At last, she thought, she was digging near the core. She was used to her own tactics, creeping like a crab towards the goal. First, they had to lay the foundations and test them for solidity. Then they had to inch slowly forwards, side-ways, whichever way it took, towards the key, the clue to what was staunching the flow of life. Julia's case was no more or less complex than others she had seen in twenty years of practice. It was as unique as they all were, but it shared the same symptoms. It was up to Julia herself to pronounce the diagnosis.

'Perhaps you'd like to talk about your father again?'

Julia looked up.

'I thought we'd done that. He left, I told you, when I was about six. That's it.'

'You were very upset when we talked about it before, weren't you?'

'Well, I suppose,' Julia said, her shoulders dropping. She sank back into the chair and stared blankly through the net to the sun straining beyond. 'It wasn't any big deal. I could tell you it was and try to hang everything on that, but for me, it really wasn't that significant. He hadn't been around much anyway. Mum thought it was a tragedy, but I was fine.'

Mary nodded, she waited a moment before speaking

again. Practised pauses, just long enough to allow thought to flow.

'In what way was your mother upset?'

'Oh, she just revered everything about him. You know, she kept his photo on the mantelpiece, and his shirts in the cupboard. That sort of thing. It didn't affect me, but I think she just couldn't let go.'

Mary nodded again.

'Has she let go now, do you think?'

'Mum?' Julia frowned. She'd never really thought about what her mother was actually feeling. She knew what she did and what she said, but what she felt was anyone's guess. Julia avoided her phone calls so that she wouldn't have to talk about insurance companies. That was about it. 'I've no idea whether she's let go or not. I don't spend much time with her now. Not since—'

Mary watched with a sharp eye.

'Since?'

'Er, about five years ago. We had a bit of a row. Quite a big row, actually. So we've been a bit distant since then. She phones me, but I think she's just happy getting on with her life. She's got a job and friends.'

Mary nodded, the lines around her lips tight.

'Have you talked to her, about the row you had?'

'No,' Julia said firmly. 'It's in the past. It's all over now. We get on fine.'

'But you don't visit her?'

Julia expelled a long breath. She closed her eyes for a moment, and opened them again. Tired eyes, Mary noticed.

'Look, I don't think my Mum's the issue. I mean, in all my – wonderings, I don't think about her, or Dad for that matter. I just think that Mum and I have gone separate ways. I don't think she understands me any more.'

'Do you think you understand her?'

Julia stared back. 'Why do you ask that? Because every

woman turns into her mother at some stage, and I need to psychoanalyse my mother to get to grips with myself? I'm not like my mother.' She shook her head, her hands interlocking. 'You don't know why I'm so sure, do you? Just believe me. I could never have done what she did, said the things she said. She was so sure she knew best.'

Mary watched as Julia stopped, breathing heavily. Her face had taken on more animation now, her eyes alive.

'What did she know best about?'

Julia was silent. Mary sat quietly, her eyes on Julia, unchallenging, observing. She saw her remove all expression from her face, adjust herself in her chair, swing her hair over her shoulders, and impose strict control on herself. She wasn't ready yet, Mary thought.

'You said you went out for dinner on Saturday, with a friend,' Mary said. 'Why don't you tell me about that?'

'Annelies? I've got you a fish.'

Julia held out her offering and smiled encouragingly. She could see a strip of a white face through the half-open door. Annelies was obviously very unsure as to whether she wanted company or not. Julia lifted the plastic bag up, and waved it gently.

'It's a very pretty one, don't you think?'

Annelies relented, and pulled open the door to her bedsit. Julia waited for a moment, not wanting to burst in too enthusiastically, then stepped inside. The kitchen was in the same state as before, several more plates of half-eaten food now stacked on top of each other on the draining board. The blind was in mid-position, allowing a little light through, but not committing itself to allowing the day in. Annelies ran a hand through her hair, and Julia saw that it was unwashed and dishevelled. Her normally round, healthy face looked sad and angular, and the light in her eyes had gone.

'Oh, Annelies! Why don't you go and have a bath and I'll clear the kitchen up for you?'

Annelies chewed her lip.

'I was going to clear up later. I was just trying to sleep, but those men are drilling again and I'm going crazy.'

'Look, you go and bath now, I'll make us coffee. Go on. I'll put the fish in the tank for you.'

Annelies relented and, picking up some clean clothes from her drawer, wandered out on to the landing. Julia closed the door behind her, and went over to the tank. The remaining fish were darting around in heartless indifference to their loss. She gently lifted the wire from the top, and lowered the opened bag into the tank, as the man at the centre had shown her. After a moment of indecision, the little fish she had bought ventured beyond the plastic boundaries, and drifted into the tank, its feathery tail waving prettily in the water. Julia sighed with contentment, her guilt eased and she removed the bag, putting the wire mesh very firmly back on top of the tank. She watched the fish for a moment, negotiating with the intruder, and decided that they were all going to be the best of friends. Now all Annelies had to do was choose a name for it. As long as she didn't call it 'Stig', Julia would be satisfied.

She noticed that the fish food she had flung across the room in shock several days ago was still dotted over the carpet. Annelies hadn't made any attempt to clear anything up since they'd ransacked the bedsit for evidence of Stig. She'd hoover for her as well.

She went back into the kitchen, flicked the blind so that it rolled up, letting the day in, and started on the washing-up. Some of the food had solidified, so it was an energetic job, but soon she had a pile of rinsed plates stacked in the draining rack, and had scoured the saucepans and heaped them up to drain. She cleared

Annelies's mountain magazines into a pile and wiped all the surfaces. Remembering that the concept of a kettle was still alien to Annelies, she set a pan of hot water on the stove to boil, then she searched the bedsit for the Hoover, finding it tucked away under the bed. She threw it round the room, satisfaction growing as the sprinkled debris disappeared and the carpet gained a new look. That was much better. She was winding the flex into a roll and edging the hoover back under the bed when Annelies returned, wrapped in a huge towel, pink flesh sticking out at either end. She looked like an uncooked sausage roll.

'You like cleaning things, don't you?' she said, wriggling into a pair of jeans and a hearty jumper. 'I hear you cleaning things downstairs sometimes. I think it makes you feel better.'

At least Annelies looked as if the bath had revived her, Julia thought. But she didn't want to be labelled as neurotic. She went into the kitchen and made them both coffee, resigning herself to drinking hers black.

'I just do a little when I need to. I spend more time at home than you do, don't forget. I've got more time to notice the dirt.'

'And I'm a dirty person. I know that. I don't mind. Stig didn't mind.'

She looked dangerously near to tears again. Julia handed her a cup and sprang over to the tank and pointed at the new recruit, identifiable by its long, floating tail.

'What are you going to call your new fish?' she asked brightly. Annelies plodded over, setting down her cup and towelling her blonde hair. She peered into the tank.

'Why don't I call it Julia, after you?'

Julia was surprised, and deeply flattered.

'Is it a girl, then?'

'Who knows?' Annelies said, reaching for a brush and dragging it through the knotted strands of her hair. 'Anyway, you bought it. Perhaps you should name it?'

'Oh, no, I couldn't.' Julia held up her hands in humility. 'It's your fish now.'

'Okay. I'll call it Julia, then,' Annelies decided, then gave Julia a curious look. 'Unless you think we should call it Fleabag, after your cat?'

Julia was fixed with embarrassment for a second, then Annelies started to giggle, a sparkle of tears in her eyes, half-anguish and half-amusement, Julia thought.

'Oh, Annelies, it's so good to see you laughing.'

'I have to laugh, don't I? Otherwise, what will I do? And I have to finish my thesis. Somehow, you see, I have to work this week, but I can't yet.'

Julia knew that Annelies was a postgraduate student, studying something to do with rocks. She usually spent her days in the University buildings. Julia had never asked her much about it, because she knew she wouldn't understand the answers. But she hadn't realized that she was so near to presenting her thesis. Stig would have known. Julia's heart hardened even further against him. It was bloody awful timing.

'Well, now you're up and dressed, you can go to the faculty today, can't you? You must have friends down there. They'll be wondering where you are, won't they?'

'Yes, I suppose so.' Annelies sniffed, and pulled her hair up into a ponytail. Even in her grieving state, with no make-up on and wet hair, she still looked lovely, Julia thought with envy. She found herself thinking that it wouldn't be long before somebody else laid claim to her heart. They'd probably been queuing in the wings, waiting for Stig to drop dead, but Annelies, being Annelies, wouldn't have had a clue.

Then she stopped her line of thought abruptly. She

herself hadn't been cured of a broken heart by taking off with somebody else, had she? It was probably what those around her thought she should do, but the thought of it had made her ill. A vision of Leo's face passed over her eyes. She didn't even know if she was ever going to see him again. They had each other's telephone numbers, but whether he would call again was anyone's guess.

'Julia? I think that perhaps having the bonfire was not such a good idea.'

Julia refocused on Annelies, now opening her curtains and sorting out some papers and putting them into a back pack.

'Listen, if Stig wants his stuff back, it's just tough, isn't it? What did he expect?'

'It's just that I've also burnt my training shoes. I must have picked them up by mistake.'

Julia began to laugh. She had thought that Annelies was having second thoughts, wishing that she could go back to where she was before. But she should have guessed that Annelies was not the 'going back' type. She'd move on, and in time she'd laugh about it.

'Never mind,' she continued, strapping on a pair of large hiking boots. 'It's a little warm to wear these, but I'll get another pair of trainers in the town. Can I get you anything while I'm there?'

'No, no. It's fine. I just need to get a few things today, but I'll go to the corner shop.'

'Why don't you walk into the town with me?' Annelies suggested, now looking brighter as she strapped her bag on to her back. 'You should get out more, you know. A walk will be good for you.'

'Now hang on, who's looking after who here?' Julia joked. 'I'm fine. I've got some forms to fill in and I've got my class later. Besides, I do go out. I went out on Saturday, didn't I? And look where that got us.'

'And this man, the one you said you had dinner with, you like him, do you?' Annelies stopped as she found that she had everything and gave Julia a disconcertingly straight look.

'Oh no, he's just a friend. Well, the brother of a friend really.'

'Ah.' Annelies nodded. 'So you won't be having sex with him, then?'

Julia gulped, having forgotten just how forthright Annelies could be at times. It was the Dutch way, she supposed. Weren't they sent away from children's parties with a balloon, a piece of cake, and a condom?

'Er, no. I won't be having sex with him. He's the last person I'd ever have sex with, to be honest.'

'Pity. I miss the sex already, you know. I suppose I shouldn't, but my body wants it.'

'Oh,' Julia said, wondering what on earth she should say to that one. 'You'll get over it. After a while, you find you don't miss it at all.'

'Yes, I suppose. Like withdrawing from a drug, yes?'

'Yes. Just like that. You just keep your legs crossed and wait for the right man to come along.'

Annelies looked tearful again for a nasty moment, but she shook her ponytail, and bounced over to the door. Julia followed her, wondering why she couldn't stop herself from making the sort of crass remarks that she had hated when she had been in Annelies's position. She just opened her mouth and they fell out. Stupid, pointless platitudes.

She saw Annelies as far as the front door, and watched her disappear down the road. Then she went back to her own bedsit and settled down with a handful of application forms she had received in response to her enquiries about Easter work at the tutorial colleges. She filled them in, and stacked them to one side. She'd have to get some more stamps to send them off, but she could go out later. At the same time, she'd pick up the bottle she'd promised for the end of term party.

She was pondering the charred heap at the end of the garden through her window, wondering if they'd done anything illegal, when her doorbell trilled. She glanced at her watch, surprised to see that it was gone three o'clock already. With any luck, it would be Maggie. Sometimes she dropped in after her lunch-time stint in the pub on the other side of the town, and she could do with a friendly chat with her.

When she pulled open the front door, it took her a few moments to recognize the strapping figure standing on the doorstep. His face was tanned and rugged, his eyes bright blue in contrast. She ran her eyes over the cropped hair, the thick jeans, the sturdy boots, with intense dislike.

'What do you want, Stig?' she asked him without ceremony.

'I need to be let in, please. I haven't got a key, and I have to see if Annelies is at home. She's not answering her door.'

'That's because she's out,' Julia retorted, and waited with clamped jaws.

'Can I come in please, and see if her door is on the latch? Sometimes she leaves it that way for me.'

'The door's locked,' Julia said, barring his way. 'Was there anything else?'

He gave her a sideways look, as if trying to work out whether she knew anything or not.

'Then I will wait inside,' he announced. 'If she's at the faculty, she'll be back soon.'

'No you won't and no she won't,' Julia said, standing tall so that she could face him out. She maintained an offensive stare. 'You're not coming into this house unless she gives you permission to, and in any case, she said something about going for a drink with somebody, some bloke she studies with, I think, afterwards. So it's pointless waiting.'

'I see,' he said tetchily. 'I will have to come back another time, to collect my things.'

'Oh!' Julia nodded understandingly. 'Your things! Why didn't you say so? I can give you those. She left them with me.'

'With you?' His eyes narrowed into blue slits. 'Why did she do that?'

'Because she thought you might come by and she thought she might be out when you did, Stig. She's been very busy, you know, out all the time, working and playing hard. Why don't you come in?'

She held the door open for him, and after a moment, he followed her inside. She led him through her bedsit, and turned the key in the back door.

'They are in the garden?' he said, his voice rising indignantly.

'Oh yes,' Julia said. 'But I hope you brought a bin bag with you. They might be a bit difficult to carry.'

Stony-faced, he followed her out into the garden, along the narrow brick path, to the black circle in the ground where a few lumps of shoe still lay intact in the ashes. Julia swallowed. She hadn't realized quite how devastating the whole scene would look a few days later. It looked as if they'd planted a bomb under the whole lot.

'There you are!' she said, trying not to allow her nerves to take over as Stig towered beside her, staring in disbelief at the wreckage. 'Do you want to borrow a dustpan and brush?'

He was silent for a long moment, then he thrust his hands into his trouser pockets, simmering gently.

'You did this?'

'Annelies did this, Stig. But in all honesty, it was my suggestion. She was going to throw your condoms in as well, but I advised her to hang on to them.' She raised her eyebrows expressively, and expelled a breath. 'Just as well, too. The week she's been having.'

'I see,' he said in a low voice. 'Then I will speak to her about this later.'

'I wouldn't call too late if I were you,' Julia prattled on. 'You don't want to embarrass her if she's got company, do you, if you know what I mean?'

'So, she hates me,' he said, his perfectly even, white teeth gritted together.

'Oh, I wouldn't say that.' Julia shook her head, her voice caramel-sweet. 'Just because you dumped her on the phone after five years together? Just because you went up the Alps with one of her friends instead, giving her half a day's notice to reorganize her life? Just because you're a total and utter bastard? No, she doesn't hate you, Stig. She feels sorry for you.'

Was she overdoing it? Judging by the heated red spots that had appeared under the tan on Stig's cheeks, she was pushing things a bit too far.

'I will speak to her about this later,' he issued, turning on his heel and striding away down the garden path.

'Close the door on your way out, won't you?' Julia called pleasantly after him.

He disappeared into her bedsit, and she heard her door slam violently. She winced in response. Thank heavens she'd persuaded Annelies to go and do some work. It would have been appalling for Stig to see her bedsit in the state it was, with evidence of her inertia littered everywhere. And Annelies might have let him in and pleaded with him to change his mind. She couldn't let her do that. She had to keep her pride, and while she was vulnerable, Julia could help her.

Her face set as she walked slowly back up the garden. If she'd had somebody to help her, when she was vulnerable, might she have dealt with things differently?

She increased her speed, and marched back to her kitchen. There could be no going back. Life could only move on. She picked up the envelopes on the kitchen table and picked out the one addressed to London. It would change her life completely, to train formally to teach. Once, in a rare moment of encouragement, Vivienne had told her she was good at it. She'd found a course that interested her – training to teach adults – and she'd thought it might be worth a shot. Things couldn't go on as they were, with Julia drifting back and forth within her walls of glass, like the little fish upstairs who was her namesake.

She grasped the envelope firmly, and let herself out of her bedsit.

Chapter Eleven

In the evening, Julia checked on Annelies before she left for her class. There was no reply when she tapped on the bedsit door and she hadn't heard her come in. Of course, she had been lying through her teeth when she told Stig that Annelies had a date that night, but she began to wonder whether she'd accidentally hit on the truth.

Mack's motorbike was already in the car park when she arrived at the adult centre. She had seen him leave on it after the very first session, and now, propped up on a side stand next to the caretaker's spindly moped, it looked even more daunting. She stopped to have a look at it in the dim light. She had no idea what the make and model meant, but it was an attractive shape, with a teardrop tank and chrome that sparkled as if Mack spent a great deal of time polishing it. There were two crash helmets strapped to the side. She wondered what it might be like to ride it. She guessed it was the sort of experience you might have the bottle to try out when you were a teenager, but if it hadn't grabbed you by then would probably remain a lifelong mystery. Looking at the size of the tank and the exhaust pipe, she decided that she was happy for it to remain a lifelong mystery.

In the classroom, she looked first for Rob, wondering if he might know by now that she'd had dinner with Leo. She spotted him deep in conversation with Sandra at the other end of the room. He looked up, saw her, smiled in a surprisingly friendly way, and carried on with his conversation. Did he know what Leo had told her? He seemed very relaxed. She took off her jacket and hung it up, wondering why she had expected him to look different, as if Leo's announcement had destined him to turn up at the class from then on sporting a leather basque and a pink feather boa. More preconceptions. She threw her scarf over her jacket on the peg.

She added her bottle of wine to the pile of plastic boxes and bags dumped on the table. Mack looked up from his conversation with Alec and came straight over to her.

'Has Elizabeth—?'

'Yes.' He grinned widely, intercepting her question. 'Two of them. Beautiful little things.'

'And – who's the father?' she asked.

'Bad news, I'm afraid. It's Wayne. One's ginger and one's a tortoiseshell, just like her mum. It was at the weekend. I was scared as hell, I can tell you. She started wailing at me and wandering around, trying to get in all the cupboards. Then I lost her completely, and finally found her in the airing cupboard.'

'She had the kittens in there?'

'I'd prepared this box, like the vet said, with old jumpers and stuff, but she wouldn't get out of the airing cupboard, so I wedged it in there and she climbed in the box and then . . .'

He broke off. She was so engrossed, she leaned forward to hear the rest. She saw that he was lost in thought. She blinked at him.

'I'm sorry,' he said, clearing his throat, and laughing. 'I'm such a stupid sod, aren't I? It was just the most wonderful thing. These little baked beans came out.'

'Baked beans?'

'Well, they looked like baked beans, but they were kittens really,' he said ironically. 'And then she washed them and they crawled around looking completely lost and then started suckling. I couldn't believe how quick that was. But now they're less slimy, I can see what colour they are. Their eyes are still closed, though. And they've got these really huge ears, like satellite dishes.'

'It must have been amazing.'

'Oh, it was. I wish you'd been there. You'd have loved it.'

Julia nodded. She wished she'd been there too. It would have been fun.

'So did you wet the baby's head?'

'What do you mean?'

'You know, I thought fathers were supposed to celebrate?'

'Oh, I did actually. On my own, you know, like a really sad bastard.'

She laughed at him.

'There's nothing sad about you, Mack. I expect you're the happiest man in Oxford at the moment, aren't you?'

'I reckon I am,' he said, his mouth curving into a sheepish smile. 'I'm so glad you understand what I'm on about. Nobody else seems to. Elsie – she's my next-door neighbour – came in to have a look at them and she said they looked like Gremlins. She's got a heart of stone, that woman. And a face to match.'

'Well, I wouldn't have said that,' Julia said reassuringly.

'No, I know you wouldn't,' he said. 'That's why I wished you'd been there. You know, it was the most fantastic experience of my life, but I just wished I'd had someone to share it with. Does that sound stupid?'

'No,' she said enthusiastically. 'And if you'd had my phone number, you could have rung me and I could have come round. We should have thought of that, shouldn't we?'

He glanced up at her, his eyes curious. He shook his hair back, and looked at her again.

'Do you really mean that?'

'Of course I do,' she said. 'I'd have loved to have been there.'

'And I thought you spent your Saturday nights on the town,' he said drily.

'Saturday?' She frowned, thinking aloud. 'Oh, I was out on Saturday night actually. Well, never mind. Any other time, I'd have been round like a shot. Cat nutters have to stick together, don't they?'

He paused for a moment, looking at the cuffs of his shirt as he readjusted them.

'You didn't miss *Family Fortunes*, surely?'

'I did actually. Sacrificed it for dinner at The Bath Place Restaurant. Still, I wasn't paying, so it was worth it.'

'Really?' He looked back to her face, eyes steady. 'Sounds romantic.'

She hesitated before answering. She hadn't really meant to talk about Saturday night, and she didn't want to have to explain it. She couldn't explain it anyway, and Rob was hovering somewhere at the back of the room.

'It was just a one-off. I'll be back on a strict diet of *Family Fortunes* next week, I expect. But I wanted to tell you, anyway, that I played winkies with Fleabag and it worked. I was amazed.'

'Blinkies,' he corrected, brightening. 'I told you, didn't I?'

'Yes.' She laughed again. 'And the really stupid thing was that I wanted to pick up the phone and tell you straight away. Isn't that daft? I must be losing my marbles.'

He nodded slowly. He looked down.

'Well, as you said, cat nutters have to stick together.'

Vivienne's arrival brought everybody's bantering to an abrupt halt. She sailed into the room, unencumbered with plastic bags, boxes or bottles, and surveyed the sacrificial pile on the table.

'Oh, no! We'll have to get this into the kitchen. We'll do an hour's work first, then we'll have our party.'

'Oh, do we have to?' Shirani uncharacteristically piped up in dissent. 'It's so nice talking like this, isn't it?'

'I'm sorry,' Vivienne declared, swirling her poncho around her shoulders, flicking it over her head and finding somewhere to hang it. The cloche hat miraculously stayed in place. 'We can't have a party for the whole two hours, can we?'

'Why not?' Mack said quietly. 'We were enjoying ourselves.' He didn't add, 'until you walked in', but it was the obvious suffix. Vivienne pursed her lips.

'Too late, anyway.' Alec held out a plastic cup with some sort of liquid in it. 'I've already started on the booze. And before you start on about driving, I haven't got a car. I don't think the bus driver's going to give a toss whether I'm pissed or not, as long as I don't deck him.'

'Alec!' Vivienne exclaimed in shock. 'What sort of language is that?'

'English,' he replied, looking cheerfully boisterous. 'Like *wot* you teach.'

Julia tried to suppress a smile, and failed completely.

'Why don't we take a vote on it?' Mack suggested in the same quiet voice. 'That would be democratic, wouldn't it?'

'I don't think a vote is appropriate,' Vivienne said, fingers twitching in an apparent urge to finger the rim of her hat. 'I get paid to run this class and run it I will.'

'But we don't pay, do we?' Alec continued happily. 'It's not as if you'd be short-changing us, and apart from you, the rest of these guys are volunteers, aren't they? So I don't see what the problem is.'

'The problem is, Alec, that I wouldn't be doing my job if I let this class descend into . . .'

184

She paused, as she sought for an appropriate word to use in front of them.

'Anarchy?' Mack suggested with a small smile. 'That's a terrifying thought, isn't it? A bunch of illiterates annexing the kitchen and firing plastic forks out the window at ladies' netball. The army would be shitting themselves.'

'Mack!' Vivienne said sharply.

'Oh, come on, woman!' Alec took up the assault, waving his plastic cup. 'Relax, why don't you? Have a whisky.'

'Whisky?' Vivienne wailed with perfect pitch. 'I didn't say you could bring whisky into the classroom!'

'You didn't give me a wine list, either,' Alec defended robustly. Julia thought it was likely that it wasn't the first drink of the day that he was enjoying. 'And Shirani's having one, so it can't be that bad.'

'Shirani?' Vivienne looked to her for allegiance. Shirani was easily the most studious, and most dedicated of the group. She shrugged back and indicated her plastic cup.

'Just a little bit. It's quite nice, actually.'

'I see,' Vivienne said grimly. 'I see I'm outnumbered.'

'Well, that's democracy for you,' Mack breathed, looking straight at her.

'Fine. Right,' Vivienne said tensely. 'Well, we'll have to get organized, then. I meant to be here earlier, but I had problems with the children. Julia, you might have at least put things in the fridge while you waited for me.'

Julia was inclined to say that they hadn't been waiting, that in fact they hadn't even noticed that Vivienne was late, but she restrained herself.

'If we're having the party now, there's no point in putting anything in the fridge, is there?'

'No, well, at least we might have found some plates and serviettes to hand round. I see that I'll have to do it myself. Never mind.' She heaved an impatient sigh. 'Let's get organized then. Alec? No, George. Why don't you take charge of the wine and Brenda and Julia can help me arrange the food in the kitchen. Come on then, let's move these bags.'

'But, Vivienne,' Mack said in a tired voice, 'why can't we just help ourselves? If we just put everything on plates on the table, and leave the drink and the cups out, then people can do what they want, can't they?'

Vivienne's eyelashes flickered, somewhere between a blink and a nervous tic. She was left squeezing her nails into her palms as Mack comfortably took over, opening the bags and retrieving the contents, while Julia stepped forward and unpacked the paper plates, distributing them in a line so that Mack could arrange the food. Shirani unveiled her home-made samosas and there was an appreciative group reaction. In seconds the conversation was buzzing again, Alec ignoring George's attempt to identify the merits of the wine that had been brought, taking the bottle from him and slopping it into a row of plastic cups. Rob took two cups and handed one to Sandra, who looked relieved to see it, and settled back into discussion with her.

Vivienne finally dislodged herself from her pose of frozen disapproval and produced a cellophane package.

'It's just as well I brought serviettes, then,' she said. 'Nobody else seems to have thought about it.'

She pulled out the serviettes, and the group obediently handed them round. Julia noticed that they were emblazoned with the Mister Men. She also noticed that the packet had already been opened and was half-empty.

'They must have set you back a bit,' Alec commented, receiving his serviette from Mack.

'Waste not, want not,' Vivienne retorted tartly.

'Oh, aren't they cute?' Brenda breathed, eyeing her

serviette and dumping two French sticks on the table for Mack to cut into slices. 'I remember when my niece was little, she used to call me Mr Forgetful. But I didn't forget the bread, even though I thought I would. I put notes everywhere after last week.'

'Drink this,' Alec said, thrusting a cup into her hand. 'And I brought a bottle of wine as well, so don't just peck at it, will you?'

Brenda flushed, and gave Alec an 'Aren't you naughty?' look. He expelled a gale of laughter and, picking up another cup, proffered it to Vivienne.

'Oh, no, no.' She held up her hands. 'I'm driving.'

'Oh, come on,' Alec said without patience. 'It's a party, Vivienne. You know, where people have fun and do stupid things. Didn't you ever have wild parties when you were young? Get off with people, and all that stuff?'

'No, I did not,' Vivienne said, without fear of contradiction.

Julia shot a look at Rob. She wondered if he still thought about the stupid thing he'd done after Maggie's party. He caught her eye, looked away. Then he looked back again. She gave him a smile, and he smiled back in acknowledgement. It was a moment of resolution, and it made her feel better. He turned back to talk to Sandra. He seemed to be asking her a lot of questions, maybe about her daughter. Leo would approve of that. As Vivienne took the plastic cup and held it out between two fingers as if it was a used potty, Mack held one out to Julia. She looked at it for a moment, then shook her head apologetically.

'I can't at the moment, I'm afraid. I'm not allowed to. It's, er, some pills I'm on.'

'Ah. Antibiotics,' Mack said instantly, putting the cup back down again and busying himself with opening the plastic dishes he had brought. What a brilliant idea, Julia thought. Antibiotics.

'Yes,' she agreed vehemently to his back. 'Antibiotics. That's right.'

He glanced over his shoulder at her, held her eye for a second, then nodded.

'Right.'

She watched him as he prepared his food and arranged the dishes so that the others could help themselves. Why that inscrutable look? What was he thinking? Did he think that she might have some sort of embarrassing sexual disease and was trying to help her cover it up?

'It's, er,' she started again behind him. 'It's not penicillin.'

He looked over his shoulder again, then stood up, and turned round. The rest of the group with the exception of Vivienne, who was very deliberately abstaining, was busy launching into the food.

'What isn't penicillin?'

'The pills I'm on.' She lowered her voice, suddenly feeling stupid. 'They're, um, not what you think.'

He quirked an eyebrow, and gave her a sardonic look. It made him look quite sexy. She'd never thought of him as sexy, but he rested his hands on the hips of his denims and she also noticed that he was wearing a black cotton shirt that made his thick, blond hair look like white gold.

'You think I think you've got the clap?' he said very quietly, but she felt as if he'd shouted it from the ceiling.

'I haven't!' she exclaimed. 'That's the point.'

They looked at each other for a moment, and she realized that his lips were twitching.

'You're winding me up,' she said. 'You know I haven't got the clap, don't you?'

'You're not the type,' he said. 'Now Vivienne's another matter.'

'Oh, go on then. I'll have a small glass, I mean, cup.' She relented. He picked up a cup for her and handed it to her.

'Sure?'

'Sure. But I mustn't go mad. I'm supposed to avoid alcohol at the moment. That's not the same as abstaining completely, is it? But I must be careful. On Saturday I overdid it a bit, and Fleabag ended up eating my neighbour's goldfish.'

'You're joking?'

'I wish I was. Poor Annelies. Her boyfriend had just dumped her, then Fleabag decided that he'd have a fish supper. She's getting over it, though. I think she's the type that will get over it.'

'But you're not?' Mack said, holding his cup, standing near her and watching her face with interest.

'What do you mean?' She frowned at him.

'It's just the way you said that. It was as if you meant that she wasn't like you.'

'Did I?'

'Yeah,' he said, peering at her as he took a sip of wine. 'But I could be wrong.'

'Oh.' She paused and thought for a moment. He was right, of course, and men being right about her feelings usually brought on an urge to contradict them. Or throw wine at them, she mused, remembering Leo's shocked, wet face. But she didn't mind it when Mack did it. 'No, you're not wrong. Not that it matters. Shall we try some of your pâté? It looks fantastic.'

Julia shifted over to the table and picked up a plate, helping herself to several wedges of bread, a slice of George's Brie, which was extremely ripe, and some pâté. It was very creamy, with small, mysterious chunks secreted into it. She smeared some on to her bread.

'What's in it?' she asked Mack, who was chewing on one of Shirani's samosas.

'Garlic,' he said, swallowing. 'Olives, chicken livers, pork, mushrooms, sage, lemon juice, olive oil and, er . . . brandy.'

'Blimey!' She looked down at the pâté. 'I didn't know pâté was so complicated. I don't know how you've got the patience.'

'It takes a lot of patience,' he agreed. 'Especially when I'm trying to read new recipes, but this one's my grandmother's.'

She nodded, slowly.

'So, how do you manage with new recipes, then? If you enjoy cooking this much, it must be very frustrating for you.'

'Tell you a secret, but don't tell Vivienne,' he said, smiling. 'It's one of the things that finally got me off my butt and into this class. I got fed up with repeating things that Gran had taught me, over and over, and some of my experiments were complete disasters. But you develop a good memory, you know, so that you can repeat what you've seen on the telly or heard on the radio.'

'The radio?' She paused, mid-mouthful, intrigued.

'The radio,' he repeated. 'There are recipes on the radio sometimes.'

'Oh.'

'And I record things, on cassette, so that I can play them again.'

She slowly chewed her pâté and pondered. He was so resourceful and so busy.

'I'm surprised you get time to work,' she said.

'I listen to the radio when I paint,' he said, offering her a plate of Shirani's samosas. She took one and nibbled on it. 'It's my lifeline, really. Though I have to try not to be influenced by what I'm hearing. You know how sometimes your mood can change, just like that?' He snapped his fingers. 'And then the moment's gone.

I have to watch that. It can change what I'm doing completely.'

'Really?' She looked at him curiously. 'You mean, it can put you off the smell of the paint, or something?'

'I mean that if you're painting sad and really getting into it, but then *The News Quiz* comes on, it really blows it.'

She nodded automatically, then almost choked on a spicy lump of potato. She gave him a startled look.

'*The News Quiz*?'

'Yeah. Or something like that. I tried turning it off, but then the silence got me down, so I've learned now to stop, have a cup of tea, then carry on when I'm in the mood again.'

She stared at him, trying to imagine him in his overalls, surrounded by tins of Apple-blossom White, seized with such a spasm of laughter that he couldn't hold a brush. What did he mean by 'painting sad'? Did he do the walls 'happy', and save 'sad' for the skirting boards? And what ever happened to Radio One?

'Why, I mean, what do your workmates say to all this? I thought cheery music was the usual form?'

'My workmates?' He looked confused for a moment. His brow cleared. 'Oh, I see. I'm self-employed, actually.'

'Ah,' she replied, trying to understand. 'You do the whole lot by yourself.'

'That's right. The whole lot.'

'I don't suppose you're any good at wallpaper, are you?' She put down her plate, having devoured as much as she felt she could, and picked up her cup again. 'My cat's busy stripping the walls in my room. I feel a bit guilty about it, but every time I stick the bits back on, he rips them off again.'

'Tell you what I could do,' Mack said, looking thoughtful. 'I could get rid of the wallpaper, and paint the walls for you.'

She smiled, thinking that it would be a lovely idea. 'I just can't afford it at the moment. But I'll bear it in mind.'

'No charge,' he said instantly, pulling himself up tall and looking down at her. 'I've got some free time over Easter. I could do it for you then.'

'Oh, you couldn't . . .' she protested.

'Yes, I could. Why not? I'm not going anywhere for the long weekend. Unless you are, of course.'

'No, I haven't got any plans at the moment. Apart from a bit of teaching, but that won't be at the weekend . . .'

She thought about it. Getting too involved with the students on a social level wasn't encouraged. They were all adults and it was thought that being too friendly didn't help the students to adapt to the classes. But hadn't she already said she'd have loved to have rung him so that she could have seen Elizabeth with her kittens? Mack didn't look like the sort of man who'd be running around with her underwear over his head the minute she left the room. She felt instinctively safe with him. Certainly, she thought, she knew more about him than she'd known about Rob when she'd dragged him back to her bedsit. She glanced over at him. He was laughing aloud at something Sandra had said, and she was smiling next to him.

'I'll have to pay you, when I can,' she said.

'No. I enjoy it. It gives me a chance to practise,' he replied, looking completely at ease. 'It would give me great pleasure to paint your walls, okay? It's up to you. It's your house.'

'Bedsit,' she amended. 'Well, a one-roomed flat with a tiny kitchen, really, but I share the bathroom. It's just the main room that's the problem. Fleabag doesn't seem to have the same urge to hang from the kitchen walls. Why do you need to practise? Don't you do this all day?'

The word 'practise' was worrying. Would everything,

including her and Fleabag, end up splattered with emulsion?

'Don't panic.' He smiled at her. 'I've done a lot of painting, but mostly on outside walls. It's always a challenge, anyway, to try and reflect the character of the room and the person.'

She nodded, pretending that she understood. She supposed that when decorating was your life, the choice of paint became very personal.

'I like magnolia myself,' she said tentatively. 'Boring, but safe, you know.'

He gave her a funny look.

'I'll see what I've got.'

Alec interrupted, thumping Julia on the arm, brandishing a freshly opened bottle of wine. Before she could protest, he'd slopped a small amount into her cup. She drew it away quickly.

'Oh, that's fine, Alec. Give the others some.'

'Are you two going to unglue yourselves from each other?' Alec slurred, waving his eyebrows at them. 'You're as bad as Kieran and Fiona.'

'We're not glued,' Julia protested quickly. She hadn't realized that the group was now indulging in a collective discussion, while she and Mack had been annexed off to one side. 'What do you mean, Kieran and Fiona?'

'Gossip.' Alec bent his head to Julia and she nearly passed out as the aroma of neat whisky assailed her nostrils. 'Guess who I saw in The Elm Tree last night, celebrating St Patrick's Day as if it was going out of fashion?'

'Oh, of course!' She nodded, remembering that it was an Irish pub. 'No wonder Kieran didn't want to come tonight. He's probably still sleeping off his hangover.'

'Yes.' Alec nodded, his thin face rising and falling knowingly. 'Kieran. And Fiona.'

Julia gaped.

'She was there too?'

'On pints of Guinness. I tell you no lies. And . . .' He sneaked a look at Vivienne, content to find her on the other side of the room, lecturing Brenda about something. 'They were together. Know what I mean?'

Mack's laugh had Julia turning to look at him in surprise.

'I'm sorry,' he said to her. 'It's just the look on your face.'

'What look?'

'As if you'd just sat on a wasp.'

Julia tried to straighten her face and look normal. She'd thought herself that Kieran and Fiona presented an intriguing match, but she'd never expected it to come to pass. It was almost as if her thoughts had been absorbed and acted on. It was a profound shock.

'Interesting thought, isn't it?' Alec gave a crooked smile, and winked shiftily. 'You don't know what me and Brenda get up to in our spare time, do you?'

'Don't be so bloody silly, Alec.'

He shrugged.

'Fair enough. I can have me fantasies though, can't I? My wife can't stop me having those. Nice, comely woman like Brenda. She shouldn't be on her own. It's not right.'

'I'm sure she's perfectly happy,' Julia responded archly.

'Maybe. But don't you think she's built for it? With those lovely arms and thick, creamy thighs?'

'Stop it, Alec,' Julia instructed. 'You sound like a dirty old man.'

'Or Vivienne perhaps?' he continued to muse, foggy eyed. 'I bet she hasn't had a good shafting in months.'

'That's enough.' Julia was suddenly serious. 'I don't

194

want to hear your opinions on everybody's sex life.'

Alec stumbled back against the table, and decided to sit on it. He looked bemused.

'I'm sorry, love. Didn't mean to offend you. You get romantic ideas about other people when you've been married as long as I have. It passes the time, you know. Take you two, for instance. Lovely couple. Tall, good-looking, and you have fun, don't you? I've seen you, you know. Giggling at each other.'

'Shut up, Alec.' It was Mack who spoke, with unexpected severity. He cast a glance at Julia's red face. 'I don't think either of us want to hear any more of this.'

'All right, all right.' His face crumpled into apology. 'I'm just an old man trying to amuse myself. Don't mean any harm by it.' He paused to swallow a hiccup. 'More wine, Mack?'

'Better not. I've got to get home on the bike. I'm sure Vivienne'll be on for a top up, though.'

Alec shifted himself unsteadily and zigzagged over to Vivienne, who had her head cast back as she proclaimed to Brenda whilst staring at the ceiling. Brenda gave him a thankful look, and stuck out her cup.

'Here y'are, darlin',' Alec sang, filling the cup. Julia shook her head as she watched him.

'Incorrigible.'

'Just ignore him,' Mack said. 'I'd better go and talk to the others, or we'll be accused of hogging each other again.'

He meandered away, finding Rob and Sandra and joining in their chat. Julia stood on her own for a moment, feeling confused. She'd been enjoying talking to Mack and she was starting to find out more about him. She hadn't particularly wanted him to go off and mingle. She had the choice now of adding herself to the Rob–Sandra group or following Alec over to Vivienne, Brenda and a silent Shirani, which meant that she'd probably end up saying something sarcastic to Vivienne. George, on the other hand, seemed content to sit at the table throwing his Brie down his throat and topping up his cup with Alec's whisky. She didn't want to get into a long, boring discussion about stocks and shares. She considered her three options.

She took her cup and slipped into a chair at the table. 'Hello, George. How's life at the bank?'

Chapter Twelve

Vivienne stumbled up to Julia later in the evening, and sank into a chair beside her. For once, Julia was pleased to see her. George was getting maudlin. Apparently, retirement beckoned, his Personal Assistant didn't understand him and his wife had a face like a horse. Julia had been listening patiently for what seemed like several months.

'Vivienne!' She shifted her own chair to make room for her to join them. 'Didn't you say that it was your anniversary yesterday? Did you have a nice time?'

Vivienne looked odd, her face flushed, her cloche hat askew. Julia realized after a quick appraisal that she was more than a little the worse for wear. She smothered a smile. Julia herself had abstained dutifully, apart from the occasional sip, and had the unusual benefit of remaining sober while those around her teetered on the edge of intoxication. It was a novel experience and worth doing, at least once anyway, to see what it felt like.

'Oh yes, my anniversary!' Vivienne exclaimed dismissively. 'Tell me, Julia. What is it about men that makes them lose interest? Why is it we women are so, so loyal? Why is it that one man is enough for us, but never for them? Woman, I mean. In their case.'

She stared down at her cup, swaying in her chair. Julia's eyebrows shot up. Alec must have really been topping her up. It was questionable whether Vivienne even realized herself how drunk she was.

'It's the eternal question,' Julia replied neutrally.

'We're not the same,' George announced, tipping more whisky into his cup. 'Can't expect us to be, can you?'

'Why the hell not?' Vivienne looked up at him, hot faced and indignant. 'What's so special about you that you have to have everything, just cos you want it? I mean, there's me, you know, stupid little me, wiping the kids' bums, sticking biscuits down their throats, clearing up the snot. I thought I was doing my bit. I thought we had a democratic household.' She shook her head wildly, cloche hat teetering. 'But, no. It's not enough, is it? We're supposed to have the energy to magic away all the jam and biscuit crumbs and be upstairs in nipple tassels and a G-string by the time they get home.'

She nodded emphatically at Julia to prove her point. Julia stared at her in amazement. She couldn't think of a single thing to say.

'We're not the same,' George repeated gruffly. 'We need . . .' He paused to reflect carefully on his needs.

'Oh, stuff your bloody needs,' Vivienne ejected, waving her plastic cup. 'I don't give a toss about them. What about *my* needs? What about those, eh?'

'Er . . .' George looked as if he was stuck on a difficult sum. 'Well, you've got children, haven't you? And a little job down here? I don't know what you mean.'

'Oh, you're full of shit!' Vivienne cried. Julia jumped visibly. She became aware that conversation had ceased around them, the others turning to watch the exchange in horrified fascination. 'Just like him. You're all bastards, the whole lot of you. Where's the wine?' She swivelled in her chair and looked for Alec. 'You, there. Where's the wine gone?'

'We've drunk it, love,' Alec said. 'There's whisky on the table. Why don't you have a snifter of that?'

'Give it here.' Vivienne lunged across the table and wrenched the bottle from George's iron grip. 'And don't call me "love"!' she called back over her shoulder to a stunned Alec. 'Bastards, all of you!'

'Vivienne.' Julia tried to lower her voice, but everybody was listening. 'Don't you think you've had enough? Haven't you got to drive home?'

'Bottoms to it,' Vivienne said as the amber liquid splashed into her cup. 'I'll get a taxi and pick the car up tomorrow. Then he'll have to walk to the station.' A satisfied smile spread over her face. 'That'll be a mind-blowing experience for him, won't it? To get out on to the drive in his beautifully ironed shirt and find that I'm not sitting in the car with the engine running like some bloody chauffeur. That's what I'll do. I'll make a stand.'

'Vivienne.' Julia dropped her voice to a whisper. 'Everyone's listening.'

'What do I care?' She swung on Julia with eyes shining. 'My life's in a heap! My husband's screwing someone else. He told me yesterday. On our anniversary, of all days. He's a bastard, and . . .' She broke off, fumbling to pick up her cup. 'And I don't know what to do!'

'Oh, Vivienne!' Julia wanted to put an arm round her, but with the audience all but gasping aloud around them, she decided it was better to play things down. 'Why don't we go and talk about this in the kitchen?'

'Perhaps,' George began, thinking hard. 'Perhaps if you get a new haircut, or lose a bit of weight, he might change his mind.'

'Shut up, George!' Julia snapped at him. 'Leave your wife out of this.'

'I just think, perhaps if she'd made a bit more effort over the years, to be attractive, it might have made all the difference. I'm only trying to help. I have some experience of this.'

'And I suppose your wife likes nothing better than ten tons of lard climbing into bed with her at night?' Julia continued sharply. 'For God's sake, George, have all-over liposuction and get a hair transplant and then lecture Vivienne about being attractive.'

George fingered his thinning black hair with concern, looking distinctly embarrassed.

'Is it really that bad?'

'Bad enough,' Julia said heartlessly and turned her attention back to Vivienne, who was now widening her eyes in an apparent attempt to focus clearly on her whisky.

'Look, Vivienne, mixing your drinks isn't a very good idea. I don't expect you normally drink much alcohol, do you?'

'Only at Christmas. And on my anniversary. Normally,' she replied quietly. 'But we didn't have a drink last night. Just a row. And he went out. That was it.'

Julia gently prised the cup out of her hands and set it to one side.

'I'll make you a nice cup of tea,' Julia said. 'Just you wait here.'

'Mack's gone to make one already,' Brenda said in a hushed voice, as if Vivienne was a hospital patient who wouldn't be able to hear.

'Good.' Julia tentatively put her hand on Vivienne's. 'I'll see you home. We can get a taxi together.'

Vivienne looked up, a wild expression in her eyes.

'I've got a better idea. Why don't we go to a night-club? All of us?'

'I'm on for that,' Sandra piped up from the corner. 'Kylie's at my mum's. I can stay out.'

'No, no.' Julia shook her head, and gave Sandra an admonishing look. Next to her, Rob's mouth was half-open, as if he was about to second the suggestion but had thought better of it. Julia frowned at him. 'You can all go if you want, but I'll see Vivienne home.'

'I can drop her off,' Mack said, appearing with a mug of tea and setting it down in front of Vivienne, who reached out for her cup of whisky before glaring down at the tea as if it was nasty medicine. 'I've got a spare crash helmet with me, strapped to the bike. I had to give someone a lift earlier.'

'I don't think Vivienne will stay on,' Julia said, looking up at him, surprised at his attentiveness.

'It's quite safe, and it'll save her a cab fare, won't it? As long as she hangs on tight.'

'I can do that,' Vivienne mumbled. 'I've never been on a motorbike.' She giggled suddenly. 'That'd surprise him, wouldn't it? If I turned up pissed on the back of a motorbike. Yes, that'd make him look up from his newspaper!'

'There is one problem,' Mack said, sounding amused. 'You would have to take your hat off to get the helmet on. Could you do that?'

She gave Mack a sloppy smile over her shoulder.

'It does come off, you know.' She reached up, and wrenched it off, revealing, to the wonder of the class, a coil of red hair that unwound itself and flopped over her shoulders.

'Blimey!' Alec exclaimed. 'You're quite a looker, aren't you? Why do you stuff it under your hat all the time?'

'Keep it under your hat!' Vivienne tapped her nose, giggling again. 'It's very red, isn't it?'

'It's a lovely colour,' Brenda gushed.

'Wish my hair was a lovely colour,' Sandra said wistfully, her blue-black strands clinging to her shoulders. 'Costs me an arm and a leg to dye mine.'

'I used to do that,' Vivienne nodded, getting into the discussion happily. 'Then I gave up. Red's red, isn't it? But David, you see, he always said that he preferred blondes. He was quite honest about it, but he settled for me.' She paused again, whimsically. 'I wonder why.'

'I think you should dump that bloody hat and let your hair down,' Alec advised knowingly. 'You look much more human with hair.'

'Oh, yes.' Sandra added herself to the group, now seating themselves in the chairs around the table. 'And red's really fashionable, didn't you know? People pay to have their hair dyed exactly that colour.'

'That's true,' Julia said, thinking of Maggie. 'I know someone who does that. And she looks terrific.'

Vivienne stuck her head on one side, then the other, flicking the thin strand around her neck like the loose end of a skipping rope.

'D'you really think so?' she said coquettishly.

'I like blondes, I must say,' George said, settling himself comfortably in his chair.

'Shut up, George!' Julia, Vivienne and Sandra shouted at the same time.

'Haven't you seen *Pretty Woman*?' Brenda said, pulling up a chair. 'She starts off blonde, but it's only a wig really, and then she gets her hair out.'

'That's not all she gets out,' Alec guffawed.

'And her hair's really this amazing colour,' Brenda continued, ignoring him. 'And that's when Richard Gere starts to fall in love with her.'

'David said we shouldn't go and see it,' Vivienne said unhappily. 'He said it was degrading to women. That's a laugh, isn't it? I wanted to see it really, but I was proud of him for making a point of principle, so I didn't argue.'

'Well, I suppose it is a bit sexist, but it's fun all the same,' Julia contributed. 'And she's got brown eyes like you too. I think Alec's right. I think you should get rid of your hat.'

'And then Richard Gere will fall in love with me!'

Vivienne said with a stupid expression on her face. 'But I'm no Julia Roberts. If I was, I'd never have married a rat like David, but it seemed like such a good idea at the time.'

They paused and, as one, held their breath as they watched her tip another measure of whisky into her cup. She stopped, and looked up at the transfixed faces.

'Well, I'm not driving, am I? What's the matter with you all? I thought you wanted to have a party?'

'It's getting late,' Julia said, hating to be sensible, but realizing that somebody would have to keep an eye on the proceedings. 'The caretaker will be round to lock up soon, won't she?'

'Balls,' Vivienne said, throwing her cup at her mouth and slurping on it.

'One for the road, then,' Alec cheerfully filled his cup again and waved the half-empty bottle at the others. There were several takers.

'Oh dear,' Vivienne expelled a hearty sigh. 'I don't know why I'm talking to you all like this. My husband, my hair.' She stopped to run her hands over her eyes, and blink around her. 'What's got into me tonight? How will I ever be able to control the class again?'

'We'll have forgotten it all by next term,' Julia assured her. 'You'll see. Another three weeks, and it will be as if nothing happened. We'll just carry on as normal.'

'But if I see you wearing that bloody hat again, I'll rip it off myself,' Alec said severely.

'I promise.' Vivienne wagged a pointed finger. 'The hat's got to go.'

'And the husband?' It was Shirani who voiced the serious question, leaning forward on to the table, looking at Vivienne with intense concern.

'The husband?' Vivienne looked confused. 'My husband, you mean?' She thought for a moment, examining the plastic rim of the cup. 'My husband will stay.'

'If it was me,' Shirani's head gyrated with sudden passion, 'I would cut off his, what you say, goolies?'

'I didn't say I *wasn't* going to cut off his goolies,' Vivienne explained. 'I simply said that he would stay. Goolies or no goolies.'

'I don't know,' Julia expelled as she tied up the bin bag in the kitchen and Mack stood beside her. 'Is this what it's like all the time now?'

'What do you mean?'

She stood up, allowing him to take the bag from her, and sighed.

'You know, Vivienne, George, Annelies, Maggie. My mum.' She paused for a moment, then added, 'Me. Doesn't anybody stay together?'

'You're getting cosmic,' he said.

'But things have changed, haven't they?' she asked him. 'Isn't this normal now?'

'No,' he said firmly. 'It's always been like this. People split up, people have affairs, and some people don't do either.'

'I wish I thought that was true.'

'Don't be a cynic. It's easy to be a cynic. It just means you can't be bothered to consider all angles of the argument,' he chided her. She glanced at him in surprise. His face softened. 'You should have seen my gran. She was broken into pieces when my grandad died. That was real love. They were together for fifty-three years and when she said that neither of them ever looked at another person, I believed her.'

'You see, I don't know anybody like that,' she said, troubled. 'I just don't think that happens any more.'

'It does,' he said firmly. 'I believe it does. It's just that people get together for the wrong reasons, sometimes.

You know, for status, or because it looks good, or because their families will approve.'

She gazed at him thoughtfully. That had been true in her case. Her mother had been delighted with Bill. He had been everything she'd wanted for her daughter. Sophisticated, educated, with a job that was important and secure. Stable, solid, well-to-do, with a respectable family and a polite manner. But it wasn't just her mother. Julia had thought it felt right too. What else was there to go on?

'But how do you ever know?' she continued ponderously. 'I mean, you could be walking past people in the street who were made for you, and you'd never know it, would you? It's all down to chance, isn't it?'

He laughed under his breath.

'D'you know what the first words my gran said to my grandad were? "How are your feet today, Mr Eaves?"'

'Really?' She smiled at him.

'She was a nurse, and he was in hospital for an operation on his bunions. Hardly the most romantic of settings, but they fell in love and when their families caused a rumpus, they just ignored them.'

'Didn't they approve, then?'

'She was from a very wealthy family. He wasn't.'

Her eyes widened at him.

'Her lot were upset enough that she wanted to be a nurse, but the war was on and she got away with it. But when she took my grandad home and they found out that he came from a long line of publicans? You can imagine the fuss.'

'That's amazing. So what happened?'

'They got married, her family disowned her and none of us have had any contact with them since. But grandad's side of the family came round eventually and my grandparents opened a pub. They ran it until he died. That's where I lived when I was little.'

She nodded, eager to hear more. Vivienne crashed into the kitchen door, rebounded from it, and lurched inside.

'Ready, then?' she said eagerly. 'You can clear up, can't you Julia?'

'Of course,' she said, pushing aside her resentment that Mack was being dragged away from her and resigning herself to her habitual duties.

Vivienne started to sing loudly. *Born to be wi-i-i-ld!'*

'Born to be mild, more like,' Mack said. 'Tuck your poncho into your trousers, if you can. We don't want to cause any accidents behind us, do we?'

'Oh. Okay.' Childlike, she turned her attention to her clothing.

'Er, Mack, shouldn't I give you my number, or something? You know, about the decorating?'

'Oh, right. Yeah. Just tell me, and I'll remember.'

'I'll write it down for you,' she said, looking around vaguely. 'I'll just find some paper and a pen.'

'Julia,' he said gently. 'I'll remember it. Think about it for a minute, will you? Now tell me what it is.'

She flushed, annoyed with herself. She told him the number, and he gave her a warm smile.

'I won't forget.'

'*I've got a Silver Machine!*' Vivienne sang under her breath. 'I'm so excited, Mack!'

'C'mon then, Barry Sheene. Let's get you home. That's if you can remember where you live.'

They disappeared. Julia heard further singing down the corridor, which faded into the distance. The outside door swung shut behind them.

She looked around at the clean kitchen, assured that they had cleared everything away, and went back to the classroom to collect her belongings. Apart from the distinct smell of wine and whisky, nobody would ever know that there'd been a party there. A most unusual party, Julia thought, picking up her file and stuffing it into her bag. She wound her scarf around her neck and slipped on her jacket. The caretaker appeared, sticking her head around the outside door.

'All finished in here?'

'Yes,' Julia said, flicking the lights on her way to the corridor.

'Have a nice party, did you?' the older woman asked, jangling her keys.

'Nice?' Julia thought about it, making her way to the outside door. 'Yes, I think so.'

Still pondering on the events of the night, Julia picked up the notepad by the telephone when she got home and looked hard at Leo's number. While she sipped at a cup of tea and fondled Fleabag's ears, she wondered what she should do with it. She didn't intend to transfer it to her address book. That would be too much of a statement. But with it left there, staring up into the room, it caught her attention every time she walked past. She could ring him, she supposed. She considered the idea.

Could it really do any harm if she saw him again? She didn't want to get involved with him, but he hadn't seemed to want to get involved himself. He'd seemed very casual, enjoying the meal with her, chatting and then going home. And he'd been quite good company. They'd dealt with Rob. They could just see each other occasionally, perhaps, on the basis that neither of them was doing anything more important at the moment.

She wavered, her hand hovering over the phone and landing back in her lap again. Should she or shouldn't she? It was Thursday, and they hadn't seen each other since Saturday. She didn't want him to think she was chasing him. Then again, she'd done nothing during their dinner to make him think she would want to chase him.

Her hand hovered over the phone again. As if by magic, it began to ring. She picked it up in surprise, shoving Fleabag away with her other hand as he prepared to pounce.

'Get off, you little bugger. Hello?'

There was a low male chuckle on the line. Her hairs rose and stood on end, one by one. Uncanny? Was it a sign?

'Leo!' she said breathlessly. 'I was about to ring you.'

There was a pause as the chuckling ceased. Then the voice spoke again.

'It's Mack, actually. Sorry Julia, are you expecting a call?'

She sat back against the wall, nonplussed.

'Oh, no. Not at all. I'm just being silly.'

He paused again.

'I just thought I'd check that I'd got the number right and report back that Vivienne's been delivered safe and sound. That's all really.'

'Oh, I see. That was nice of you.' She gathered her thoughts again quickly. 'Did her husband see you drop her off?'

'Well, I waited while she let herself in, just to make sure she didn't choke on her own vomit on the doorstep, and I just saw the door open and this figure appear. She started singing at him and the door closed. I've no idea what happened after that.'

'I'd love to be a fly on the wall now.'

'Yeah, me too. Poor Vivienne.' She heard him sigh. 'I could hear her behind me, yelling "Wheeee!" into the wind. She's going to be so embarrassed about this next term.'

Julia considered his statement, and decided that what surprised her about it was that while it would be easy to snigger over Vivienne's fall from grace, he was more worried about her frame of mind when she sobered up. So was she.

'We'll just have to act as if nothing happened and if any of the others mention it, we'll shut them up.'

'Yeah, I think so too. I think the class is really important to her. Oh, hang on a minute. Elizabeth's here.'

'Put her on,' Julia quipped. 'And I'll get Fleabag to talk to her.'

She cradled the receiver in her neck, listening to him having an absurd conversation with his cat. It was funny to hear his voice soften. He cleared his throat, and came back to her.

'Look, I mustn't keep you. I wondered if I should pop round on Saturday, to see what to do with your walls?'

'Are you sure about this, Mack? I feel really bad about you doing it for free.'

'Don't,' he said. 'I really don't mind. Shall I come round in the morning?'

They agreed a time and she told him her address, hoping that she was doing the right thing. She wasn't intending to clear it with the landlady first. Dr Gimble had actually said that she could make small improvements if she wanted to, and a lick of paint on the walls would definitely be an improvement. She'd write to her afterwards and tell her. If anything, it would put the value of the place up, not down.

'I'd better go then,' Mack said. 'Leo might be trying to get through.'

She noticed that he'd remembered the name. But he relied on his memory for most things.

'Okay, see you on Saturday.'

She rang off and sat back to look at the walls. The paper had been painted over before, but it was in a shade of milky coffee that was starting to look stale, and the strips of wallpaper that she'd tried to stick back on had only made it worse. The glue had seeped through, leaving dark patches, like sweat stains. Yes, she confirmed to herself, it was the right thing to do, and Dr Gimble would be very pleased about it, especially since she wouldn't be landed with a bill.

She picked up the notepad again. Filled with a burst of confidence, she pressed out Leo's number on the phone, and waited. The phone rang several times, then there was a click. She was about to launch into her justification for ringing, when she heard the distinctive whirr of an answering machine. She hung on, curious to hear what he might say about himself.

'You've reached Leo Karr. You know what to do.'

There was a bleep. It took her by surprise. That was it. Minimalist, she thought fleetingly. Then she realized that she was still on the phone, and the recorder was running. She'd have to say something. She took an unsteady breath.

'It's Julia Cole. I was wondering if you'd be free at any time to get together. Just for a drink, or a walk.' She cringed. 'Or anything.' Actually, not quite anything, but she couldn't really qualify that to the machine. 'There's no urgency. It doesn't matter if you're too busy. Goodbye.'

She lay back on the carpet and stared up at the ceiling, noting that it was very quiet upstairs and that Annelies appeared to be out still. Unless she'd cast herself off Magdalen Bridge, that was a good sign. If Annelies could still circulate in the world after her own personal disaster, then Julia could do it too. That was if Leo decided to ring her back.

'So, they're coming on Easter Saturday, then?'

'Not if I can help it.'

Maggie looked over the table at Fabian, staring

belligerently down at his meal. She'd wondered all along if it had been a mistake to agree to let him take her out to dinner, but he'd been very persistent and she'd finally agreed. She'd managed at least to persuade him to take her to a quiet Italian restaurant in Summertown, although he'd suggested a much busier restaurant in the town centre at first. He seemed to be euphoric in his decision to declare his feelings for her, but she wasn't ready to respond, or to be seen with him publicly. She still had a few friends at the University and if they stumbled over her they'd ask awkward questions. She wouldn't be able to answer them. She still didn't know what she was doing.

Fabian made her laugh. It wasn't just that. He was considerate, bright and he was very attractive, not in a way that she could describe to anyone else, but he had sex appeal. He could be surprisingly mature with her and he listened to her, not tactically, not to appease her, but because he was genuinely interested in what she had to say. Their relationship had been changing since they'd started sharing the house, but when he'd approached her, after the party, and told her how he felt about her, she'd been moved beyond words. She'd told him to go away and sober up, but he'd taken her hand, led her up the stairs into his room, and told her again. She'd started to believe him. Then, before she knew it, he was touching her, carefully, as if she was fragile and might break, and kissing her softly. She'd been lonely, drunk and flattered. And she'd been sexually aroused. She'd tried to leave, but he wouldn't let her. So she'd given in to her feelings and stayed with him for the night. That had been the beginning.

She had thought, afterwards, that he would be horrified with himself. He'd see her the next day and be embarrassed, awkward and clumsy. But he hadn't been.

He'd been happy. That had surprised her almost more than his first approach. And he'd taken her back to bed, to appreciate her with a clear head, he'd said. He'd worshipped her body, the skin she'd agonized over, the dimples in her flesh that she'd wanted to blot out. He'd made her feel like a goddess.

But her dizziness was subsiding now, and Pete, in his decision to end their marriage, had only succeeded in forcing her to live through it again, over and over. She was still writing it down, to purge it from her system, she told herself. But she was living in a vacuum at the moment, caught between the past and the future. The present was so unreal, she could hardly believe it existed.

She looked at Fabian again as he toyed with his pasta, at the effort he'd made to look nice for her. And he did look nice in a jacket and tie, it made him seem much older. Older? It put him in his mid-twenties at least, she thought roughly. While she was old enough . . . She stopped herself again. Fabian kept telling her that age was immaterial. But she knew that it wasn't. Whatever Fabian thought now, it wasn't immaterial. The fact that he didn't recognize that was evidence enough that the gap was like a chasm between them.

Looking at him now, his face troubled, his eyes cast down, she could only think of him as a boy. But his reaction to his parents' intended visit reminded her that he *was* only a boy. She picked up her glass, appreciated a sip of the wine and set it down again carefully.

'Fabian? Your parents will think there's something wrong if you put them off, won't they? Isn't it better just to go through with it?'

He laid down his fork, and ran a hand through his thick hair.

'I don't know why they can't leave me alone. I'm only

212

going to hear Sara this, and Sara that. I don't need it at the moment. I don't care about bloody Sara and her career in publishing. Sara's not me.' He looked at her with soulful brown eyes that made her stomach buckle. 'And I don't want them interfering with us.'

'Why should they do that?' Maggie went cold for a moment. 'You haven't told them, have you?'

'Of course not,' he reassured her gently. 'Think about it, Maggie. They're going to come up and treat me like a child. That means that you're going to think of me as a child. And there's something else. When you see my mother, you're going to wonder why you're spending any time with me at all.'

'She's not that dreadful, is she?' Maggie joked, deciding that she could probably already guess the answer to her question.

'It's not so much that. It's that you keep saying that you're three years older than her. When you meet her, it'll be all motherly stuff. You know what I mean, you'll start on about your three kids, then you'll think, "Blimey, they're all older than Fabian and I'm a sodding grandmother."'

She smiled at him. He was bright, all right. She'd known that she'd go through all those processes when they arrived.

'But all of that's true, isn't it? It won't go away just because you don't want to think about it.'

'But that's my point. All you ever do is think about it. You never let yourself go completely. You never leave it behind you. It's like we're there in bed and Pete's lying right there between us.'

She blanched, holding her glass tightly. That was something she had felt so strongly herself that she'd almost expected Pete to walk in on them, to bounce Fabian down the stairs. Being with somebody else, in such intimacy, was so alien to her that she couldn't explain it. Not to Fabian, to whom twenty-nine years of marriage was as unimaginable as waking up one morning to find out that he'd started his periods.

'You're writing about him, aren't you?' Fabian said, leaning his elbows on the table and looking at her quizzically.

'What – how do you know that?'

'I haven't read anything, don't worry. I wouldn't dream of nosing through your private things. It's just that you've been locked in your room, typing away all day, and whenever you come out, or I interrupt you, you look as if you've just arrived from another planet.'

Maggie expelled a long, slow breath.

'If that's how it looks,' she said. 'It's because it's how it feels. It is another planet, Fabian. You wouldn't understand it.'

'Then take me there,' he said, his eyes urgent. 'Show it to me. Help me to understand.'

She shook her head at him, trying to find the words.

'You won't understand it by looking, love. You've got to live it, day after day, and not know anything else beyond it to understand. You could never get close.'

'I could try,' he said, taking her hand. 'How can I get close if you don't let me try?'

'No. You're on the outside, looking in. You've got to be on the inside looking out, and to know that what's outside is beyond you to understand.'

'I know that not everybody lives their lives like my parents do, Maggie. I can imagine it, can't I?'

'All right. Imagine this. Imagine hiding from the milk-man because you can't afford to pay him. Looking forward to Friday nights because it's fish and chip night. Looking for toys for the kids down at the jumble sale and hoping they're not going to be too beaten up to give them as Christmas presents. Rolling your last ciggie and knowing you can't afford another pack of baccy.' She looked down. He stroked the back of her hand with his thumb.

'I know it's been hard, Maggie, but it's over now. It's not hard any more. Your life has changed. You've changed.'

'No,' she was vehement. 'That's just it. I haven't changed. Not one bit.'

'You must have done.' He sat back. 'Look at the things you've done, how your life's been enriched. The things you understand now, that you never understood before.'

'Like Kandinsky,' Maggie mused aloud.

'Yes.' He seized on her comment. 'Just like that. Like Kandinsky. How can you say you haven't changed?'

'I'll tell you something,' Maggie said, looking squarely at the eyes which watched her so carefully. 'The only moment that I came close to understanding Kandinsky was when I was on the phone to Pete and I looked at that poster you've got up, of the couple on the horse. I saw how much love there was in that painting. It was Pete that made me see it, not Oxford, not any complex explanation that anyone could give me. No long words,' she finished softly. 'Just Pete.'

Fabian withdrew his hand slowly, and picked up his wine, taking a long draught. He waited a moment for Maggie to compose herself.

'You still love him, don't you?'

She looked at him in surprise.

'Of course I still love him. I'll always love him. That's never been the point.'

'Then what *is* the point?' Fabian said, sitting forwards. A flash of anguish passed over his eyes. 'If you love him, you'll have to go back to him.'

'Things aren't that clear-cut, Fabian,' Maggie said. 'It's

215

possible to still love someone, but to have to move on. For you both to move on. It doesn't mean the love is dead.'

'I don't understand.' He shook his head in a resigned manner. 'That's not what love is in my book.'

'And what is love, in your book?' Maggie said testily. 'A burst of adrenalin? A hard-on? Tell me about it, in your twenty-one years of experience.'

Fabian's face hardened. Maggie quailed as he leaned forward, his eyes sparkling in a manner she'd never seen before.

'That's not fair and you damned well know it! If you insist on treating me like an adolescent, that's up to you. But I don't remember you complaining when I did have a hard-on. I remember you saying that Pete hadn't had a hard-on in living memory. Not one brought on by you, anyway.' He ignored her sharp intake of breath. 'And I don't remember you throwing my age in my face when I brought you to orgasm, twice actually, in the same night. I remember you melting in my arms and remembering who you were. That's right, Maggie, who *you* were. Who you are now. Not a grandmother, not somebody three years older than my mother, not Pete's wife, but yourself. A woman. Get it? A woman.'

He broke off, his breath shallow. He took an agitated sip from his wine, and set the glass down clumsily.

'Don't go silent on me. Nobody can hear us, and what the fuck if they can anyway? You enjoy sex with me, Maggie. I'm old enough to turn you on, aren't I? So why the hell aren't I old enough to deserve just a little, a tiny portion, of your damned respect?'

She sat motionless, the blood drained from her face. He picked up his fork, and tried to play with his food. Then he threw the fork down. She jumped.

'Forget it, Maggie. Just forget it.'

Levering a twenty-pound note out of his wallet, he

flicked it out and laid it on the tablecloth. Then he rose shakily from his seat.

'Where are you going?' she asked him weakly.

'To get pissed,' he said. 'To spend my time with people who are less insulting than you.'

He stormed away. She waited, hearing him push his way through the door and disappear. She stared down at the twenty-pound note, sitting crudely on the marsh-mallow-pink tablecloth. She picked it up, and put it away in her handbag. Then she motioned the waiter to come over, and pulled out her cheque book.

'Can I have the bill, please?'

He nodded and dissolved again. She tried to hold her pen, her fingers shaking. She stopped and finished her wine in one mouthful. Then she tried again. She would have to give it a couple of minutes, then she might be able to write.

Chapter Thirteen

Mack arrived at the time they'd agreed on Saturday morning. Julia heard the guttural roar of his motorbike engine in the road and seconds later he pressed her bell. She hurriedly shoved a pair of stray socks into a drawer and went out to let him in.

He was pulling off his crash helmet as she opened the door. She watched him heave it from his head, shake his hair back into place and look up. He smiled when he saw her.

'Right house, then.'

'Come in.'

She led him through to the kitchen. He glanced around him at her arrangement. Not intrusively, she thought, but she had the impression that he noticed everything. He wandered over to her back door, and looked out at the garden.

'Nice place.' He nodded. 'You could stick a couple of chairs out there, you know, on a day like this. It'd be lovely.'

'I'd never really thought of that.' She paused, kettle in hand, and followed his gaze out on to the patchy mess of grass and path. 'I suppose if I thought I'd stay here long enough, I might bung some paving slabs down or something. Just here, by the door. It'd be quite private.'

'You don't think you'll be here long, then?'

'Oh, I don't know.' She plugged the kettle in and heaved two mugs from the cupboard. 'I assume you'll want tea?' He nodded. 'I've applied for a course. In

London. I don't even know if they'll offer me a place or not, but if I get on to it – and *if* I decide to do it – I'll have to move back down there again.'

He absorbed her words, looking from her back out to the garden again.

'So you were in London, then? Before you came up here to University?'

'That's right. All that was missing was the bowler hat and black umbrella.'

She picked two tea-bags from the box and dropped them in the mugs.

'I can't imagine you doing that,' he said, looking at her thoughtfully. 'You don't strike me as a London type.'

No, she supposed in her jeans and a sloppy jumper, her hair falling all over her face, she didn't look like a London type at all. Not any more.

'Well, I'm not really an Oxford type either. I don't really know where I belong at the moment. But then, who does?'

'And you said *if* you do this course. What might make you change your mind?'

She paused to cross behind him to get the milk from the fridge. She hadn't talked this through with anybody yet, not even Maggie, and her thoughts were still a muddle.

'I might do it, I might not. I'm not sure if it's really me or not.'

'What's the course?'

She glanced up at him and decided that he only seemed casually interested. It made it easier to think aloud.

'It's a teaching course, training you to teach adults. I'd work in Further Education and hopefully be able to carry on literacy teaching too.'

'Sounds like you.'

'You would say that,' she bantered. 'You only know me as a teacher, don't you?' He didn't answer, but unzipped his leather jacket and shrugged it from his shoulders. 'Oh, just dump that anywhere. I haven't got any proper coat hooks, I'm afraid.'

She noticed that he was wearing his pale blue denim shirt. It was flattering to his colouring and made his skin look healthy. But he'd just got off a motorbike, she reminded herself. He would look healthy. She could smell the cool spring air on his clothes and hair.

'Shall I open the door?' she said suddenly. 'Let some fresh air in?'

'If you like.'

She unlocked the door and pushed it open. A breeze wafted into the small room, bringing with it the scent of early hyacinths. Fleabag appeared from nowhere, and trotted dutifully up the path towards them. Mack instantly dropped to his haunches in the doorway, and held out a hand.

'Hello, Fleabag,' he greeted him in a warm voice.

Fleabag hesitated just before he reached the stranger, stalked the last remaining steps, and pushed out his nose to sniff the hand before committing himself. After a split second of careful analysis, he threw himself on the ground and stuck his paws in the air.

'He wants his tummy tickled,' Julia said, watching the display indulgently. 'But watch out. He may be cute and fluffy, but his claws are like meat hooks.'

Mack laughed quietly.

'I'm used to being savaged, don't worry. Elizabeth's really moody. One minute it's all love and snuggles, the next, she doesn't want to know me. My gran had a weird phrase for it. She used to call it get-away-closer.'

'Get-away-closer,' Julia mused. 'Your gran was a bit oblique, wasn't she?'

'You bet. She was full of phrases. She had another one I always remember now that's a bit more straight-forward.' He stood up suddenly, reminding Julia that he was very tall, taller than Rob even, and gave her a serious look. She had the vague feeling that she was about to be given a piece of advice. She shrank back towards the kettle.

'What was that then?'

'Success can only be guaranteed with hindsight.'

His words drifted on the air. She waved her hand at the kettle to pick it up, and missed it completely, her eyes still on his. They'd taken on a peculiar, hypnotic quality. No, it wasn't his eyes particularly, it was because he had an odd ability to make comments that were relevant to her life. She found the handle of the kettle, and laughed.

'Something of a philosopher, wasn't she?' He inclined his head in agreement. 'You, er, I suppose you think that applies to me doing this course, do you?'

'I think you can apply it to anything,' he said. 'Your work, study, aspirations.' He paused, then added, 'Relationships.'

She held his eyes for a moment longer, then looked away. She concentrated on making them both tea, remembering from the class that he took his with milk but no sugar, and handed him a mug. By this time, he had draped Fleabag over his shoulder like a diminutive sack of coal. Fleabag was purring loudly, his paws sticking out at all angles, his body totally relaxed into the broad shoulder. Such a strong shoulder, she thought, able to carry so many burdens without bending.

'So, er, let's go and look at the walls, shall we?'

'Yeah, the walls,' he said.

She took him through to her main room. She'd tried very hard to make it tidy for him. The best feature of the room was the bay window at the front, which made it seem light. And unlike the bedsits above, she had a high ceiling which gave the impression of space. Around the walls were dotted a couple of old prints she'd picked up in the past. She hadn't thought to take them down, as he was probably only going to give her an opinion on the work that needed doing today, but they were only held up by panel pins she'd nailed in using the marmalade jar as a hammer and could be removed easily enough. There was a single bed in the corner, which she draped with a coverlet and threw cushions over during the day, a two-seater sofa, her wardrobe, a chest of drawers, her wonky bookcase and the television, stuffed away in the corner.

'Not exactly Blenheim Palace, is it?' she said disparagingly.

'It's okay.' He walked over to one of the walls, and stared closely at one of her prints. It was one she'd had framed cheaply and was intending to deal with properly when she had more cash.

'That's, er—' She got no further.

'Edmund Dulac. From the *Arabian Nights*,' he said. 'Do you like Dulac, then?' He spotted another similar print further along the wall and went over to it. She watched him. 'Yes, you do. You've got two, which is more than a coincidence.'

'Three, actually.' She found her voice. 'One's stacked away in the kitchen. I found it a couple of years ago, but haven't had it framed yet.'

He gave her a look over his shoulder, one of muted pleasure, she thought.

'He's great, isn't he?'

'Oh, yes. I like him.'

'It's the romance, isn't it? The magic of him. The detail of those little faces and they're all different.'

She was silent as she watched him drink in the features

of the prints she'd hung. He was nodding to himself, as if reaffirming something. She wanted to ask him a question which started with 'How do you know . . .' but she stopped herself just in time, trying to squash her irrelevant surprise. He looked at the prints as she had done, when she'd first seen them and decided to buy them. With childlike wonder.

'So, what do you think of the walls?' she said briskly. He stood away from the pictures, looked down at the carpet for a moment as if composing himself and turned his attention to her walls.

'You're right. They need painting,' he replied.

'Okay, so what shall we do?'

'Well, we could paint over the paper again. That's up to you. Stripping it is a big job, but it shouldn't take too long. I can hire a stripper and do it in an afternoon.'

'Hire a stripper?' she quipped. He gave her an elaborately exasperated look, and she remembered, with a flush, how good he was at that. Now he was in her home and not at the centre. She'd have to be careful what she said. She pulled her face into neutrality again.

'Right. And then what?'

'Then, I'll paint your walls for you. I think . . .' He gazed around him again, assessing the four walls. 'Yes, this one here. This is the one I'll make interesting.'

'Interesting?'

'If you don't mind, of course. I don't want to do anything you don't want.'

She sat down on the corner of her bed, and frowned at him.

'What exactly do you mean by "interesting"?'

He turned and looked at her again, resting his hands on his hips. He scrutinized her, as if trying to read her mind.

'Do you trust me?' he said finally.

'Er, in what way?' she said, eyelashes fluttering unintentionally.

'If you trust me, I'll make this wall interesting and do the others in magnolia, as you wanted. I should tell you, perhaps.' He paused, assessing her again. Her legs started to feel warm. 'You see, I'm not a decorator now. I started that way, but I do other things now. More adventurous things.'

She swallowed, not wanting to make any suggestive remarks now. Adventurous could mean whatever you wanted it to mean.

'Explain,' she said curtly.

'Well, I did the underpass in one of the estates. And I've done the walls at the Youth Club. And the Community Centre asked me to do the outside. I've done a few other things too, but the underpass is probably the best. I don't suppose you've seen it, have you?'

She gaped at him.

'Are you talking about murals?'

'In a word, yes.'

'Oh. Oh, I see.'

'No, you don't,' he said pleasantly. 'You'd have to see my work, then you'd understand. I do whatever's required. I wouldn't do anything here like I did at the Community Centre, or at the underpass. This is a private house and it's yours. I'd paint something about you.'

'Now just you hang on a minute,' Julia said, getting up and flicking her hair over her shoulders. 'I don't want my life splattered all over my bloody wall. It's bad enough having to live it. What the hell would you put on there, anyway? You don't even know me!'

'I know a bit about you,' he replied calmly. 'But I wouldn't paint anything you wouldn't like. Just the things you love, things that you'd like to have around you. Some reflections of the person you are.'

She stuck her hands on her hips and glowered at him.

'Which would be what, precisely?'

He took a breath before answering her and looked away from her, as if eye contact was too uncomfortable.

'Your cat, for one thing. But that's obvious. There's poetry, you love that. And being fair is important to you. Fairness, and being kind to people. You've got problems to deal with of your own, but you've always got time to help somebody in trouble.'

She sank on to the bed, unable to speak. His voice continued to roll over her.

'You think that you don't do anything important, but you don't realize how important you are to the people around you. You think that if things go wrong, it must be your fault, but you're wrong. You're a powerful person, but you don't realize it. You've got love inside you, but somebody's stopped you from feeling it.'

She looked down at her hands to hide her blurred vision. She laughed.

'You're not talking about murals now, are you?'

'Perhaps I'm not.'

'Mack.' She swallowed hard. 'I don't know where you've got all these ideas from, but I can tell you that I'm very straightforward. The rest is just your imagination.'

'Yeah.' She relaxed as she felt him turn his attention away from her. 'It's my imagination.'

'I, erm.' She screwed up her thoughts. She looked up at him. He had his back to her, apparently engrossed now in the state of her wallpaper. 'I'd like you to do a mural, if that doesn't sound too crazy. God knows what Dr Gimble will think, but I suppose if it isn't what I like, you'd paint over it for me, wouldn't you?'

'Of course I would,' he said, not turning round. 'As I said, I won't do anything you don't want. If you don't like it, we can just get rid of it.'

'You're sure about that?'

He swung round to face her, his lips twisting again in humour. He held out his hands.

'Hey. Trust me.'

She smiled at him, her stomach knotted in an odd mix of sorrow and laughter. She looked down again, getting herself together.

'Okay, so—'

'So, I'll get a paper stripper and get rid of this gunk first. Okay with you?'

'Yes, why not?'

'And, if it's not inconvenient, I could do that today?'

'Er . . .' Her brain raced. She had no plans – when did she ever? – but she'd assumed that he'd have a look, then come back next weekend. But there was no reason why he couldn't start on it now. Except that she hadn't been prepared to heave her furniture around today. In some way, she'd expected life to go on exactly as it was, stale coffee-coloured walls and all. 'Well, I suppose we might as well do it today. Yes, why not?'

She nodded firmly, got up abruptly and took herself into the kitchen to find her mug of tea. Tea would help. It would give her a moment to think before anything started happening. She was picking up her mug when she thought she heard the phone ring. She put her head on one side. Yes, definitely.

She dropped her mug, and raced into the other room, aware that her sudden dive for the phone probably looked a bit strange.

'It's Fleabag,' she explained as she landed on the floor and groped for the receiver. 'He's a sod. He'll get it before I do, if I don't . . .' She stuck the plastic under her chin. 'Hello?'

'Julia?'

'That's my name, don't wear it out,' she said with a

sudden attack of flippancy. 'Who's that?'

'It's Leo. Leo Karr. You telephoned me in the week and left a message.'

She collapsed on her knees, her face reddening, suddenly conscious of Mack standing a couple of feet away, examining the collage which was her wallpaper with apparent fascination. Her heart started to thunder.

'Hi!' she said, trying to sound natural. 'How are you?'

'I have to apologize for not getting back to you. I've had a difficult case this week and I was working all hours.' He paused, as if waiting for her to tell him that she understood.

'That's okay,' she said. 'I understand.'

'But I'm free this weekend. Blissfully free, actually. I could come up at any time.'

She smothered a gulp. The pendulum was swinging wildly. Yesterday, when she'd seen Mary Hanson again and talked about Leo, she'd decided that she was very relieved that he hadn't rung her back. Privately, she'd been decidedly miffed. But now he was telling her that his weekend was at her disposal. That was unnervingly keen. She closed her eyes, and tried to think, adrenalin rippling across her stomach.

'Well, it's a bit tricky, actually. I've got—' Was there any other way to put it? 'I've got the decorators in, and I should be here for – them, I think.'

'Over the weekend?' He laughed, and she remembered how intriguing he looked when he laughed. Surely Mack wouldn't mind if she went out? 'I suppose they're charging you overtime, are they?'

'Not at all. It's free, actually. Someone I know. Er, a friend.'

'A friend?' Leo said in a plain chocolate voice. 'So, I've got competition, have I?'

227

She laughed lightly. Competition? *Competition?* Her body curled up into a ball of tension.

'No, no. It's just someone I know who's going to do some stripping for me.'

He laughed again, and she closed her eyes and grimaced.

'Look,' Leo said, taking control with ease. 'Why don't I drive up to Oxford today and take you out to a country pub somewhere? I remember that The Trout was always the place to go on a fine day like this. Would you like that? You said you fancied a walk. We could go over Port Meadow. I haven't done that for years.'

She glanced at Mack's back. He was edging himself away from the phone, she thought, not wanting to look as if he was pointedly leaving the room, but moving away from her all the same.

'I'll just check that it's okay with my – the decorator.' She shoved her hand over the phone, and called out to Mack in a loud whisper. 'Mack? Do you mind if I go out today?'

He turned and looked at her with badly concealed amusement.

'It's probably better if you do. Then I can get on with the job.'

She nodded, wondering why she'd hoped he was going to say that it was imperative for her to stay in and help him. She removed her hand from the mouthpiece.

'No, that's fine, Leo. We could do what you suggest.'

'Give me your address, then.'

She gave it, aware that she'd got into the habit recently of dishing out her address to strange men. He assured her that he'd find her.

'I'll see you in about an hour and a half, then,' he said and hung up without dithering.

She put the phone down and put a hand over her eyes.

Now she would have to tart herself up while Mack shredded her wallpaper around her. It had been a very bad idea.

'I'll just pop out and get the wallpaper stripper,' Mack announced. 'That way, you can get ready while I'm gone, can't you? If we can just shift the furniture first, I'll be able to get behind it.'

Leo arrived half an hour late. It wasn't his fault, she thought, knowing that the traffic leading into Oxford could be a nightmare on a Saturday, but it had given her an extra thirty minutes of tension. Mack had disappeared after they'd heaved her wordly goods into the centre of the room and he'd been gone for almost an hour. That had given her just enough time to examine the contents of her wardrobe, get changed three times and end up in her jeans and a loose white shirt. She'd thrown a thick cardigan over the top, and tried to hit the uneasy balance with her make-up that was never happily achievable with a daytime date, somewhat closer to Mia Farrow than Joan Collins. Mack had returned with an implement that looked like a metal detector, and nodded at her casually.

'You look nice,' he'd said and turned his attention to making the contraption work.

She'd hovered around him from then on, one eye on her walls and one eye out the window, waiting for Leo's car to sweep into a parking space in an expensive manner. He hadn't disappointed her. She'd finally identified him grinding to a halt in a well-polished Rover, somewhat out of place in her road. She'd immediately launched into an absurd conversation with Mack, trying to quell her nerves. He'd turned and looked at her indulgently.

'Just go and open the door, Julia. I take it Leo's arrived?'

The doorbell rang, confirming the suspicion. She'd considered trying to look flabbergasted, but settled for honesty instead, heaving a series of deep breaths as if she was going into labour.

'He means a lot to you, this Leo, then?' Mack asked her casually, hoisting the metal detector in the air.

'No, nothing at all. I mean, I hardly know the man. We've only had dinner once. And now he's here,' she flapped. 'I don't know why, really.'

'It's been a long time, then, I guess?'

She pursed her lips at him, waiting to feel indignant, but the feeling didn't come. She just nodded slowly instead. The doorbell rang again, insistently.

'Go and answer the door,' Mack instructed kindly, setting down the wallpaper stripper.

She obeyed. Leo was not as she expected. He looked comfortable in jeans and a dark blue cotton jumper, a jacket slung over his arm.

'The traffic was a bastard,' he said. 'Sorry I'm a bit late.'

'Come in,' she said, deciding that it was the obvious thing to say next. He followed her through. She let him into her kitchen and immediately felt embarrassed.

'I thought we could have lunch out,' Leo said, still focused on her. 'If we walk at a reasonable pace, we'll make it while they're still serving.'

'Fine,' she said. 'Er, Leo, this is Mack. He's doing my walls. Mack, this is Leo.'

Leo looked around, and found Mack walking towards him with his hand outstretched. Julia watched them come together and shake hands. Mack was taller, more at ease, it seemed. Leo looked tense as he gave an acknowledging nod. It was very strange, seeing two men in her bedsit, greeting each other, after such a long period of being on her own inside it. And they contrasted with each other overtly, Leo with his neat dark hair, Mack

230

with his straggly blond locks. They seemed to jump away from each other after they'd shaken hands, as if one of them had a joke buzzer attached to his palm. Leo immediately looked back to Julia.

'Ready, then?'

'Right. I'd better leave you a spare key, Mack, in case you need to pop out for anything.'

She ferreted through a kitchen drawer and pulled out the keys, handing them to him. She hesitated. Was she going completely mad, giving the keys to her home to a man she hardly knew? He gave her a small smile, as if he knew exactly what she was thinking. She dropped the keys into his hand, and he immediately placed them on the table.

'I'll just leave them there. It's unlikely I'll need to go out.'

'Okay, well, um.' She shuffled towards the door. 'Bye then, Mack. We won't be long.'

'Come on,' Leo said firmly as she loitered.

'I'll look after Fleabag for you and I'll just let myself out when I've finished,' Mack said casually, returning to his metal detector and giving it his full attention.

'So you're having the walls repapered, are you?' Leo asked as they followed the tow-path alongside the Isis in the direction of the pub.

They hadn't been able to talk much in the town. It was nearing lunch-time and the traffic was growling slowly through the streets as they walked, lessening a little into Jericho, but Leo hadn't attempted to start a conversation until they'd entered the flat expanse of Port Meadow and strolled down the wide path leading to the river. It was a dry day, the mud accrued from a temperamental month's weather forming a solid crust, and it was quite easy to walk on. Along the tow-path, the brittle twigs were budding, little green and white dots sprinkling the brown around them. That, and the warm sun, gave her spirits a boost.

'Mack's going to paint them,' she said, walking beside Leo. She realized now that he wasn't as tall as she'd remembered him, but he was bulky. He had all the solidity of a Renault Espace.

'You're very trusting, leaving him your keys.'

'He's trustworthy,' she replied shortly.

'Defensive,' he observed. 'Must be a good friend.'

Of course, she thought, this was how it was with Leo. He liked sparring. It was in his blood. But she'd stood up to him the first time they met and she wasn't worried about doing it again. In fact, he seemed to like it. It was possible that she even liked it herself.

'He's not what I'd call a close friend, but I know him pretty well,' she lied. She didn't want Leo to know that Mack was a student at the class. When she'd told him about her voluntary work before, he'd seemed interested, but she didn't want him sticking labels on Mack. Mack was, well, Mack.

'So you must be intent on staying in Oxford then, if you're redecorating.'

'I might, but I might not,' she hedged. 'I haven't really made up my mind yet. I'll see what happens.'

'So you're not going to talk about it, then.'

She glanced up at him. His eyes were trained on the path ahead, but he seemed to be concentrating hard on what she was saying.

'I might, but I might not,' she said, happily thwarting him. 'I'll think about it.'

'Ah. And what would you be thinking about? A career move of some sort?'

'Why don't we talk about you instead?' she said decisively, shoving her cardigan on to her other arm, and wondering why she'd brought it with her. 'Where do you go from where you are now?'

'You don't like talking about yourself, do you?' he commented, walking steadily on. 'I'd thought you were just being cautious, but I detect a mental block.'

'You know lots about me,' she defended. 'You know about my class, where I've studied, what I did before, and you've even seen my glamorous bedsit. What more is there to say?'

'You tell me.'

'No. We're going to talk about you now. We can come back to me if it's still light when you've finished.'

'But I asked first. That's the way it works.' She felt him shoot her a sideways glance. She hid a smile.

'You mean there are rules to this?'

'Absolutely.'

'And what if I cheat?'

'That's just it.' He stopped, and she ground to a halt beside him. He peered ahead into the distance. 'Where is this bloody pub? We should be there by now.'

She laughed at him.

'You've forgotten how far it is. We could go to The Perch instead, if you haven't got the stamina.'

'The Perch? Oh yes, I remember. That's lurking in the bushes somewhere up here, isn't it?'

'Depends how much you want to see the peacocks at The Trout. Do you think you can make it that far? You could have driven, you know, and bagged us a table. I could have met you over there.'

'Let's go and see the peacocks,' he said, starting to walk again. 'And I've got plenty of stamina, if you don't mind. I may be thirty-five, but I'm not saving up for my incontinence pads yet. I was going to say that I don't know anything about you. What you want, or what makes you tick.'

'Ditto,' she said neutrally.

'That's just what I mean. You always throw my questions back at me.'

'And you don't like that, do you? You prefer people to be trapped in the witness box with the judge banging his hammer and saying "Just answer the question, please".'

He shot her another glance. She felt it, but kept her eyes ahead.

'Funnily enough, I think that's why I like you,' he said. 'You're quite a challenge.'

'Really,' she retorted. 'Good exercise for your grey matter, then.'

They paused to edge past a young couple with a pushchair trying to negotiate the uneven turf and she stepped behind him. They continued for a while in single file, the path thinning to a strip on a raised patch of river bank. He had a nice figure from behind, she decided. His jeans were quite close-fitting, showing up a nicely firm rump and powerful legs. His hair was thick and black against the neck of his jumper, brushing it silkily. Yes, he was masculine, and attractive in his own bumptious way, and somehow she didn't doubt his stamina. But she didn't think she liked being thought of as a challenge. It suggested that she had to be overcome. The path widened again.

'Tell me what *you* want, Leo,' she demanded as he waited for her to catch him up. 'Be brave and kick us off.'

'Okay.' He thought for a moment. 'All my life I thought I wanted money. To be secure, and never to have to worry about the bills. And I wanted a good job, status and a nice car. I wanted a challenging career and to do something that was in some way constructive.'

'So, aren't you doing all those things?'

He nodded, flicking his jacket over his shoulder.

'I chose to join a set of chambers that defended, rather than prosecuted. That wasn't just a lucky break, I pinpointed them and went for them.'

'You usually get what you want, don't you?' she said airily.

'Most of the time. But there's Robert, for a start. He's got his own ideas, as you know. I don't want him to be doing what he's doing right now, but I can't stop him. And,' he took a deep breath. It was a strange sound, as if he was sighing. 'There's what might come under the loose heading of my private life.'

'Oh. Relationships, you mean.'

'Whatever.'

She fell silent, wondering what to say. Every possibility seemed embarrassing. 'Oh, you'll meet someone, don't worry.' Or, 'There's nothing wrong with you, is there?' Or, even worse, 'I'll go out with you if nobody else will.' They reached the remains of Godstow Abbey, a heap of stones which heralded the imminent arrival of the pub.

'When I see Rosie – she's Robert and Emily's daughter – I know what I'm missing. She's there in my life now, constantly reminding me of what I haven't got.'

'So, er. You'd like a family, then?'

'I've even thought of marrying Emily and legally adopting Rosie. But – Emily and I are too different.'

She swallowed. He really was serious about it. She'd often sat with friends in the past, and had 'One day . . .' conversations, but he was actually getting out the battle plans. She suddenly felt like a target.

'I'm not sure if I'll ever get married,' she said quickly, spotting the pub through the trees and deciding that she might have a lager after all.

'Oh, you will,' he said confidently. 'When you meet the right man.'

Chapter Fourteen

The pub was packed. The University term had recently ended and Julia identified several crowds of students enjoying a peaceful pint. The Easter holidays would skid past, she thought sympathetically. Before they knew it, the bomb of finals would have dropped on them. A handful of people had draped themselves over the low wall edging the river, looking impossibly relaxed. Alongside them, the weir threw refreshing spray into the air and crashed into the river unrelentingly.

They collected drinks from the dark interior of the pub and took them out into the garden which stretched away to the back, narrowing towards a copse of trees. A trestle-table had just become free and they headed for it. Julia dumped her cardigan on the slatted seat, and squeezed into the space, while Leo managed to thread his legs under the table opposite her. A peacock came to investigate, squawked at them and stalked off to find his friends.

'I think I'd forgotten how nice this place was,' Leo said, sipping his bitter and putting it down with a twisted face. 'And how awful the beer is.'

'Are you a real ale buff, then?'

Of course, he would be, she thought, remembering how picky he was about wine.

'I like beer to taste like beer,' he replied.

'We could have gone somewhere else. Still, it's probably worth having to sit opposite your grimaces just for the atmosphere here.'

'It's not Rob's angelic face, I know, but it's not so bad, is it?' He looked at her strangely, then got up again. 'I think I should go and get some lunch for us. No, you stay here, or we'll lose the table. Will anything do you?'

'Oh, er, yes. Good idea.'

'I'll pay,' he said.

'Good,' she replied without conscience.

She watched him walk back to the pub. Well, he said he was wealthy, didn't he? It was fair enough. She was in dire financial straits now. It was just as well that one of the colleges she'd sent her CV to had come back to her and asked her to tutor next week. With any luck, she'd have three students a day for A level revision, and as the college liked the students to be taught individually, that would mean more money. She'd have to dig out some old novels and a couple of Shakespeare plays to prepare, but she'd probably enjoy that. It might even lead to more work. She'd have to take as many hours as they offered. For now, at least, she would just relax. She stretched her legs out under the table and took a deep breath of spring air. It was good to be out, away from the confines of her flat.

She took a sip of her lager, wrinkling her nose as it fizzed at her. It was annoying that Leo had mentioned Rob's name. It would be nice to draw a veil over the whole stupid incident, but at least he'd been kind enough not to rub her nose in it by reminding her of the fact she'd spent the night with him. She gazed over at the river and thought of the friendly smile Rob had given her at the class party. She didn't even think about him as 'gorgeous' Rob now. Whatever spell she'd temporarily been under had been broken long before Leo had gone into graphic hormonal detail. It must be hard, she thought, with a moment of sympathy for Leo, to have such a fantastic-looking brother, whatever his sexual proclivities. She wondered if Leo habitually tried to get off with Rob's leftovers. There was Emily, who he'd decided to marry, but for some reason changed his mind, and now there was her. But then, she'd said herself to Mack that meeting somebody was all down to chance. Perhaps in years to come, she'd be saying to her children, 'Guess how Daddy and I first met? Well, first I copped with Uncle Rob, but he was gay, and anyway, *nothing* happened, so Daddy thought he'd step in himself. Isn't that romantic?'

Oh, no, no, no. She pursed her lips and stuck her glass in her mouth, gently sucking up the lager. She wasn't exactly looking for Sir Galahad on his white charger, but there had to be a more auspicious beginning to a relationship than this. She thought back to when she had first met Bill. She'd had an instinctive feeling, straight away, that he was somehow important to her. He'd been appointed to her department and she was busy photo-copying a mass of papers when he walked into the office. She'd turned round, looked at him and the photocopier had jammed. For the first couple of weeks, she didn't even think he'd noticed her, but then one Friday evening, when a group from the department had adjourned to the pub, he'd ended up sitting beside her. They'd been talking politics and she'd been finding it hard to get a word in edgeways, but finally she did. After she'd delivered her piece, Bill turned round to her in surprise and said, 'Why are you wasting yourself? You should go to university.'

That was it. They talked to each other all night, ignoring the others and staying on after the rest had gone on to eat. The following week, he'd asked her out properly. And after it was all over, only then, did she take up his advice.

And she was still here, she thought wryly, gazing

around at the scattered bodies, sprawled over the grass in T-shirts and jeans, jumpers under their heads, basking in the sun. She wondered what Bill would think if he saw her now. She hadn't spoken to him for five years. Did he ever stop what he was doing and wonder where she was, how she was? If she was alive or dead?

'Shepherd's pie. Not very original, but it was the best of what was left. We've left it a bit too late.'

Leo placed the plates on the table, and handed her a knife and fork wrapped in a serviette.

'Thank you,' she said, suffering a pang of guilt. 'It's nice of you to buy me lunch.'

'Nice of me?' He sat himself down, and arranged his plate, looking at her curiously. 'I've obviously left you alone for too long. You must have been brooding.'

'What makes you say that?' She tried to look as if she hadn't been brooding.

'Because you've just said something complimentary to me, even if it is only about the lunch, and so far, I consider that to be out of character. Your mood's changed.'

'Don't be silly. I'm just getting my breath back after the walk.' She tackled her shepherd's pie with her fork. 'You should have gone into Psychology, not the Law. You've obviously got a fascination with it.'

'It's very similar. You have to have an interest in the workings of the human mind to want to go into Law. You have to look at people, what motivates them, how they usually behave, what is and isn't within their capabilities. You have to develop an insight into human nature.' He stabbed a pea. 'Just like studying English, really.'

'Incredible. You've almost managed to make it sound interesting,' she said. 'I tried to read a book on Land Law once. Someone at the college had left it lying around, so I picked it up. I was in a coma by the end of the introduction.'

He laughed, the green smears across his irises catching the sun.

'Well, there's law and law, of course. Some people are fascinated by Land Law, believe it or not. But it's always been Criminal Law for me.'

'I can see why that's different.' She chewed thoughtfully. 'So do you do this all the time, then? Analyse people you meet?'

'I'm afraid so.'

'But you ask a lot of questions.' She pointed her fork at him. 'You're like a medium, giving messages from beyond the grave. You squeeze information out of people first, then present it back to them.' She nodded decisively. 'That's it. I've got you sussed now. The problem is that most people forget what they've told you, so it looks as if you're amazingly perceptive. But the truth is that you've just got a good memory.'

He laughed again, swilling his beer around in his glass.

'It's not that simple, I'm afraid. I get a sense of what's going on in people's minds without talking to them. It's something I've been trained to look at. It's in the expressions, the body language, the way people react without knowing it.'

She shook her head firmly.

'No. Sorry, I don't believe it. That's just guessing.'

'Call it guessing if you like.' He pondered, laying his fork down, and taking a sip of his beer. He looked at her steadily. 'For example, I can tell you that your friend is in love with you.'

Her fork fell with a clatter. She stared at him.

'What friend?' Who did he mean? He hadn't met any of her friends, unless it was someone at the party? She hastily swallowed a mouthful of lager. 'Who are you talking about?'

He smiled. 'Don't look so alarmed. You're obviously

totally oblivious to it and that's because he's hiding it from you. But he's in love with you.' He nodded slowly. 'I'm quite sure of it.'

'Leo,' she said, a little unsteadily. 'You're not talking in an indirect way about yourself, are you? Because if you are, I have to tell you—'

'Relax,' he said calmly. 'It takes me a little longer than this to fall in love, although I do like you, obviously. No, I'm talking about your decorator.'

'Mack?' She blinked. 'Mack!' She shook her head strongly. 'No, you're wrong about that.'

'No, I'm not,' he said, picking up his fork and continuing with his meal. 'I could sense it the minute I walked in.'

She stared at him for a moment, thrown into confusion. 'How could you sense it?'

'His eyes.' He swallowed. 'His body language, the way he looked at you, the way he looked at me. The way he shook my hand. The fact that he's painting your walls for you for free. Hadn't that struck you as a little over-generous? At the weekend? In his own time?'

'Oh, I see.' She relaxed again, her shoulders dropping, and gave him an easy smile. 'No, you don't understand. He's practising.'

'Practising?'

'He, er, he does murals.'

'Murals?' Leo looked deeply concerned.

'Yes. He's done an underpass and some clubs, mostly outside walls. So he's going to do one for me.'

'Tell me you're joking.'

'No, I'm not. So you see, that's all there is to it. He obviously saw the opportunity to practise his – mural – skills on my wall, and jumped at it.'

'Right.' Leo finished his meal and laid his cutlery down, touching his mouth elegantly with his serviette and giving her a steady look. 'However, that's got nothing to do with everything I've said. Mack's in love with you, Julia, and for some reason he doesn't want to tell you. I stand by that analysis.'

'No, you're wrong,' she asserted, leaving the remainder of her food as she found that her appetite was fast disappearing.

'Men can sense when they're being sized up as competition,' he continued smoothly. 'And I was definitely being sized up.'

'Oh, that's rubbish,' she protested vehemently. 'Men are always competing with each other. They love doing it for no reason at all. It's how they pass the time when they're not trying to get someone into bed. It's got nothing to do with being in love. Anyway, you were the one who suggested that my decorator might be competition for *you*, on the phone, weren't you? You're just assuming that Mack's doing the same. It's absurd.' She adopted a prim expression. 'You're being very silly, Leo.'

He laughed aloud, and shook his head at her.

'Well, you obviously don't feel the same way about him, anyway.'

'Of course I don't.' She flushed. 'I don't feel that way about anybody.'

'Good. Well, if Mack the friend-that-you-know-pretty-well and sometime decorator isn't in the running, perhaps I've got a chance.'

The sun disappeared behind a cloud, giving her a sudden chill. She picked up her cardigan and put it around her shoulders.

'A – a chance to do what, Leo?'

'Don't be disingenuous, Julia.' He lowered his voice to a murmur. 'I'm thirty-five, single, and very nicely set up. I've reached a point in my life where I seriously want to think about committing myself to somebody. I've got something to offer, I think. A comfortable home, a safe income, perhaps I'm even quite good company at times. That's not for me to judge. But I didn't drive all the way up to Oxford just to recharge my car batteries.' He paused. She sat, stunned. 'I'm just being honest with you, Julia. I'm too old to play the mating game and I don't have time endlessly to follow up false leads.'

She couldn't say a word. She watched him, waiting for him to say something that might bring her voice back into action.

'I have the impression you've been let down in the past,' he continued quietly, flicking her a glance. 'Very badly, judging by your reaction at the party. I just want you to know that I'm being sincere. I'm a reliable person and I wouldn't let you down.'

'I—' she croaked finally.

'I think we might suit each other,' he said, assessing her again. Suddenly, he smiled at her. 'You've got a sharp mind, you're witty and you can stand up for yourself. I admire you and I've already said I like you very much. You're also a very attractive woman. I hope you don't mind me saying that to you.'

'I'm speechless,' she said, leaning on the table. 'I – I really don't know what to say.'

'You're at a crossroads at the moment,' he said. 'You don't know which way to go next. I wondered if you might have been thinking yourself about commitment, about a family.'

She grabbed her lager and took a deep slurp, holding on to the glass for strength.

'You think what I really want is a baby? That I've been hanging around, waiting for someone to offer themselves as an impregnator?'

'It sounds crass if you put it like that. I don't mean that

it's the obvious solution, but aren't you tired of being on your own? Haven't you thought about opening yourself up to someone?'

'But, Leo.' She tried to steady her racing thoughts. 'You've said yourself that you like me, but you're not in love. I respect your honesty. But I feel the same. I don't know what I think about you at the moment, but I'm not in love. You must know that too. Doesn't that mean something?'

'It means that we've only spent a short time together,' he said earnestly, his eyes probing hers. 'And it's difficult, you being in Oxford and me in London. I work long hours and that makes it tricky for me to make arrangements during the week. But I think if we did spend more time together, something would come out of it. Something deeper and more enriching.' He watched her reactions. 'Don't you think that's possible?'

She looked back at him, at his solid shoulders, stooped as he leaned towards her, his thick hair, ruffled in the breeze, his honest eyes. She felt an unexpected surge of respect for him. It took courage, to speak as he was doing. He deserved more than a flippant knee-jerk reaction from her. But how could she voice her fears? How could she explain what she was going through, without plummeting in his estimation? Her indecision, the pills the doctor had put her on, her counselling sessions. He saw her as the person she was sometimes, the sparky character who'd thrown wine in his face, who'd bantered with him in a restaurant. How could he possibly understand the person she was the rest of the time, her paralysing doubts, the inadequacies she felt?

'Leo, I, er—' She chose her words with care. 'When I phoned you, in the week, I think I might have given you the wrong impression. Perhaps that I was looking for the same things as you. I had no idea that you felt like this about – your life.' She paused. 'I'm not looking for those things at the moment. I'm still trying to make sense of my own life.'

She stopped. He was nodding gently at her, absorbing her words, watching her face. Surely, she thought, with his self-proclaimed powers of perception, he'd realize that she was telling the truth.

'I think you've got a great deal to offer,' she continued softly. 'And I do like your company. But the problem's *me*, not you. I don't feel as if I've got anything to offer at the moment.'

'I've rushed you,' he said levelly, sitting back and picking up his glass again. 'I've gone in like a bulldozer. I'm sorry.'

'No, it's all right. Don't apologize. I'm very flattered. But I think it's going to take me a very long time before I think about committing myself to anybody. I'm trying to be as honest as I can.'

'Look.' He pushed a hand through his hair. She noticed for the first time that his fingers were long and slender. He *was* an attractive man. Why was she deliberately blowing it with him? Why couldn't she say something different? Couldn't she at least leave her options open? He composed himself. 'Why don't we start again and pretend that I never opened my mouth and blurted all that out?' He looked at her with clear eyes. 'I should have been more sensitive, and I'm sorry. I'm afraid when you're used to jumping on the facts and throwing them at people, it becomes a bit of a habit.'

'Yes. I understand.'

They sat quietly as the clouds gathered overhead and blocked the promising early rays of sun. She gathered her cardigan around her, noticing that the crowd around them had thinned out.

'Leo? I'd still like to do this from time to time,' she

ventured. Get-away-closer, she thought suddenly. She was doing it right now. Mack's gran had been spot on.

'Yes, why don't we?' he said. 'Shall we have another drink before we go?'

She pulled herself out from the table.

'I'll just have a Coke, but I'll get you a beer. And I insist on getting this round.'

Julia didn't think about the fate of her walls again until they reached her house and she turned the key in the door. It was late afternoon by the time they headed back home. After one more drink at the pub, they'd walked back by the river, then lingered in the town for a while. Leo hadn't brought up the subject of his future intentions again and she'd been able to enjoy her time with him. But somewhere at the back of her mind, while they slipped back into bantering mode, was a wedge of discomfort.

She paused on the doorstep. He wasn't exactly waiting to be asked in, but she wondered what to do. If he stayed the whole day, it would be something of a statement in itself. And what might he think to do later, if he was still in Oxford at bedtime?

'I'm going to call in on Robert now,' he said, pushing his thumbs into the pockets of his denims.

'Oh, are you?' Now she knew he had other plans, she wasn't so sure that she wanted him to go. But she didn't know what else to do with him.

'I rang him earlier, so he's expecting me. We're going to try and have a meal together without it ending in a row.'

'That sounds nice.'

'You'd be welcome to join us, of course.'

She managed to maintain a friendly smile while the nightmarish vision flitted across her mind of the three of them grouped together socially, while the fact that she

246

had got off with the gay brother and just had lunch with the straight one was buried under polite conversation.

'No, I've got to get organized here. I've got some things to do,' she said vaguely, trying to sound convincing. She had an urgent date with the television, or a book perhaps. She had work to prepare for her revision classes. Anything was better than playing her role in a bizarre love triangle.

'You'd better go and see what's happened to your walls, then.'

'Yes. Mack will have gone, I expect.' She spotted his motorbike parked in the road as she spoke. It wasn't worth commenting on. Especially if Leo was still obsessed with the absurd idea that Mack was concealing his undying love for her. 'Well, tell Rob that Vivienne got home safely. He'll know what that means. And remember what I told you about Sandra. He's been talking to her a lot recently. Just give him a chance to explain.'

'By which you mean, don't bulldoze him,' Leo said, giving her a wry smile. Before she could move, or say anything, he'd bent towards her and brushed her cheek in a kiss.

And he turned and went. She found herself watching him make his way to his car, open the door and climb in. He hadn't said he'd call, or asked her to call him, or anything. He'd just walked away. She stepped into the hall and closed the front door. She waited until she heard his car pull away, then released a long breath, wondering how long she'd been holding it in. Since about one o'clock that afternoon, probably.

Fleabag danced over to her as she pushed her way into the bedsit. Her legs were starting to ache from the hours of walking, and she suddenly felt tired. Too much fresh air, she told herself. She squatted down and rubbed

Fleabag's ears as he head-butted her hand. Her radio was playing quietly in the corner, on Radio Four, as she'd left it. She wandered inside, bracing herself for disaster. If she'd known that she'd be out today and would come home as tired as this, she'd have put off any ideas of decorating for another century. The last thing she needed now was to have to pick her way through piles of wallpaper.

She peered through into her main room. Mack was engrossed with shouldering her wardrobe back into place. The walls were stripped of paper, but there was no evidence of it anywhere else. The carpet was clean and the Hoover was still lying in the middle of the room. And apart from her wardrobe, he'd put everything back where it was before. He seemed to be so preoccupied with heaving it back against the wall that he hadn't heard her come in.

'Mack?' she said, quietly enough to avoid making him jump.

He looked over his shoulder at her, seemed surprised to see her, and pulled himself away from the wardrobe. For an instant, he seemed put out by her sudden arrival. He shook back his hair, and smiled at her.

'Hi there.' He glanced behind her. 'On your own, then?'

'Yes, Leo's gone now. Mack, thank you so much for clearing up as well.' She walked into the room and looked around. Apart from the sorry state of the walls, she could continue her life as before. 'I was expecting to have to do it.'

'It's no bother. I'm sorry you've got to live with these surroundings for a bit, but if you can put up with it, I'll get back and paint them as soon as I can.'

'Oh, it's fine. You've done a great job. I can't believe you've been so quick.'

'It's just as well I did strip the walls. D'you know, there were four layers of paper on here?'

'Really? Well, Dr Gimble will just have to be grateful then, won't she?'

'Did you, er—' He stood a little awkwardly. 'Did you have a nice time?'

She ran Leo's words through her head again. Something about Mack's body language. She was no psychologist, but he seemed to her to be behaving in the way he'd always behaved with her. Leo obviously had an overactive imagination. She felt comfortable with Mack and she liked being with him. She wouldn't feel like that if he was in love with her. She'd know.

'I had an interesting time,' she said non-committally. 'Can I make you a cup of tea? I should have shown you where everything was.' She stopped, glanced at her watch, and saw that it was gone six o'clock. 'And have you eaten anything? You've been here for ages.'

'Oh, no. It's okay, really. I had a cup of tea mid-afternoon, but I'm often an erratic eater. Especially when I paint, you know. I just lose track of everything.'

'That's all very well,' she said sternly. 'But you haven't been painting today, you've been waving that machine around and getting rid of wallpaper. I hardly think it's fascinated you so much that you've forgotten to eat.'

'Well, I just wanted to get it done before you came back,' he said, smiling at her again. 'And I've achieved my objective, haven't I?'

'Then I insist on paying for a take-away,' she said. 'Unless you've got to get back?'

He seemed disturbed again and she wondered what she'd said. He looked at her, putting his head back, and blinking.

'I'm sorry, Mack. I'm not thinking. It's Saturday night after all, and you've probably got plans.'

'And if I don't get to watch *Family Fortunes* on my own telly, it'll put me on the wrong foot for the rest of the week? No, a take-away would be great. But I'd have to pop home first, feed Elizabeth and check on the kittens.'

'Of course.'

'And I could pick up a take-away on the way back.'

'But I want to pay.'

'No, I can pay.'

'No,' she insisted. 'You're doing all this for me, for nothing, so it's the least I can do. And seeing as I was treated to lunch today, I don't see why I shouldn't pay for supper.'

'I suppose there's some sort of logic in that,' he said. 'Although Leo seems to end up out of pocket.'

'Oh, he can afford it,' she said dismissively. 'Don't worry about him.'

'I wasn't,' Mack commented, and walked past her to collect his jacket and crash helmet. 'So what shall we have?'

Julia hesitated. She knew what she really fancied eating now, she could picture it, and she'd even thought of the dishes she wanted.

'What would you like?' she asked, denying her craving and being polite.

He laughed at her, pulling his jacket on, wrenching up the thick zipper with vigour.

'That's a cop out. You're paying, so you can choose.'

'Can I?' she said happily. 'In that case, it's got to be Indian.'

'I'm so glad you said that.' He arranged his crash helmet ready to put on, pulling out the straps and leaving them hanging over the sides. 'I fancy something really challenging, but I don't know how hot you like it.'

'I like it really hot,' she said, feeling less tired suddenly. 'But let's get a combination and play ping-pong. I tell you what, why don't I ring and order and it'll be ready by the time you come back?'

'Brilliant,' he said drily. 'Just tell me where you're going to ring, so that I turn up at the right restaurant.'

She gave him the name of her favourite restaurant and they enthused about it for a moment. She gave him some cash to take with him and after his initial reluctance he took it and headed for the door.

'Why don't you just order what you want, then?' he said, his voice muffled through the padding of his helmet. 'I trust you. Tell them I'll pick it up in about half an hour.'

He vanished through the door.

Julia busied herself with warming plates, giving Fleabag unnecessary attention, and pushing the switch on the kettle on repeatedly, until she heard the roar of the motorbike engine as Mack returned. She wondered if he'd taken her spare keys, but noticed that they were still lying on the table, apparently untouched. She went out to the hall to let him in.

'It's a bit squashed.' He held out a plastic bag, flicking his crash helmet off with his other hand. 'The panniers aren't really big enough.'

'Panniers?' This was a new word to add to her vocabulary.

'The plastic boxes on the side of the bike,' he explained, following her through. 'I strapped them on so that I could carry things today.'

She dumped the plastic bag on the table, and began to fish out the foil containers.

'This smells fantastic.'

Mack produced something wrapped in paper from inside his jacket, and unravelled it to reveal a bottle of wine.

'I know you're not supposed to, really,' he said, putting it on the table. 'So I got a low-alcohol one. I

251

thought a sip would be nice. You could save the rest.'

She stopped as she was sharing Prawn Vindaloo between the two plates.

'That's really sweet of you,' she said.

'You left your pills out. On the floor, by your bed,' he said. 'I had to move them, because I had to slide the bed out to get to the wall behind it. But you'll find them on the mantelpiece.'

She looked up at him, spoon in hand.

'Oh.'

'You're wondering if I knew what they were,' he said. 'The fact is, I do know, but you shouldn't worry about it. I just thought I'd say that to, er, clear things up.'

She blinked at him uncertainly. The pills were very private and led to the sort of questions she didn't want to answer. She should have thought of putting them in the bathroom. That was stupid.

'I don't think I want to talk about it, Mack,' she said quietly.

'Talk about what?' he said casually. 'Have you got a corkscrew? I've got a Swiss Army knife, if you haven't.'

She reached into a drawer in the unit and picked out the corkscrew, handing it to him. He busied himself with opening the wine, all conversation about her pills apparently forgotten. She was starting to realize that Mack was like this. He wouldn't push her on anything that was difficult for her. It was as if he knew when to speak, and when not to. He was very unlike Leo, probing her for information.

'Actually,' she began, continuing to serve the food. 'I'm seeing a counsellor at the moment.'

He paused, held out the bottle and put his head on one side.

'Got any glasses?'

'Oh, yes.' She picked two from the cupboard. 'It's, er,

all very dull really. I've just been going through a bit of a bad patch, but I'll be fine. And I think the pills are starting to work now. I felt quite good today, walking by the river. I won't bore you with it, but I just thought I'd say something. You've seen the pills, after all.'

'I didn't need to see the pills,' he said, tipping a small amount of wine into each glass. 'I guessed you were under the weather, anyway.'

'How did you know that?' She looked up at him.

'Let's just say it takes one to know one.' He handed her a glass, took a sip from his own and gave her a small smile. 'I had a bad patch myself a few years ago. It's nothing to be worried about. It'll pass. Sometimes things catch up with you, don't they? Things you've tried not to think about, in the hope that they'll go away?'

'Yes. Yes, it's something like that.'

'It made me re-evaluate things. And that's when my art really started to take off. It gave me the confidence to do what I really wanted to do. I know that sounds stupid. I expect the last thing you feel at the moment is confident. But I came out the other side in control of my own life again.'

She took a slow sip from her wine and gazed at him thoughtfully.

'And that's when you stopped decorating and started painting?'

'That's it. I'd been too scared to express myself. Every time I'd tried to express anything before, it'd been laughed at, or ignored because I couldn't spell it properly. But in art, there wasn't any need for words. I could paint what I felt, without worrying about it. And I found that people liked what I did. It was fantastic.'

She pondered a moment longer over his sincere face, then turned her attention back to the meal and laid the plates out on the table.

'But those pills are a bugger to get used to.' He smiled at her. 'Have you been through the Ronnie Biggs stage yet?'

'Ronnie Biggs?'

'Yeah. Unable to finish a sentence.'

She found herself stopping to laugh. It felt wonderful.

'Mack?' she said, as she arranged the cutlery for them both. 'I don't suppose you'll take me to the underpass and show me what you did?'

Chapter Fifteen

'I'm sorry.'

Fabian looked up from the files strewn across his desk and gave Maggie a bleak stare. The desk was heaving under the weight of paper, Maggie thought. He seemed to be trying to do everything at once. She'd seen the light under his door when she'd got up in the night, unable to sleep, and thought about making herself a pot of tea. It was gone two in the morning, and his eyes looked small and tired, his face pale. Since their scene in the Italian restaurant, they hadn't spoken, apart from mundane necessities. He'd seemed to be avoiding her, spending all day in the library and all night in his room. It was what he should be doing at this crucial stage in his degree anyway, but Maggie also knew that it was personal.

'Can I come in?'

He nodded and pushed his chair away from the desk, stretching his legs.

'I've made you a cuppa. And I've brought you this back. I didn't know how to give it to you without it seeming rude.'

She put the twenty-pound note that he had left on the restaurant table on his desk. He looked at it for a moment, then picked it up and put it in the pocket of his jeans.

'So you paid, did you?'

'I wrote a cheque. It's okay, it won't bounce.'

'You can't afford to do that.'

'I'll negotiate it with the bank later, don't you worry

about it. It was a lovely meal, anyway. It was worth it.'

'Shame about the company, though, I suppose.' He stared down at his notes, scrawled in an untidy hand, filling the page in front of him. The desk lamp cast a vivid arc of light across the paper. He screwed up his eyes, and rubbed his face with his hands.

'You've had enough, love. Why don't you get some sleep, now?'

'I can't sleep,' he said blankly.

'You can't burn yourself out yet.' She tentatively sat down on the corner of his bed, pulling the oversized men's shirt she usually wore to bed around her collar bone. It was cold in the room, as well. She guessed he hadn't noticed. 'You've got to pace yourself. Little by little. Imagine it's a Chinese meal and do it in small bites.'

He shook his head, a cynical smile on his lips.

'This is nothing like a Chinese meal. This is, without doubt, the worst experience I've ever had.' He looked at her, his tiredness overcoming him, his eyes sad. 'I'm not going to make it, Maggie. I'm going to have to defer. Or jack it in.'

'You can't do that,' she insisted. 'You've got to forget Sara and do it in your own way. Any degree's better than no degree.'

'That's all right for you to say.' He leaned back in his chair, casting his head back and staring up at the ceiling. 'It was different for you. Just going to university at all, let alone Oxford, was an incredible thing, wasn't it? I mean, regardless of your result.'

She considered being indignant, but decided that, on balance, he was right. Back on the estate, if she'd said she'd been to Oxford, she might as well have said that she'd been to Jupiter. Nobody would ever think to ask her what class her degree was, and it wouldn't mean a great deal to most of her friends if she'd told them. Even

Pete hadn't tried to understand just how much it meant to her that she'd achieved an Upper Second. A good one too. Her tutor had told her she was a borderline First, but she hadn't told Pete that. She knew what it had taken her, but nobody else did.

'But my family are different,' he continued in a weary voice. 'My grandfather was here, my father and my sister. They all walked out with Firsts. Every single bloody one of them. Even my mother probably would have got a First if her family had thought that women should go to university. But they sent her to a posh secretarial college instead.' He snorted. 'That's a laugh, isn't it? Seeing as she's the one piling the pressure on.'

'It's probably because she doesn't understand what you're going through,' she said, trying to be sympathetic. Encouraging him to feel resentful would only stir him up even more. He had to stay calm now. 'Have you thought of trying to explain it to her?'

'What's the point?' He closed his eyes, head lolling. 'All she knows is that Sara managed it. And if Sara managed it, there's no reason why I can't.'

'But you're not Sara,' Maggie insisted steadily. 'You know that and that's all that matters, surely?'

'They don't see it that way,' he said drearily. 'For them, it's like some sort of IQ test. They think that because I did well in my A levels, it came as easily to me as it did to them. But that's not what it was like. The truth is, I shut myself away and worked like hell to get them.'

'But everybody does that,' Maggie said. 'They're hard to do well in. I found them really hard too.'

He opened his eyes and looked at her, shaking his head slowly.

'No, you don't know what I mean. You found them hard because you were juggling your job, your husband, your kids, your grandchild and your exams all at the

257

same time. I'm saying that I crammed for eighteen hours a day, practically for the whole two years. It was all I had to do, but I nearly killed myself. I was so scared of failing, of letting them all down.'

She held her mug of tea and watched him. His eyes were focused on a distant point in the corner of the room. She stayed silent. He needed to talk about this.

'So the lie continued. I got a place here, my reports were excellent, my grades were predicted to be straight As, and when I got them, it was as if it proved the point. But it was a lie. I didn't dare to tell anyone that it wasn't me that had done it. That it wasn't meant to be.'

'But you're here now,' she said softly. 'And you've survived this far, haven't you?'

'By the threadbare seat of my silk boxer shorts,' he said, heaving a harrowed sigh. 'But now, it's show time. This isn't the same as being at school. I just can't get to grips with it all. There's too much of it.'

He stared down at the papers again, his face now very white.

'Fabian? You're not saying anything that I didn't say last year. Everyone else was saying it too. And we all really meant it. Oxford does that to you. Everybody feels like a fraud here, but nobody is. They took you because they wanted you, and whatever you get in your exams, nothing will change that.'

'Words, words.' He shook his head. 'I hear what you're saying, but I think they really took me because I was part of a family tradition.'

'That's crap,' she said bluntly. 'I wasn't part of any bloody tradition, was I? And they were fool enough to take me.'

'And you did really well.' He put his head on one side, and looked at her. There was a flicker of admiration in his eyes. 'You were really meant to be here, Maggie. That's the thing. You had the brain for it, estate or no estate. But I don't. My brain isn't up to this. I can't swot my way through finals. I've left it too late for that. And I'm not going to get by on my searing intelligence, am I?'

'Who says your intelligence isn't searing?' She smiled at him warmly. 'You're a very perceptive man, Fabian. I call that intelligence. What you said to me really made me think. Nobody's been quite so brutally honest with me for a very long time.'

He blinked at her, wavering.

'What did I say that was so profound?'

'That you felt used. Not in those words, but that was the gist of it. And that I was labelling myself. That's true too. I *am* a grandmother. That's just a fact and I can't do anything about that.' She paused. She'd had time to reflect. It had been a curious time, passing his words through her head. 'But I am a woman too. And I want to thank you for reminding me of that.'

'A very attractive one,' he added, cautiously. She felt a warm flush in her stomach.

'I want to thank you for seeing me for the person I am, Fabian. Back home, I've always been Pete's wife, or the kids' mother, or Charlotte's granny. It – it's a bit of a shock, to suddenly look at yourself on your own, with no tethers around you holding you down, and try to work out what it is that you are.'

'That's what you've done for me.' He sat up and his eyes gained more life. He leaned towards her. 'I've been trying to explain it to you. You're the only person I've ever been able to be honest with. You don't think I've ever told anyone, anyone at all, about my A levels, do you? Even my mates at school thought I was just being over-cautious, working such long hours. Nobody knew how frantic I was. But now you know. And you don't mind, do you? It doesn't make any difference, because you take me for what I am, money or no money, degree or no degree?' He held her gaze urgently. 'When you look at me, you don't see my family's name, or my posh school, or my bright prospects. You see a man, a young one, perhaps, but a man. One who loves you.'

'Oh, Fabian.' Her fingers drifted to her mouth. She felt breathless. 'You mustn't say that. You've got to be careful.'

'What? That I love you?' He sought for words. 'But that's what I feel. Don't throw it back at me, Maggie. You don't know what I feel. You know how *you* feel, how you see yourself, but how can you possibly know how I see you? You've got to tell me that you don't know that.'

'But . . .' She put her hand in her lap, and tried to hold on to her mug. She could see from the quivering reflection of the light in the surface of the tea that her hands were trembling. 'You see, one day, Fabian, you'll meet somebody, somebody perhaps a little like me, but closer to your own age. I know you think it's irrelevant now.' She held up a hand to stop him interrupting her. 'But in time, you'll understand why it's important. It's not just arithmetic, you see.'

She chewed her lip. Only through writing about Pete, about their marriage, had she begun to understand herself. 'It's about sharing, the same experiences, the same music, remembering the same moments in history.' She looked at him pensively. 'It comes down to the irrelevancies in life. The programmes you watched on the telly, remembering the theme tune to your favourite kids' programme. Who presented *Blue Peter* when the kids were young. What happened at the Red Lion twenty years ago. Where you were when Kennedy was shot – no, don't laugh, Fabian. I mean it. I was young, but I remember it and Pete does too. Who was at number one when you bought your first record, that's the sort of thing you share. You don't realize it's important, but it is.'

She stopped, beseeching him with her eyes.

'And that's more important than anything else, is it?' he said. 'And how often did you and Pete sit down and talk about *Blue Peter* presenters? Daily? Weekly? Once a month?' He threw his hands in the air with impatience. 'Come on, Maggie. You've said enough about Pete for me to get a clear picture of what was going on. He didn't talk to you at all, did he? About anything? Not literature, politics, your feelings about life, or anything. Not even *Blue Peter*. You're kidding yourself about how it was, because you're writing all about him and it's making you nostalgic. I suppose the summers were long and hot and it always snowed at Christmas when you were married to Pete as well?'

'I'm still married to Pete,' Maggie said quietly. Fabian paused for a moment, then leaned forward again.

'You can re-invent the past for yourself, Maggie, but it's not going to change it. If you don't believe me, go back to him. Go back to your estate, and try and carry on as if nothing's happened. I swear to you, you'll last about a week and you'll be back again.'

She held on tightly to her mug, watching him, listening to him in silence.

'You've changed, Maggie, and he hasn't. It doesn't matter that you're back working in a pub at the moment. That's all part of you trying to do just what you did before, to hang on to the past. But it's not there any more. It's not there for you. Only on the pages you're typing. Pete's not there for you any more, Maggie.' He ran a hand over his face and looked away. 'You're on your own now, Maggie. Why don't you just accept it?'

Maggie awoke slowly, wondering what the delightful sensation was that had stirred her from sleep. She was being kissed, softly, preciously and it felt wonderful. She moved a little, and kissed the sweet lips back. Her hand wandered carefully over the firm, strong shoulder to rest on the wide back, brushing over the soft skin. She melted away. Her body felt formless, as if she was drifting on a thick cloud around a warm sky. And her skin still burned from their lovemaking in the night. Again, she felt the weight of him shift over her, crushing her excitingly against the sheets, his body hard against hers.

Fabian pulled his head from hers and her lips grew cold again. Her eyes fluttered open. He looked as if he was listening for something.

The loud hammering on Maggie's door across the corridor came again.

'Bugger it,' he whispered. 'Bloody Naomi. I thought she was staying with Graham last night.'

'Shhh,' she hushed him.

They froze, Maggie tensing her body. They heard Naomi's voice calling through her door, and knocking again. Then they heard Maggie's door being opened. Maggie's eyes were wide open now and dark with fore-boding. Her bed hadn't been slept in. Surely, if Naomi hadn't worked out what was happening before, she would do now. And she'd know where they were. Then Maggie's head shot from the pillow to strain with anguish as she heard a conversation taking place in the hall, right outside their door.

'I'm not sure where she is,' Naomi was announcing casually. 'Did she know you were coming?'

'No,' came a female voice in reply.

Maggie shut her eyes in horror and wriggled under Fabian. He looked down at her with intense concern.

'What is it?' he whispered.

'Jesus, Mary and Joseph on a speedboat.' Her face was as cold and white as snow. 'It's Kay.'

'Who's Kay?' he hissed.

'My bloody daughter!'

'Are you sure?'

'Of course I'm sure, you stupid git.'

They froze again, their bodies locked into rigid immobility, as Naomi next pounded on Fabian's door.

'Fabian?'

They stared into each other's eyes. Fabian's pupils were as black and dilated as Maggie's now, responding to the fear inside her. He raised his eyebrows in an urgent question. What the hell were they going to do?

'Say something,' Maggie mouthed at him. 'Or she'll come in.'

The knocking came again. Maggie twisted her face anxiously. If Fabian didn't utter something, anything at all, even a squeak, which was all he looked capable of, Naomi would stick her head round the door. It was the way she did things and they both knew it. She saw his lips moving, his eyes blank as he fought the fog in his brain.

'Hang on, Naomi,' Maggie called loudly. Fabian twitched in shock on top of her. There was a moment's pause, then the door crashed open, flung wide on its hinges.

'There you are, it's . . .'

Naomi's voice died. Fabian twisted his body round, exposing Maggie beneath him, both of them naked. Maggie saw Naomi's face melt into a blob of expressionless shock. Beside her stood Kay, her daughter, the smile which she had evidently prepared dropping away, her mouth opening to gape at the sight of her mother in a strange bed, pinned down by a lad who bore an uncanny resemblance to Pete Sampras.

'Kay,' Maggie said, sitting up and pulling the edge of the sheet over her breasts. 'I didn't know you were coming. You should have said.'

'Obviously.' Kay's face set like a cliff face.

'Would you close the door please, Naomi?' Maggie continued. 'I don't like to have an audience when I make love.'

'God Almighty!' Kay emitted between her teeth.

'And make Kay a cup of tea, would you, love? I'll be down in a minute. That's if you intend to stay and talk to me, Kay?'

Kay nodded slowly, her mouth a firm line.

'You bet I want to talk to you.'

There was a pause in which nobody moved. Maggie raised her eyebrows at Naomi.

'Naomi? The door, please?'

Naomi jumped. She looked as if she was about to faint, or vomit. She pulled the door closed, and it clicked shut. Maggie waited as she heard the two sets of footsteps make their way down the stairs. She heard the living-room door swing shut behind them. Only then did she breathe out.

'Oh dear,' Fabian muttered, his expression unreadable. 'I don't think Naomi had guessed, do you?'

'No.' Maggie sat up and pulled herself away from Fabian. 'I think that's a safe bet. We obviously over-estimated her.'

'What are you going to do?' He looked worried as he swung his legs over the side of the bed and got up slowly.

'I'm going to have a quick shower, get dressed and go downstairs to talk to my daughter.' She glanced at her watch. 'We overslept, didn't we?'

'That's because you kept me awake all night,' he said, his eyes warm. She sighed at him, pushing a hand through the soft strands of her hair.

'I think you'd better stay up here, if you're in that sort of mood,' she instructed. 'I don't think Kay's going to be able to cope with any more graphic displays of your amorous intentions. I'll get Naomi to bring you up a cuppa.'

'That's if Naomi's still talking to me.'

'Well, if she's going to get virtuous, I'll bring you a cuppa myself,' she said firmly. 'You're not in the doghouse, Fabian. I've just got to think of Kay. She'll only be able to cope with so much at a time.'

'Okay.' He inclined his head. He watched her as she swung from the bed, and pulled on her shirt, the sleeves flopping over her slender wrists. 'Maggie?'

'What, Fabian?'

'You seem – I don't know.' He shook his head at her. 'Calm.'

'Yes,' she replied, thinking. 'I am calm. It's odd, isn't it?'

Maggie took her time to shower thoroughly, and dress in her own room. She put on her jeans. They did fit her and they did look nice on her figure. She really believed that now. She pulled on the bottle-green sweatshirt she'd bought with her college crest on it and sat down at her mirror. Carefully, she applied her make-up in the usual way. She left her hair to dry naturally, swinging it over her shoulders. She wasn't young. She knew that as she looked at herself in the full-length mirror on the back of the door, but she was Maggie. And she felt very good about being Maggie today.

Assured that Fabian was secured in his room, she went down the stairs. She pushed open the door to the living-room. Kay was sitting on the edge of the sofa, a mug in her hand. Naomi was draped on an armchair, a book on her lap. Maggie wondered if they'd said anything to each other at all. Kay was older, at twenty-four, and Maggie knew that she wouldn't think she had anything in common with a girl such as Naomi. The concept of university, of studying, of Oxford, was something Kay wasn't interested enough in to think about. She had a good job as a sales rep, a company car and she had a steady boyfriend who she'd probably marry soon. Even Maggie's voyage of discovery hadn't encouraged her to think beyond her next bonus, or the savings she was collecting to put down on a house.

And she looked so much like Pete with that expression on her face, Maggie thought, that it was uncanny. She had Pete's colouring, his dark brown hair, now winged away from her face in soft waves, his pale eyes and more of his stature than hers. She was a good six inches taller than her mother and she was more angular. Maggie stopped to appreciate that her daughter was looking good and that she was obviously taking care of herself, and that if it wasn't for the pallor in her face brought on by shock, she'd be looking satisfyingly healthy. Her slick trouser suit and her Cuban-heeled shoes looked new. She was doing well, and as her mother, Maggie was pleased. Maggie glanced at Naomi, who was pretending to be engrossed in her book, her face pinched.

'Naomi?' she said softly. 'Haven't you got some work to do upstairs, love?'

'Right.' Standing up abruptly, Naomi left the room, slamming the door closed behind her. Maggie gazed after her. She probably couldn't expect any other reaction. She turned back to Kay. 'I see she's made you tea, then?'

'What's going on?' Kay asked abruptly.

Maggie walked over to the armchair that Naomi had vacated, and sat down.

'I think you know the answer to that.'

'How long has it been going on for?' Kay demanded.

'Oh, a few weeks, I suppose,' Maggie said, trying to remember. 'But I think the undercurrents were there before that.'

'You've got no shame, have you!' Kay declared, shaking her head, the corners of her lips down-turned. 'What do you think you're doing?'

Maggie put her head on one side, and considered Kay's expression. However much she'd feared a confrontation like this, run it through her head and iced over with horror at the thought, it didn't occur to her now to be anything other than honest. And she didn't feel horror, now that it was really happening.

'I think I'm enjoying myself, Kay.'

'Look at you!' She ran her eyes coldly over Maggie's body. 'In jeans and your stupid University top. You think you're young, don't you? Well, you're not. You're old, Mum. It's disgusting. It's – perverted, that's what it is.'

Maggie held her head up and listened. The words bounced off her like boomerangs.

'And what about Dad?' Kay continued. 'What d'you think he'd say if he knew you were shagging that kid?'

'Did your dad think about me? When he started shagging Daphne?' she replied impassively.

'That's different. That's completely bloody different. You left him, didn't you? To go off and do your own thing. He had every right to find happiness wherever he could. But I can see now just what you've been doing. I suppose you've been slagging about ever since you came down here, haven't you? For years, even when you used to go back and visit Dad?'

'Kay.' Maggie linked her fingers together and looked down at them. 'There's so much that you don't understand.'

Kay slammed her mug down on the coffee table beside her. The liquid slopped across the table surface.

'How dare you talk to me as if I don't understand! Who d'you think looked out for Dad while you were swanning about down here, pretending to be a teenager, pretending to be posh? We did. Me, Terry and Jason. Your kids, Mum, remember us? We looked out for him, we cooked for him, had him round to visit, tried to cheer him up. Because you crapped on him, Mum.' She stopped, her cheeks spotted with red. 'You just crapped on him.'

'That's enough,' Maggie said firmly. 'You will not speak to me like that, not here, in my home.'

'This is your home, is it?' Kay glanced around distastefully. 'Well, fine. If this is what you want.'

'In all the time I was here,' Maggie said, looking Kay straight in the eye. 'I was never unfaithful to your Dad. Never. After my course, when I went home, he told me he was seeing Daphne. Our lives went separate ways then, but I was never unfaithful.'

'You really expect me to believe that?' Kay said, shaking back her hair, her lip curling sarcastically. 'After what I've just seen upstairs. God, you were enjoying it, weren't you? That lad, slavering all over you!'

'Yes, I was enjoying it,' Maggie said evenly. 'That's why I was doing it.'

Kay pulled a contorted face, her disgust unconcealed.

'I suppose you can't get a man of your own age. That's why you've got to seduce a boy.'

'He seduced me,' Maggie replied factually. 'He was very insistent about it.'

Kay stood up, teetering on her heels, and looked down her straight nose.

'I don't think I want to hear any more of this. It's revolting. And to think that Dad wanted me to talk to you!'

Maggie looked at her, the mask dropping, her curiosity aroused.

'Dad sent you?'

'No, he didn't *send* me,' she said with emphasis. 'But he

thought if I talked to you, you might get on the phone to him and put him out of his misery. But you've obviously had more important things to do, haven't you, than talk to your own bloody husband.'

'He wants a divorce, Kay,' Maggie said in a hushed voice. 'A divorce.'

'Well, he'll want one now, won't he? When I tell him about this!'

'He wanted one before. He rang me and told me.'

'He didn't know what to do,' Kay said impatiently. 'You don't think he's serious about Daphne, do you? For God's sake, get real, Mum. She's a pain in the arse. He knows that. She was just there for him when you weren't. She's gone back to Brian now. They're moving off the estate, getting a transfer.'

'What?' Maggie stood up. 'I didn't know that. He didn't tell me that.'

'Well, why the hell should he? You've been keeping your own life pretty damned secret, haven't you? Why should he keep you informed about what he's doing?'

'But, but he wants a divorce!' she said stupidly, staring at Kay's face, twisted into ugliness, trying to understand. 'Why does he want a divorce if he's not with Daphne? What's happening, Kay?'

'Why should you care now? Do you know, the poor bastard was even having second thoughts about it? Wondering if you might come home?' Her eyes glittered. 'Poor stupid sod. He's got no idea what you're doing down here, what you're really like.'

'Then—' Maggie's throat constricted, the band across her chest squeezing her rib cage into crushing pain. She held out a hand to Kay, trying to touch her arm. 'You – you mustn't tell him about this. You mustn't tell him what you saw. Do you understand?'

'I'll tell him what I damned well like.' Kay shook her

arm away roughly. 'And if you lie about it, he'll know. I'll tell him everything.' She stopped again, her chest heaving. 'You've blown it, Mum. You might have had a second chance, but you've really blown it. I just think you should be clear about that.'

'Kay?'

Kay reached down to pick up her handbag, tossing the linked chain of the strap over her shoulder. She strode to the door.

'Kay! Where are you going?'

'Home,' she issued, turning to look acidly over her shoulder. '*My* home. Where I belong. At least I still know where I belong.'

'Don't tell Pete!' she cried painfully. 'You can't tell him. Not if he's been having second thoughts. You mustn't. Let me talk to him.'

'Just shut up, Mum,' Kay yelled. 'You're pathetic. And don't you ever, ever try to contact me again. Or Dad. Just go back upstairs and shag your little toy-boy. You've got your own life to live now, so just stay the hell out of ours!'

She stalked out and crashed the door behind her. Maggie heard the front door slam. She stood for a moment, staring after her daughter, then sank back into the armchair, too numb to move. In a moment, she would get up and make herself tea, and take one up to Fabian. In a moment. When the pain across her chest had subsided.

Chapter Sixteen

'What do you think?'

'It's fantastic.' Julia gazed around at the swirls of colour arching across the wall of the underpass. A long strip light set on the concrete ceiling threw a harsh light over the mural, but the daylight streaming in from either end of the tunnel brought out the muted tones of the painting and accentuated the brightness and the joy of it. She shook her head slowly, stepping forward to see the detail more clearly. It had been painted with a bold brush, the characters thick-set and alive, but within the boldness was a fascinating fineness of detail. Behind the figures was an abstract design which filled the wall with activity. Laid over the design, the figures themselves were so real Julia almost felt she could talk to them. They were people she saw every day, at the bus stop, on the street, chatting in the supermarket.

She walked slowly along the wall and stopped to examine the face of an old woman more closely. Something about the face was different, as if she'd been painted with more care and more precision than the others. She turned to Mack.

'This one – who is she? Is it somebody you really know?'

Mack walked up to her and stood beside her, assessing his own work.

'What makes you think that?'

'There's something about her,' Julia pondered, considering the woman's eyes. Something stirred inside her.

There was something very familiar about the face, now that she thought about it. 'It's somebody I've met myself. I'm sure about it. Is she local?'

Mack laughed softly at her elbow.

'You haven't met her, although I wish you could. You'd have liked her, and I think she'd have liked you as well.'

She absorbed his words and finally the penny dropped. She turned to him.

'This is your grandmother, isn't it?'

'The same.' He smiled again, looking wistfully into the one-dimensional, painted face. 'It's only an image of her. I could never capture her spirit in a painting, but it's like her. It's how I remember her, anyway, before she became ill.'

'Oh. But you have captured her spirit, I think,' Julia said assessingly. 'She's like you, isn't she? She's got your eyes.'

'I've got hers, I think. Apparently my mother had them too.'

Julia looked at him. He kept his gaze ahead, as if the painting was drawing him back into his memories.

'Don't you remember your mother, then?'

He shook his head.

'She gave me to Gran to bring up and disappeared. I think she went to Australia with some bloke she met, but nobody was ever very sure. I stayed with Gran until she died.'

'When was that?'

'She was ill for nearly two years, but she died when I was nine.'

Julia looked back at the mural, not wanting to stare at Mack. It was no wonder that his grandmother was so significant to him. She'd been his mother.

'W-what happened then? After your grandmother died?'

He walked away. She sensed him looking over his work, but felt that he wasn't seeing it.

'I went to a home,' he said in a flat voice.

'A children's home?'

'Yeah. Pretty awful place. And I went off the rails, to coin a phrase. I stayed that way for quite a long time.'

'What about your father?'

'Nobody knows who he was. I don't think my mum knew either. I think that's probably why she dumped me on Gran. Can't blame her, really.' He turned back to her suddenly, the light from the end of the underpass silhouetting his tall figure. 'So that's the story of my life.'

She nodded. For a moment, neither of them spoke.

'It's funny, though,' he said, walking towards her again, his voice echoing down the empty tunnel. 'How you picked out my gran. Nobody else has done that. She's in all my paintings, you know. It's not deliberate, but I always find an excuse to put her in. Stupid, isn't it?' He stopped alongside Julia, and looked at the figure again. 'If she'd lived, I'd never be at the class now. She knew I had problems with reading and writing and she did what she could to help me, but after her, nobody noticed. So then I just covered it up, pretended I wasn't interested, bad-mouthed the teachers, you know the sort of thing. That's when I bothered to turn up for classes, which was practically never. So I managed to get through school and out the other side without a single qualification to my name. Pretty clever of me, don't you think?'

He gave Julia a sideways glance. His mouth was smiling but his eyes were expressionless.

'You don't have to answer that,' he said. 'It happens. I'm not the first, and I won't be the last. I'm not making a big deal out of it. Shall we go now?'

Julia lingered a little longer, drinking in the vibrancy around her, then she nodded at Mack and they walked together out of the underpass and up a pitted concrete slope to the road where Mack had parked his motorbike. It was peaceful on the estate, the Sunday atmosphere pervading. Only a handful of people walked past them and the traffic was sporadic. Mack squatted down to unlock a latch below the seat, and unhooked the two crash helmets that were attached. He grinned at her as he handed her back the spare helmet.

'Feeling brave enough for the journey back?'

Julia flushed, taking the crash helmet from him. She'd panicked when Mack had taken her at her word and turned up expecting her to climb on to the machine and be ferried to the underpass.

The previous night, they'd eaten the take-away, talked nonsense and finally adjourned to the main room to watch *Family Fortunes*. Mack had been easy company, and they'd become engrossed in the show, shouting out their own answers and falling about at the contestants' suggestions. It had been fun. Then Mack had insisted on going. She'd been tired and was happy to spend the rest of the evening on her own, before flopping into bed. Before he left, he'd asked her if she meant it when she said she wanted to see his work. She'd assured him that she had and let him out.

Then, late on Sunday morning, while she was standing outside her back door and thinking that it would be a great idea to put some chairs outside and enjoy the spring sun, he had arrived on his motorbike, handed her his spare crash helmet and announced that now was as good a time as any to see the underpass. It had taken him a good half an hour over a cup of tea to persuade her to climb on the back of the bike.

The reality had been totally different from her fears. It was exhilarating to feel the wind battering her face as she tried to look ahead over his shoulder, and as they left her bedsit further and further behind, she'd started to feel quite heady. It hadn't been a long journey, but for a novice like herself, it was far enough.

Now she eyed the flat leather seat again and flicked back the ends of her hair, raising the crash helmet over her head.

'No problem,' she said, immersing herself in a sea of foam padding which smelt of a combination of diesel and fresh air.

'Okay.' He smiled again, tossed his hair away from his eyes and pulled on his crash helmet. His eyes were still smiling at her as he threw a leg over the motorbike, hoisted the machine into an upright position, kicked up the side stand with the heel of his boot and motioned that she should get on behind him. Earlier, she had gripped unsteadily under the seat with the ends of her fingers, but it had felt a bit insecure. Before he flicked the key in the ignition, she called over his shoulder.

'Do you mind if I hold on to you?'

'Be my guest,' he called back.

She tentatively wound her arms around his waist. It struck her that if he was facing the other way, they would be in a passionate clinch. But then, if he was facing the other way, they'd be heading straight for a ditch. They rode for a while, Julia not moving from her position, finding that it felt quite nice to be wedged up against such a broad back and that she felt unexpectedly safe.

He pulled up at a junction, steadying the motorbike as he waited for the traffic to clear. She shifted herself and looked up. A thought suddenly occurred to her.

'Mack?'

'Yes?' He glanced back at her over his shoulder.

'I was just wondering.' She stopped. Would it be an imposition? Yes, it probably would. She shook her head at him. 'No, it's all right.'

'Sure?'

'Yes. Just carry on.'

He nodded and turned back to assess the main road. She had thought that she might ask him if she could be taken to see Elizabeth and her kittens. But that would mean him allowing her to see his home, and although they'd talked about it casually enough before, it couldn't be at her request. He'd have to ask her some time, then she'd go. And at the back of her mind, she was mulling over her weekend with him. He'd been in her own home, seen how she lived, they'd shared a take-away and sat in front of the television together, and today he'd turned up unexpectedly and they'd gone out. She could rationalize each of the experiences, but it added up to spending the weekend in each other's company. When Leo had seemed to be suggesting that they do something similar, she'd turned hot and cold and sweaty all over. She and Mack should be careful. They mustn't intrude on each other's company too much, otherwise the classes would become difficult.

They reached her house and Mack pulled the motorbike into a space outside. She disentangled herself clumsily from the contraption, hopping on to the path, and getting her balance back. The ground felt oddly flat and boring under her feet. Having initially stared at the tiny footpegs on either side of the machine in horror when she'd first climbed on, she'd got used to the feel of them. It had been exciting. She shook herself back into shape. Mack stilled the engine, and climbed off too, taking the helmet from her, and stooping to attach it under the seat. She watched him, her skin tingling.

'Mack? Thanks for that. It was quite an experience, what with one thing and another.'

'Yeah. It was,' he said quietly, keeping his eyes on the latch that he was locking.

'Do you, er, I wondered if you wanted to pop in for a cup of tea.'

'Another one?' He removed his crash helmet, and eyed her quizzically.

'It's just that I was going to put a couple of chairs out the back, as you suggested, and enjoy the sun for a bit. It's up to you.' She hovered, feeling suddenly self-conscious. She was treating him as if he didn't have a life of his own. No doubt he had things to get on with, perhaps arrangements with friends. Or even a girlfriend. She couldn't be sure of anything. And she had reading to do for the classes next week. She just wanted to put off thinking about work for a little longer.

'Well, perhaps just for a bit, then,' he said.

He followed her inside. As she twisted the key in her door, there was a noise upstairs. Annelies's bedsit door swinging shut. They heard footsteps bounding down the stairs towards them and Annelies appeared, looking gorgeous in a flimsy T-shirt and a cut-off pair of denim shorts, her hair plaited like a sumptuous Harvest Festival loaf. But Julia instantly saw that her face was pale, and her eyes were red around the rims.

'I thought it was you,' Annelies burst out. 'I've got to talk to you!'

'Annelies, this is Mack,' Julia said quickly, in case she hadn't noticed the figure standing beside her. 'Er, he was just coming in for a cup of tea. Do you want to join us?'

'Oh.' Annelies looked at Mack, and flushed.

Julia watched her face curiously. Annelies was prone to many expressions, but looking abashed wasn't one of them. Her eyes took on a strange quality, she held out a slim hand to him politely and gave him a shy smile. Julia glanced back at Mack. He inclined his head, a lock of gold hair swinging forwards, and took the small hand in his. His eyes, too, seemed distant. He blinked a little

277

unsteadily, then straightened himself again. After a lingering moment, he looked back at Julia and seemed surprised to find her watching him. He cleared his throat.

'I should be getting off,' he said, inching away towards the front door.

'No.' Annelies and Julia spoke at the same time. Julia frowned at Annelies, wondering if she was purely imagining the fact that Annelies seemed to have perked up since she descended the stairs. 'If Annelies doesn't mind, Mack, let's all have tea together. It's a lovely day to sit in the garden.'

'Oh, yes,' Annelies said energetically. 'And I have to get my legs brown, don't I, Julia?'

Julia gave Annelies's legs a quick appraisal. They may have been lacking in a tan, but they were in perfect shape. Mack was looking at them too, as Annelies had suggested.

Julia quickly opened the door and held it open for the others to follow her. She busied herself with preparing the teapot and some mugs on a tray, while Annelies and Mack organized some chairs and arranged them on the uneven ground in the garden. They left the back door ajar so that the warm, fragrant air would filter through. She waited for the kettle to boil as the two of them sat outside and began a conversation.

'Ah! You see that little cat? He ate my fish!' Annelies said, without any sign of distress. She heard Mack chuckle.

'Julia told me about that. How many fish have you got?'

'I have six,' Annelies bubbled, now seeming quite happy. 'Do you like fish?'

There was a pause. For a dangerous moment, Julia had an instinct that Mack was going to say something like, 'Only with tartare sauce.' She heard the heavy zip of his jacket, and the sounds of him taking it off. Annelies was silent. Julia wondered suddenly if she was appreciating the view of Mack in his nicely fitting white T-shirt. She threw four tea-bags into the pot.

'I like all animals,' Mack replied. 'I've got a cat myself. She's just had kittens.'

'Oh, how sweet!' Annelies exclaimed. Julia poured boiling water into the teapot and stirred it vigorously. 'Perhaps if I show you my fish, you'd show me your little kittens!'

Julia plonked the teapot on to the tray with a clatter.

'Tea's up!' she shouted a little prematurely. She staggered outside with the tray and dumped it down on the grass. She squatted down and set about pouring the tea into the mugs. 'I haven't got any honey I'm afraid, Annelies. Do you just want it black?'

'No.' Annelies leaned back in her chair, stretching out her legs, and puffing out her chest. Julia realized with horror that she wasn't wearing a bra, and that two pert nodules had appeared through the thin material of her T-shirt. 'I think today I will do things the English way. Why not? I'll have what you have, Julia.'

'Fine.' Julia passed around the mugs, noting that Mack didn't meet her eye as he took his and sat back, and that Annelies stopped to pull her plait back around her shoulder so that the glossy strands sat prettily over her collar bone, before taking her mug. Julia set the free chair as straight as possible on the lumpy grass and sat down, clutching her mug. They were all vaguely facing towards the end of the garden and as Julia sipped her tea she realized that the blotchy black mess which was left over from the sacrificial bonfire was still very much in evidence.

'Did you want to talk to me about something, then, Annelies?' She relaxed into her chair.

'First, I will enjoy the sun and the company,' Annelies announced. 'Then I will tell you about the terrible thing that has happened.'

It couldn't be that terrible, Julia deduced, if it could wait until the sun and the company had been enjoyed. She remembered the red-rimmed eyes and the expression of need when they'd first arrived, but now Annelies seemed quite happy. She felt a little less sympathetic.

'Annelies is studying rocks,' she told Mack. 'And she climbs up and down things in her spare time.'

Annelies gurgled a laugh.

'I'm a geologist,' she corrected. She opened her wide blue eyes to Mack. 'I like to climb things. Do you climb things?'

Julia felt an odd thud in her stomach. Her imagination was definitely on over-drive. Either that, or Annelies was making a suggestive remark. But then, it could be losing something in translation.

'I stick to riding things,' Mack replied equally obliquely.

'And what do you ride? Horses?'

'No, the motorbike's mine. You might have heard it when we pulled up.'

Annelies sat forward.

'That wonderful machine? That is yours? But that must be so exciting. When I was younger, I had a boyfriend who had a Harley Davidson. They are so much more fun than cars, aren't they?'

'Yeah. They are. Mine's a Suzuki, one of the GS series, if that means anything to you.'

'Not really.' Annelies sat back again, pouting prettily. 'But you could show me your machine, couldn't you?'

Julia now felt decidedly hot under her shirt. She undid a further button, and allowed the neck to rest open, aware that perhaps a small glimpse of her cleavage would be visible. She couldn't compete with the pert nodules, but she did have a pair of breasts too, and it was irritating her that every time Annelies bounced backwards and forwards on her chair, her neat breasts bounced in perfect rhythm. Ungenerously, Julia had concluded that it was the main reason for her sudden transformation into the human metronome. There could be no question about it any more. Annelies was flirting with Mack, and if Mack was too naïve to see it, she wasn't.

'We went out on the motorbike this morning,' Julia said casually. 'It's fantastic.'

'Glad you enjoyed yourself,' Mack said, flicking Julia a glance as she fingered her neckline and briefly exposed the white scalloped edge of her bra cup, allowing her cotton shirt to fall modestly back into place.

'Would you take me for a ride one day?' Annelies asked. 'When you are not so busy, perhaps?'

'Sure, why not?' Mack smiled. 'I don't see why not, do you, Julia?'

'No.' Julia blinked back her neutrality. 'You could take Annelies to see your little kittens at the same time, couldn't you?'

He paused, sipping his tea and holding Julia's uncertain gaze, before answering.

'I thought perhaps you might like to come round and see them some time. They're growing very quickly. Their eyes are open already. It's worth seeing them before they change.'

'Me?' Julia laughed. 'I don't know if I'll have time, I'm afraid. I've got some teaching work lined up, and . . .' She thought hard. 'Things.'

'Things?'

'Yes, things,' she said firmly. Mack shrugged, and

looked back at Annelies. 'Any time you're free, just let me know.'

'We could go today. Perhaps this evening?' Annelies sat forward again, body jiggling. 'If it is to be so sunny, that would be nice, wouldn't it? If you have no plans with Julia, of course.'

'No.' Julia waved her hand dismissively. 'No plans.'

'Then we could ride out into the country.' Annelies gained enthusiasm. 'When the sun is setting and the fields are pretty. What do you think?'

'Okay.' Mack laughed softly. 'I don't mind.'

'What about the terrible thing that has happened?' Julia asked politely. 'Don't you want to tell me about that?'

'Oh, it is Stig.' Annelies slumped back in her chair, and pointed her eyelashes at the rim of her mug. She did look genuinely downcast now. 'I don't know if I even want to think about it.'

'What's he done?' Julia softened her voice. Now Annelies seemed unaware that Mack was also listening, despite the fact that he was gazing over at the blossoming cherry and appeared to be transfixed by it. Annelies turned her eyes to Julia and she saw that tears were welling there.

'He – he telephoned me. And he said that he is going to prosecute me.'

'Prosecute you? For what, for God's sake? You haven't done anything wrong!'

'For burning his things.' Annelies sounded choked. 'He said it wasn't legal, what we did, and that he will have me sent to prison for it.'

'What a load of balls!' Julia stuck her mug down on the grass and sat up stiffly. 'He's got a bloody nerve, after what he did to you!'

'I don't want to go to prison.' Annelies's eyes rounded with sorrow.

'You won't go to prison. He's just threatening you,' she said firmly. 'And in any case, if anyone's going to take the rap for this, it'll be me. It was *my* suggestion and I told him as much when he was here, so he's got no right to take it out on you. He's just being a nasty coward. Don't you worry about it.'

'But . . .' Annelies swallowed. 'He said that he's seen a solicitor and they've told him that he can do this. He said I damaged his things deliberately and that he can prosecute me. He says I am just a criminal.'

'And he's just making empty threats,' Julia told Annelies confidently. 'He can't do that, I'm sure of it. You're not a criminal, Annelies, any more than I am.'

She paused. Annelies took a tremulous mouthful of her tea, looking unconvinced. Mack shifted in his chair, reminding Julia that he was absorbing the exchange.

'Julia?' he said quietly. 'Why don't you ask Leo about it? You said he was a lawyer, didn't you?'

She stared at him, computing his suggestion. She shook her head.

'There's no need. Stig's just bluffing. There's nothing he can do about this.'

'Are you sure?' He asked the question softly, without alarm, and his words drifted over to her on the breeze. She frowned at him, thinking hard. No, she wasn't sure, but it seemed so ridiculous, so unfair. After all that Annelies had been put through, it surely couldn't be legal for Stig to throw this at her as well? Mack gazed at her steadily. He was so calm, she had to consider the possibility that he was right. She didn't know the law. What if she was wrong? She expelled a long, exasperated breath.

'No, I'm not sure. But I do know that if anyone's going to be prosecuted for anything at all, it's going to be me, not Annelies. That's only fair.'

'But he doesn't hate you!' Annelies whined. 'He hates me! It is me he wants to have in court.'

'Then we'll put him off that course of action straight away. Perhaps if he realizes that you're not going to be hurt by what he does, he'll forget about it. If he rings again, you must tell him that you had nothing to do with it. I bet you he'll drop it straight away.'

'But . . .' Annelies sniffed nobly. 'I can't afford to defend myself. I haven't got any money left and I had to buy some new trainers because the others were burnt.' She stuck her feet out prettily to display the new trainers. 'And that was the rest of the money I had.'

'I can lend you some money,' Julia said. No, you can't, a voice returned in her head, because you haven't got any. It was irrelevant, Julia decided. She must say whatever she could to stop Annelies from fretting. 'And if it'll make you feel better, I'll speak to somebody I know who's a lawyer. He'll be able to advise me.'

'Yes, please,' Annelies said meekly. 'Please find out from your lawyer. I don't think we really know whether Stig can do this or not, do we?'

Julia pursed her lips and nodded in assent. It was a disconcerting turn of events, most of all because it meant that she would have to initiate contact with Leo again, and after their lunch together she wasn't sure how she felt about that. What if he graciously gave her advice, then decided that she owed him something in return? Wouldn't she herself feel that she owed him something – another dinner? A peck on the lips? Her hand in marriage? Nevertheless, she'd have to do it, for Annelies's sake, and after all, she had got her into this mess in the first place.

'I'll deal with it, don't worry. And if Stig rings you again, just give him my number, and I'll deal with him.'

'Thank you.' Annelies sniffed, and sat back again,

gazing at Julia with gratitude. 'You are very brave, aren't you?'

'Brave?' Julia echoed in surprised. 'No, I'm not brave at all.'

'Yes.' Annelies nodded, flicking her plait over her shoulder. 'Stig can be very frightening, when he's angry, but you're not scared of him, are you?'

'No, I'm not scared of Stig.' Julia smiled.

Fleabag distracted them by leaping on to Annelies's lap, and flopping down to wash his paws, as if her bare legs were an ideal venue. She patted his head. Julia watched her. She herself thought of Annelies as brave. Julia could never go pot-holing, or mountaineering, or sky diving, or whatever it was Annelies spent her life doing. She'd even quailed at the thought of sitting on Mack's motorbike, even though the seat was as wide as a park bench and he was undoubtedly an experienced rider. There were other things that Julia was afraid of, although the counsellor was helping her to unravel the knots. But Annelies could have no way of knowing that. If Bill himself walked through her door, Julia would shake like a leaf, but Stig was a different matter. He had no power over her feelings.

Before long, Annelies set down her mug and announced that she would go to the faculty to spend the afternoon working.

'You will come back here at seven, to collect me, yes?' she said to Mack. Julia felt an odd qualm in her stomach again. She'd wondered if Annelies might have forgotten the suggestion in the face of her other preoccupations. Mack inclined his head and gave her a small smile.

'If you say so. You'll have to wear jeans and a thick jacket and gloves, if you've got them.'

'On such a beautiful day?' Annelies sparkled. 'I want

to feel the wind against my skin, so I can wear my shorts, can't I?'

'I'm afraid I wouldn't let you near the bike dressed like that,' Mack directed pleasantly. 'You have to think about how your skin would feel if somebody pulled out on me unexpectedly, and you ended up sliding down the road on it. Sorry to be blunt, but you have to be prepared, otherwise it's no ride.'

'Oh.' Annelies looked crestfallen for a moment, but she cheered up. 'Well, you know what you are doing, don't you? I'll feel safe with you. Seven, then.'

She bounced away, Julia turning her eyes from the jiggling breasts, although she wasn't convinced that Mack had done the same. They heard the door close as Annelies let herself out of Julia's bedsit, then Mack stretched his legs and let out a long breath, gazing out across the sunny garden.

'She seems like a nice person,' he said, putting his head back, closing his eyes and absorbing the rays of sun on his face.

'She's all right,' Julia said. 'You seemed to get along very well.'

'Yeah,' he said, not opening his eyes. 'We did, didn't we?'

Julia silently picked up her mug and drank the remaining lukewarm slops of tea, peering at Mack as she did. His face was composed, neutral, almost as if he was asleep, but she guessed that he was passing quite lively images across his brain.

'She went out with Stig for a long time, you know,' she told him. 'Over five years. It's only just finished, and I think she's still in shock.'

'Ah,' Mack said under his breath.

'I think she might be on the rebound,' she suggested tentatively. He opened his eyes sleepily and cast her a look from under his lashes. Dark lashes, she noticed, despite his fair hair, and the sun was slanting into his irises, making them look very blue.

'Are you warning me off?' he asked in a lazy voice.

She sat up straight and edged forward on her chair, keeping her voice low.

'I'm just telling you that she's been very upset. It's not surprising if she's being a bit—' She stopped, trying to think of a suitable word.

'A bit what?'

'A bit – friendly.'

'Ah,' he said, still watching her through half-closed eyes. 'Friendly.'

'Yes,' she continued sincerely. 'And I think she's a bit confused. I think that's why she was . . .' The words stuck in her throat again. 'I think she was flirting with you, Mack. So that's all I'm saying.'

'That's very observant of you,' he said mildly. 'I thought so too.'

She cast him a sharp glance. He seemed quite unperturbed.

'So I'm just saying that you should be careful, that's all.'

'Okay,' he said. 'I'll be careful. Anything else?'

She looked at him, wondering why she couldn't voice what she was feeling. She didn't want Mack to take Annelies out on his motorbike, or to take her home to see Elizabeth's little kittens. But she couldn't simply open her mouth and say that. It would sound – odd.

'Julia?' Mack sat up, and put down his mug. 'Is there some reason why you don't want me to take Annelies out on the bike tonight?'

She glanced at him, wide-eyed.

'Of course not,' she said, more curtly than she intended. 'There's no earthly reason why you shouldn't, is there? I just thought I should tell you that she might be a bit unpredictable. I shouldn't take what she says too seriously at the moment.'

He frowned at her.

'What do you think she might say to me, then?'

'I've got no idea.' Julia got up quickly, gathered her mug and Annelies's and put them back on the tray. Mack stood up too, stretched like a cat that had just woken up after a snooze, and reached for his jacket.

'Thank you for the tea, Julia. Do you want me to wash these things up?'

'I can manage.' Julia walked ahead of him back into the kitchen. 'I've got all day to do it, haven't I?'

She dumped the tray and ferried the mugs over to the sink, turning the tap on so that it splashed loudly against the plastic bowl. She tried to stop herself from acting like a sulky child, but it was so difficult. She couldn't even understand why she felt sulky.

'Well, I'll be off then. Thanks for coming to see the wall.'

She turned round and forced a smile.

'I'm glad you showed it to me.' Then, as he reached her door, his jacket slung over his shoulder, she added, 'Perhaps you should show it to Annelies as well?'

He nodded slowly, his eyes unreadable as they held hers. She bit her lip firmly to stop herself from ejecting any more nonsensical remarks and widened her smile to look magnanimous.

'Have a nice time tonight.'

'I'll give you a call about the painting, shall I?' he said.

'My room? Yes, why don't you do that? I'm busy teaching during the day next week, but apart from that, you can come and do it when you want.'

'And don't forget to ring Leo, will you?'

'I won't,' she said.

She kept up her smile until he had let himself out. Then she crashed the mugs into the sink and plunged her hands into the hot water, staring out the window at the three empty chairs. What if Annelies really was on the rebound? What if they went out together and things developed? What if they ended up in bed together? She fixed her eyes on the white cherry blossom splattered over the twigs. What would Annelies think of Mack, sexually? Would he be a good lover? Was he as attractive without his clothes on as he was in them?

She blinked at the tree, her throat tight. She had allowed herself to think of him as a man. Not as a subject she was teaching in her class, somebody who needed her help, but as a man, in all three dimensions. And she found him attractive. She let her breath go and stirred the soapy water around with her fingers, wallowing in the sensation. What of it?

He mustn't ever suspect that she'd started to think about him in this way. And now that he had met Annelies, his attention would be diverted elsewhere. She should be encouraging them to see each other, not throwing cold water on the idea. It would be safer all round if she stopped thinking about him completely. He could finish off her walls, but apart from that, they'd better stick to meeting in the class.

And in any case, she had to ring Leo now. If she was going to think about a man at all, it should be him. Wasn't he the one, after all, who had expressed interest in getting to know her? Hadn't he made it plain enough that he wanted a relationship? She pondered for a moment, filling the mugs with water and tipping it back into the bowl. Then she wiped her hands on a tea towel, and wandered through to find Leo's telephone number.

Chapter Seventeen

A pair of heavily mascaraed eyes blinked at Julia across the desk.

'What do you mean? I thought Cathy loved Heathcliff?'

'Yes,' Julia said carefully, fingering her copy of *Wuthering Heights*. 'But what sort of love is it, do you think?'

'It's, er . . .' The girl tailed away, paused to pick a blob of eyeshadow from the corner of her eye, shook back her hair and settled back to think. She stared down at the opened copy of the book on the desk. 'It's quite strong.'

'Yes. Anything else?'

'Er, she doesn't really love Edgar. That's because she really loves Heathcliff.'

Julia nodded, gently shifting herself on the hard, wooden chair. It had been a long session. A furtive glance at her watch told her that they had ten minutes to go. Ten long minutes. Like many of the revision students she had taught, Harriet was in front of her because her parents thought it was a great idea, not because she particularly wanted to spend her Easter holiday considering the merits of Emily Brontë. They had just about got to grips with the opening chapters in the last hour and fifty minutes, but Harriet was pretty weak on anything that she hadn't read in the slim revision guide which Julia had spotted wedged in her bag. Julia was becoming gradually more convinced that she hadn't actually read the novel.

She couldn't blame her. There were far more inter-esting things to do at seventeen. Julia herself had found it impossible to settle into her A levels, and having scraped through them had fallen into the first job which would pay for her to move away from home. Perhaps in another five years, Harriet would pick up *Wuthering Heights* and read it because she wanted to. Perhaps in ten years she'd fly off to university as a mature student. And then she might end up sitting opposite a seventeen-year-old in a revision college, wondering what on earth it had all been about. Julia suppressed a sigh. In the small room, the air was still and she could tell that Harriet's optimum concentration level had peaked and disappeared, although it was difficult to pinpoint the moment when it had happened.

'How do we know that Heathcliff *does* love Cathy?' Julia persevered, trying to look wide awake. 'Does he actually say so?'

'He kisses her.' Harriet brightened, sitting forwards. 'On the moors, and the sky's a reflection of their love for each other, as passionate as the kiss they share.'

'Not bad.' Julia smiled. 'Which version of the film have you seen? Just don't tell me you're basing your analysis on the musical, please.'

Harriet looked indignant for a moment, then slumped again.

'How do you know I've seen the film?'

'Ah!' Julia tapped the side of her nose. 'Read the novel and then you'll find out.'

'But Joseph says that the baby's got Heathcliff's eyes,' Harriet protested, her eyes narrowing. 'So they must have kissed, mustn't they?'

'Oh dear.' Julia sighed aloud. 'I suppose you'll have worked out from the revision notes that Cathy dies about half-way through? You're not going to get many marks in the exam if you start proclaiming about the final dramatic scene on Cathy's deathbed.'

'Shit, does she?' Harriet looked startled.

'It's all in the book,' Julia said, giving Harriet a wry look. 'You haven't got much time, I know, but you're going to have to read it.'

Harriet put on a disgruntled face, picking up the novel and flicking through the pages.

'But there's so much of it. I've got loads to do before the exams.'

'Well, I can give you some tips, but your examiner's going to be able to tell if all you do is spout from the revision notes. They do read them as well, you know.' Harriet looked suitably horrified. 'Why don't we finish up now, and you go off and read what you can before tomorrow.'

'But I'm going out tonight,' Harriet said woefully.

'Not any more,' Julia decided. 'Get as far as you can, and we'll talk about your impressions tomorrow.'

'At least tell me which chapter to read up to?'

'Absolutely not.' Julia shook her head. 'Let's see what happens.'

'Tell me how it really ends, then?'

'That, at least, you can get from your guide,' Julia said with assumed patience. 'All I'm going to say is that it's very romantic and worth reading on for.'

Harriet crashed her bag on to the table in response, shoving her pad and book inside, her face set into a sulk. Quite a pretty face, Julia thought, but ruined by her current expression. She waited quietly while Harriet threw her bag over her shoulder and stomped out of the teaching room. The door swung shut behind her.

'Bye then,' Julia muttered under her breath. 'Thicko.'

She gathered her own notes together and packed them away, pushing her biro back into her handbag. Harriet probably wasn't thick, just distracted. And Julia's remit was to bung as much information into her brain as humanly possible during the intensive week. The head of English at the school would be horrified that she'd actually sent a student away to read the text. Earlier in the day, she had suggested to one of her other students, in reply to a bluntly posed question from him, that it was actually fucking possible to understand Chaucer, and that reading *The Wife of Bath's Tale* was probably his best option if he wanted to survive the exam. She'd thought he was going to faint. It wasn't what she was supposed to do at all, and Harriet's reaction had been depressingly predictable, but the alternative was to monologue at her for nearly two hours a day while she wrote down her comments verbatim. It would hardly make Harriet a better student. Thank God the first day was over, though, and she had survived.

Julia slipped away from the school without encountering any of the other tutors and out into St Giles. It was another fine afternoon and she decided that she would walk home. She stopped to cross the wide road and wondered whether Maggie would be at home. It was a short bus ride up to Summertown, but she hadn't spoken to Maggie for some time. They hadn't phoned each other recently either, which was quite unusual. Julia knew that she herself had been preoccupied. There had been Leo, and the end of term at the class, and now the revision course to prepare for. And there had been Mack too. All thoughts of Maggie had fled her mind.

She hovered on the pavement. Maggie had once said that sometimes even your closest friends had to be shut out while you pieced your head back together in the right order. That was probably what Julia had been doing to Maggie recently, but could Maggie have possibly been doing the same thing to her? Julia turned towards the town and began to walk home. She would ring Maggie soon and find out how she was.

As she was nearing home, Julia decided to take a detour and stopped off on the main road to see Mr Hussain.

'You are looking lovely, my dear,' he said, brown eyes widening at the sight of her smart clothes.

'The truth is, I'm bushed,' she said, placing an assortment of unwanted items on to his counter and picking up a newspaper. 'I'm teaching again. Rewarding, but hard work. And sometimes, just hard work.'

'Like my business.' He grinned, piling her items into a thin plastic bag.

'I don't suppose you've managed to talk to your wife again, have you?' she asked, pulling out her purse.

'Now, I think I am getting somewhere,' he said, nodding expressively. 'She has met another lady who has also been to a class like this.'

'Not Shirani?'

'No, it's a cousin of hers who she hasn't seen for a very long time. They talked about it and I think perhaps she might come. But I may have to come with her.'

'It might be better if you don't,' Julia suggested politely. 'She could be a bit inhibited if you're there, don't you think?'

'But Miss Cole—' Mr Hussain leaned forward and whispered over the counter to her. 'I think I need a little help as well.'

'Oh.' She blushed stupidly, and nodded eagerly to show that she understood. 'Please do come, both of you. Ring the number I gave you and somebody will talk to you about it.'

He cleared his throat and poked the till as several people came into the shop. She paid, took her bag and gave him a broad smile as she left. He had already turned to rearrange the shelves behind him.

She ground to a halt behind Mr Henderson as she turned into her street. The pavement had been successfully demolished and a deep trench now ran alongside a narrow strip left for pedestrians. It looked as if a giant mole had attacked the path in the night. She found herself putting out her hands to either side, ready to catch him as he teetered dangerously near the edge of the trench. A car screeched past them and as Mr Henderson stared after it, his trajectory changed to head straight for the hole in the ground.

'Mr Henderson!' she exclaimed quickly, diving to the side of him.

'Eh?' He twisted round in shock and teetered the other way, falling against a thick hedge and remaining safely wedged at an angle in the twigs. Julia lost her balance, slipped over the edge of the hole, and stuck one leg into it up to the knee. Her polished shoe was greeted with a wet squelch and a cold sensation.

Mr Henderson watched her with startled eyes as she smiled sweetly, pulled her leg gauchely back on to pavement level, and stood in front of him with one leg stockinged and elegant, the other looking like a well muddied golf-club.

'How are you?' she asked loudly.

He looked down at her brown foot and back at her face. Then he heaved himself out of the hedge, and fell forward into her arms.

'I'll see you home,' she announced. 'These pavements aren't safe. You've got to be very careful.'

'What's that?' he yelled down at her from his rug of hair.

'Be careful!' she bellowed.

'You should be careful,' he shouted at her, looking at her foot again. 'These pavements are dangerous!'

'Yes. Let's get you home.'

She saw him to his front door, waved him inside and plodded on home, her foot making a disgusting noise as it slid in and out of her shoe. If one of those workmen had the nerve to call her sweetheart again, she'd follow Shirani's advice and head for the goolies with the garden shears. She stopped as she reached her front path. There was a very smart car parked outside her house. She had a closer look, her pulse rattling. It was a Rover and she had an ominous feeling that it was Leo's. She'd left him a message about Annelies, but he hadn't got back to her yet. He wouldn't just turn up, surely? She peered into the window of the car, her stomach vaulting over. She was sure it was his, but he was nowhere to be seen. Perhaps he'd gone for a walk, or a pint at the local, while he waited for her to come back? Or perhaps he'd got out of the wrong side of the car and disappeared into the workmen's trench?

She let herself in to the hall, and stopped as she reached her door. She could hear voices from upstairs. Annelies. Annelies and ... Stig? No, too friendly. Annelies and Mack? She stiffened, trying to eavesdrop. The voice was too dark to be Mack's. She felt a flicker of relief. Perhaps she'd invited a friend home from the faculty. That was her business, she thought, pushing open her door. Then she stopped as she heard a male laugh.

Annelies and Leo. There was no question about it. She held on to her key and turned to tromp up the stairs, her shoe farting at her with every step. Annelies must have heard the bell and let him in, or found him on the doorstep. Either way, if he was responding to their call for legal aid, he'd reached his intended destination. She paused as she was about to rap on Annelies's door and listened. They had gone quiet, probably because they'd heard a noise which sounded like somebody blowing raspberries outside. She knocked.

'Come in!' Annelies called robustly.

She opened the door. It was indeed Leo, looking official but handsome in a dark suit and tie. It made his hair look very dark, almost black, and his eyes were striking as he glanced up at her. She felt an incongruous flutter of shyness on seeing him again, coupled with acute embarrassment that one of her legs was plastered with mud. He was sitting on one of the stools in the kitchen, next to a mug of black coffee. Annelies was perched on a stool opposite him. She swung her ponytail around her head as she greeted Julia cheerfully.

'I found your lawyer waiting in his car when I came home,' she said. 'So I have given him coffee.'

'He's not *my* lawyer,' Julia corrected a little brusquely. 'Hello, Leo, how are you?'

'Fine. Enjoying coffee as nature intended. I got your message and as I was free this evening I decided to drive up.'

'I see. Well, you've met Annelies, so hopefully she's been telling you about her problem. What do you think she should do?'

Both Annelies and Leo looked at Julia with an element of surprise. She wondered what she'd said. She supposed perhaps she'd been businesslike to the point of rudeness in her welcome and cursed herself. She slipped her bag from her shoulder and tried again with a smile.

'It's very kind of you to drive all this way.'

That must have been it. Annelies brightened and jumped from her stool to collect a cup from the draining board for Julia. She poured thick liquid into it from a glass cafetière.

'We have been talking so much, but not once about my problem,' she announced happily, handing Julia the cup. Julia looked at it suspiciously. 'Sit down, here, on this stool.' Annelies patted the stool next to her.

'You look so smart today, Julia, doesn't she, Leo?'

'Er, have you got any kitchen roll, or some tissues?' Julia said. 'It's just that my foot's covered in mud, and I'd better get it off before I smear it all over your kitchen.'

'I don't mind mud,' Annelies said, finding a roll of paper and handing it to Julia. 'I like to get covered in mud. It's fun.'

'Yes.' Julia perched on the edge of the stool, and cleared most of the mud away from her shoe. Her tights would just have to stay wet and diarrhoea-brown until she could get them off. 'I had great fun falling into the hole in the pavement. I laughed till I cried.'

As she was cleaning her shoe, she hoisted her leg on to her knee, revealing several inches of slim thigh. The job finished, she handed the lump of soggy tissue back to Annelies who dropped it in her bin without a word of complaint. Then Julia noticed that Leo was looking at her legs. A warm flush crept over her cheeks as he looked up at her.

'It's the first time I've seen you in a skirt,' he said. 'It suits you.'

'It's supposed to be worn without the mud.' Julia picked up her cup, wondering why his attention bothered her. She had legs, she just didn't choose to use them very often. Although many of the tutors at the college did turn up in jeans, Julia had decided that she needed to start from the outside and work her way in. Wearing a skirt and jacket was a blatant self-confidence boost, and she'd chosen her bright red jacket to make sure that any lingering self-doubts were chased away. She was glad she was smart now. It made it easier to pit herself against Leo. 'So anyway, Leo, why aren't you working all hours, like you usually do?'

'The case finished unexpectedly early, as I was telling Annelies. I got the gist of your problem, and thought I'd come up and find out more about it.'

'The personal touch,' Julia said. 'Do all your clients get such an attentive bedside manner?'

He raised a dark eyebrow at her and she swallowed her words. Why was she talking about beds? The flush in her cheeks grew warmer.

'I wouldn't mind a lawyer at my bedside.' Annelies laughed, touching the back of Leo's hand. 'But I wouldn't be able to afford twenty-four-hour service.'

Julia looked at her in amazement, then looked at Leo. He was smiling back at Annelies. What had got into Annelies recently? She seemed to be using every man who walked through the door for target practice. Julia hardly wanted to see her in widow's weeds, but shouldn't she be displaying a little more grief than this? A coy smile here and there would be enough to demonstrate that she wasn't going to suffer any permanent damage on account of Stig. She didn't have to get off with every man that Julia introduced her to.

'I can always arrange a concession,' Leo said drily, and Julia gulped a mouthful of what tasted like melted tar and instantly suffered a timely choking fit. As she choked, Annelies collected a glass of water and stuck it on the table under her nose.

'Drink this,' she instructed.

Julia nodded and, eyes streaming, swished the water around her mouth to dislodge the grit stuck to her palate. 'I'm all right,' she said huskily, holding out her hand to dispel alarm. Judging from the way that Annelies's eyes had swivelled straight back to Leo, the alarm was not severe.

'So, how long have you been here, Leo?' Julia croaked at him.

He glanced at a bulky wristwatch. 'About an hour, now. Time flies, doesn't it?'

'When you're having fun,' Annelies finished for him. 'I know that expression. You people have so many expressions that I find difficult, but I know that one.'

'But your English is excellent,' Leo said sincerely. 'It must be, to be writing a thesis in the language.'

'Yes, in Holland we all speak English very well,' Annelies said factually. 'We have to, because nobody speaks Dutch. Apart from you, Leo. You're the first Englishman I've met who can speak my language. I mean, properly, not just well enough to find marijuana in Amsterdam.'

'You speak Dutch?' Julia almost shouted in surprise.

'Yes,' he replied calmly.

'You never told me that!' she accused.

'You never asked,' he parried.

'You're not just saying that?' she said, and regretted it instantly. It sounded ridiculous.

'Why? Just to impress your friend?' Leo gave a low laugh. 'My mother's Dutch, but I don't suppose you ever talked to Robert about it either, did you? She's back living in Amsterdam now.'

'I haven't talked to Rob much at all,' she replied a little defensively. It was annoying for him to bring Rob up again, almost as if he was reminding her that he hadn't been her first choice of escort.

'Robert speaks Dutch too, but not as well as I do,' he said, unhindered by modesty. 'We were brought up there when we were young, but we moved to England when I was about ten. Robert was only four then. He didn't go to school in Holland.'

'But Leo did!' Annelies informed Julia. 'And I know the school that he went to. Isn't that incredible?'

'Not really, seeing as you come from Amsterdam,' Julia said flatly. 'So I suppose you were talking Dutch then, before I came in?'

'Mine's a little rusty,' Leo said, now looking as if modesty had occurred to him. 'And Annelies insisted on using her English.'

'Yes, I need to speak it all the time,' Annelies nodded. 'I have to be sure that my thesis isn't full of mistakes.'

'But I've told you before, I'll proof-read it for you,' Julia protested, increasingly feeling forgotten.

'Leo has offered too!' Annelies smiled. 'Aren't I lucky? Perhaps I should ask Mack as well, then I will have three brains to help me.'

'No, don't ask Mack,' Julia said quickly.

'Why not?'

'Just – just trust me. Don't ask him to read your thesis, please.'

Annelies looked at Julia in confusion, then her eyes cleared. 'Ah, I know what it is.' She paused to pat Leo's hand again. Julia watched in fascination. Annelies looked deeply into Leo's eyes. 'This friend of yours is seeing a man called Mack. And he is seeing her. But neither of them have said anything to each other about love. Isn't that typically English?'

'Annelies!' Julia exclaimed.

'No, no.' Annelies wagged her finger at Julia. She turned back to Leo. 'Julia doesn't want me to ask him to read my thesis. And she didn't want me to see his little kittens. I know. She didn't tell me, but I know why. No, Julia, be quiet. I know you people don't tell anybody what you're feeling, even your good friends. But Leo,' she shook her head at him. 'What do you do with a woman like this?'

'Annelies, you don't understand,' Julia began.

'And she has had dinner with this man,' Annelies continued to tell Leo happily. 'He took her out to The Bath Place Restaurant. It's in the town, Leo, and it is very expensive, and then she was so drunk, she let her cat eat

301

my fish. The next day, she told me about the dinner and I asked her if she would have sex with this man.'

'Annelies! Stop right now!' Julia leaned forward urgently. Annelies brushed her aside.

'English, English! You think sex is something you do in the dark with your socks on. Sex is nothing to be ashamed of, is it Leo?'

Leo flashed Julia a glance. She had paled beyond recognition, and had now resigned herself to staring bleakly into her cup of melted tar.

'So,' Annelies bubbled on. 'She said, no, she would not have sex with this man, never, ever. So I thought, what sort of man is it, that she doesn't want to have sex with?'

'Oh God.' Julia put her head in her hands.

'And then, I met the man. He came round on his motorbike and we had tea, out there in the garden. And he is a gorgeous man, I have to tell you that, Leo. Quite beautiful, and with very good shoulders and deep eyes, like a river. And then I knew.'

'What did you know?' Leo asked casually.

'That she was in love!' Annelies announced triumphantly. 'And after I had been out on his motorbike and seen his kittens and his paintings, I knew that he was in love too.' She nodded her head to make the point. 'So there it is. I think it's the English way, to sleep with people you don't like and to be a virgin with people you are in love with, isn't it? You must tell your good friend, Leo, that she mustn't be repressed like this, she must let this man into her life. Don't you think?'

'Oh God, Annelies, you've got it all wrong,' Julia moaned into her fingers. She waited with her eyes closed for Leo to denounce Annelies's account, and to explain that he was in fact the man who had taken her to dinner, the man who she had fervently announced that she would never have sex with. She should have told

Annelies that Mack was not the same man who had wined and dined her, but it was too late now. Leo would say something instead. She waited and nothing happened. She peered through her fingers. Leo was watching her with an expression of interest.

'Julia?'

'What,' she replied ungraciously.

'Don't you think you should listen to Annelies? She seems to have everything worked out for you.'

Julia plucked her fingers from her face, and gave Annelies a tired look.

'I'm sorry, but you've really made a mistake, Annelies. There's nothing between me and Mack. And when I went out to dinner it was—'

'Interesting, I'm sure,' Leo interrupted bluntly. 'But I still wonder if Annelies might not be right, Julia? After all, your friends usually know what's best for you, don't they?'

Julia stared across the table at Leo. Was he being sarcastic? He looked fairly genuine, but how could he be? Only a short time ago, he'd been suggesting that they'd make a good couple. If she'd agreed with him, they could be out choosing mobiles for the nursery by now.

'But—'

'And only somebody who cared about you like Annelies would try to be so helpful, surely?'

Annelies beamed at Julia, happy with Leo's response.

'Yes, you're a good friend, Annelies,' Julia said automatically, her emotions heaving. 'Thank you for your insights. However, I have to tell you that neither Mack nor I feel that way about each other, nice though the idea might be. He's not somebody I've met in that way. You don't understand our relationship, I'm afraid.'

'How did you meet Mack, Julia?' Leo enquired, lifting his coffee cup.

'Yes, tell us!' Annelies added, oblivious to any possible complications that her enthusiasm was arousing.

'If you must know.' Julia laid her hand on the table and looked at them both seriously. 'Mack is a student at the basic skills class I teach at.'

There was a pause as her words sank in. She hadn't wanted to reveal private details of Mack's life to either of them. That was his business.

'That explains a great deal,' Leo said.

'What does it explain?' she said, sitting up, adrenalin suddenly firing through her system. 'You don't know anything about Mack. You've only met him once.'

Leo nodded at her slowly.

'Exactly. It explains your very defensive response to any questions about him. And it explains why you don't want Annelies to ask him to read her thesis.'

'Obviously,' Julia replied tartly.

'What is this?' Annelies looked at Julia searchingly. 'He's in your class? The one where you teach illiterates?'

'A stark choice of vocabulary, Annelies.' Julia gave her a sharp look. 'Mack's not illiterate at all. He's had an interrupted schooling and he missed out on the sort of education that we were all lucky to have.'

'That isn't what I mean.' Annelies waved her fingers in the air. 'Please, don't tell me about these problems as if I don't have any sympathy for them. I'm talking about his paintings. The things I saw in his house. I just find it difficult to believe that he has had problems like that. There is so much talent, so much expression.' She shrugged at Julia.

'It also explains why you reject your feelings for him,' Leo said. Julia stared at him.

'What do you mean by that?'

'By what?' Annelies looked troubled now, glancing from Julia's tense face to Leo's, which seemed quite relaxed.

'You seem to be suggesting that even if I did feel something for Mack, which I don't, I'd reject it because of – of who he is?'

Leo had the decency, she thought, to look a little abashed now.

'I'm sorry, Julia, I'm speaking out of turn. I've got a habit of doing that, I know. I didn't mean to offend you.'

'I'm not offended,' she said, holding on to her empty glass, and wishing that it was still full of water so that she could throw it over him. It was as well that the jug of melted tar was out of reach. 'I just wish you two would stop trying to create something out of nothing. I can't make it any clearer than it is. Mack is a student in the class and that's how I know him. He offered to help me redecorate my bedsit, so he came round here.' She articulated her words carefully. 'And he'll be coming back, just to warn you, to finish painting the walls. Now can we talk about something more interesting? Stig's impending prosecution of Annelies, perhaps?' She eyed Leo sternly. 'Isn't that what you came up here to discuss?'

'I came up for a number of reasons,' Leo said, sitting back on his stool with perfect balance. 'One of which was to enjoy an evening away from my work.'

There was a moment's silence. Annelies was looking at Julia with some concern and she was aware of it, but she couldn't meet her eye.

'Well,' Annelies began uncertainly. 'I'm not going to work this evening. Perhaps, Julia, it might be sensible if I spend a little time with your friend? Perhaps we'll be able to talk then about the law? Will you join us?'

Julia glanced at Annelies. She seemed oblivious to the incongruity of the fact that she was inviting Julia to spend the evening with the man who'd taken her out and kissed her on the cheek only the previous weekend. She stared over at Leo. He smiled at her.

'Yes, do join us. I was thinking of eating out this evening. We could all go together.'

'Oh yes, let's do that!' Annelies bounced on her stool.

'I, um. I've got to have a bath first.' Julia peered down at her mismatched legs. One wouldn't look totally out of place on the pages of *Cosmopolitan*, she thought, allowing herself a futile moment of self-admiration. The other looked as if it belonged to a rugby player.

'Will you be quick, then? I'm starving.' Annelies still seemed cheerful, although Julia felt the urge to wring her neck becoming stronger.

'We could go on ahead, perhaps?' Leo suggested, looking at Annelies. 'I was thinking of walking down to Café Coco. We could have a glass of wine and talk about your legal problem first, and Julia could join us to eat when she's ready.' He glanced at Julia again, his eyes vaguely amused. 'Would that suit you, Julia?'

'By all means,' Julia said, picking up her coffee cup, and finding herself committed to draining it. She took a tiny sip and, aware that Annelies was still watching her, tried to look as if she'd enjoyed it. 'But don't wait for me to eat, will you? I need a long soak and I've got a couple of things to organize. I wouldn't want Annelies to starve.' She smiled with tight lips at Annelies. 'See you later. Thanks for everything.'

'Everything?'

Annelies was just too nice, Julia thought with regret, to be treated with sarcasm. It wasn't her fault if she'd thrown herself into a delicate situation with her climbing boots on. And she was still trying to deal with the odious Stig. And it probably wasn't her fault that Mack obviously fancied her. Or that Leo obviously fancied her. It was just as well she'd never introduced her to Rob. He'd probably have shot straight back into the closet again and bolted the door. Julia stood up, scraping back her stool.

'Enjoy your drink, both of you.'

She let herself out and went down the stairs, sighing inwardly as she went into her own bedsit, thinking of the two of them jaunting off to Café Coco, drinking wine, talking about Holland, sharing an interest in Annelies's legal predicament. He'd driven all this way to see her, she'd thought. But perhaps he did just want to spend an entertaining evening away from his work? He didn't seem too upset to be faced with Annelies as a substitute.

She sat on her sofa and stared at her naked walls as she kicked off her shoes. Did she care that Annelies was muscling in on Leo? She got up wearily and replaced the phone on the hook from where Fleabag had removed it sometime in the day. He blinked green eyes at her proudly.

'Bathtime, wonder cat,' she said, grabbing at a jumper and jeans to take into the bathroom with her.

She soaked herself in a warm bath until her skin began to wrinkle, watching Fleabag as he ate the last remaining green shoot on her yucca plant. From the hall, she heard the sound of Annelies and Leo leaving the house. The door slammed shut behind them. She expelled a long breath, wallowing in the bubbles. She was feeling incredibly tired now, as if the last few volts from her spare batteries had seeped out into the bath water and were wafting away from her. It made it difficult to be annoyed about Leo and Annelies. Or perhaps it wasn't just that she was tired? She thought about it, watching Fleabag idly as he stared disconsolately at the brown stub left standing in the pot plant. She had enjoyed Leo's company, and it was fun to spar with him, but wasn't there still something missing? Yes, he looked dashing in a dark suit, and his hair was nearly black, but even so . . . ?

'What do you think, Fleabag?'

Fleabag yawned at her expansively before turning his attention to her toes, sticking out of the remains of the bubbles.

'Hmmn. You might be right.'

So, she did like Leo. That was agreed. But even though they might have continued to go out on dates, she still felt that she wouldn't have wanted to take it any further with him. In which case, surely it was a very good thing that Annelies had been in to receive him when he'd arrived?

The bath water was now lukewarm. She ventured the hot tap, but the tank refused to oblige with any more hot water. Reluctantly, she climbed out. At least she still had the bathroom to herself, she thought, towelling herself down and throwing on her jeans. She pulled on a loose jumper, and hoisted Fleabag from the empty bath tub, where he had reclined on the damp ceramic left by the water and was happily plastering black hairs all over the white surface.

'C'mon, you.' She stuck him under her arm.

She ambled lazily back into her bedsit and over to the telephone. She looked down at it, wondering whether or not to make the call that she'd been thinking about. She decided that she would. Mack had given her his number and she'd written it down. She flicked through the notepad and found it. She took a breath and pressed out the number. The phone was answered after a couple of rings.

'Mack? It's Julia. I just thought I'd ring and ask when you'd be free to come back and paint for me.'

'Hello,' Mack said, sounding surprised to hear her voice. 'I've been thinking about that. It's up to you. I don't know if you've got any other plans or not. Just tell me if you have.'

She relaxed back against the wall. In the background,

she could hear the tiny squeaks of Elizabeth's kittens mewing. Her stomach curled.

'Annelies said she saw your kittens,' she said, disappearing off at a tangent.

'Did she?' He paused. 'What else did she say?'

'Nothing.' Julia thought back to what Annelies had actually said. 'Except that she said you'd got some paintings in your house. She said they were very expressive.'

'Oh, right.' He didn't seem to want to be drawn on the subject. 'How were your lessons?'

'My lessons?'

'You said you were teaching this week, during the day.'

'Oh, yes, I did.' She mulled over the last session with Harriet. 'I've got a girl mugging up on her English A level. It's pretty painful. She's supposed to have actually read the books, but she hasn't. I sent her off tonight to read *Wuthering Heights*, but I expect she'll be down the pub with her friends by now.'

'*Wuthering Heights*?' he said with interest. 'I didn't know they set books like that for exams?'

'Do you know it, then?' She cradled the receiver under her chin.

'I listen to a lot of books on tape, when I'm painting, you know. Things I get from the library, or buy. It's fantastic, isn't it? I love the way it ends, the way it all comes full circle.'

'Yes, it does.' She sat up, pulling herself away from the wall. 'I tried to tell Harriet that, but she's only seen the film. Everybody thinks that it finishes when Cathy dies, don't they?'

'I thought that to start with, but when I realized what happened later, I was just amazed. The way Catherine is with Hareton.' He stopped. She could imagine him looking for the right words. 'She's awesome. It's a great story, isn't it?'

'When do you want to come round, then?'

'How about Friday? It's a long weekend, isn't it?'

'I'm working right through to the weekend, but I'm free on Saturday. How about coming round on Saturday morning?'

He rang off and she sat for a while looking at Fleabag while he scraped his claws down the bare walls, thwarted by the lack of wallpaper to peel. She wasn't in love with anybody. People around her were just being silly. She liked being on her own with Fleabag, at moments like this, when she could be her own boss, eat what she wanted, watch TV, or go to bed with a book. And now she had no intention of disturbing Leo and Annelies. Let them spend the evening together enthusing about canals. She shifted herself and wandered back through to the kitchen, pulling a loaf and some cheese from the fridge and dumping them on the table. She switched on the grill. While it was warming up, she found the bag of elastic bands she'd bought in her lunch-hour, opened it, and picked one out. She waved it at Fleabag as he hovered over the lump of cheese on the table, caught her eye and thought better of it.

'This is the end of the road for you, young man!'

She laughed at his expression, then took the elastic band over to the telephone and fastened it securely so that the receiver was bound into place. That would put an end to his stint as a receptionist. Now her answerphone might have a chance to pick up the occasional message. Maggie would be proud of her.

By the time she had eaten her way through her cheese on toast, her eyelids were drooping. She climbed into bed with *The Wife of Bath*, pausing to reflect that it was the best company she'd had between the covers for some time, and fell asleep with the lights on and the volume spread out over her chest.

It must have been several hours later that she heard the front door slam loudly. She opened her eyes in shock. Energetic voices echoed up the stairway. She pulled herself up in bed, blinking at the brightness of her overhead light. She waited, listening. Annelies's flat door opened, then closed. There was a silence, broken only by a peculiar, rhythmic twanging sound coming from the corner of her room where the phone was.

A low rumble of laughter rippled across the ceiling like thunder. She stared up. Should she have mentioned to Mack that Leo was here and that he was spending the evening with Annelies? What if Mack was keen on Annelies? What if he was hoping to take her out again? After all, she'd seen his house now, and his 'little' kittens, and his 'expressive' paintings. A bolt of energy shot across her stomach.

She sat still as the feeling passed, deep in concentration. She knew that feeling. She'd felt it before, but it was a long, long time ago. She gaped at Fleabag as he continued to strum the elastic band on the telephone like a double bass. What she was feeling was so alien that she'd forgotten its power. It was jealousy.

Chapter Eighteen

'It's the most amazing thing I've ever experienced!'

'Why don't you tell me about it? Why did you think it was amazing?'

Harriet launched herself forwards on the desk, shoving her head into her hands, forgetting for a moment that she was a complex teenager prone to frequent and unexplained mood swings, and gazed at Julia with shining eyes.

'I couldn't put it down. Once I'd got past the middle bit, you know, when Cathy's dead, and Heathcliff's finished head-butting his tree and all that. I nearly gave up, but I remembered what you said about the ending being romantic. So I was trying to work out what the romance was going to be. It couldn't be Linton, I knew that.'

'How did you know?' Julia smiled and leaned back in her chair.

'He's such a wimp, such a snivelling git. No way! Even a crusty old virgin like Emily Brontë couldn't have made him the hero. So I read on, and on. And then I realized. It was the hunk.'

'The hunk?'

'Hareton, although it's not a very hunky name, is it? Not like "Rock" or "Flint", but he's really sexy. He's strong and healthy and manly. Great choice, Emily. I nearly wet my knickers.'

Julia laughed aloud.

'So which parts did you find romantic?'

'All of it. I was so stirred up, I even turned my CD off. I couldn't listen to anything. And after I'd finished reading the book, I wanted to do something with it to get closer to it, oh, I don't know, put it in a sandwich and eat it, or something. Do you know what I mean?'

'Yes.' Julia nodded, delighted. She tried to smother her grin of triumph. 'However, you're going to have to be a bit more precise. When it comes to writing an essay about it, you'll have to pinpoint moments in the novel to make your case for you. So, try again. Think about the moments you remember.'

'Well,' Harriet screwed up her eyes in thought, the blue smears of her eyeshadow mingling with the grey shadows around her eyes. When she said she'd stayed up all night to finish the novel, Julia guessed that she wasn't exaggerating. 'There's the moment when Heathcliff comes back and Cathy throws herself all over him. That's quite sexy, isn't it? But I didn't like the bit when he broke into her bedroom. Far too melo-dramatic.'

'Okay, that's a good description to remember for your essays. Anything else?'

'The best bits are at the end. Catherine's been such a bitch to Hareton, you know, taking the piss because he can't read. But then, she helps him and it's just . . .' She put her arms around her body and hugged herself dreamily. At that moment she looked about twelve years old, Julia thought with a niggling feeling of affection.

'Perhaps you can find the bits you liked in the book again?' Julia nudged her copy towards her. 'And put some notes in the margin, so that you'll find them again.'

'Okay.'

Harriet went quiet, leafing through the pages, her concentration totally absorbed as she skim-read.

'Here!' she announced, bending the book on its spine

and laying it in front of her. 'This is great. Catherine's reading and Hareton's watching her and he becomes totally fascinated by her hair and reaches out and touches one of her curls.' Her eyes flicked through the paragraph urgently. 'Oh, no. That's not it. When she realizes what he's doing, she says, "Get away". She's still being a bitch at this point, but she likes him really.'

She turned the page, and read on, flicking ahead.

'Get-away-closer,' Julia said to herself, under her breath. For a fleeting moment, she had an idea what Mack's grandmother must have meant. She realized that she had thought aloud, but Harriet was too engrossed with searching through the lines to notice. She straightened herself, and waited patiently.

'Ah, here you are. Lockwood's come back to call and he's gone to the Heights to look for Nelly, and he sees Catherine and Hareton. He's sitting, trying to read, and she's leaning over his shoulder, correcting him.'

'And, what's romantic about it?'

'What's romantic about her teaching him to read?' Harriet looked up at her in disbelief. 'What *isn't* romantic about it?'

Julia stared back at her, her blood stirring. She blinked unsteadily back at the blue and grey-ringed eyes demanding an answer to an apparently straightforward question. Julia tried to think of a response, something suitable for an A level student, something that Harriet could write down and remember for her exam. She thought hard, but her thoughts were fading and becoming as merged and obscure as the patterns she had seen splashed across the underpass.

'It's, erm.' She frowned down at her copy of the book. 'Tell me what page you're on.'

'Three hundred and thirty-eight,' Harriet read. She looked up again, her bounding enthusiasm diminished for the first time. 'You really don't think that's very romantic, do you?'

'What I think,' Julia said, squinting at the page, 'isn't important. It's what you think that counts.'

'Heart of granite, you,' Harriet said. 'Read that bit there, where she's bending over him and her hair's mingled with his. And she won't let him kiss her until he gets the words right.'

Julia read. It had been a long time since she'd read the novel through attentively. She remembered the events, the structure, the characters well enough to teach Harriet. But she'd clearly forgotten some very poignant moments. She reached the end of the scene and looked back at Harriet. She cleared her throat.

'Yes, it's very touching.'

'Say it as if you mean it,' Harriet said.

Julia gave her a firm look. It was always difficult trying to be formal with the revision students. Not only were they on holiday, they were away from the authority of their schools, and knew that they could get away with most things. Harriet's attitude had extended from informal to flippant and Julia didn't really mind. But now she was uncomfortable under the younger woman's scrutiny.

'Harriet, teaching anybody anything doesn't have to be romantic in the slightest. I'm teaching you and it's not romantic.'

'That's because we're both straight,' Harriet said, chewing on the end of a fingernail. Julia must have paused a little too long before answering. 'Aren't we?' Harriet's eyes grew round. 'Why are you looking at me like that?'

'Stop messing around, Harriet. All I'm saying is that the romance between these two isn't particularly because she's teaching him.'

'But it's how they come together,' Harriet complained. 'He'd just stay out on the moors shooting rabbits all day and she'd sit upstairs with her Latin epics if it wasn't for this.'

'But they'd still get together in the evening, wouldn't they?'

'Great. You mean, he'd bring the rabbits home, she'd make a lovely stew out of them and they'd sit round the table and eat it. It's hardly the stuff of romance, is it?' She sniffed inelegantly. 'That's pretty much what my mum and dad do. It may be reality, but you don't want to read about it, do you?'

Julia's lips twitched.

'Some literature isn't romantic at all, you know.'

'I know. I'm doing Philip Larkin for the exams as well.' Harriet looked down at her nail with an expression that suggested she was sorry to have chewed it off. 'But it's nice to think there might be a Hareton out there somewhere, isn't it?'

'Let's get back to the text,' Julia said, glancing over some notes she had made. 'How did you get on with the dialogue? There are some difficult passages of dialect, especially when Joseph's speaking, aren't there?'

'You mean all that Chinese?' Harriet swung on her chair. 'I just ignored that and read on to the good bits.'

Julia sighed, pushing back her hair and hooking it behind her ears. Harriet was starting to sound like somebody who'd missed a night's sleep. Julia watched her go back to the book, turning pages backwards and forwards, glancing over them and smiling to herself, happily ignoring Julia's attempts to direct her.

'What about this bit?' Harriet continued without looking up. 'Catherine puts primroses in Hareton's porridge. That's romantic, isn't it?'

'It depends how you like your porridge. I prefer sugar

on mine,' Julia quipped. Harriet's mouth turned down at the corner. Julia smiled at her. 'Why don't you make a note of the page so you can find the quote again?'

Harriet pursed her lips and picked up a biro, scrawling an illegible note on an otherwise unblemished sheet of paper. When she had finished, she put her pen down again, rocked back on her chair and looked at Julia critically.

'Are you married?'

'Er, no.' Julia looked back to her own notes quickly.

'Got a boyfriend?'

Julia looked up at Harriet with an eloquent expression.

'No,' she said clearly.

'Oh.' Harriet rocked the chair again. Julia pretended to be engrossed. 'You are straight, aren't you?'

'Yes, Harriet, I'm straight.'

'Right. Why haven't you got a boyfriend, then? I've got a boyfriend and I'm half your age.'

Julia sat up and pushed her notes away, picking up her pen and fingering it. She could lean over the desk, she supposed, and stab the pen into Harriet's panda eyes, but that wouldn't really achieve anything.

'Why do you want to know, Harriet?'

'I'm just curious.' Julia steadily held her gaze. A slow, pink flush crept across Harriet's cheeks. 'I'm sorry,' she muttered. 'I didn't mean to be rude. I just don't understand why you didn't think Hareton was much of a romantic hero.'

'The thing is, ' Julia decided to be big-sisterly, rather than disapproving. 'I actually teach at a literacy class, one where people come to improve their reading and writing. They're people in genuine need of help. I just don't think it's that constructive to see that sort of teaching as romantic. It's – it's patronizing, to the student.'

'Oh.' Harriet raised her eyebrows, genuinely surprised. 'Okay. I see your point, I suppose. If you say it's not romantic, then it's not.'

'No.' Julia pulled her notes in front of her again.

'Although,' Harriet said, fixing her eyes in the corner of the room and chewing on the end of her pen. 'If Hareton turned up at your class, *then* it would be romantic, wouldn't it?'

It was nearing five by the time they finished the session. Julia waited while Harriet packed up her things, and flounced away, this time stopping in the doorway to look back.

'Julia? You're an okay teacher.'

'No, Emily Brontë is an okay writer, Harriet. That's why you enjoyed your lesson.'

'Oh. I suppose.'

Julia concentrated on arranging her notes and putting them back into a wallet folder and clearing the desk. When she was sure Harriet had gone, she sat back in her chair and stared across at the window that looked over St Giles. The traffic was gathering outside and they had wedged the window open for the lesson, to let in the warm air and stop them both from nodding off.

But Julia had been in no danger of nodding off. She had realized just how totally lacking in wit and perception she had been when she'd talked to Mack last night about the novel. She had enthused about it to him, delighted to find that he could share her passion for the story, but she'd missed the point completely. And if she'd been so dull as to miss it initially, he'd even made it clear for her, in an unguarded moment. Catherine and Hareton. How could she have been so blinkered not to see what it might mean to him? And to her?

She sat very still, watching the thin net curtain

flickering against the window-frame in the wind.

She packed away her papers in her bag, hoisted it over her shoulder and left the school by the narrow stairs which led out into a side street. She walked out into the bustle of St Giles and turned towards Summertown. She waited for a bus in the Banbury Road and took it as far as the nearest stop to Maggie's house.

She got off and walked slowly through the suburban streets, appreciating the sprinklings of blossom splashed across the trees which hung over her head and adorned the safe, walled gardens of Maggie's area. She reached Maggie's gate and pushed it open, peering into the dining-room window as she approached. It was quiet, but it was a room they hardly used. She pressed the bell.

After a while, the door was opened. Naomi blinked at Julia, then appeared to recognize her.

'Hello, Naomi. Is Maggie there?'

'God knows,' she said, walking away from the front door and leaving it open for Julia to find her own way in.

'I thought she might be working tonight?' Julia ventured as Naomi headed for the living-room and closed the door behind her. Julia stared at the door in surprise. 'Hello Julia, nice to see you,' she muttered under her breath. She turned to the staircase and made her way up, pausing on the landing. It was quiet upstairs. Often when she visited, Maggie would be typing in her bedroom and Julia would be able to hear the rattle from outside the door.

She tapped on Maggie's bedroom door. The door swung off the latch and opened an inch. Julia called to announce herself and pushed the door open. There was no sign of Maggie. The room was tidy apart from the desk, where her typewriter stood with a page still in the roller, a wedge of piled-up papers untidily gathered next to it. Julia walked in and picked up the top page, smiling to herself. Probably another saucy story. She read a paragraph and her smile faded.

She put the page down again quickly. This was very private and she had no right to read it without Maggie's consent, but it was clear that Maggie was writing about Pete. From the size of the stack of paper, she'd been doing so for some time. That might be one good reason why she hadn't called.

Julia left the room, closing the door behind her and ensuring that the latch clicked. She pounded down the stairs and stuck her head around the living-room door. Naomi was locked in a clinch with a young man who looked like a cross between a human and a grasshopper. He looked up with irritation at the intrusion.

'Er, I'm sorry. I take it Maggie's at the pub tonight, is she?'

'What Maggie does or doesn't do is fuck-all to do with me,' Naomi blurted with a great deal of edge, looking over her shoulder. 'Is that all you want? We're busy.'

Julia expelled a breath, taken aback. Naomi wasn't famous for her maturity, but relations in the house seemed to have hit an all-time low.

'Thank you for your help,' Julia said politely, and closed the door.

Outside, she decided that it was worth popping in on Maggie on her way home. She had to go near the pub on her way back to the town anyway, so she decided to walk.

The pub was on the main road, on the edge of the town. When Maggie had been looking for bar work, she'd told Julia that she'd tried to avoid the busy student pubs. She'd been lucky enough to talk her way into a job at a pub which was a comfortable mix of town and gown. Outside, a number of bodies had already gathered at the trestle-tables positioned along the pavement. Julia pushed her way through the wooden swing door leading to the lounge bar. It was a low-beamed room, adorned, like most of the Oxford pubs, with a combination of rowing blades and College crests. Maggie was serving two men in grey suits. Julia stopped for a moment to consider her. She looked lovely, as she always did when she worked, but she also looked tired.

Julia approached the bar. It was quieter inside. There was a paved garden at the back, bordered by trees and bushes, and she suspected that most of the early drinkers were making the most of the weather. A couple were sitting near the window, but apart from them and the two men who now made their way through the glass-panelled door which led out to the back terrace, they were temporarily alone. Maggie looked up with an expression of polite enquiry, recognized Julia, and relaxed into a warm smile.

'Hello, Julia. Fancy seeing you here.'

'I know. What's a nice girl like me doing in a place like this? I might as well have a small lager, now I'm here.'

'This one's on me, then,' Maggie said, sliding a glass from the rack above her head. 'It's lovely to see you. I kept meaning to ring you and somehow I didn't get round to it. I hope you don't mind. You look as if you've been working.' Maggie nodded at the smart jacket.

Julia slipped on to a high, cushioned stool at the bar and dropped her bag on the floor.

'Yep. They're paying well, and I might get some more work with them after Easter. How are you?'

Maggie flicked the tap with her finger and expertly handed Julia the full glass without spilling a drop of the lager. She laughed as she picked out her handbag from under the bar, took out some money and put it in the till.

'I don't think you really want to know.'

'What's happened to Naomi?' Julia asked, sipping the cool drink. 'She's changed.'

'Yes. Not Mousey Naomi any more. Now Fabian calls her "Rodent with Attitude".' Maggie laughed again. 'He's a funny lad.'

'Where is he? I called round at your house first, but there was no sign of him.'

'He's at the library. Or he's down the pub, but I hope he's still at the library.'

Julia nodded.

'It's that time, isn't it? Is he coping with it all?'

Maggie paused as she picked up a towelling bar mat and began to wipe the varnished surface of the bar.

'No. But I hope he'll see it through anyway. He's suffering from a bad case of parental pressure. It makes me think about the way I was with the kids. You know, I may have wanted the best for them, but I let them be themselves. But these two—' She shook her head. 'I don't think they've got any idea what they're doing to him.'

'Oh.' Julia mused over the bubbles in her lager. 'I didn't get any of that from my mum. I suppose I'm lucky. She never really noticed what I did, unless it involved a potential husband. But I suppose that's natural, in its own way. I suppose mothers just want their kids to have the sort of relationships they never had, don't they?'

Maggie gave her an odd look, and set about rolling herself a thin cigarette.

'Is that what your mum wanted for you?'

'I think so.' Julia swallowed a mouthful of the lager. 'I've been thinking about my mum. I think that's why she was the way she was, you know, after Bill.' Maggie leaned forward on to the bar so that Julia could continue in a quiet voice. 'She wouldn't allow me to let him go. She'd never moved on herself, so she didn't see why I should. That's why she did – what she did.'

Maggie nodded and, watching Julia thoughtfully, lit the bent end of her cigarette.

'Have you told your mum that?' She exhaled, pointing a thin jet of smoke away from the bar. 'Have you talked to her recently?'

Julia looked up in surprise.

'No. We hardly talk at all, unless she rings me to ask what I'm doing. And then she only wants facts. Anyway, she wouldn't want to hear what I'd want to say to her. She's so wrapped up in her own way of doing things, I think it's too late.' Julia fingered the stem of her glass and considered Maggie. 'I mean, you wouldn't want Kay's advice about how to live your life, would you?'

'Funny you should say that,' Maggie said. 'I've had a dose of Kay recently. You'd be surprised at how much it shook me up. You shouldn't underestimate the power you've got over your own mother. She may think it's her place to tell you what to do, but when the roles are reversed . . .' She suppressed a shudder and flicked her ash into a polished glass ashtray.

'What's got into Kay, then?' Julia looked at Maggie with concern. 'I didn't think she'd had much to say to you recently.'

'Well, she's got plenty to say now,' Maggie said, looking away from Julia and rearranging the ashtrays into a line along the bar in front of her.

'Has something happened, Maggie?' Julia watched her. 'Is that why Naomi's turned into the teenager from hell suddenly? She was really offhand today.'

Maggie stopped arranging the ashtrays and looked at Julia thoughtfully, as if she was considering whether or not to tell her something. Julia raised her eyebrows in a silent message of encouragement. Maggie let out a long breath.

'Yes. A lot's happened. The thing is . . .' She stopped as a group of young students burst into the room, chatting loudly to each other. Maggie instantly put on a bright

323

smile, and readied herself for the order. Julia sat with her drink and waited, watching Maggie's act of professionalism, marvelling at her ability to get on with what needed to be done as if she hadn't another thought in the world. Something was wrong and it wasn't just Naomi's rudeness and Maggie's tired eyes that suggested it. Now Julia remembered how pensive Maggie had been when she'd been round to the bedsit and they'd drunk tea and chatted. It was Julia who had chatted, Maggie had been unusually passive.

She'd come looking for Maggie to talk about Mack, but she could see that now wasn't the time to burden her with her formless thoughts. Maggie looked as if she was in need of some support, and perhaps, after receiving so much support herself from Maggie, it was time she returned the compliment. The boisterous crowd moved off and followed the trail to the back terrace. Maggie busied herself with rearranging bar glasses.

'Maggie? You were going to tell me something?'

Maggie walked over to her and leaned on the bar intimately.

'If I asked you to do something for me, Julia, would you do it?'

'Anything,' Julia said firmly, sitting up to listen.

'Can you come round to dinner this Saturday?'

Julia blinked in surprise, and then found herself laughing at the intensity in Maggie's face.

'That's hardly a huge favour, is it? Of course I'll come, if you want me to. Are you cooking something special?'

'I'm not cooking, love.' Maggie picked up her dead cigarette and lit the end. She flicked the top of the gold lighter, looked at it thoughtfully for a moment, then set it down. 'Fabian is.'

'Ah, I see,' Julia said. 'You want me to be a guinea pig.'

'It's a bit more complicated than that. His parents are

coming up on Saturday, and much as his mother wants to take him out to a swish restaurant, Fabian's insisting on cooking for them. Naomi and Graham are going to be off exploring each other's anaemic bodies in the Lake District, so I'm going to be there on my own.'

'I see. And you've got to eat with them, I take it?'

'I need some moral support, Julia. I can't face those two on my own.'

Julia smiled, nodding at her. After a moment of sensing the muted urgency in Maggie's tone, Julia stopped smiling and widened her eyes. She took another delicate sip of her lager, and looked into the glass as her thoughts fell together. She seemed to have been making a habit of missing the point recently, but in this case, at least, she finally thought she had got it.

'Maggie?' Julia kept her voice low. The couple near the window burbled at each other in the background. 'Maggie, is this because of you – and Fabian? Is it what I think it is?'

'Yes, Julia, if what you're thinking is the most absurd, unlikely thought that's ever crossed your mind, then yes, that's what it is. And Kay knows, which is why she gave me a piece of her mind, and by now Pete will know as well, which will just make him all the more determined to go through with the divorce.'

'Oh God,' Julia's voice was hushed. 'I'm so sorry, Maggie. I had no idea any of this was happening.'

'How could you, if I didn't tell you?' Maggie gave her a reproving look. 'Now, are you going to turn up on Saturday and help me out of a hole or not?'

'I'll be there,' Julia said. 'If you don't think it'll look a bit odd.'

'I don't think there's any possible permutation of people around that table that could look odder than just the four of us tucking into a plate of Fabian's pasta and tomato soup speciality and trying desperately to find something to talk about.'

'Do *they* know as well, then?' Julia asked.

'Bloody hell, no. And they're not going to find out, as long as I don't give the game away by saying something stupid. That's why I need somebody there to keep things neutral.'

'And Fabian wouldn't say anything, would he?' Julia sought confirmation.

'No way.' Maggie shook her head confidently. 'He didn't even tell them when he broke his nose. It's not that sort of family. They're more, oh I don't know, business associates, I think.'

Julia gave a grim smile. 'You're going to need me there. I'm so glad I dropped by tonight. I wouldn't have wanted you going through that ordeal on your own.'

'Well, I got myself into this mess. And I think Fabian might be working himself up to tell them that he's going to drop out of finals,' Maggie said, her eyes worried. 'I've got to stop him doing that. If he has a huge scene with them now, he'll be out for sure. He won't be able to cope with the collective fury of his parents on top of every-thing else.'

'I can help out there,' Julia said, thinking aloud. 'We'll just keep things jovial, if we can, and he won't get a chance to interrupt. But we'd better have a couple of bottles of wine at hand, hadn't we?'

'I've already bought them,' Maggie said earnestly. 'I might just drink them before they turn up.'

'I'll come round early,' Julia insisted. 'And we'll have a glass together before the meal, shall we? Then you'll be fine.'

'Thanks. I really appreciate this.' Maggie gave Julia a small smile, her face less tense. 'I have to say, I'm relieved. I thought you'd be shocked, but you're not, are you?'

'Shocked?' Julia thought about it, playing with her glass. 'No. Should I be?'

'I don't know. I just thought you would be. I expected everyone to be shocked. Naomi is, Kay is, Pete will be, by now.' She tapped her cigarette nervously. 'God knows what Pete's thinking. I thought he'd have rung me, to vent his wrath, but he hasn't. It's all gone dangerously quiet.'

'When did you see Kay?'

'Sunday. She caught me on the job.' Julia laughed, putting back her head. Maggie shook her head at her, but her eyes were smiling. 'You shouldn't laugh. You should have seen the look on her face.'

Julia laughed again, trying to stop herself, but the picture in her mind was getting gradually worse.

'I'm sorry. I can't help it. Oh, poor Fabian. I can just imagine him, hopping around, trying to get his socks on.'

'Not very elegant, is it?' Maggie watched Julia with an expression of bemusement. 'And Kay told me that I was a pervert.'

For a moment, Maggie watched Julia as she tried to straighten her face, but she saw that her shoulders were shaking, and soon the lines cleared on her face and she began to giggle with her.

'Oh, you're champion,' Maggie said, brushing the corner of her eye. 'I should have told you a long time ago. You'd have saved me a few grey hairs.'

'I thought Lady Grecian was doing that for you,' Julia said in an unsteady voice. 'You'll have to compare notes with Fabian's mother, won't you?'

They looked at each other and Julia snorted again. Maggie moved off to serve a handful of customers who had come into the bar, and Julia sipped on her drink, musing to herself. It was about time that Maggie was the subject of some appreciative male attention, she thought, swilling the clear liquid around in her glass and considering with a smile that Maggie would say exactly the same thing to her.

It was several minutes before Maggie returned to her. She looked brighter when she did.

'So how's Rob, then?' she asked Julia. 'Is he behaving himself?'

'Oh yes,' Julia said, realizing that her clumsy encounter with Rob was becoming more and more distant. 'We're on holiday from the class now, but I've got one of the students to paint my bedsit. I've been teaching him for a few weeks now. He's full of surprises and it turns out that he does murals as well, so I thought I'd let him do one for me.'

'That's adventurous of you,' Maggie said, raising an ironic eyebrow. 'What's he like?'

'Handsome,' Julia said, with a slight smile. 'Intelligent. Artistic. Intriguing. Honest.' Her voice softened as she gazed at the frothy circle around her glass. 'He's quite unique.'

Maggie's eyebrow remained raised. She paused for a moment, before commenting.

'And how old's this lad?'

'Oh, far too old for you,' Julia teased. 'He must be in his thirties.'

Maggie chuckled quietly under her breath, wiping her hands on a tea towel.

'You can laugh, Julia, because I'm not your mum. How would you feel if it was her?'

'My mother?' Julia peered at Maggie over the rim of her glass, and set it down again. 'Don't be daft. My mum's still in mourning. I don't think she's got any sensation from the waist down.'

Maggie drew a sharp breath. Julia glanced up, and straightened her face.

'All right, I'm being a bit harsh. But she's still hankering after Dad and that's a fact. God knows why. It's as if she stopped living when he left. I don't think she even sees herself as a woman any more.'

'I think you should talk to your mum about all this,' Maggie said firmly.

'No, Maggie. Bad idea.'

'It's up to you,' Maggie said, readying herself to serve two more customers who had walked in. 'But in my opinion, until you sort things out with your mum, you're not going to be free to let yourself feel what you really want to feel now.'

'Which is what, exactly?' Julia asked.

'Love,' Maggie said, walking away.

Chapter Nineteen

'You look smart today, Julia. Are you working?'

'I've been teaching this week.' Julia settled herself opposite Mary Hanson and crossed one knee over the other. 'I finish with this student tomorrow, but I've got some more hours lined up next week. It'll keep the wolf from the door. For now.'

Mary nodded. As she sat before the wide blue eyes, Julia felt the energy drifting out of her body. Somehow the momentum she'd picked up this week seemed inappropriate in the little room. It was more the sort of room to sit back and sigh in. Mary seemed to be waiting for her to do just that. She felt a flash of irritation.

'I suppose you want to know if I feel better for it? I do. It's got me out, communicating with the rest of the world, and I'm earning some money. I expect my self-esteem's risen a millimetre because of it.'

Mary nodded again. The hint of sarcasm at the end of Julia's last sentence hung in the air.

'Is it different from your voluntary work? In the way it makes you feel?'

'Yes. It makes me feel richer.'

Mary picked up a biro and turned it over in her fingers. Her eyes rested on Julia thoughtfully.

'What about the bank holiday weekend coming up? Have you got any plans for that?'

Julia stared at Mary. She never said what she expected her to. By now she'd have thought they'd be hammering on about the past again, sifting through meaningful moments in her life. What did the bank holiday have to do with anything?

'I've got someone coming round to paint my walls on Saturday, and I'm going to dinner in the evening with a friend. Maggie. I think I mentioned her to you before.'

'That sounds nice.' Mary's thin lips stretched into a smile.

'Nice?' Julia pondered the word. 'I don't think nice is going to be an appropriate word for either of those arrangements.'

'Why's that?'

Sod it, Julia thought. She should have just smiled back and agreed. It was all too complicated to explain. But she supposed she should be trying to explain something to Mary. She wasn't exactly giving her much to go on. She'd have to be Madame Arcati to piece together the truth from the snippets Julia was throwing at her.

'Well, the thing is, Mack's coming to do the walls. He's one of the students at the voluntary class I teach at. It's, er, a bit difficult to explain, but I think I like him.'

'Mack. I think you talked about him before.'

'No, I don't think so.'

Mary paused, turning over her pen.

'I think you said that his cat had had kittens. You seemed quite moved by it.'

'Oh. Did I say that?' Julia felt her cheeks grow warm. She was underestimating Mary. Just as she underestimated everyone else. She sat back in her chair and sighed. 'Yes, now I think about it, I might have mentioned him. It was the way he was about the kittens. Almost as if they were his babies. I'd never seen a man react like that before over reproduction. It was quite a shock.'

'Don't you think men get broody?' Mary gave another small smile.

'Hell, no. It's the quickest way to make yourself single that I know of. Start talking about a family. Amazingly effective.'

'Did you talk about a family to Bill?'

Mary watched Julia change. Her face paled and her pupils widened. Her grip tightened on the wooden arms of the chair. Mary waited a few minutes. Julia sat back, but her expression stayed the same. The breeze lifted the net curtain, wafted it in the air, and dropped it again. Mary cleared her throat.

'What about dinner at Maggie's? Why shouldn't that be nice?'

Julia gradually regained animation. Mary saw that her eyes were overly bright, as if they were stinging. Julia pushed a strand of brown hair out of her eyes, and let out a long breath.

'You, er.' She pinched her fingers together in her lap. 'You're wondering why I didn't answer that, aren't you?'

Mary knew that her question about dinner in the evening hadn't even been heard. She was stuck on the last one. She blinked at Julia and waited for her to carry on.

'I – I could tell you something.' She stopped and looked up with an expression in her eyes which took Mary aback. She was adept at masking surprise, and she did so. She had observed many different expressions in Julia Cole's face since they'd begun their sessions, but she'd never seen guilt before. It was overwhelming. 'I could tell you the same story I told Maggie, couldn't I? I could tell you what I wanted you to hear, but it wouldn't be the truth. One day, I think I will be able to tell you what really happened.' Her voice dropped to a whisper.

Mary swallowed. Moving on from here was difficult.

'Perhaps you'd like to tell me the story you told Maggie?'

Julia laughed humourlessly.

'The story? All right. Sit comfortably, and I'll begin. Once, I had a relationship with a fantastic man called Bill. I loved him and he loved me. Or so I thought. We lived together, happily. Then, one night, he suggested we went out for a meal. He wanted to talk to me, he said. I thought we were going to make plans for our future, so I made sure I looked beautiful for him. But he told me that he wanted to leave me and live with somebody else. He did.' Her voice was so quiet that Mary had to strain to listen. 'What he didn't know when he left was that I was pregnant.'

She stopped. The soft brown eyes which had been holding Mary's throughout dropped suddenly to her lap. Mary waited, her pulse slowing. Truth or fiction? Which was it?

'I'm sorry,' Julia said, standing up slowly. 'I think I'm going to throw up.'

'Hello there,' Mack said, shaking back his hair as Julia opened the door and tucking his crash helmet under his arm. 'I thought for a moment you'd forgotten I was coming this morning and gone away for the weekend.'

'No, no. I was expecting you. I just got held up. The, um, I spilt something.'

She stood back and allowed him in. She watched him saunter easily into her hall, unzipping his heavy jacket, putting his head back and looking at her coolly as he always did. He wasn't to know that she'd been twitching around her flat all morning waiting for him to arrive and that when she'd heard the bell she'd been thrown into panic. She'd run around, trying to make the place look casually lived in, as if she hadn't spent hours carefully arranging things in a way that might make her seem interesting to him.

'Where's the paint?' she said as they went through to the kitchen.

'I've got to nip out and get it. There's a place up the road that does a good deal. I thought we'd better just talk through what you want me to do again before I get stuck in.'

'Fine. And I can pay for the paint at least, can't I? Tea, then?'

He nodded. She nipped around to the kettle, hoping he'd spot the *National Geographic* she'd borrowed from Annelies and left lying on the table. She couldn't pretend to be as energetic as Annelies, but at least she could pretend to show an interest in the elements. She watched him drop to his haunches to stroke Fleabag, his voice changing to an unmanly coo. Her stomach turned over. His fingers were strong, ruffling the black fur, his shoulders stretching under his T-shirt.

'How did you get on with your student?' His blue eyes emerged from beneath the white-gold mop of hair. 'Did you get her to read *Wuthering Heights*?'

Julia flushed, concentrating on shuffling a handful of tea-bags.

'Yes, she read it. Quite enjoyed it in the end. Sugar, or not?'

'I thought you knew how I took my tea?' He glanced at her from the floor.

'I do, don't I? Stupid of me. I'd forgotten for a moment there.'

'So she liked the way it ended, did she? The way it all comes full circle?'

'Who?' She looked up, flustered.

'Your student. Did she like the ending? Where Catherine and Hareton—'

'She particularly liked Joseph. She was fascinated by his dialect, so we spent most of the time on that, actually.

334

You know, unravelling it and trying to make sense of his speeches. So, milk? Yes, you take milk. Fine. What colour do you want to paint the walls, then?'

She flipped the tea-bag in and out of the mug at record speed, leaving a pale beige liquid in the mug. She passed it to him, and whipped her hand away as soon as he'd taken it so that he couldn't see that her fingers were trembling. She hopped back to deal with her own mug and peered at him as neutrally as she could manage. He sipped his tea slowly, too polite, it seemed, to mention the fact that there wasn't any tea in it.

'How are you getting on with your pills?' he asked her, a flicker of concern in his eyes. 'Are they giving you gyp?'

'My pills?' She laughed, a little too manically. 'No, they're fine. Why d'you say that?'

'It's nothing, really. You just seem a bit agitated this morning. Perhaps it's just the shock of doing all that teaching last week.'

'Yes, that's exactly what it is.' She hadn't thought to deny the fact that she was agitated. Mack was too good at observing her. He'd proved that before. 'What about your week? How was it for you?' She gave him a bright smile. He was watching her with a quiet studiousness that was unnerving.

'Oh, pretty much the same as ever. You know, painting. Doing things that need doing. And, um. Well, something quite interesting happened.'

'It did?'

'Yeah. It seems the wine I bought managed to impress the right person after all.'

She stood with her mug in the air and stared at him.

'The wine you bought in Tesco's?'

'Yeah. You remember, when you saw me in there and found it for me? Seems like a long time ago now, doesn't it?'

'Yes,' she breathed. 'It does.'

'Well, it turns out it did the trick.'

She waited for him to go on. She should have known that something would be happening in his life. Just because she'd been working through her feelings for him in the last few days didn't mean that he felt anything similar. He'd never given her any indication at all that he saw her as more than a friend. He'd been complimentary, yes. But he was a man. Why shouldn't he flatter her, just to exercise his flattery skills if nothing else? She'd done nothing to show him it meant any more to her than that. But watching his dark blue eyes grow distant, she had a sudden urge to burst into tears.

'This woman, the one who came round that night, well, I thought she'd never get in touch again. But she did, this week, and—'

'God, is that Annelies?' Julia interrupted quickly, slamming down her mug and lurching across the kitchen to wrench open the door. 'I thought I heard her coming down the stairs, didn't you? I haven't seen her for a couple of days and I was wondering how she was.'

The hall was silent. Julia stuck her head out, and took two deep breaths.

'No, not her. I was sure I heard a door.'

Mack stood up. He leaned back against her table and blinked at her.

'I thought I heard the front door,' he said. 'Someone must have been going out.'

'Oh, that's all right then.' Julia shut her door and raised her eyebrows. 'As long as she's going out and not upstairs pining. That's the spirit, I say.'

'Julia?'

'Well, wouldn't you say so too? You took her out, didn't you? That perked her up. And now Leo's showering her with attention, so there's no excuse for her to be miserable.'

336

Mack was silent for a moment, sipping his tea, and pondering the floor. Julia pushed her hair behind her ears, and tried to stop herself behaving so erratically. He must be noticing it. But she'd had to stop him before he went into details of his love life. She couldn't hear them now. And she'd had to tell him about Annelies and Leo. Just in case he was nurturing any intentions towards Annelies. She couldn't cope with that either.

She retrieved her mug and kicked open the back door to let some air into the kitchen. A low drizzle was moving over the garden. It was turning the remains of Stig's charred belongings into a black, soggy heap. She bit her lip miserably as she stared over the rough grass at the mess. She'd thought it would solve something, but it hadn't. It couldn't. Not while she was still at war with herself. And now Mack had found someone else. Suddenly, him doing anything to her walls at all, let alone a mural, was pointless. She didn't want him to splash echoes of herself all over her flat. How could he, when he had no idea what sort of person she really was?

'Listen, Mack.' She turned round and faced him. 'About the mural. I know your work is fantastic, and I'm sure it would be beautiful, but I'm starting to think it's not such a good idea.'

He stood up straight again, stiffening his neck. His face was expressionless.

'I had a feeling you might change your mind.'

'Did you?'

'Yeah. Don't worry about it. People often do. It's quite a dramatic thing to have done. It's not very trendy any more, and people get twitchy. You've got to trust someone a lot to let them draw pictures all over your walls, haven't you?'

'Trust? This isn't about trust, Mack, it's just—'

'Yeah, it is.' He put down his mug and rested his

337

thumbs in the pockets of his jeans, his eyes on hers. 'It's all about trust.'

'I – no. No, it's not.'

'It is,' he continued easily. 'I told you I'd paint something about you. That's what's scaring you. If I'd said I'd do a scene out of *Gone with the Wind* you'd probably have been fine.'

'Actually, I hated that film.'

'So did I.' He half-smiled, and straightened his face again. 'No, it's something I said. I'm trying to work out what it is.'

'Look, don't wear yourself out looking for underlying reasons for it. The truth is, I've got cold feet and Dr Gimble would probably throw me out if I did it without her permission and I like magnolia anyway. I'm sorry, but that's all there is to it.'

He thought for a moment, chewing on his lip while he considered her.

'Okay,' he said finally.

'And seeing as I only want magnolia, it's hardly fair to ask you to do it, is it? I mean, it's a waste of your talents. Any old painter and decorator can come and slap magnolia on my walls. I can do it myself, in fact.' She nodded at him. 'Yes, I'll do it myself. It'll be therapeutic for me.'

'Therapeutic,' he repeated.

'Yes,' she said, sure of herself. 'It's just what I need. But I couldn't have done it if you hadn't come in and stripped the walls for me. I'm really grateful.'

'Grateful,' he repeated flatly.

'Yes,' she said, becoming disturbed by his lack of reaction. 'And seeing as you haven't gone ahead and bought any paint, I haven't put you out too much by changing my mind, have I? And—'

'Go on,' he said quietly.

'It's just that there's no reason for you to – to—'

'Be here,' he finished for her. He watched her face as he finished his tea. He took his mug over to the sink and put it on the draining board.

'No, it's not that exactly. It's just that I don't owe you anything, do I? Financially, I mean. I'd hate you to be out of pocket on my account. That wouldn't be fair.'

'God forbid that you should owe me something,' he said in a low voice, picking up his jacket and walking towards her flat door.

'Look, you don't have to go just yet,' she said quickly, putting out a hand to him. His subdued intensity was worrying her now. He turned and looked at her as he opened the door.

'There's no reason for me to be here now, remember?'

She stared at him mutely as he gave her one last searching glance and let himself out.

Julia threw herself on to the sofa after she'd heard Mack's bike roar away, stared at her bare walls and allowed blankness to wash over her. What had that all been about? Now she'd rudely sent him away, with no reason for him to come back, or to ring her, or for her to ring him, and term at the basic skills class wasn't due to start again for a couple of weeks. That's if he bothered to turn up again. That's if he had any regard left for her at all.

Why had she done that? Why had she buggered it up when what she'd really wanted was to be around him, to make him feel welcome, to encourage him to stay in the flat as long as possible, so that she didn't go through the same ache of missing him when he wasn't around. And now the ache had started already and he'd only been gone ten minutes. She felt the tears wedge in her throat, but she couldn't cry. A thump on the door of her bedsit ensured that she had to swallow back her frustration and wander over to open it.

Her eyes shot open in surprise to see an elderly lady standing in the hall, her baby-soft white hair trapped in a bun, her face pleated into a smile.

'Dr Gimble!' she ejected, subconsciously edging her door closed another inch to peep round the side. 'Good grief, I didn't know you were coming!'

'I don't want to intrude on you, Miss Cole, but I've just been showing the bedsit across the hall to a new tenant and I thought it might be a good time to introduce you to each other.'

A shadowy figure appeared at Dr Gimble's elbow. Julia's spirits hit rock bottom. Now, to add to her list of depressing eventualities, the bathroom was no longer hers to hog. It was back to sharing again. But at least it was a woman she'd be fighting over the hot water.

'This is Martina,' Dr Gimble said, as a young woman stepped forward and offered her hand. Julia tried to juggle with the door, but it was no good. She couldn't exactly wind her arm through the tiny gap. She'd have to open it, be brave and hope that Fleabag had climbed into the wardrobe and locked himself in there. In fact, as the two women in the hall smiled faintly at her in the gloom, she realized that the obvious thing to do was to invite them both in. After all, Dr Gimble had trusted her to look after the place without checking up on her every five seconds. The least she could do was to show her that she wasn't running a spanking parlour.

'Why don't you both come in?' she suggested, to broader smiles, as she opened the door wide with a confidence she didn't feel.

'Thank you. Martina's training to do social work, at Oxford Brookes,' Dr Gimble explained, puffing a little as she made her way to the table and instantly sank into one of Julia's chairs. She gazed down the garden through the gap left by the open door. 'Have you been gardening?'

'Er, just a bit. You know, pulling up weeds and things.' Julia ran round to the kettle, remembering that Dr Gimble had good eyesight, and that there were the remains of a bonfire out there. She couldn't be sure, but she could guess that bonfires weren't a very good idea in terms of hanging on to your tenancy. 'Tea, both of you?'

'I can't stay, I'm afraid,' Martina said. Julia glanced at her. She was quite plain, devoid of make-up and, by the looks of it, an expensive hair-care routine. That was good. That meant she'd be quick in the bathroom. 'Your bedsit's nice. Very homely. Have you been here long?'

'A year in July,' Julia said, wondering how she could distract Dr Gimble. She was leaning forward now and staring down the garden with a frown.

'Come and see the other room.' Julia nudged Martina out of the kitchen. Dr Gimble followed them. Once Julia arrived in the middle of her main room, she realized what she'd done. Dr Gimble stopped in the doorway, and gazed around the walls with an expression of bewilderment.

'I thought I'd freshen the place up a bit,' Julia explained, leaping across the room and flinging her hand out at the walls expressively. 'Do you know there were four layers of paper on these walls? Four? I mean, that's a lot, isn't it?'

Martina nodded uncertainly and looked at the older woman beside her. She had wandered over to one of the walls, and was running her hand over it.

'Did you do this yourself?' she asked Julia, an eyebrow raised, not in a very friendly manner, Julia thought.

'Oh, God no. I got a professional in to do it. I wouldn't have dreamt of just ripping it off without asking you. I

341

mean, I know I didn't ask you, but I wouldn't have done it myself.'

Julia watched with a slow pulse as Dr Gimble frowned down at the telephone.

'An elastic band?'

'Oh, that. The receiver kept falling off. I just kept knocking it off without realizing it. So I thought an elastic band would . . .' Julia could hear her voice fading. '. . . stop that happening.'

Dr Gimble nodded slowly, her lips pursed. She stepped back to gaze at her walls and a high-pitched squeak came from the carpet. She jumped. Then she steadied herself and bent down painfully to pick the small plastic mouse up from the carpet. It was covered in tiny bite marks and sticky with spit. She held it out between two fingers.

'What's this?'

'It's – it's my sister's.'

'Your sister's?'

'She's got a baby. She brought it round to see me, and I let her play on the floor for a bit. You don't mind, do you? I know we're not supposed to have babies here, but she was only visiting.'

'I thought you said you were an only child?' Dr Gimble asked, still looking confused.

Bloody good memory, you, Julia thought with a combination of respect and hatred. Of course, she was an academic. She had healthy brain cells. Just because she'd retired didn't mean that she'd been delivering lectures one minute, and gone off to crochet blankets and dribble into her soup the next.

'She's only a cousin really, but I think of her as a sister. That's what it's like when you're on your own, you know. You try to make the most out of your relations.'

'Ah. Well, that's nice for you. Where does she live, this cousin of yours?'

'Oh, in Whit-church-bridge. D'you know it? It's a very small town, just outside Wessex. Sussex.'

'I see.' Dr Gimble wandered over to Julia's sofa and sat on it. She looked as if she was thinking. Julia held her breath. 'And when she left the squeaking mouse behind after this visit, did she also forget to take her cat with her?'

'Cat?' Julia's eyes opened into circles. 'She doesn't have a cat.'

'So whose is the cat?' Dr Gimble continued calmly, pointing over to the bed, where Fleabag was draped over a cushion, his paws outstretched, as if he was trying to imitate Superman.

'Aagh!' Julia jumped. 'Where did that come from?'

'The pet shop?' Dr Gimble suggested. 'Or maybe the animal sanctuary?'

'Shoo!' Julia pulled the cushion away from under Fleabag's body and he slumped on to the coverlet, staring up at her in disgust. 'Get out of here! It comes in sometimes, this one. It must be because I left the back door open. I'll have to lock it from now on, just to make sure he doesn't get in again.'

Martina shifted awkwardly and Dr Gimble sat quietly on the sofa, her head on one side, as they both watched Julia attempt to eject her own cat from its home. Finally, she picked him up inelegantly, strode through the kitchen with him, and threw him outside. She slammed the door on him and mouthed an apology through the glass, turning back to her visitors with a firm look and slapping her hands together.

'There! It won't happen again.'

'Miss Cole,' Dr Gimble began elegantly. 'I don't mind you having a cat. You're on the ground floor, you've got access to the garden and your furniture is your own. I wouldn't say the same to the other occupants, because it

343

wouldn't be so convenient. That's why I told Annelies she could keep fish, but nothing else. At least the cat explains the fact that when I telephoned you in the week, you appeared to pick up the phone and have trouble with your breathing. I assume that the elastic band has helped to remedy the problem.'

'But—'

Dr Gimble put up a hand. Julia felt her head descend into her shoulders. She was mortified.

'Neither do I mind you making changes to the decorations. I'm a little more concerned about the bonfire, but it appears that there hasn't been any major damage. At least you are trying to do something with the garden and that pleases me.'

'I'm sorry,' Julia said in a small voice, feeling about ten years old.

'All I would have liked is that you'd have asked me,' Dr Gimble said. 'I trust you, and you must trust me. I'm not a tyrant and I like to think that the tenants in this house are responsible people. In future, if you are going to adapt the tenancy agreement to suit yourself, perhaps you would just pick up the telephone first and advise me of what you intend to do? The same applies to you, Martina. Just ask, and it will be granted. Within reason.'

'Thank you,' Julia said, wondering how she could recover her dignity.

'What's more, if I'd known you were decorating, I'd have offered to pay for the paint. It's about time these flats were brightened up.'

Julia nodded, offering to help Dr Gimble as she rose from the sofa, but finding that her help wasn't needed. She showed the two women to the door, and waved them off.

'See you soon,' Martina said, giving her a sympathetic grimace over her shoulder.

After they had gone, Julia threw herself on the carpet and stared at the phone. The day had started full of promise, turned surreal by half past ten and become a living nightmare of humiliation before it was midday. Now what she really wanted to do was rip off the elastic band, dial Mack's number and hear his voice. But after her appalling display this morning, she suspected her voice was the last thing he'd want to hear.

She pulled herself up lethargically and plodded out through the kitchen to rescue Fleabag. He was still sitting exactly where he'd landed, and was blasting an indignant miaow at her through the glass.

'I'm so sorry, little one.'

She opened the door for him and he scampered in, stopping to look over his shoulder at her and miaow again, before diving back on to her bed and resuming his position of repose. She let out a very long sigh as she collapsed on the bed next to him. How could she rectifiy the situation? What could she do? She rubbed Fleabag's back for inspiration. After a moment, she sat up.

It was an idea, but it could be a very bad one. She could invite Mack to come to dinner with her tonight at Maggie's. She thought about it carefully, getting up and beginning to pace around the room. On the one hand, Maggie would probably welcome another body around the table. Any distraction from her relationship with Fabian would be good. On the other hand, Mack might be insulted. He might think she'd asked him to make up the numbers. No, on the other hand, Mack probably had a date with the woman he'd impressed with the bottle of wine from Tesco's.

She expelled a noise of anguish, clutching her hair with her fingers. This was just so, so bloody typical. The one man she had managed to fall in love with, the only man in years, was just forming a relationship with somebody else. She stopped pacing, her body suffused with a swell of conflicting emotions. And how was it, exactly, that she'd managed to fall in love with Mack? After all, if she'd been quick off the mark, she might have booked her place in the passenger seat of Leo's rather smart Rover. A spot that she now suspected Annelies might be the favourite to fill. She stood still, gazing over the bare walls, at the last things he'd touched, feeling stupidly sentimental.

Mack was Mack. He was everything that he was. She couldn't explain it to herself any more than she'd been able to describe him to Maggie. He filled a need in her. Being with him made her feel complete. All of those things were true, but the point was, what the hell was she going to do about it? Was she too late? She took a shallow breath and edged closer to the phone. Her nerve ends were tingling. What if she asked him as a friend? It would be a gesture. He wouldn't have to make anything of it. He didn't need to know how she felt. They could have a fun, sociable evening and at least she would have shown her gratitude for all he'd tried to do to her walls.

She dropped to her knees and crawled purposefully towards the phone. She pulled off the elastic band and lifted the receiver. She pressed out Maggie's number.

'Maggie? It's me. Listen, I know it's late to ask you this, but would you mind if I asked somebody else to your dinner?'

Maggie laughed back down the line at her.

'The more the better. Bring the whole street round if they're free. I'm counting down the seconds here. I'm starting to understand what it must feel like to be on Death Row.'

'Well, I thought I'd ask Mack. I'm not even sure if he'll be free, but I'd like to ask him. Just as a friend, you know.'

'A friend?' Maggie snorted. 'Whatever you say, lass.'

'No, really. He's going out with somebody else now. He told me this morning. So it'll just be to thank him for all the time he's put into thinking about decorating for me.'

'He's not, is he? That's a bummer,' Maggie said with feeling. 'Isn't he at least going to do that Muriel for you?'

'I changed my mind. Long story. He'll probably have something else planned anyway, but can I ring you back and let you know what he says?'

'Sure thing.'

Julia took a deep breath, and dialled Mack's number. She waited, her eyes closed, begging him to be there. After a long while, the phone was picked up. His voice sounded weary.

'Hello?'

'It's Julia. I'm sorry about this morning. I was a cow.' She rattled on, not wanting him to interrupt. 'I want to thank you for everything you've done. And I'd like you to come to dinner this evening with a friend of mine, her lover and his parents. So, I need to know if you're free and whether you'd like to do that.'

There was a long silence after she'd finished her speech. She hadn't exactly thought it out carefully and produced any drafts, but it had been honest and that was a start.

'I'll come,' he said finally. She let out an audible breath.

'Good. And don't worry, I understand that you're seeing somebody else. I'd just like you to come as a friend. Is that all right with you? I mean, she won't mind, will she?'

Another long pause. Julia waited silently for him to respond.

'No,' Mack said. 'I don't think she'll mind. What time do you want me to come round?'

'Make it six-thirty, if you can. I know it's a bit early, but Maggie's nervous, so we need to get round before

Fabian's parents arrive and get her drunk.'

'Right.' Mack sounded as if he was smiling. 'Sounds interesting. I'll be there at six-thirty. You've got it bad, Julia.'

'What?' She frowned at the phone.

'Nothing. I'll see you later.'

He hung up. Julia mused over the phone afterwards, wondering why her spirits were flying so high again just because she'd spoken to him. He had that effect on her. And she'd blurted Maggie's situation out to him. That didn't seem to matter. He had that effect on her too. And she was in love with him. And now she knew they were going to be together for the evening and she prayed with all her heart that she wasn't going to find the strength within herself to sod it up again.

Chapter Twenty

'Are you sure you've got it all under control?' Maggie looked up from her magazine as Fabian arrived in the sitting-room and fell into a chair. He'd showered and made something of an effort for his mum and dad, she thought approvingly. They'd like that. He'd abandoned his jeans for the evening, and was in chinos and a loose white shirt. She'd also caught a whiff of aftershave. The same one he'd worn when he'd taken her out to the Italian restaurant.

'Stop flapping, lass,' he said with a heavy accent. 'You'll get yer tea when it's good and ready, and not before.'

She stared at him. There was something that reminded her of Pete in his mimicry. He couldn't know it. He'd never met him. It was as well for both of them that they were as unreal to each other as fictional characters. He gave her a warm smile and she gave a tense smile back. She'd kill for a drink. Until he'd declared the kitchen out of bounds to her, she'd been in there every five minutes, not to check on his own very individual way of making lasagne, but to open the fridge, look at the wine and wonder if it was too early to open it.

'By the way,' Fabian said, getting up and walking over to her. 'I haven't told you how gorgeous you look.'

'Oh.' She self-consciously pushed her fingers through her hair. 'I wondered whether I should tie it back. You know, just so that I don't look—'

'Look what?'

'Wanton,' she said seriously. His brown eyes widened at her as if to see whether she was joking or not. 'All right, not quite wanton. I just don't want to look like mutton dressed up as lamb. God knows what they'll think.'

'That's a point. They might think that something really kinky's happening. Like you're sleeping with me. Or worse.'

'Worse?'

'Are you telling me your fertile imagination can't come up with anything that's worse than sleeping with me?'

'I didn't mean it like that.'

'Don't worry about it.' He smiled. 'You look gorgeous. And you'll probably give my dad a hard-on. That'll bring back a few memories for him. Mum won't like it, but he'll be happy.'

Maggie stood up and, as Fabian reached for her affectionately, pulled herself out of reach.

'I think I'll have a glass of wine now.'

'What's the matter, Maggie? What did I say?'

Maggie reached into the fridge, picked out a chilled bottle of white wine, and held it to her chest like an old friend.

'It's all the talk about sex, Fabian. It's too much. I don't like it.'

'But you're horny. What's wrong with that? You should be happy about that. Shouldn't you? Have I put my foot in it again?'

'I just don't like the idea of your mum sitting here while you and your dad see me as some sort of bit on the side. I'm a family woman too, Fabian. It's not funny. I don't want you to think of me as horny.'

'Why the bloody hell not?' Fabian looked astonished.

'Just not today.' She fumbled for the corkscrew and set about opening the wine.

'Okay,' Fabian said. 'I'll start again, shall I? God

Maggie, you look gross. I don't know how we're all going to keep our food down if you insist on sitting at the same table.'

'That's better.' The cork flew from the bottle. Maggie poured a large glass. 'Want one?'

'Better not just yet. I can't hold it like you can.' He glanced at his watch. 'On second thoughts, they could be here any minute. I'll have one.'

'I thought they weren't coming till seven thirty?'

'Dad's really anal about being on time. He always allows an extra half hour for any journey he makes. You never know when he'll arrive, but he's got an irritating habit of being early.'

'Thanks for warning me,' Maggie muttered, taking three large gulps from her wine.

'What about Julia and this bloke she's bringing?'

'What about it?'

'What's going on there?' He wandered into the kitchen and bent down to peer through the dark glass of the oven door at his mysterious effort.

'He's just a friend of hers. I've never met him.'

'Ah. More "friends" to add to the gathering. I suppose they're knobbing each other as well then, are they?'

Maggie sighed elaborately and took herself back to the sitting-room to stare at the poster on the wall. *Couple Riding* looked as in love today as they ever were. They had no inhibitions, no fear of what others might say. But that was probably because they were sure about what they were doing. You'd have to be pretty bloody sure of it to get on a horse and ride off together, Maggie decided, trying to picture herself and Fabian doing the same and finding herself wanting to laugh aloud at the thought. The doorbell rang.

'Shit. Where's my wine?'

'I'll get the door,' Fabian called, in no hurry as he

pulled a bowl of washed salad from the fridge and stuck it on the draining board.

'Where did I put that bloody glass?' Red-faced, Maggie flew into the kitchen, her eyes darting all over the place.

'Here it is.' Fabian handed it to her, his eyes dark with concern. 'Maggie, will you calm down? It's my mum and dad coming to dinner, not Tony and Cherie sodding Blair. Just be yourself.'

Maggie finished her glass and refilled it, slopping wine on the kitchen unit. She took another sip.

'Do I really look all right?' she asked Fabian as he sauntered out of the kitchen. Fabian turned and assessed her. She'd worn her long, black skirt, but with a sedate round-necked top and gold earrings.

'Very catalogue. Mum will approve. Can I get the door now?'

'Go on, then. Sod off.'

Maggie waited, her head throbbing, her knees dissolving, as she heard the door being opened and voices coming through the hall. She closed her eyes and let out a long breath. Thank God. It was only Julia. She readied herself with a smile as Julia came through to the sitting-room, followed by a tall, broad-shouldered man, with a cracking pair of blue eyes and thick blond hair. Maggie's eyebrows shot up uncontrollably. Julia had been right. He was handsome, to say the least. And Maggie was mature enough to look beyond a pretty face. He had the build of a man who could make an early night seem like a very good idea.

'Hello, love.' Maggie gave Julia a quick hug. And she looked lovely too in a pair of slim cotton trousers and a linen blouse, although her eyes showed that she was nervous. That would be Mack's fault, Maggie guessed.

'This is Mack, Maggie.'

'Hello there.' Maggie resisted the urge to throw her arms around him as well. He looked like the sort of man you could hold on to when your bowels were turning to water.

'Hi. Nice hair,' Mack said with a relaxed smile.

'Thank you.' Maggie flicked it over her shoulder. 'I can lend you a bottle if you like.'

'I'm stuck with Barbie's spare wig, I'm afraid. Had it all my life.'

'Looks pretty good to me.' Maggie flashed Julia an approving glance to make her point. 'It's good of you both to come. I'd better get us all a drink.'

'Just a small one for me, Maggie,' Julia said, wandering through with her into the kitchen.

'Hey, out of there!' Fabian leapt through and ushered them both out. 'I've got a salad dressing to make. I'm not having you two taking over. Get back in the living-room, where you belong.'

He winked at Julia. At least he didn't seem daunted by the forthcoming encounter, Julia thought in surprise. She'd got the impression from Maggie that he'd been the one person who was dreading his parents coming more than Maggie herself. They obliged by grabbing the bottle and a handful of glasses and retreating from the kitchen. Mack was standing over the Kandinsky poster, squinting at it.

'Pretty, isn't it?' Maggie said, pouring him a glass and presenting it to him.

'Yeah. Nice.'

They stood for a moment, sipping wine. Julia realized she had things she'd like to say to Maggie, but couldn't in front of Mack. Maggie looked as if she needed to blurt a few things out herself, while she still had time. Mack took his wine and wandered towards the kitchen door.

'You all right in there?'

'Er, yes. Pretty much,' they heard Fabian respond, not sounding sure. 'Is it three parts vinegar and one part oil, or the other way round?'

'Let's have a look.'

Mack disappeared into the kitchen. Maggie and Julia raised their eyebrows at each other and smothered smiles.

'My, things have changed,' Maggie said in a low voice. 'Can you imagine a time when the women stood around drinking while the men went off to debate the merits of the salad dressing? Come to think of it, you probably can. It's me, isn't it? My generation never did anything like that.'

'I'm not sure my generation make a habit of it.' Julia peered at the entrance to the kitchen to make sure they couldn't be overheard. They heard Mack and Fabian talking to each other, safely preoccupied. 'It's more of a special occasion thing. It reminds me of Bill. He used to cook on a Saturday night, which for some reason made it fair that I cooked every other night, washed up, hoovered and cleaned the loo. I don't think it ever entered his mind that the equation of responsibilities wasn't perfectly balanced.'

Maggie took another sip of wine and pondered Julia's face. Talking about Bill hadn't seemed to distress her. She'd never heard her mention him in passing like that before. And she never brought him up, apart from that one time, when they'd both been pissed in the early hours.

'Mind you,' Julia went on quietly. 'Mack's different. I think he really enjoys being in the kitchen. And he lives on his own, from what I can make out, so he's used to all the other boring jobs as well.'

'Quite a catch,' Maggie said.

'Yes.' Julia pursed her lips. 'If it wasn't for the fact that he'd already been caught, things would be going very nicely.'

'Are you sure about that?' Maggie glanced over her shoulder again. 'He seems very comfortable with you.'

'Well, I'm not exactly sure. But there's a woman in his life one way or the other. I didn't really give him a chance to explain. I just didn't want to hear it and have to put on a happy face. I'm not very good at putting on happy faces at the moment.'

'You will be, Julia,' Maggie said affectionately. 'It'll all come right, you'll see.'

Julia gave Maggie a rueful glance and turned to gaze at the Kandinsky.

'I've never really looked at that properly before. It's lovely.'

'It's Fabian's.' Maggie followed her gaze. 'Bloody thing. If it was mine, I'd have taken it down by now.'

'Why?'

'Because, it reminds me of Pete and I don't want to think about Pete at the moment. Especially not tonight.'

'Oh, Maggie.' Julia touched her arm. 'Is it really getting you down?'

Maggie pondered her glass of wine.

'Yes, love. Now it's really getting me down.' She sought for words, and lowered her voice to a whisper. 'Have you ever had the feeling that you're in the wrong play? That the lines you're speaking aren't yours?'

'What are you two whispering about?' Fabian bounced in and stood with them, glancing happily from one to the other. 'Me, I hope?'

'Of course. What else could we possibly have to talk about?' Julia said.

The doorbell went again. Maggie jumped visibly, knocking Julia's arm. There was a hushed silence. Mack put his head around the side of the door, and looked at the three frozen figures. They stared back at him.

'What's the problem?' he asked. 'You're not expecting the Jehovah's Witnesses, are you?'

'I'll go,' Fabian said, his face visibly paling. He walked

out of the room, carefully shutting the door behind him.

'I wish it was the bloody Jehovah's Witnesses,' Maggie muttered. 'At least I could tell them to bugger off.'

'I told Mack about it,' Julia said quickly to Maggie. 'I hope you don't mind. I thought it would be simpler that way. Otherwise God knows who'd say what.'

'I don't mind. I don't care,' Maggie said, knocking back her glass of wine. 'I'm going into the kitchen. You two just stay here and introduce yourselves.'

She fled away and Mack let her pass before coming out to stand next to Julia. For a brief moment, they were alone. Julia flicked her eyes from the door that led out to the hall, to the kitchen door which Maggie had subtly kicked shut behind her, wondering which was going to burst open first. Suddenly she felt a finger softly brush the end of her nose. She jumped, and stared up at Mack.

'What did you do that for?' she demanded in a hoarse whisper.

'Because I wanted to. You've got that sort of nose.'

She was still blinking up into his eyes, trying to fathom why he should want to touch her, and how incredible it had made her feel, when the door to the hall swung open, Fabian in mid-sentence.

'Well, I've never noticed that there was mould on the wallpaper down there, Dad. You'd have to get on your hands and knees to see it.'

'But it should be dealt with,' a strident voice instructed from behind him.

'Then it's probably why the rent's so cheap. You can't have everything, you know.'

'Didn't you inspect the house before you all signed the lease agreement?'

'Er, Dad. This is Julia, a good friend, and her boyfriend Mack. They're going to join us for dinner this evening.'

Julia shot Fabian an alarmed glance at his introduction of Mack as her boyfriend and he coloured violently as if he'd only just realized what he'd said. Then she turned her attention to the tall man she expected to walk through the door, only to have to drop her sights a foot and a half to focus on the short, portly man who burst into the room behind Fabian, his body bristling with energy. Apart from a pair of dark brown eyes, he was nothing like Fabian. His hair was wavy and thin and started growing half-way over his scalp. He was wearing a pair of spectacles, lodged on his nose so that he could peer at them over the top, a tartan patterned jumper with a shirt and tie visible above the V neckline.

'How d'you do. Call me Charles.' He strode over to shake both of their hands. Despite his height disadvantage, he seemed undaunted by the fact that Julia literally looked down on him, and Mack had to stoop to shake his hand. 'You must meet my wife. Vanessa? Where's she got to, Fabian?'

'Fabian, is this the jacket we bought you for your twenty-first?' Fabian's mother arrived from the hall clutching a Barbour in one hand. She was taller than Julia and now she could see where he'd got his height, his dark looks, and his big nose from. She held the Barbour up in front of Fabian's face. 'What the hell have you been doing to it? There's a cigarette burn on the sleeve.'

'Mum.' Fabian cleared his throat. 'Can I introduce you to Julia and her *friend* Mack. They're going to eat with us this evening.'

Vanessa looked up from the jacket, and failed to disguise her disconcertion.

'But Fabian, I thought we were going to take you out. Just the three of us. Your father wants to talk to you about your exams.'

'No, Mum,' Fabian said politely, turning a deeper

shade of red. 'I told you on the phone that I was going to cook for you, and that I wanted you to meet someone.'

'What's this, Vanessa? You didn't tell me that!' Charles bristled robustly. 'We'll stay in, then. Why not? It makes a change for you to actually want us to meet someone, Fabian.'

He turned and winked at Julia, taking her completely off her guard. She was so shocked, she winked back in a reflex action. He seemed happy enough that she had.

'Yes, I see what's going on now. Don't you, Vanessa?'

Vanessa had proffered the jacket to Fabian again and was pointing to the black-edged hole on the sleeve. She looked at her husband in irritation.

'What's going on, Charles?'

'Fabian's got himself a girlfriend, haven't you, son? Isn't that what this is all about?'

'What? Just before your finals?' Vanessa looked at Fabian in horror.

'No, it's not that at all,' Julia said quickly, deciding that it must be time to pull Maggie out of whichever bottle of wine she had dived into and present her. That way she had a small chance of altering the direction of the conversation. 'Fabian, why don't you get your parents a drink and drag Maggie away from that salad dressing?'

'Who's Maggie?' Charles demanded cheerfully.

'The northern woman,' Vanessa advised him, looking further displeased.

'Er, okay.' Fabian slipped off into the kitchen.

'Both students, are you?' Charles asked with an expression of pleasant enquiry. Julia decided he must be either very broad-minded or blind. Couldn't he see that they were both thirty-something?

'I was, but I graduated last year. I was a mature student.'

'University, or the poly?' Vanessa asked, picking her

way forward and sliding suspicious glances at the tatty furniture.

'They're both universities now, actually,' Julia said evenly.

'Ah, so you were at, what's it called now? Brookes?'

'Er, no. I was here, at Oxford.'

'I see.' Vanessa seemed gratified at least with that answer. She turned to Mack, running her eyes over his casual trousers, his loose shirt and his unkempt hair.

'And you must be an academic. You look like one.'

It might have been an attempt at flattery, Julia thought generously. The other option was that it was a delightful way of telling him that he looked like a long-haired git.

'Not a bit of it.' Mack smiled.

'Ah.' Vanessa inclined her head, waiting for clarification. Mack broadened his smile. Clever boy, Julia thought, her admiration for him swelling.

The door to the kitchen was pushed open and Fabian arrived with a bottle of wine and two extra glasses. Julia saw in horror that he had a smear of Maggie's dark lipstick on his cheek. She couldn't imagine that Maggie had grabbed him in a passionate clinch, now of all times. Perhaps he had grabbed her and missed. Or he'd grabbed her, but she'd got away. Maggie appeared behind him.

'Hello, ducks. Mrs Gough, I'm pleased to meet you at last. Makes a change from me being Fabian's receptionist, doesn't it? Mr Gough, it's a pleasure.'

Charles was momentarily stunned and it showed. Then he held out a hand warmly.

'So you're the older woman who shares the house. Not a bit how I imagined you, I have to say. Call me Charles, won't you?'

'Maggie?' Vanessa looked at Fabian with a frown. 'You're sure this is Maggie?'

'No, Mum. I'm not a hundred per cent sure. It could be David Starkey. What do you think?'

'I don't want your sarcasm, thank you.' Vanessa took a glass and held it out to be filled. Then Julia saw that her eyes roamed his face, and alighted on the smear of lipstick. Her grip on the stem of her glass tightened.

'We were just talking about the mould in the hall, Maggie. You must have noticed it?'

'Yes, I have. But you know what landlords are like, out to screw every penny out of you and give you nothing back in return. This one's no better than the rest.'

'But I'm a landlord myself.' Charles stood squarely holding his wine glass. 'I've got two properties in London I let out. I'd notice mould if I saw it. You have to tell him about it.'

'We have, but he's not interested. It is a student house, you see, and if we didn't take it, there'd be others that would.'

'And that sofa's such a disgusting colour.' Vanessa snorted at it. 'Can you believe that such a thing exists? It looks as if it's come straight off a council estate.'

Julia immediately shot Maggie a glance and saw her stiffening. Maggie had told her it reminded her of the curtains back home, in her house, on her estate.

'So where are you from, Maggie?' Charles asked. 'We toured the Dales a few years ago. They were quite beautiful.'

'Aren't they? But I'm not from the Dales, I'm afraid. I come from Leeds. Lived there all my life.'

'There are some quite smart areas in Leeds now, aren't there?' Vanessa decided to risk perching on the edge of a chair. 'And there's the university, of course. I suppose your children must be at university now, mustn't they, Maggie?'

'No. I'm the only one in my family to give it a bash,' Maggie said. Julia saw that she was trying to look casual, but her eyes were giving her away. They were too bright. 'They're all working now.'

'Well, you don't look old enough to have grown-up children. You look far too young and sprightly,' Charles said, collapsing on the sofa regardless of its disgusting colour.

'She's amazing, isn't she?' Fabian said, leaning against the wall. Vanessa gave him a sharp glance.

'So where have you driven from today?' Julia asked, smiling at Charles and deciding that he was the best bet for an uncomplicated response.

'Hampshire. We live just outside Winchester.'

'It's a lovely town,' Vanessa said. 'So full of culture and history. Like Oxford. I couldn't live anywhere that wasn't beautiful.'

'Nice to have the choice.' It was Mack who spoke quietly from where he stood.

'Where do you live, Mack?' Vanessa turned ostensibly polite eyes on him.

'Blackbird Leys. You might have heard of it. It's famous for its joyriders. We've been on the news a few times.'

There was a silence.

'More wine?' Fabian said, waving the bottle in the air. Apart from Julia, everybody in the room stuck their glasses out to be filled.

'Is that – yes, it's a Kandinsky, isn't it?' Vanessa said, peering at the poster from the sofa. 'So few people understand modern art. It must be yours, Fabian?'

Julia glanced at Maggie. They locked eyes without expression. Fabian seemed oblivious to the under-current.

'Yes, it is. I brought it up from school. You must have seen it in my study when you came to see me there.'

'No, I don't think so,' Vanessa said innocently. 'But I

do love Kandinsky. The Russians are so expressive. Still, it's not to everyone's taste. Some people still seem to prefer the Spanish boy with the tear in his eye type of decoration.' She gave a small laugh. 'I don't suppose you'd want to hang a Kandinsky on your wall, would you, Mack?'

'Nope,' he said, pausing to sip at his wine. 'I prefer Braque.'

Vanessa's smile slipped.

Maggie laughed, and turned it into a short cough. 'Braque?' she said, turning an ironic eye on Mack. 'I can't stand the Cubists, myself. I don't know what you see in them. You give me a Picasso and a Braque painted during their period of collaboration and I'll swear that you can't split a hair between them.'

'But that's so unfair,' Julia said, catching on to the twinkle in Maggie's eye. 'It's clear that the influence of Cézanne on Braque sets him apart.'

'Bollocks!' Maggie said, flicking her hair back with passion. 'Cubism denies the existence of the human spirit.'

'Ah,' Mack said quietly, his lips turning into a smile. 'So you're an Expressionism woman yourself, are you?'

'Absolutely,' Maggie said, fixing Mack with a stare that pleaded that she was now out of her depth and begged him to go on.

'You prefer the rough expression of human emotion portrayed by Munch, or Van Gogh, I suppose?'

'Too right I do,' Maggie said, applauding him with her eyes.

'Can't say I agree.' Mack shrugged. 'It ignores the fact that every person is capable of deceit. It's what sets us apart from the animal kingdom. Now, the Impressionists understood that. Don't you agree, Mrs Gough?'

'Er . . .' Vanessa glanced at the animated faces around her, blinking erratically. 'But what about Mondrian? Where does he come into this?'

'Oh, do me a favour!' Maggie guffawed, shooting a demanding glance at Mack to elaborate on her behalf.

'Is it the Neoplasticism you admire in Mondrian, or his later Cubism?' Mack gave Vanessa a questioning look. She was speechless and stared back at him.

'Not everyone likes to have an advert for L'Oréal stuck up on their walls,' Mack said softly. 'Not even in Blackbird Leys.'

'Shall we eat now?' Fabian said, lurching towards the kitchen.

'So, how is it you know so much about art?' Charles asked Mack as they tucked into the tiny portions which Fabian's diminutive lasagne allowed them.

'Well, I'm a bit of a painter, actually,' Mack said, looking back down at the shreds of lettuce on his plate.

'Are you, by Jove? D'you hear that, Vanessa? Even you should have been slightly reticent about getting into an argument about art with an artist.'

'I didn't know he was an artist. He wouldn't tell me what he did,' Vanessa defended, her lean cheeks now flushed from Fabian's constant attempts to fill up everyone's glasses. Julia had realized that getting the bus over from her flat had been a very good idea. Nobody should be driving after the amount they were drinking, including Charles, who Julia thought was enjoying the voyage to oblivion along with the best of them. And it wasn't as if Fabian's meal was going to provide much blotting paper, tasty though it was.

'I don't remember you asking,' Mack said, glancing up, and smiling pleasantly. 'I'm sorry.'

Julia remembered the way that Mack had dealt with

Vivienne. Politesse. He was good at it. Vanessa fumbled with her fork.

'So where do you exhibit, Mack?'

Julia glanced at Mack, sitting beside her. He seemed unperturbed by the question.

'My first exhibition will be in October. In London. Perhaps you might even manage to drop in and say hello. I'd love to see you there.'

Vanessa's eyes widened into saucers.

'You're exhibiting in London? Good heavens, why didn't you say so?' Julia noticed the sudden flutter of Vanessa's eyelashes, and the enthusiasm in her eyes, just as she was subsiding from the shock of Mack's announcement herself. 'Which gallery?'

Mack named a gallery which Julia had never heard of, but that had Vanessa's eyes all but leaving her head on stalks.

'Really? I say. You must have really impressed somebody.'

'Yeah. I think it was something to do with a bottle of wine.' He smiled at Julia. She put her fork down and stared at him.

'The Fleurie?'

'Yep. The same.'

Julia felt a rush of relief as she looked into his eyes. He seemed to sense it, his eyes warming back at hers.

'So the woman you impressed was—'

'Impressed enough to ask me to do large-scale canvasses of my work. And they want to take photographs of the murals I've done. But this only happened this week.' He glanced around at his captive audience shyly. 'It's been a big breakthrough for me.'

'Tremendous!' Charles said, giving Mack a gracious nod. 'Good for you, man. You don't get anywhere in this life if you don't try. That's what I always say.'

'That's what I've been trying to tell you, Fabian.' Vanessa turned to him with luminous eyes. 'If you want success, you have to work for it.'

'Really?' Fabian pretended to look astonished. Maggie chuckled.

'I think he knows that, Vanessa,' she said. 'I don't think anyone could have tried harder than Fabian's done. He's off in the library all day and spends all night ploughing through mountains of paper in his room.'

Vanessa looked at Fabian.

'It doesn't sound as if you're very organized. You should be revising by now. I know Sara was. She was very well prepared.'

'Well, Sara's Sara, isn't she?' Fabian gave his mother a curt smile.

'But I mean—'

'Ah, I see,' Charles said, holding out his glass for another refill as Mack proffered one of the bottles he and Julia had brought with them. 'I was wondering what all this stuff was about you wanting us to meet someone. It was Mack, wasn't it? You knew your mother needed something interesting to talk about at her coffee mornings.'

'Charles!'

Charles turned and winked at Julia. Julia stared back, unwilling to collude this time. She suspected Fabian's mother could be an uncomfortable enemy.

'Oh, come on Vanessa. I just hope you were taking notes when we were all discussing Cubism. You'll have forgotten it all by the time we get home.'

'Charles, that's quite enough. You've had too much to drink.'

Julia couldn't remember Charles entering the discussion at all, but he seemed happy to think that he had.

'Anyway,' Vanessa said, narrowing her eyes at her

husband. 'I thought you were going to talk to Fabian about his finals.'

'He seems to have it all under control.' Charles smiled magnanimously at his son. 'You'll get through all right. And if you don't, you'll just have to pick up the pieces yourself. You'll survive. Nobody's going to go to war over it. But I'm worried about that mould near the door. Is there any sign of it upstairs? Is the bathroom properly ventilated?'

'Actually, now that we've all finished eating, I've got something I want to say,' Fabian said, taking a deep slug of his wine, and refusing to meet anyone's eye.

Julia went cold. Under the table, without being conscious of doing it, she reached for Mack's hand. He took hers and squeezed it. Her eyes flew to Maggie's. She was staring sideways at Fabian.

'What's that, then?' Charles asked, leaning back in his chair comfortably.

'There's no pudding,' Maggie said, laughing. 'That was it, wasn't it Fabian?'

'No,' he said. He turned his knife over on his plate. 'It's more important than that. Mum, Dad, there's something that I want you to know.'

Maggie stood up and began to clear the plates.

'Sit down, Maggie.' It was Vanessa who gave the order. 'I think we have a right to hear this, don't you?'

Maggie sank into her seat, her face pale, her eyes startled. The room fell silent.

'The thing is—'

The doorbell rang. Maggie sank back into her chair in a moment of utter relief.

'Leave it,' Fabian said in a low, commanding voice.

'No, love. I'd better get it.'

'Leave it.' Fabian swung round and stared at her. The bell rang again.

'Look, I'll get it,' Julia said, standing up. 'I'm the nearest to the door, aren't I? I'll just get rid of them, then come back.'

Fabian issued an impatient sigh. Julia slipped her hand from Mack's and skipped from the room, stopping in the hall to push her hair from her face and take a deep breath before turning the catch on the door. For a moment she didn't recognize the figure standing on the doorstep. Then she did.

'Come in,' she said, pulling the door open. Lost for words, she pushed open the door to the dining-room, where the assembled company were silent, waiting for her to return.

'Maggie?' Julia said, grabbing Maggie's attention as she fumbled with a napkin. 'It's, um. It's Pete.'

Pete Ridley stepped into the room, glanced around him, and turned his eyes back on his wife.

'Hello, Maggie,' he said.

Chapter Twenty-One

Fabian was the first to react. He stood up, dropping his napkin on the table, and straightened his shirt.

'Sit down, Fabian,' Maggie said.

Julia stood next to Pete, biting her lip awkwardly. Vanessa arched an eyebrow in Maggie's direction, looked to her son and rested her eyes on Pete.

'I'm sorry, you're all having tea. I'll wait in the other room,' Pete said.

'Tea?' Vanessa opened her eyes in ridicule. 'I thought we'd just had supper.'

'We've just finished,' Maggie said, ignoring Vanessa. 'I'll come through with you.'

'Aren't you going to introduce me to your friends?' Pete asked.

Julia glanced sideways at Pete. He was quiet, not ballistic, as Maggie had thought. It was difficult to tell from the stretched expression of calm on his face whether or not he was biding his time. His dark hair was damp, the drizzle which had engulfed the day still droning on outside, and it had touched the shoulders of his jacket. His pale blue eyes hadn't left Maggie, but Julia saw that he was curling and uncurling his fingers.

Maggie stood up. 'Pete, you'll remember Julia. You met her that one time you came down to see me at college. And her friend Mack, Mr and Mrs Gough, and Fabian.'

Julia thought Maggie sounded calm, but she could see her hands trembling as she indicated the people seated around the table.

'Ah, you must be Maggie's husband.' Charles stood up and stuck his hand out over the table. He was six inches shorter than Pete, even at full stretch. Pete shook the hand loosely.

'Nice to meet you,' Pete said.

Charles reached for the wine. 'You'll have a glass of this, won't you? And do join us. Fabian, get another glass.'

'No, I'll come through,' Maggie said, working her way around the side of the table. 'We can talk in the other room, Pete.'

'Thank you,' Pete said, looking at Charles over Maggie's head. 'I will join you.'

'We'll need another chair then, Fabian,' Charles said, boring Fabian out with a demanding stare as he seemed to be doing nothing but sitting and gazing into space.

'No, Pete,' Maggie said in a firm voice. 'We'll go through and talk first.'

She touched Pete's arm and he stiffened. His lips tightened. Then he turned on Maggie.

'What's the matter, Maggie? Worried I won't be able to keep up with the conversation? You don't have to hide me out back. I do know how to behave in company.'

'But I would like to talk to you, Pete. And I'd like to do that privately.'

She nudged him towards the door. After a moment of immobility, he allowed himself to be led from the room, burning a long stare at Fabian as he went. The door swung shut behind them. Unable to stop herself, Julia let out a long breath.

'Ah, well. A little domestic strife in the air, I think,' Charles said, shrugging. 'We'd better leave them to it. More wine, everyone?'

'You were going to tell us something?' Vanessa turned to Fabian with apparent levity. Julia slipped back

369

to her chair and exchanged silent glances with Mack.

'Oh, forget it. Not now, Mum.'

'But I thought it was important to you. Come on, Fabian, you were about to make an earth-shattering announcement, weren't you?'

Now Julia was sure that Vanessa was being disingenuous. There was an odd look in her brown eyes. It was almost sadistic. Fabian was agitated, darting looks at the door. He started to stand up and sat down again.

'Shouldn't you go and see if Maggie's all right, Julia?'

'She'll be all right,' Julia said as soothingly as she could muster. 'I'm sure she and Pete have got things to discuss.'

Fabian looked as if he wanted to dissent, but clammed up.

'Oh do come on, dear. Tell us what important decision you've come to. We're all ears.'

Fabian turned to his mother and assessed her expression. Colour rose in his cheeks.

'What do you think I was going to say, Mum? Why don't you stick your neck out for once. Say something risky. Say something that other people can disapprove of. Go on, tell me what you're thinking.'

'I only meant—'

'I'm all ears.' Fabian tapped his fingers on the table elaborately. 'Come on.'

'Look, Fabian,' Julia interrupted, pushing back her chair. 'I think Mack and I should go now. It's been a lovely evening and the lasagne was delicious, but I think we should leave you to chat.'

'We're not going to chat,' Fabian said, his deep brown eyes glinting at his mother. 'We're going to wait for my mother to commit herself.'

Vanessa shifted in her chair. She stared around the table haughtily.

'Well, whatever it was you were going to tell us was

obviously thwarted by the arrival of Maggie's husband.'

'You think so. And why might that be?'

'Because – because.' Vanessa stuck out her chin. 'Because you're obviously having it off with that woman. That's why.'

There was a silence. Charles blinked at his wife, his glass stuck in his mouth. Fabian threw back his head and bellowed with laughter.

'Having it off,' he repeated, shaking his head. 'Mum, you're precious. Yes, of course I've been having it off with Maggie, but that wasn't my big announcement.'

Julia wanted to dive out of the room now, pulling Mack after her by whatever she could grab hold of.

'Really?' Charles finally detached his glass from his mouth. 'What, you and the northern woman? In bed? I say!'

'Shut up, Charles. You can pat your son on the back later, when I don't have to witness it. What is it you were going to say, Fabian?'

'I'm leaving Oxford,' he said slowly and clearly.

'What, after finals, you mean?' Vanessa's face went from pink to white in no less than a second.

'No, before finals. I'm jacking it in. It's done nothing but make me miserable from the moment I set foot in the place. I've had enough of it, and I'm not going through with it. If it wasn't for rugby, and Maggie, I'd probably be swinging from the shower rail by my belt by now.'

Julia watched Fabian's face as she tried to subside into her chair. He was serious. She'd never realized how serious he was about it.

'That's total nonsense and you know it,' Vanessa said factually. 'You'll carry on as usual, get yourself organized properly and come out with a first. Nothing's going to stop you from doing that.'

371

'Apart from me jacking it in, of course,' Fabian said calmly.

'You can't. I won't allow it.'

'Try and fucking stop me.'

'I'll get Sara to come up. She'll talk some sense into you.'

'Oh, Sara. Of course. I'd forgotten about her. If Sara sets one foot into my house, I'll wring her fucking neck, is that clear?'

'Fabian! Don't use that language with me. I'm your mother!'

'Really?' Fabian whistled. 'Then as my mother you should care about my happiness, shouldn't you? Doesn't it bother you that I've been totally bloody miserable for the last five years? Ever since I started my A levels? Don't you give a shit?' He shook his head at her. 'No, you don't, do you? I think you'd actually prefer it if I was swinging from the shower rail. That would be more bloody honourable than giving up, wouldn't it?'

'Look, everyone calm down please,' Charles said, laying his hands on the table reasonably. 'Fabian, if you were unhappy, why didn't you tell us?'

'Why d'you think?' Fabian said with a smirk.

'I wish you had. We could have thought this through. Perhaps you'd have been happier somewhere else, where the pressure was less intense.'

'Sara could cope with the pressure. It's what builds your character. You tell him, Charles.' Vanessa's eyes were straining.

'Then you do it, Mum,' Fabian challenged her. 'Go on. Do what Maggie did. Or Julia. You give up everything you've got, risk your home, your income, your marriage, and come here, and you get the bloody Oxford degree. If Sara can do it, I don't see why you can't. But you haven't got the balls, have you?'

Vanessa gaped back at him.

'No answer? I thought not. So stop lecturing me about it. Just get off my bloody back and let me live my own life.'

'Look, we really must go.' Julia stood up quickly, tugging at Mack's arm. He rose beside her. She gave Fabian a rueful look. 'I'll call you tomorrow, Fabian. You know we'll stick by you, whatever you decide, don't you?'

'Thanks,' Fabian said.

'Goodbye.' Julia nodded at Charles and Vanessa, who was too busy glaring at Fabian to notice. They left the room quickly. Julia picked up her jacket and handbag from the hall, and they let themselves out of the front door. There was a murmur of voices coming from the sitting-room.

Outside, the drizzle had thickened into a steady rain. They walked quickly away from the house without speaking, and reached the Banbury Road. Then Julia stopped, closed her eyes and took a long breath.

'Mack, I'm so sorry. I had no idea it was going to be as bad as that.'

'Hey, don't worry about it.'

'No, I'm really sorry. I didn't just ask you so that you'd be an extra in some sort of bizarre drama. I actually wanted to see you this evening.'

He put his arm around her shoulder. She looked up at him, allowing his arm to rest there. He smiled at her.

'So what would you like to do now?'

'Now?' Of course. It was still only mid-evening. She felt brighter immediately. His hand stroked her shoulder through her jacket.

'How would you like to see the "little" kittens?' he said, imitating Annelies. 'They're not going to stay little forever.'

She laughed at him, a tentative feeling of happiness rising inside her.

'I'd love that. And you can show me your Braque posters. You have got Braque on your wall, haven't you? Even though you live in Blackbird Leys?'

'Nope. As it happens, I can't stand Braque.' Mack smiled as they walked towards the bus stop.

'Let's get out of here,' Maggie said, a good while after she'd heard the front door close. She knew Julia and Mack would have left. Fabian would be trying to fend off his parents in the dining-room. Correction, his mother. His father seemed reasonable enough. She just hoped he had the strength to hold her off with one hand while he tried to get through to his dad. She'd broken up the dinner party, but it was no longer a collective gathering. Now it was a family affair. And she had to get Pete away from the house, somewhere where they could talk and she could think.

'Let's walk,' Pete said.

Maggie picked up her coat and umbrella in the hall and led the way out of the house. Pete hovered at the dining-room door, as if he wanted to throw himself inside and shout something.

'C'mon, Pete. Let's walk into town.'

Maggie opened her umbrella and they walked together over the wet cherry blossom, ground into the pavement in a soggy mass. It reminded Maggie of confetti, trampled and redundant. She slipped her arm through Pete's. His arm stiffened, but he didn't push her away.

'Here. Get under this brolly. You'll catch your death,' she said.

'Would you care if I did?'

'That's a daft question and you know it. I've never stopped caring about you.'

They walked on steadily, purging the adrenalin from their systems, silently being close. They didn't speak for a long time, allowing the darkness to wash around them, the rain to splash against their ankles and the cars and pedestrians to sweep past. They reached the town, and walked on down Cornmarket, past the garish lights thrown on the glassy street by McDonald's, and on down the High Street.

'I hate this bloody town,' Pete said, breaking the silence finally as they stopped at the University outfitters. In the window, the effete mannequins were modelling a selection of University gowns.

'You see that one?' Maggie pointed out a black gown with a hood lined with white fur. 'I wore one of those for graduation. I wish you'd have come.'

Pete considered the sight silently for a moment.

'I bet you looked like a right prat.'

'I did.' Maggie laughed loudly, the weight lifting from her chest. Suddenly, it was good to hear his mockery. 'I've got a photo you can see. You can throw darts at it if you want.'

'I wouldn't want to do that,' Pete said quietly.

They turned away from the shop window and walked on down towards Examination Schools. Maggie thought of pointing it out to Pete. She could tell him about the excitement she felt when it was all over, about the flour and the champagne and the hangover the next day. But the memory filled her with bitter disappointment. He wouldn't want to know what he'd missed. He missed it because he didn't want to be a part of it. They reached the stone steps of the building and it was Pete who stopped. He gazed up at the locked doors.

'Is this where you did your exams?'

'Yes, Pete. This is where it was.'

'Bet it's grand inside.'

'It is. Bloody scary. All oil paintings and chandeliers. I nearly crapped myself when I first went in.'

Pete relaxed his arm suddenly. It felt as if she was holding on to her husband again, not a lump of rock.

'I'm proud of you, Mags. You do know that, don't you?'

They walked away slowly, on towards Magdalen bridge.

'You've never said that before,' Maggie said, emotion lodging in her throat. 'I had no idea you were proud of me.'

'Course I am.' He took a ragged breath, staring ahead at the narrowing bridge as they approached. 'I wouldn't have had the guts to do what you did. Or the brains.'

'That's bollocks. You're one of the brightest men I know.'

'I couldn't read a book like you did, or write one of your essays. I wouldn't have understood what the lecturers were talking about. You're cleverer than I am, Maggie. You always have been. It's why you got bored.'

'It's not about being clever. It's about exploring. That's all. And I was never bored with you, Pete. Not all the time that we were talking. It's just that you stopped talking to me. I didn't understand why you did that.'

'Oh, heck.' Pete shook his head. They stopped on the bridge under an ornate lamp, and peered at the river lurching below them. They watched it in silence for a while.

'Maggie?' Pete began.

'Don't, love,' Maggie whispered, squeezing his arm. 'I know why you've come. I know what you want from me. Just don't ruin it now. Not just yet.'

'Why him, Maggie? Why that lad? There must have been others who've looked at you. Why did you do it with a kid? He'd never come close to knowing what sort of woman you are, what makes you tick.'

Maggie thought for a moment. Fabian had come close. But not close enough. He never could have done. Pete was right.

'I think that was why,' she said softly, glancing sideways at Pete. 'What about Daphne? Why in God's name did you pick her, of all women?'

'Hell, don't talk about that now. I'm not proud of myself. I want you to know that. She's a strong woman, that Daphne. I was alone and she was determined. I don't know what it was all about. It wasn't about me. I think it was about Brian.' He flicked his wife a curious glance. 'She wasn't a patch on you, you know. For talking, that is.'

'You always told me to stop gassing.'

'But it always made sense to me, what you said. You could talk about anything. Not just curtain rails and pedicures. I've never met a woman like you for having opinions. I don't think Daphne had an opinion on anything. Not that I could make out, anyway.'

'And now they're moving away.'

'Aye. Getting off the bloody estate.'

'Just as we should have done, years ago. I wanted to, you know.'

'You never said. I thought you were happy?' He snorted at himself. 'Of course you weren't bloody happy. We wouldn't be in this mess if you had been. Are you happy now?'

'Are you happy, Pete?'

'Happy?' Pete rubbed at his face roughly with his hand. Maggie saw how tired he was. He guffawed. 'I've got one of those brochures. From the college. Like the one you had. I thought I might do an evening class, like you did. I thought that might make me happy.'

Maggie felt tears swim in her eyes. Pete's face danced around her.

'I wrote a book,' she blurted out. 'About you. A whole book. I was happy when I was writing it.'

'You never did.' He looked at her distantly. 'You're a one, aren't you?'

'Pete,' she choked, her heart full of love. 'I know I've changed. I know I'm not the same old Maggie who used to live with you, but don't you think we could try again?' The tears spilled down her cheeks. She gulped. 'I can still do the things I want to do, but with you. I could write more books. I enjoyed that. Just don't divorce me, Pete. Please don't divorce me. You can't. Not while I love you this much.'

Pete lifted a finger slowly, put it to her cheek, and wiped away the tears.

'Don't cry, lass. You're my wife and I won't see you unhappy. Not any more.'

She threw herself into his arms, dropping the umbrella. The rain hammered on to their heads, but held by her husband like this she felt dry and safe. She heard his muffled voice, strangled with emotion as he stroked her wet hair.

'Any road, it's not you who's changed, Maggie. Not one bit. It's me.'

'Oh my God, they're incredible!'

Julia dropped to her knees and put a hand out to the tiny creatures, mewing helplessly into the air. She cradled a kitten in her hand, held it up to kiss its head. Then she placed it carefully in her lap. It crawled into the warmth of her thighs.

'Here. Take the other one as well. They get freaked out if they're not together.'

Mack gently lifted the ginger kitten up and put it with

the other. The two kittens fused into a small mass of downy fur.

'Ah. I think one of them's weeing on my leg.'

'Don't worry about it. They've only got tiny bladders.'

Julia looked up at the room again from where she knelt, glad to have the distraction of the kittens. His 'expressive' paintings, stacked against the wall, around the room, were more vibrant than she'd been ready for, even after seeing his work on the underpass. Now she understood why Annelies had thought, after visiting his flat and seeing his paintings, that he was in love with her. He'd painted Julia, from memory, into three of the canvasses. He'd shown her when they'd come in. She'd been shocked beyond words to see her own image staring back at herself. The confusion had evolved into a stammering attempt to explain to Mack how flattered she was. She still felt her cheeks glowing with appreciation of his skill and his attention. There was no doubt now of his talent, of his ability to capture a face in his memory and reproduce it in his own style. And there was no doubt that he had been thinking about her often. Much more, initially at least, than she'd been thinking about him. But that had changed.

'I still can't get over what an incredible memory you've got,' she said, gazing at the images around the room.

'Can't you?' He flopped beside her, tickling Elizabeth's head as she rubbed against him. 'I've had to use it all my life, remember.'

'Of course,' she said slowly. She considered him for a moment. 'Earlier on, at Maggie's when we were bluffing about art, you said something I thought you meant.'

'Really?' He smiled. 'About L'Oréal?'

'About deceit. You said it sets us apart from animals. Do you really believe that?'

He gave her a long look, then settled himself to lie on the floor with his head propped up on one elbow.

'Don't you?'

'I'm asking you.'

He looked down at the floor, and blinked in thought.

'I understand deceit. I've been deceiving people all my life. It's how I've got by. In little ways mostly, and sometimes in bigger ways.' He lifted his deep eyes to hers. 'Stopping people in the street to ask them the time, pretending I didn't have a watch. Asking people's opinions about instructions, timetables, getting by on images and patterns. Getting friends to read letters for me, pretending my eyesight was bad, that I couldn't afford new glasses. I even got round France on deceit.'

'I remember. You said you were in France.'

'I went when it all got too much. I couldn't speak French, you see. Ideal.'

'I think I understand.'

'Nobody thought it was weird that I had to ask people about everything. Buses, trains, places to camp, menus. Because I was English, of course, and the French are used to the English asking them stupid questions. I think they'd be gutted if we didn't. Gives them something else to grumble about while they're lobbing boules around. I picked up a bit of French, in the vineyards, but I could never write it. It didn't matter.'

'You worked in a vineyard?'

'A couple of them. In the summer. Beaujolais region. It's pretty down there. Some time I'd like to show it to you.' He shot her a glance as if he'd been thinking aloud, and hadn't meant to. She nodded and smiled. 'Then I stayed in Lyons. That was where I did all my thinking. Then I decided that it was time for honesty. It was time to come back and make something of myself. So I came back, wandered around for a bit, landed in Oxford, and decided to stay here and paint.'

'And to do something about reading and writing?'

'That came much later.' He gave her a lazy smile. 'Honesty comes in stages, doesn't it? It's one thing to make a decision to be honest, it's another one to get on with doing it. I got labouring jobs around here, did some voluntary painting, for a youth club, one of the sports centres, then they gave me the underpass to do. It wasn't till then, when I was standing there, looking at my grandmother's face on the wall, that I could hear her voice in my head.'

'Don't tell me. Get-away-closer.'

He laughed. It was a wonderfully happy sound.

'Nope. It was the success and hindsight one.' He shook his head with a sigh. 'My old grandmother. She didn't half talk some crap.'

Julia stroked the tiny heads in her lap, watching them indulgently as they snuggled closer to each other.

'I've been deceitful too,' she said quietly.

'I know,' he said. She looked up at him, her eyes mirroring her guilt.

'How do you know?'

'Because you've been so unhappy. People get unhappy when they're pretending. You must have noticed that.'

'Pretending what? What am I pretending?'

'You know. Pretending what you're doing's a really good idea, when you know deep down that it's not. Like, I don't know, jobs and relationships. And where you live. That sort of thing.'

'Oh, just little things, then,' she said ironically.

'Yeah. That's when people get worn out. Not with what they're doing, but with the pretence.'

He stopped and dropped his gaze to the kittens as she stroked them soothingly. Julia considered his face. So peaceful. So honest.

'There's something I'd like to tell you,' she said. He nodded. 'It's about a relationship I had once.'

'If you want. I'm not going anywhere.'

'It's – I've never told anybody the truth about it. Not since it happened. I've been covering up, to try and make myself look good. Basically.' She gave a half-laugh at her summary. 'But it's caught up with me and now I think I've got to face what I did.'

He didn't speak. He just carried on watching her. She swallowed.

'I went out with a bloke, called Bill. It doesn't really matter what his name was, but anyway, we lived together and I thought I loved him. I – I always panicked about what I'd do if he changed his mind and went off somewhere else. It was because he seemed to be so much better than me, you know, more educated, better-looking on the grand one to ten scale, more ambitious, successful. And my mother thought he was ideal for me. I wanted to make her happy.' Her mouth became dry. 'One day he said he was leaving, going off with someone else. I let him go. I fell to pieces. My mother rang him and she – she told him I was pregnant.'

She paused, waiting for a reaction in Mack's eyes. He continued to watch her without expression.

'I – when she told me what she'd said, I was horrified. You see, what she'd told Bill was a lie.' She cleared her throat. Her cheeks were burning with the memory. She must continue now. 'I – somehow I found myself swept up in the illusion. I loved him so much, you see. At least, I thought I did. There was no life without him. I – I thought if he came back, perhaps I would become pregnant, that fate would step in and save me. He – er – he came back to me.'

Unshed tears rested in her eyes. She forced herself to look Mack in the eye.

'He – he seemed resigned to staying with me. I thought we could make it work. I tried to make him happy, but we had friends, you see. Mutual friends, at work. He – he told them I was expecting a baby. The web of lies spread, beyond me, beyond us. I was trapped. I'd trapped myself.' She gulped in a breath, her pulse thudding at her ears. Again, she felt the shame sweep over her. 'I – you see, I wouldn't have thought I could be so base. That I would ever go for the oldest trick in the book. It was so desperate, so – so terrible.' She dropped her eyes. A tear edged its way down her cheek. She brushed it away with impatience.

'Weeks passed. I – I don't need to tell you that nature didn't find a way to save me.' She raised her eyes to the ceiling. The voices came back, haunting her. 'Our friends asked me questions. They all knew, they were all waiting for something to happen, for me to do something – something that would be normal under those circumstances. I had a choice. Either I could pretend in some ghastly melodrama that I'd lost my child, or – or I had to be honest. To show myself for what I was.' She stopped again to wipe her eyes on her sleeve. Mack put a hand towards her. She shook her head. 'No, let me finish. I – I confessed. To Bill and to the others. I was disgusted with myself. I tried to explain it, but . . .' She swallowed again, painfully. 'My shame was complete. Bill left. I lost my friends. I – I knew I'd never have instigated the lie myself, but once it was in place, I went along with it. I was weak, and I think for a while I was almost mad. After that, I hated myself. I couldn't believe that I'd stooped so low. I couldn't live with the mortification. Everybody around me knew.'

She searched Mack's face for a sign that her words had filled him with disgust, that he'd been politely waiting for her to finish before backing away from her. His eyes remained peaceful.

'It was five years ago.'

He nodded.

'After that – after Bill had gone, I couldn't face what I'd done. I had to get away, to find another way. To start again. It's what made me leave London, to come here and to try to rebuild myself.'

'Blimey. I've got the bionic woman in my flat,' Mack said, smiling at her. 'Is there anything else?'

'Yes. I've dealt with it by not talking about Bill. By making it seem that it was the fact he left me that did the damage. But that's not it. It was my own pain, over my own actions. And I've tried to blame my mother for it. But I spoke the words and did the damage when I could have denied what she'd said. I cut her out of my life because I couldn't face what we did. What I did.'

'Does she know you feel like this?'

'No. But I'm going to tell her. It's about time I was brave enough to apologize to her.' She chewed on her lip. 'She was wrong to do what she did, but she's been very unhappy for a long time. I could have talked to her about that, instead of running away. Perhaps then things would have been different.'

Mack watched Julia's face for a moment longer. She felt his eyes on her and gazed at him sadly.

'I know all about shame, Julia,' he said. 'I've lived with it for years.'

'Perhaps that's something else that sets us apart from animals,' she said with a half-laugh.

'There's another one that I've just thought of,' Mack said, adopting a serious expression.

'What's that?'

'We're not scared of Hoovers.'

She stared at him blankly for a moment, then her face creased into a smile. She laughed aloud. God, how good it felt to laugh, to have shed the burden at last. Mack's eyes softened pensively.

'I let humiliation get the better of me for far too long,' he said. 'But I'm doing something about it, by coming to the class. I've taken control. Just as you have, with your degree and your teaching course.'

'Oh yes, the teaching course.' She gave a long sigh, and smiled at him tentatively. 'Thank you for encouraging me to do that.'

'You're a great teacher. Why shouldn't I encourage you? I was only telling the truth.' He winked at her and she felt a rush of pleasure.

'And you're not biased?' she said coyly.

'Only a very little. Anyway, why should I want you to move down to London unless I thought it was the right thing for you? Shot myself in the foot there, didn't I?'

'Well,' her blush returned to warm her cheeks. 'I'm not exactly sure what my plans are going to be. That depends on . . .'

'On?' His eyes teased her.

'A few things,' she said, looking down again.

'On the other hand,' he said casually, lolling on the floor, 'my art might take me to London. There's the exhibition there later this year, and it's the heart of Cool Britannia after all. I wouldn't want to miss out on all that. I might just think about moving down there. But that would depend on . . . a few things.'

She looked up at him and saw that he was smiling.

'Well, it is a good course,' she said.

'Naturally.'

'It really is, actually.' She sat up, thinking. 'You start off in lectures, just to get the foundations in place, but you get out into classes very early. They believe that practical experience is very valuable. And if I was lucky, I'd get a placement in basic skills teaching so that I can carry on with—'

'Julia?'

'What?' He'd stood up. She gazed up at him.

'Would you like to come to bed with me?' he asked, holding out a hand to her.

'Now?' She looked at him in confusion, her heart shooting up into her mouth.

'No, tomorrow night at seven thirty-five.' He lifted an eyebrow at her. She felt a warm glow spread over her stomach.

'I – it's been a long time for me. I'm a bit out of practice.'

'Me too,' he said.

'I – I don't know how adventurous I can be. I suddenly feel stupidly shy.'

'Well, I could leave the vibrator in the drawer for now.' His lips curved at her. He shook his head at her in gentle reproof. 'I just want to hold you, Julia.'

'I – are you sure? After what I've told you?'

'Especially after what you've told me. I was starting to wonder where your halo was.'

She took the kittens in one hand and placed them on the floor next to the tortoiseshell cat. Elizabeth immediately set about them with a rough tongue.

'Mack? This won't stop you coming to the class, will it?'

'You're the tutor,' he said, taking her hand and looking at her in a way that made her feel dizzy. 'I'll do anything you tell me to.'

She allowed him to put his arms around her, to feel his way down her back, to pull her close against his hard body. For a precious moment, she pushed her fingers up into his hair, in the way she'd imagined, and looked deeply into his eyes. Then he kissed her slowly and her body melted into his, his arms tightening around her with a possessive strength that sent a bolt of excitement through her. Without warning, she felt herself being hoisted into the air. She opened her eyes in shock and squealed loudly.

'Mack!' She began to giggle. 'What are you doing?'

'Time for some adult education,' he whispered in her ear as he caught her up in his arms and carried her towards the bedroom.

Linda Taylor's second novel

Going Against the Grain

will be published later in 1999

Louise is not sure where her life took the wrong turning, but it's not shaping up as well as she might have hoped. She's just turned 32, her job for a party planners – the latest in a long line of occupations – has little to recommend it, and she watches helplessly as her dynamic elder sister charges up the career ladder.

Scatty, disorganised and very bad at co-ordinating her wardrobe, Louise can't help feeling that she needs to get it together – even her boyfriend is part-time. But then she discovers she's succeeded at one thing: getting pregnant.

Life changes dramatically: a baby is the last thing her feckless boyfriend wants. But it's the one thing her sister, settled and content in a relationship, yearns for. Louise must decide who she is going to defy.

Also available in Arrow paperback

Close Relations

Deborah Moggach

The three Hammond sisters have each chosen their own paths. Louise leads a seemingly perfect existence in Beaconsfield with her venture-capitalist husband, messy teenage children and Smallbone kitchen. Prudence, who has successfully forged a career in publishing, is having a fruitless affair with her married boss. And Maddy, always the square peg in the round hole, has just met and fallen in love with a lesbian gardener.

When their father, Gordon, has a heart attack and then runs away to live in Brixton with a young black nurse, Dorothy – his wife – is released like a loose cannon into her daughters' lives.

As passions run high, relationships break up and dramatic developments look set to change them all for ever. For better or for worse.

'A compassionate family comedy . . . Moggach writes of the calamity of love and the devastation of divorce. A novel of comic appeal and topical wit' *Times Literary Supplement*

Close Relations was a major drama serial for BBC 1.

Chloë

Freya North

Chloë Cadwallader is in a quandary. Her beloved godmother has just died and left Chloë a letter instructing her to give up her job (*lousy*) and her boyfriend (*never good enough for you*) to travel the four countries of the United Kingdom during the four seasons of the year.

Heavens. How can Chloë deny a godmother's last wish?

Off she goes, with a tremor of doubt and a letter marked *Wales*, to a farm deep in the Black Mountains where she finds a selection of eccentric animals and the best looking man she's ever laid eyes on.

As subsequent seasons unfold, so too does Jocelyn's mission to teach her goddaughter to stand on her own two feet, celebrate the beauty of Britain and discover love, lust, life (and a man for each season).

'Read of the month . . . settle down and indulge' *Cosmopolitan*

OTHER TITLES AVAILABLE

Close Relations	Deborah Moggach	£5.99
Every Woman Knows A Secret	Rosie Thomas	£5.99
Chloë	Freya North	£5.99
Chasing Dreams	Susan Lewis	£5.99
Camellia	Lesley Pearse	£5.99
The Moonbathers	Deborah Lawrenson	£5.99
Moving In	Elisabeth Leigh	£5.99

ALL ARROW BOOKS ARE AVAILABLE THROUGH MAIL ORDER OR FROM YOUR LOCAL BOOKSHOP AND NEWSAGENT.

PLEASE SEND CHEQUE/EUROCHEQUE/POSTAL ORDER (STERLING ONLY) ACCESS, VISA, MASTERCARD, DINERS CARD, SWITCH OR AMEX.

EXPIRY DATE................................ SIGNATURE....................................

PLEASE ALLOW 75 PENCE PER BOOK FOR POST AND PACKING U.K.

OVERSEAS CUSTOMERS PLEASE ALLOW £1.00 PER COPY FOR POST AND PACKING.

ALL ORDERS TO:
ARROW BOOKS, BOOKS BY POST, TBS LIMITED, THE BOOK SERVICE, COLCHESTER ROAD, FRATING GREEN, COLCHESTER, ESSEX CO7 7DW.

NAME ....

ADDRESS ....

....

Please allow 28 days for delivery. Please tick box if you do not wish to receive any additional information □

Prices and availability subject to change without notice.